CHRONICLES OF THE SENTINELS
SENTINELS
RETRIBUTION

Jon Wasik

http://jonwasik.com

Cover Art by Shupeipa

https://www.fiverr.com/shupeipa

Chapter Illustrations by Beck Wasik

https://www.instagram.com/darksyd3ofm00n/

ISBN-13: 978-1-7349361-2-4

For my sister Tanya

Through highs and lows, ups and downs, you never once doubted I'd become an author

Thank you for believing

Also by Jon Wasik

The Sword of Dragons
Rise of the Forgotten – The Sword of Dragons Book 1
The Orc War Campaigns – A Sword of Dragons Story
Burning Skies – The Sword of Dragons Book 2
Secrets of the Cronal – The Sword of Dragons Book 3

Chronicles of the Sentinels
Legacy
Retribution
Book 3 *(Coming August 2022)*

ACKNOWLEDGMENTS

This novel has been a passion project of mine for a long time, and I owe some amazing people for helping me bring it to light!

First and foremost, a shout out to my wife, Beck, for their endless and undying support, encouragement, and help. Beck was one of my first beta readers for Chronicles of the Sentinels, and helped me ensure I did the LGBT+ community justice throughout the entire trilogy. In fact, every part of this crazy creative endeavor? They've been there for me with ideas, feedback, encouragement, and love. I know it's a cliché to say this, but I truly am beyond fortunate to have someone like Beck as a part of my life!

Thank you to Wayne Adams from VtW Productions for his support, ideas, and most importantly his enthusiasm! He pushed and prodded and pulled me to make the best novel I possibly could!

Thank you to Jen Immer and Sean Carter for helping me with cultural terminology.

Thank you to all of my Facebook, Instagram, and blog followers for enduring my social media ineptness! I struggle with it to this day, but you all are incredibly supportive!

And as always, to the Welts family for their constant support. Especially my best friend of over 20 years, Nick. You've endured beta reads, story ideas, frustrations, and celebrations with me. Thanks for always being there for me!

A NOTE FROM THE AUTHOR:

Chronicles of the Sentinels contains a diverse cast – representation and inclusion are important to me, and as it happens, is an important part of the story told in this trilogy.

It is my sincere hope that what I have written is respectful and accurate, and I've had a lot of help in ensuring I've done so. However, I am still human and will inevitably make mistakes. I hope you enjoy the story you're about to read, but if I have portrayed anything inaccurately, I would love to hear from you!

You can contact me through my website, http://jonwasik.com

CHARACTER REFRESHER

When last we left our intrepid heroes, the Barrier, a mystical field protecting all of Earth from magic, had been dispelled, and magic had returned to the world and many of its inhabitants. The Sentinels, guardians of the Barrier and stalwart defenders of Earth from the ravages of the Babylonian god Marduk, suddenly found themselves in need of fresh blood amongst their ranks, and have a new mission — prepare to defend humanity from a god.

No pressure, right?

Christopher Tatsu — The hero of our journey, Chris is a young college graduate who, after a fateful graduation party, discovered that not only was magic real, but he was also able to use it. After being forced by the demigod Nabu into dismantling the Barrier, Chris learned that he is a descendant of one of the creators of the Barrier, Tattannu. All the souls of Tattannu's descendants joined together into the Barrier over the course of four thousand years, and now those souls reside within Chris, giving him the powers necessary to one day destroy Marduk. As such, he asked to join the ranks of the Sentinels. His powers are based upon the arcane, which currently manifests in the form of golden energy beams, plasma balls, and an occasional lightning strike (Palpatine eat your heart out!)

Oh yeah, and Chris is the biggest repository of geek knowledge and pop culture references west of the Mississippi.

Emmanuelle Dubois — Another hero of our journey (there's a few,) Emmi is likewise a recent college graduate. After she and Chris completed their last finals, she was invited to an end-of-term bash by her boyfriend. Her boyfriend, it turns out, was really Nabu, and he used her to ensure the destruction of the Barrier. Along the way, Emmi discovered that she can shapeshift into various animals, her favorites being a black housecat, a bald eagle, and a black panther. After being abducted by Nabu and forced to endure untold tortures, Emmi trains to become a Sentinel while struggling to overcome emotional trauma.

Alycia Taylor — Alycia met Chris and Emmi four years ago and has been an inseparable friend ever since. She and her father

Thomas immigrated to the United States from Australia in pursuit of the man they thought murdered her mother, one demigod known as Nabu (he really pissed off a lot of people...) While Alycia was not privy to the details of her father's role as a Sentinel, she came up to speed very quickly after Nabu tried to murder her and her friends to destroy the Barrier. Since then, Alycia has discovered that she has conjuration and enchanting powers, to include summoning shields and imbuing elemental powers into objects. Her experiences creating clothes and props for cosplay has proven to be invaluable when combined with her powers. Now she trains with Chris and Emmi to join the ranks of the Sentinels.

Thomas Taylor – Alycia's father and leader of the United States division of the Sentinels, Thomas is ex-military and transitioned directly into working for the Australian Sentinels. Two decades ago, Nabu escaped from Thomas's facility, killing almost everyone, including his wife Mia, or so he thought. It turns out that Mia served Nabu and helped the demigod escape. Now Thomas must find a new path for the Sentinels to protect Earth from the wrath of Marduk, while he simultaneously searches for the whereabouts of his long-lost wife.

Shara – Although Shara looks like a cross between an anime and Tolkien elf, if you value your own life, you'll never call her an elf. Stranded on Earth in the early 1940's thanks to a joint venture between Nazis and rogue Sentinels, Shara has lived amongst humans for eighty years, and for most of that time, she has served the U.S. Sentinels. Some say the growing trend for colored hair (especially blue) comes from her influence (she grew tired of dying her hair to look 'normal,') and thanks to the invention of colored contact lenses, she no longer needs to wear sunglasses inside. Once the Barrier fell, Shara was able to cast magic for the first time since arriving, and shapeshifted into a gryphon to help defeat Nabu. Now she is helping Chris, Emmi and Alycia learn to harness and control their powers, and is preparing them for the day that they may join the ranks of the Sentinels.

Nabu – A demigod, Nabu is the embodiment of the Babylonian god Marduk. His mother, later deified in the Babylonian pantheon, was human. Nabu has lived for four thousand years, despite the Barrier blocking magic and, by extension, Nabu's powers. After forcing Chris to destroy the Barrier, Nabu was apparently killed by Chris's newfound, god-destroying powers. Of course, nothing is ever that easy, and while Nabu's body was disintegrated, his spirit remained. Now Nabu inhabits a young Scottish woman's body, which has given him a considerable advantage in moving unseen by the Sentinels.

Mia Taylor − Long-thought dead, Mia was seduced by Nabu's powers of persuasion, and has served as a leader amongst the cultists for two decades. She had become so lost in her service to Nabu that she forgot she ever had a husband or daughter, until that fateful party in the hangar. Once those memories started to resurface, she broke away from Nabu's hold just enough to ensure she survived the Battle at Babylon. Her current whereabouts are unknown.

Babbar Nurin − A gnome who fled to the protection of Earth's Barrier, Babbar has been a thorn in the Sentinel's collective sides, since his favorite past-times included peddling magical artifacts around Earth. The U.S. Sentinels, led by Shara and Thomas, finally caught up to him and arrested him after raiding his underground mansion in the Rocky Mountains. Later, they convinced him (politely) to aid them in their fight against Nabu, to which Babbar agreed only if they protected him from Nabu and Marduk.

Ninazu − Better known as Nina, she is a tiny little green dragon, only about a foot long. Babbar found her egg just before it hatched a century ago, and she immediately imprinted upon him and has been a loyal companion ever since. Her abilities, completely unhindered by the Barrier, include invisibility and the creation of portals. No one knows why, but Nabu was terrified of her upon their one and only encounter.

Oh yeah, and she loves to hoard bottle caps. If you value your hand, don't try to take them away from her.

Abigail Turner − Abby is the heart of the Sentinels, and her bubbly personality has an uncanny knack for cheering up even the most despondent team member. She is the tech wiz, the 'gal behind the chair,' and an occasional flirt with Shara. Abby lost the use of her legs in an incident involving a monster (no, really,) and was saved by the Sentinels. Unsatisfied with her life prior to then, she decided to join the Sentinels and help them protect the world.

Tiana Jones – One of the elite members of the Sentinels, Tiana is a talented pilot, able to fly both fixed-wing aircraft and helicopters. She is also the best sharpshooter on the team. After serving four years as an Air Force pilot, Tiana wandered from job to job, unable to find something that truly satisfied her need for action and adventure. When the Sentinels approached her for a job, she very nearly turned them down, until she learned the truth of their existence. Since then, she has been one of the most valuable members of the team. She flew the Sentinels to Babbar's Rocky Mountain home, and later acted as sniper in the Battle at Babylon, helping finish Nabu off with perfectly timed shots.

Marisol Rodriguez – Usually one of two U.S. Sentinels on night shift, Marisol joined the Sentinels specifically because of her fascination with magic, and her desire to see more of it. As such, she is one of the few Sentinels anywhere who is both accepting of Shara's presence, and more recently, accepting of Chris, Emmi and Alycia's powers, and Chris's decision to dismantle the Barrier.

Jered Becker – Another stalwart member of the Sentinel night shift, and one of the few survivors from Nabu's attacks, Jered is the embodiment of the rest of the Sentinels from around the world in his distrust towards anything magic, including and perhaps especially Shara. He specifically works the night shift so that he never has to actually take orders from Shara, and he *really* doesn't like Chris, Emmi or Alycia. Most recently, he has disappeared from Sentinel Tower in Denver. Tom insists that Jered still is working his night shift, but from another, secondary facility.

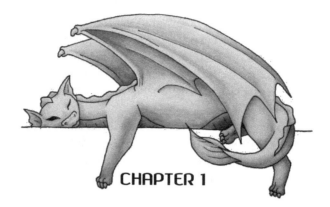

CHAPTER 1

Christopher Tatsu ran for his life!

Wind whipped through his short black hair as he booked it across a stony surface in the woods, fir and aspen trees whipping by. His heart thundered in his ears and his breathing was heavy. He had only run for two miles, but damn if the altitude of the Colorado Rockies still hit him hard.

The path came upon a series of boulders, one of which was directly in his path and eight feet high, so he leapt and crawled up, his combat boots gripping the rough surface and his hands grasping at any deformity he could to get him up and over as fast as possible.

Once atop the boulder, he glanced at his watch, and cursed. Time was running out, and he still had a quarter of a mile to cover!

Sweat dripped down his tanned face, darkened from eight weeks spent out in the wilderness far to the west of Denver, deep in the Rocky Mountains where no one else lived and few campers treaded. His white t-shirt was soaked in all the disgusting places, and his pants felt heavy and oppressively hot.

Why the hell *are we forced to wear pants?!*

Almost ten weeks had passed since Chris had first learned the truth about magic, which meant it was now the hottest part of summer. Ten weeks since he found out about Babylon and the existence of magic and god-like beings. He had fought his first battles then – *him*, Chris, a college graduate, a mechanical engineer, had fought and killed and nearly been killed in a conflict that had decided the fate of the Earth and altered the course of humanity.

It sounded crazy even in his thoughts.

And yet it was all true, every bit of it. Gods, magic, a mystical shield against magic, one which Chris had dismantled.

The Barrier, erected four thousand years ago to block all magic and prevent the Babylonian god Marduk from forcing a mass sacrifice of human lives and gaining power, had fallen at Chris's hands. He had learned the truth then, about his destiny and the legacy of his ancestors. Now the spirits of all of one man's descendants fueled his soul.

So when he came across two immobile targets, one of which held a faux-hostage, he didn't reach for the semi-automatic pistol strapped to his right thigh like he was supposed to. Instead, he touched the golden core of energy deep within him, drew power from it, from those millions of souls, and released a carefully controlled golden beam of arcane energy upon his targets. The forest echoed with a deafening thunderclap, and his targets, thanks to pin-point accuracy, had smoking holes in their heads, while the dummy hostage was completely unharmed.

They were mannequins, after all, not actual living people. He hadn't taken a single life since he had ended Nabu, Marduk's half-breed son, in the sands of Babylon. These were training dummies, with the 'bad guys' dressed in all-black tactical gear, and the occasional hostage dressed in random assortments of clothes.

As he passed by the dummies, the pungent smell of burning rubber and plastic stung at his nose, momentarily occluding the otherwise pleasant scents of flowers, trees, and grasses.

Glancing again at his watch, he grinned at the time he had just made up. If he had slowed enough to draw his pistol, he would have fallen further behind. *Let's see the old bastard lecture me for that,* he thought with a grin.

The smoking dummies were the last of the course, it turned out, and a few minutes later, Chris barreled around a set of cones marking the final turn of the obstacle course, and one of the cabins came into view. It was an old log structure, like everything else in the Sentinel training complex, built who knew how long ago.

Passing by another pair of trees, he crossed the finish line and stamped to a slow walk, approaching a wooden picnic table where his two best friends, Emmanuelle Dubois and Alycia Taylor, sat cheering him on and clapping. He glanced at his watch and smiled. He'd finished the course thirty seconds faster. Pressing the button to stop the timer on his watch, he stopped before his friends, who both stood up and cheered louder, while he took a deep bow between heaving breaths.

The bow turned out to be a mistake, as blood rushed to his head and the world tilted, threatening to throw him down. Steadying himself, he laughed and huffed out a breath. "Thank you, thank you," he smiled. "I'll be here all week."

Alycia, shorter than him by a few inches, stepped off of the seat she had stood upon and clasped him on the shoulder, flashing him a smile with golden brown eyes lit up in amusement. "I hope not," she remarked through her Australian accent. "This is our last weekend here, after all."

Returning her smile, Chris took a moment to take in her visage. Alycia's skin was darker than ever, thanks to their time spent outdoors ever since her father Thomas Taylor had sent them here to train to become Sentinels. She, like Chris, had lost weight and gained a lot of muscle from their physical training, and he couldn't help but think she looked more attractive than ever. Especially since she wore a light-blue tank top. Like Chris, she wore khaki pants, something their trainer insisted on during their PT sessions to get them used to strenuous conditions. Likewise, she had a pistol in a tactical holster, except it was on her left hip, since she was left-handed.

Emmi likewise stepped down, but otherwise kept her distance. Unlike Chris and Alycia, her skin hadn't burned in their first week, since she already had spent time outdoors exercising even before Sentinel training. At most, her tan and, more noticeably, her freckles had darkened since their arrival. Emmi's furious red hair, cut short several months ago, was quickly growing back and was pulled into a tight ponytail much like Alycia's brown hair, and she wore a forest-green tank top and yoga pants, the latter of which she insisted on no matter what their trainer demanded. She also had taken off her tactical holster, leaving it on the table.

Emmi's most recognizable feature these days was her facial scars, one of Nabu's little 'gifts' from battle ten weeks ago. Two scratch marks on her right side, starting on her forehead and raking down to her cheek, with the inner-most one having scoured down in front of her eye and cleaving her eyebrow, though thankfully not injuring her actual eye. She also had three claw marks on her stomach, which was why she now favored tank tops rather than her usual sports bras.

"Where's Miyagi?" Chris asked, huffing another breath out and searching for their trainer. Miyagi wasn't his name, but Chris had taken to calling the old man that since their very first meeting. Unfortunately, their trainer didn't see the amusement in it, nor was he as endearing as Daniel-san's teacher. He had no sense of geek culture, and probably had never seen a single movie in his life.

"I don't know," Alycia frowned, looking back towards the cabin. "I thought he'd be back by now, I-"

Alycia's eyes widened, and she reacted instinctively, the familiar press against Chris's soul signaling her use of magic a moment before a blue wall of light snapped into existence behind him. Something thunked against it, and he spun around, finding an arrow suspended in mid-air, halted by Alycia's barrier.

"Good," an old man's voice called out from the woods. Their trainer, a man named Benson (he never told them if that was his first or last name) appeared from behind a tree. He held in his left hand a compound bow, and he already had another arrow in his right hand. "Your reaction times are getting better," he added, nodding to Alycia with a stoic expression. Alycia let the shield dissipate, and the arrow fell noiselessly into the grass.

But then Benson turned to Chris and emotion found the craggy old face, his white beard creasing down into a scowl. "Tatsu, on the other hand," he growled. "You dropped your guard. *Again!*"

Chris felt the burn of embarrassment, but after eight weeks of training, he'd had it with the old codger. "I finished the course," he defended.

Walking towards them, Benson slid the second arrow into a quiver strapped on his hip and shook his head. "This is your final week, the course is *never* over Tatsu. And I told you, no magic on the run!"

Splaying his hands out in exasperation, Chris asked, "Why the hell not? It saved me time." Patting the pistol on his thigh, he added, "Why use a gun when I can use magic?"

Benson was close enough now that Chris could easily see the sharp blue of his eyes and the stubble of hair on his scalp, in need of another shave. "Do ya really need another lesson in that department, kid?"

God dammit, stop calling me kid! He thought it, but even his defiance would let him go only so far.

"Magic might not always be around, you've already seen that,"

Benson stalked past Chris and the others towards the cabin, but then stopped and whirled around, surprisingly spry. "What happens if the Barrier returns? What're you gonna do then?"

He couldn't help it, and before he could catch himself, he let it slip out, "I'll dismantle it again."

The look of outrage on Benson's face would have made Chris laugh if the circumstances had been better. As it was, as their trainer and one of the persons who would decide whether they joined the ranks of the Sentinels or not, Benson had some measure of control over Chris's future.

And he wasn't afraid to use that fact to his advantage.

Pointing a finger to his left, Benson ordered, "Run the course again!" Chris's thumping heart cried.

"But sir," Emmi protested before Chris could say anything. "We're due to have our final magic lesson with Shara after lunch! He'll need to eat, and-"

"Then run it with him," Benson spat. "In fact, all three of you, get to it now!"

"You're gonna make us miss lunch again?" Alycia asked, frustration and anger edging her voice.

Ignoring her question, Benson growled out, "Don't make me repeat myself. Get to it, kiddos, and if you want to have time for a snack after, ya better make it a snappy run."

It was bad enough that Benson hated Chris, more than most other Sentinels he had met. Chris was wildly unpopular for dismantling the Barrier. But for Benson to take it out on Emmi and Alycia? That stripped away Chris's inhibitions.

"No," he stated, shaking his head. "No, I'll run the damn course again, just let them go get some food. We've all worked har-"

"It's not your place to question my orders, boy," Benson snapped back. "Life's a bitch, and it ain't gonna get any easier now that magic's made a comeback. So get used to it, all of you. You get one day off before your test, so that means today's your hardest day." He stalked towards Chris, rage suddenly contorting his face. "And don't you ever tell me no again, ya get me?" He was nose to nose with Chris when he finished speaking, the perpetual whisky stink on his breath washing over Chris's face and making him gag. "I give orders, you follow 'em, or you may as well go home now and not worry about the test."

That was a threat that always snapped Chris back in line. He hated Benson. Hated him almost as much as he hated his father. *No, he thought, more. At least Father only ever ignored me or treated me with stoic nonsense. He didn't retaliate.*

But Benson was right. Chris had dismantled the Barrier, and magic had come back to Earth. Thousands of people the world over suddenly could use magic, the range of their powers varying widely. Chaos followed, as one might expect, with 'normal' people feeling afraid of those with power. Countless countries had declared martial law during the intense magic storms that occurred when the Barrier was merely cracked, and many kept that martial law in place following the fall of the Barrier.

The world was in chaos, and the United States wasn't faring much better. The Sentinels, being the only group with any experience concerning magic, was having to step up and try to contain and control the worst of it.

Yet for all of that, Chris knew the worst was yet to come. With the Barrier gone, Marduk would be able to influence Earth again, maybe even come personally oversee the sacrifices necessary to give him power. With eight billion humans, Earth would be a veritable smorgasbord.

And it was all Chris's fault.

The guilt weighed on him daily, as did the fear. But for all of his hatred towards his father, he had instilled one vital personality trait in Chris – a need to take responsibility for his actions, especially his mistakes.

So he wanted to be part of the Sentinels more than anything. His college career was long over, having passed his final exam (which he only found out about after returning to the United States following the Battle at Babylon,) but he didn't care anymore about finding a job as a mechanical engineer. Now he had only one goal.

So Benson's threat held a lot of weight with Chris.

With a clenched jaw, Chris nodded, and with exaggerated subservience in his voice, he said, "Yes, sir!"

Together with Emmi and Alycia, Chris turned towards the forest. He pressed a button on his watch to restart the timer, and then after drawing in a deep breath, he led the charge.

CHAPTER 2

For all of the physical training Chris had done over the past eight weeks, immediately going on another two and a half mile run was grueling. Emmi and Alycia could have easily outpaced him, but after only a half mile, he was forced to slow down, and they stayed with him. Even after he insisted they go on to ensure Benson didn't have a reason to lecture them, they stayed with Chris.

They ignored the training dummies this time, and instead focused on keeping an even pace.

By the time they rounded the final turn, Chris's hands shook and he felt ready to fall down, light-headedness beginning to set in. His legs screamed fire, but he wouldn't give up. He *couldn't* give up. Chris would never let Benson have that satisfaction, not today, not ever!

When they crossed the finish line, with Emmi and Alycia encouraging him every step of the way, his 'run' had slowed to a crawl, and the instant he was over Benson's imaginary threshold, he collapsed to his knees and lowered his head. Darkness edged into his vision, but he managed to stave off passing out.

Alycia was at his side in an instant, kneeling next to him and coaching him to breathe. Emmi stalked past Benson, who snapped at her, "Don't give me stink eye, girlie."

"Don't call me girlie, old man," she retorted. A few seconds later, she was at Chris's side with a water bottle. He pushed off of his hands to kneel upright and sucked down as much water as he could in one short breath, but it caught in his throat and sent him into a coughing fit. It was warm from sitting in the sun, but he didn't care, it was water! So after he regained control of himself, he slugged down the rest.

When he opened his eyes, Benson stood staring at a stopwatch shaking his head.

"What?" Chris breathed between drinks.

"That was unacceptably slow," Benson remarked, looking at Chris with unimpressed eyes.

He huffed. "Screw you, I just ran five miles straight."

"And I didn't hear any gunfire," Benson added, and then he motioned to the picnic table behind him. The trio followed his pointing finger, and Chris felt a void open up inside. A holstered pistol sat on the table. "And Ms. Dubois, you committed the worst offense yet!" His voice rose in pitch and volume at that. "You left a goddamn loaded firearm unattended!"

Emmi's already flush face deepened in color, and she looked down. Chris knew what was coming next, and he wanted nothing more than to step in between Benson and her, to keep him from laying in on her, but the moment he tried to stand, his legs gave out on him.

"You never leave a loaded gun unattended!" Benson's voice had turned to a veritable roar and he stalked closer to her, while she shrunk down, shying away from him. "Jesus Christ, what if you did that in public and a kid got 'hold of it? Worse still, this was training for combat, and you left your damn weapon behind! What were you going to use to defend yourself, harsh language?"

"She doesn't need guns," Alycia retorted hotly, expressing Chris's growing rage when he had no energy left in himself to express it. "Neither does Chris!"

"Stay out of this," Benson reeled on her. "You've done better than them, but that doesn't mean you get to mouth off to me."

"Go to hell," Emmi whispered.

Chris knew she didn't mean for Benson to hear, but she'd whispered it the moment he'd finished shouting at Alycia. "The hell did you just say, girlie?"

Her eyes flashed in rage. "Stop calling me girlie!"

Benson stalked closer, and she didn't back down right away. Pressure pressed against Chris's inner soul, pressure that he recognized coming from Emmi. Her eyes flashed a bright green, and he knew that she was moments away from shapeshifting into an animal.

"Emmi, no," Chris managed a hoarse-voiced caution.

"Go on," Benson chucked his chin out at her. "Go ahead and turn into a bear, or a tiger, or whatever. Maul me all you like, you'll never get into the Sentinels then..."

Emmi's temper faltered, but she had already summoned power into her body, and as they had learned from Shara, once she started a transformation, she had to use that energy someway. So she backed away, and the green in her eyes enveloped her body. Instead of turning into a vicious predator, she shrunk down into a tiny shape, and when the green glow receded, a squirrel stood in her place. An instant later, squirrel-Emmi darted away, dashing into the forest with incredible speed.

"Emmi!" It was Shara's voice, calling from the cabin as she ran out the door towards them. Had she felt Emmi's powers and come running? Chris glanced at his watch, switching it over to show the time, and realized that it was more likely due to their session with Shara starting in two minutes.

The squirrel was already long-gone, disappeared into the flora beneath the trees. Shara stopped beside Benson and planted her hands on her hips. Her cerulean-blue hair was pulled back into a ponytail, revealing her long, pointed ears, and unlike when Chris had first met her, she didn't wear colored contacts, and her sunset-violet eyes sparked with anger. "What'd you say to her this time?"

Benson quickly turned defensive, as he always did in Shara's presence. "Girlie got mouthy with me," he defended, folding his arms. "So I told her off."

"You were a jackass," Alycia stated.

"No need for that," Shara lectured, cutting off Benson's retort. As much as Chris liked Shara, that accusation and his ability to breathe normal again made him want to defend Alycia, but he didn't need to. Shara pointed a finger at Benson and she continued, "But she's right." Pointing at her ears, she continued, "I heard what you said to her, and I told you to stop berating her."

Chris glanced at Alycia and asked through his eyes, *but she didn't want him to stop berating us?*

Alycia saw his expression and shrugged, but he saw that she was as pissed off as he was about all of this. The end of training couldn't come soon enough, for any of them.

"Coddling the kids ain't gonna prep them for what's out there," Benson mirrored Shara's stance, hands-on-hips and all, as he glared at her. This was an unusual turn of events – Benson never stood up to Shara. He respected rank, and as the second-in-command of the Denver-based Sentinels, Shara's rank held great sway with him.

"After what she went through, the last thing she needs is a man shouting at her or insulting her or tearing her down," Shara shouted. Pointing a finger towards the cabin, she commanded, "Now get your ass out of here while I try to undo your screw up!"

Benson was taken aback. "I, what, screw up?"

"Now!"

He clamped his mouth shut and glared back at Shara defiantly. Finally, with a grumpy huff, he stalked off towards the cabin, muttering under his breath. "I heard that," Shara shouted at his back.

Sighing and pinching the bridge of her nose, Shara shook her head. "If he wasn't the best trainer we had..." Then she seemed to remember Chris and Alycia were within earshot, and she looked at them. "I'm sorry, guys, I really am. I know he's a veritable asshole."

"You can say that again," Alycia grumbled.

Chris stood up with some help from Alycia and he nodded. "Why can't you guys find someone else?"

"We're not exactly openly recruiting just anyone," Shara shook her head. "Our options are limited, and he was a drill sergeant for the U.S. Army before joining the Sentinels, so he's kind of our only option at the moment. Unless we sent you overseas, but Tom wanted to keep you all nearby."

Shara's eyes darted towards the forest, and Chris swore her ears perked up. "Emmi didn't go far," she said a second later. "I'll go get her. You two be sure to drink some water, and then start on meditation."

"Yes, ma'am," Alycia and Chris said simultaneously.

There was another press of energy against Chris's soul, while a lighter-green glow engulfed Shara for a second, and then she was a tiny chipmunk-type creature. It wasn't actually a chipmunk, since its fur was navy blue, but that was likely because Shara always favored shapeshifting into creatures from her home world.

Once transformed, Shara bolted off into the woods after Emmi.

Knowing that Benson might come back after they headed for the grove where they meditated, Chris stopped by the table to grab

Emmi's holstered pistol, and then they stalked past the cabin, snagging fresh bottles of water from a cooler in the shade as they went.

There was a part of Chris that knew that Benson had been right to be furious at Emmi. Chris hated firearms on a good day, and he was more appreciative now than ever at just how deadly a gun could be. That's why he always preferred using magic over guns – as deadly as arcane magic could be, he could always dial back the power and 'set it to stun,' so to speak.

Their first days of training had been all about firearm safety and use, and it had been drilled into their heads to never leave a loaded weapon unattended. But Chris couldn't forgive their trainer for laying into Emmi so harshly like that. Into all of them.

Chris and Alycia walked in silence, and he suspected she was fuming over Benson as much as he was. "I can't wait to be done with him," he growled.

"Yeah," she nodded curtly, her Australian accent a little thicker, like it always was when she was angry or flustered. "I think I'm gonna have to give Dad an earful about him."

"I'd offer to be present when you did," Chris grinned, "but I don't think that'd help matters."

Tom hadn't quite forgiven Chris for dismantling the Barrier. Most of the Denver Sentinels didn't, for that matter. Those that survived Nabu's attacks, anyway.

Three had died in May; one in the hangar when Chris first learned that magic was real, and two in the Sentinel headquarters when Nabu used one of the Sentinels to betray them. Now Chris, Emmi and Alycia were setting up to take the place of those fallen Sentinels.

It was a strange world they lived in now. Magic was real, when it hadn't been for four thousand years of human history. Mythological gods were real, and one threatened every human on Earth. And Chris was apparently the one chosen to stop Marduk.

After trouncing through another open field, Chris and Alycia came upon the small grove of aspen trees with a clearing in the middle just big enough for them, Emmi, and Shara to sit in and meditate. It was peaceful there, with birds chirping in the distance and a breeze blowing through the trees, which swayed patiently against it. There was no undergrowth here other than soft grasses, so Alycia sat down, folding her legs into a pretzel beneath her. Chris set

Emmi's pistol and two bottles of water down, and then used the nearest tree to stretch out his legs before he joined Alycia.

Silence fell upon them as they focused on their breathing, and Chris in particular had to fight against a post-marathon high. He placed his hands on his knees and closed his eyes, and drew in a deep breath for four counts, held it for seven, and exhaled slowly, imagining his tension and anger radiating out with his exhalation. Who knew that a breathing exercise Emmi had taught him would one day be what helped him center himself?

Emmi did, of course, he thought wryly.

While repeating the exercise, he tried to keep his excitement down. This was always his favorite part of the day. Meditation and centering himself, focusing on that golden core of energy within, was the best part, next to sleeping. It meant something wonderful and exciting was coming.

It meant he could talk to his sister again.

Each of the trio had different powers, and they had learned that their magic abilities drew energy from different sources.

Emmi's, being tied to nature, drew from the life force of plants and animals. That had worried her at first, since it might have meant hurting other creatures, but Shara assured her that it was nothing so terrible. It was borrowed energy, and never enough to hurt anyone or anything.

Alycia's was vastly different. As one who could conjure and enchant, Alycia's powers came from an endless source outside of 'our realm,' as Shara had put it. It made using her powers more difficult than Chris or Emmi's, but apparently it also meant that she could tap into an endless supply and, theoretically, never run out of energy to use.

Chris's, being arcane based, apparently depended upon his own soul. Or at least, normally that's what it meant. This would normally limit how much of his powers he could use before tiring, but Chris was special. Four thousand years ago, his ancestor, Tattannu, had tied his soul to the Barrier, and ensured that he, along with every single one of his descendants, would contribute to the Barrier upon their deaths, their souls joining it and powering it. They were intricately interwoven, so that when Chris had used the Dragonstone to dismantle the Barrier, those souls transferred to him.

Tens of thousands, if not millions of souls powered Chris's magic.

Including his sister's soul.

After finishing his initial breathing exercises, he changed to a more metered breath, four counts in, four counts out, and reached inward towards his golden core. If he had successfully purged himself of his frustrations, then it meant...

Warmth washed over Chris's being. He was in a swirling void of grays and whites, and before him was a golden sphere of light, with tendrils of electricity lancing from the outer shell inwards towards the pinpoint of light in the center.

All around him, he could see shadows of people moving about. The souls of Tattannu's descendants. Not just those directly related to Chris, but from all branches of Tattannu's family. After four thousand years and countless generations splitting off in all directions, it was a dizzying number.

From the haze of those milling souls, one figure stepped closer to the golden core, and materialized into a solid visage.

Elation filled Chris, and a smile stretched across his face, both in the metaphysical world and in the real world. "Naomi," he said.

Naomi Tatsu was slightly shorter than him, pale-faced and slender, with long, straight black hair, and deep, dark eyes that could gaze into his soul even when she was alive.

"Hello again, Chris," she said, though this time it was not with a smile.

He tilted his head to one side. "What's wrong?"

She paused, glancing at the golden sphere. "You're here again."

A frown drew down his brow. "Well, yeah. Like I am every day."

Her gaze shifted away from him, off into the ether, before she looked at him again, her face one of absolute seriousness. "What about Emmi?"

Surprised by her question, he asked, "What do you mean?"

"I mean why didn't you go try to find her?"

This was completely unexpected. Usually when he came to talk to Naomi, they spent the time catching up more and more on what had happened in life since Nabu had killed her ten years ago. Chris had told her all about what was going on with Mom and Dad, school, meeting Emmi after Naomi passed away, and going to college.

She had never before asked about something that had just occurred. "Wait, you can see what happens around me?"

With a nod, Naomi replied, "Sometimes, in flashes."

That was a little disturbing, and thinking back to some of his private moments over the past ten weeks, his face flushed considerably. "I, um. Well. That is, I don't know what…"

"Chris, if there's one thing I can tell you with absolute confidence, it's that the people in your *life* matter more than you can ever know." She drew closer to him and lightly touched his elbow.

"I know that," he nodded. "But how many people get a second chance to visit with those they've lost?"

A smile crossed her face then, as beautiful as ever. "That's true."

"Besides, I'm just following Shara's orders," he added. "She wanted us to come meditate. I only get moments with you when we do this."

"I know," she replied, her smile faltering a little bit. Then she looked off into the ether again. "Speaking of, looks like it's time for me to go."

His smile vanished completely. In here, within his inner-self, he could always sense when other magic users were nearby, so when he looked to his left, he wasn't surprised to see two green spheres slowly approaching.

Naomi squeezed his elbow, and then turned away, walking into the mists of the other shadows. A second later, Chris brought himself out of his meditation.

CHAPTER 3

Just as Emmi and Shara walked into view, Chris's eyes fluttered open. He watched them approach, but his mind was still in the dream world. Still with Naomi and her strange behavior. Why had she been so stand-offish?

Emmi's face was drawn down, her eyes staring at the ground before her while Shara guided her. Wondering how long it took Shara to find Emmi, Chris glanced at his watch and noted that he'd been talking with Naomi for almost an hour.

He silently hissed out a surprised breath. Sometimes a minute in dreams cost him an hour in real life. Sometimes a minute in real life gave him an hour of dreams. Would he ever learn to control that aspect? Or was he doomed, like every other human on Earth, to never control it?

Shara rubbed the top of Emmi's back, but they didn't speak to one another. He suspected that any words would have been exchanged before coming to the grove.

Distinctively keeping her eyes off of both Alycia and Chris, Emmi passed between them and sat down in her customary spot, folding her legs like a pretzel. A second later, she spied the holstered pistol to Chris's right, and then clenched her jaw.

Darting her eyes up to him, she nodded and reached out a hand. "Thanks."

Passing it over to her, he nodded. "No problem." He then handed her a bottle of water as well, and she gratefully took a sip from it.

Shara sat across from Emmi in their tiny circle and cleared her throat. "Alright. I have to tell you all something, and I meant to tell Benson, but…" She glanced towards the cabin and scowled. "Maybe for once I'll let the grumpy bastard find out the hard way." Looking again to the trio, she continued on, "I have news that may not exactly be welcome. Your final evaluation is being moved up to tomorrow."

A jolt of surprise sent tingles down Chris's extremities, and he and Alycia protested at the same time.

"I know, I know," Shara raised her hands defensively. "I argued against it, but circumstances have changed."

She sighed deeply, clearly hesitant about something. She studied the grasses in the center of the circle while mulling something over, but then nodded to herself and looked up. "Nabu's cult has apparently regained strength." Chris blinked incredulously, but listened intently. "And by regained strength, I mean they have more members than ever before, as best as we can tell. As I'm sure you've seen on the internet," she looked pointedly at Alycia, who always spent considerable time on her smart phone in the evenings, scouring for signs of her mother's whereabouts, "violence has exploded all over the world with riots, civil wars, coup d'états, and more, ever since the Barrier came down." She glanced knowingly at Chris.

Shara continued, "Apparently Abby found evidence that some of this is being instigated by Nabu's former followers." Abigail Turner was the 'gal behind the computer,' as she called herself, the computer whiz for the U.S. Sentinels who manned the ops center on weekdays and during emergencies. "Before you ask," she warded off Alycia's incoming question, "she hasn't found your mother yet, but it seems likely that Mia is orchestrating things.

"In any case, pulling world leaders from the Sentinel Council now is a tricky business at best. Some that were supposed to come observe your final test have already canceled their trip to the States. Others insisted we get it done now, because we can use all of the help we can get. And others still want…" Shara paused and shook her head, her face betraying her disbelief in what she was about to tell them. "Others want you three, especially you, Chris," she nodded at him, "thrown in a cell for your part in dismantling the Barrier. They're blaming you for everything going on in the world, and as they've all begun briefing their respective countries' leaders on the truth about magic, their leaders are blaming you, as well."

A lump formed in Chris's throat, and he audibly gulped it down. This was highly unexpected news, and suddenly the world felt like a much smaller, more claustrophobic place. "Which, um…which countries?" he asked.

"Tom didn't give me specific names," she shook her head. "But it's getting dicey out there. It's like the year 2020 all over again, maybe worse." The trio grimaced at one another. Shara visibly hesitated again, and added, "I wish that was all of the bad news."

Chris felt his face grow pale and he groaned. "What else?"

"We think that some of the new cultists are magic users."

Inwardly, Chris felt his growing tension ease just a little bit. That wasn't actually a surprise to him. Estimates still varied widely, but internet sources indicated at least five percent of the global population could use magic, probably more. That meant there were a couple hundred million magic users out there, and it was no surprise that some would find out about Nabu and Marduk and decide to worship them.

"And," Shara continued, re-twisting the knot in Chris's stomach, "they've attacked the British Parliament building."

"What?!" Alycia gawked at Shara wide-eyed.

"When?" Chris asked.

"Last night," Shara replied. "Casualties were light, but there's a lot of damage. The attacker, and it was a single person with magic, was spotted by a couple of witnesses. Her powers were incredibly strong, and based on witness descriptions, it was arcane powers." Chris blanched. Did that meant the Sentinels intended to send him after whomever did it?

"Well," Chris breathed. "I, uh. I guess they're V for Vendetta fans, eh?"

His attempt at humor was the only way he knew to deal with the shock and fear, and his efforts earned a giggle from Alycia. Shara frowned, and looked at Chris inquiringly. "Some pop culture reference I don't know yet?"

"It's a comic book," Emmi stated.

"Graphic novel," Chris corrected. "And a movie. You should at least watch the movie, it's entertaining and, considering where things are going, might be somewhat relevant."

Shara nodded. She'd actually been curious to learn more about all of the pop culture references that Chris and Alycia continually exchanged, and had started to watch some of the shows and movies in the evenings to catch up.

Emmi brought them all back to the topic at hand. "So what do we do tomorrow?"

"You test out," Shara replied. "Benson and myself will be judging, along with Tom, the Brazilian Sentinel leader, the Japanese Sentinel leader, and the Australian Sentinel leader. The foreign leaders are all arriving in Denver today, and will be here late tomorrow morning."

The knot in Chris's stomach twisted even more, and he sighed. All of the tension he'd worked out through meditation was back, and then some.

"That said," Shara nodded, "my lesson plan for today remains the same. Practice what you already know. *When* you pass," she emphasized her confidence in them, "You'll be the first magic-capable Sentinels."

"Other than you," Emmi pointed out.

Shara smiled. "True, but you all have an advantage over me on that one." Shara was a powerful shapeshifter, but she had admitted to them that it took considerably more effort for her to transform on Earth than it did on her world. She suspected that because she had to draw energy from nature and life on a world that she had not learned on, it was more difficult.

"So the question remains, do you all want to go off on your own, or do you want to watch each other work?"

Chris looked to the others, who looked to him with the same uncertainty he felt. Emmi in particular looked frightened and despondent. Thinking back to Naomi's words, he said, "Let's help each other out, cheer one another on." He nodded at Emmi. "I think we're all nervous about tomorrow, so let's build each other up."

The smallest hint of a smile crooked at the corner of Emmi's mouth, but she didn't meet Chris's eyes. Alycia nodded her support.

"Then let's get to it. Who wants to go first?"

Chris volunteered, and the four of them left the grove. All three of them had spent considerable time and effort over the past eight weeks honing the abilities they'd already shown, but Shara had likewise encouraged them to explore new possibilities with their powers.

As Chris used mostly arcane powers, or so Shara called it, she indicated that he was limited to raw power in his magic. At first, he thought that meant he could only ever attack directly, and he'd spent time learning how to better aim and, more importantly, control the output of his powers. He hoped to avoid over-powered attacks like what had happened to the reception desk at Nabu's complex in Babylon.

Now, he could control the diameter of the beams he projected from his hands, right down to near-laser widths. He had learned to control the intensity and duration better, too. They setup empty soup and soda cans on boulders for him, and he spent the first few minutes that morning burning holes in some, and disintegrating others completely, while trying not to cause collateral damage around or, more importantly, behind the cans. Mostly he was successful, but the first can he disintegrated, he had used a bit too much power, and a tree behind it splintered bark off and was left with a scorch mark.

The next power he used was one he rarely had a use for, and that was electricity. Inspired by the countless sparks he'd endured leading up to the battle at Babylon, and having cast it a couple of times against Nabu, Chris was actually afraid of casting bolts of lightning. They were at least as powerful as his energy beams, but much harder to control. Sometimes when he tried to send a bolt of lightning at a can, at the last second it arched in another direction, obeying the laws of physics and finding a closer path-of-least-resistance, and in the past, he'd fried a few trees as a result.

This time, however, he managed to stay on target, and he sent three root beer cans flinging away into a melted heap.

Next came the plasma ball, and as usual, Alycia quoted at him, "Remember, a plasma ball is a wizard's bread and butter!" It was a line from the live-action Sorcerer's Apprentice, and he grinned at her.

These were sort of in between lightning and the energy beams, easier to control where they went, but a little harder for him to control their intensity. The first can he tried it on was blown apart, but the boulder it was set upon took collateral damage. He cursed at himself, and was reminded by Shara to clear his mind. He went through a couple of breathing exercises, and then tried again, this time successfully damaging a can without hurting the innocent boulder underneath.

The last can he was to smash with a plasma ball was a Mountain Dew can, and right before he cast his spell, a grin stretched across his face. He glanced back at Alycia, and then clapped his wrists together and curled his fingers before thrusting the palms outward together and shouting, "Ha-dew-can!" His joke distracted him, and the boulder took damage, but the can was absolutely obliterated, and Alycia practically fell over laughing.

Turning with a self-approving grin and laughing along with Alycia, his humor died a second later when he noticed the puzzled looks on Shara and Emmi's faces.

"It's from a video game, sort of," he explained. "Street Fighter. Hadouken." They still looked puzzled. "I...you know what? Never mind."

"That was great," Alycia beamed, wrangling her laughter.

His final ability was one that he had zero confidence in, but decided to try out anyway. As a conjurer, Alycia had been able to summon barriers with ease since the very beginning, but Chris had no such defenses, no way to defend against incoming attacks except with attacks of his own. Instead, he expanded upon the idea of the plasma ball, and only a week ago had the idea to surround himself with energy to protect himself.

His first attempt had been disastrous. So he stepped away from the others, *far* away, and found the circular scorch mark in the grass where he'd tried every time.

Once there, he looked back at the others, and Alycia and Emmi cheered him on.

Drawing in a deep breath, he looked inward, sought out the golden core within, and touched it, drawing power from it.

The difficulty came in controlling the shape of his powers. The energy beam had come naturally to him, but all other forms, being more complex, took more effort and will power. To entirely surround himself with such power? That was another thing altogether.

While drawing power out of that core and into himself, he began to imagine projecting it outward from his skin. The power was only too eager to leap out of him, and he tensed while he caught it, trying to keep it under his control. The idea was to project a constant stream into a sphere, creating a shield.

And for one brief moment, a golden sphere of energy *did* appear around him. He'd done it!

For one second. And then it exploded outward in a great wave, scorching earth and sending out a pressure wave, short-lived but still enough to blow back his friends' hair.

He sighed in defeat. Would it ever work? Could he ever learn to control it enough that he wouldn't endanger his friends if they were nearby?

A second later, he noticed a few small clumps of grass were on fire, and he quickly stomped them out. "God *damn* it," he grumbled.

"Don't give up, try again!" Shara shouted from their safe spots.

But no, he wouldn't. Shaking his head, he stalked towards them once the last little fire was out. "I don't want to be responsible for starting a brush fire," he explained once he didn't have to shout anymore. "I don't think I'll ever have the control necessary."

"Hey," Shara caught him on the shoulder and forced him to look at her. He took the opportunity to stare into her violet eyes, lost in them as he always was and drawing courage. "You're doing better than almost any arcane caster I ever knew on my world. Most of them take years to get to where you are now. And none of them, as far as I know, ever thought to use their powers as a shield, so you're already ahead of the game in ingenuity." She gave him a warm smile, and he felt his cheeks flush. "Don't give up, okay?"

He nodded. "Alright. If you think I shouldn't give up, I won't. But I think I've had enough of the spotlight today." He looked at the others, but then paused when he noticed Alycia's smile had vanished, replaced by a saddened look.

Chris was about to ask her what was wrong, but Shara turned to them and said, "Alright, who wants to go next?"

Alycia noticed Chris staring, and then a resolute expression hardened her features. "I'll have a go," she volunteered quickly.

The first abilities Alycia ever displayed were protective barriers, conjuring walls of light that stopped everything from bullets to knives to, as Benson had demonstrated, arrows. The only thing they hadn't been brave enough to try yet were magic attacks from Chris.

Today, Alycia challenged that. She stepped away from the group, towards Chris's burn circle, while pulling on fingerless gloves, and then she stopped and turned around. He wondered what the gloves were all about, but then he was surprised when she said, "If magic users are out there wreaking havoc, I have to be sure I can stop them," she said. "So, come on, Chris," she glared at him. "Hit me with your best shot."

An old 80's song passed through his head, but he ignored it and instead set himself nervously in front of her. "Um, are you sure?"

She glared at him. "I can take it. Do it."

There was a hard edge in her voice, as if she was pissed off at him for some reason, but he didn't know why. Not at first. Then it clicked in his head, and he glanced at Shara. Was Alycia jealous of the attention Shara had just given him? *No, idiot*, he thought to himself, looking into Alycia's golden-brown eyes. *If anything, it's the fact that you blushed.*

Annoyance crept into him. Certainly he liked Alycia, and he'd been nursing a crush for four years, far too afraid to admit his feelings to her. But they weren't dating, right? So he was free to blush from compliments from another girl he liked, or even flirt with her, wasn't he?

He knew she wasn't psychic, but the anger and determination on Alycia's face grew more intense, and she closed her eyes just long enough to create a blue barrier between them.

"Do it," she demanded.

Drawing on his golden core, he thrust his palm out and unleashed the weakest beam of energy he could.

The blue-white shield crackled with energy, golden tendrils of lightning playing across its surface, but it didn't budge.

"That's it?" Alycia asked. "That didn't even register on me, come on!"

He grit his teeth, and unleashed another, stronger blast. This time there was an audible boom when his attack hit her shield, but the shield held.

"Seriously?" she mocked, frustration in her voice. "Come on, ya ratbag, I thought you were supposed to be powerful!"

He didn't know what a ratbag was, but the insult still got to him, and so he let loose a much stronger blast.

Alycia's shield flared brightly, the boom was as deafening as a bolt of lightning, but suddenly some of his golden energy came barreling back and slammed into him, sending him tumbling back and knocking the wind out of him with a "whuff!"

The ringing in his ears took almost as long to stop as the spinning world did, but when it all cleared up, Emmi and Shara stood over him with shocked and concerned looks on their faces.

"Are you alright?" Emmi asked. "Chris? Can you hear me?"

He blinked. "Uh, yeah." His voice sounded distant to himself. "I, uh, what happened?"

Shara and Emmi grabbed his arms and hefted him back onto his feet. He stared at Alycia, who fumed at him, not a lick of concern in her expression. Her shield was gone, but he didn't know if that was because he'd overpowered it, or if she had dispelled it.

However, with a great big grin stretching across her face, she closed the distance between them and lifted her gloved hands up. They were navy-blue like her tank top, but he just now noticed runes embroidered in them.

"It worked!" she exclaimed with excitement. "I wasn't sure what was going to happen, but it worked!"

"What worked?" Emmi asked.

But Shara knew, and she gaped at her. "You placed a defensive enchantment on your gloves!"

"Yup," Alycia beamed. "I mean I knew it would work, but I didn't know if it would do exactly what I wanted it to do, and it did!"

Glancing back and forth between Chris and Alycia, Shara commented, "It redirected a fraction of Chris's attack back at him."

"Exactly." Her smile soured a second, turning into a scowl. "I hoped I could goad him into doing enough to get knocked on his ass."

His face turned pink for an entirely different reason now.

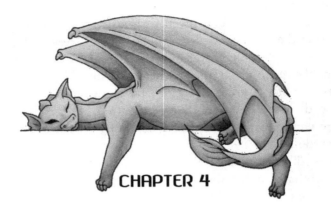

CHAPTER 4

Emmi helped Chris up onto his feet, but then she covered her mouth with her hand, a poor attempt at hiding her grin.

Brushing himself off, Chris tried desperately to hide his embarrassment, but the rushing sensation in his chest and his rosy cheeks made that practically impossible. Thankfully, Shara didn't laugh, and instead only admired Alycia's handiwork.

"I swear, you kids impress me every day," Shara shook her head. His blush vanished, and he was sorely tempted to tell her they weren't kids, but then stopped himself. They weren't exactly sure how old Shara was, but she was at least around a century old, so he supposed that to her, most people on Earth were still 'kids.' "Enchanting through embroidery takes considerable concentration and patience, because you have to focus for the entire time you're embroidering. Did you do it by hand or by machine?"

Alycia replied, "No sewing machines here, so all by hand."

Shara very carefully and very gently held Alycia's hand so that she could examine the embroidery, and she whistled appreciatively. "Chris was right, you really do have incredible talent."

And once again, Chris felt himself blush. Alycia's earlier scorn towards him vanished in a heartbeat, her face turning slack as she looked at him with surprise. He had, in fact, mentioned that to Shara, but it had been months ago, when they barely knew Shara. She definitely had a good memory.

It occurred to Chris a second later that Shara had said that specifically to help de-escalate the tension between him and Alycia.

After a moment of stunned silence, Alycia shrugged. "Anywho, now that I know it works, I'm gonna start trying other enchantments on clothing to see what I can make happen."

Shara eyed her cautiously. "Just be careful. When some enchantments go wrong, it can be disastrous for the enchantress."

"Duly noted," Alycia nodded.

Once Shara was done examining Alycia's gloves, it was Emmi's turn to practice her magic. This was something she always excelled at and seemed to take great joy in. Shapeshifting into animals had become her favorite thing to do, and by now, she could do it with almost no delay. She first shapeshifted into her famous black panther, which he always found to be a striking form with her lightning-blue eyes contrasted against the deep, black fur.

Next she transformed into a bald eagle, the very first form she had ever shapeshifted into, and she took off into the sky, her giant wingspan eclipsing the sun for a second. She swooped about, gaining altitude and then diving towards them only to pull up at the last second, blowing their hair in a rush of wind.

It reminded Chris of his first dreams, and their subsequent battle at Sixteenth Street. It reminded him that ever since Babylon, he hadn't had a single prophetic dream. Were his dreams an anomaly resulting from the cracks in the Barrier? Or would he someday have visions again?

A couple of terrified sparrows took issue when eagle-Emmi drew too close to their nests, and their size and mobility allowed them to harass her with impunity. She screeched in complaint, and dove for the field. As soon as she was low enough, she shape-shifted into a tiger and roared, scattering the birds back towards the trees.

Another green glow engulfed her, and then she was a fox, reddish-orange fur and black tailed. She trotted over and yipped up at them. Shara grinned, and asked, "Want to try some water forms?"

Emmi's tail became a blur of excitement, and she hopped and yipped excitedly.

Looking at Chris and Alycia with a grin, Shara said, "Meet you by the lake!" and she ran from them until she was far enough away to safely shapeshift into a gryphon!

This was always his favorite form to witness from Shara's world. As big as a Clydesdale horse, her gryphon form consisted of a giant eagle front-half and a great lion back-half, with shimmering white-gold feathers merging flawlessly into the like-colored lioness flank.

She was gorgeous!

Gryphon-Shara let loose a roar and took to the sky, her massive wingspan larger than any living creature's on Earth. Emmi, anxious to keep up, directly shifted to a falcon form and took off in pursuit.

Which left Chris and Alycia alone.

They smiled awkwardly at one another, and somehow Chris lost total control of his heart rate. It thumped with annoying intensity against his chest, thundered in his ears, and for reasons he couldn't begin to fathom, distracted him so much that he couldn't think of a single thing to say.

Alycia, thankfully, at least knew enough to motion towards the lake and said, "Shall we?"

"Uh, yeah, yes," Chris nodded dumbly, and they fell into step alongside one another.

The afternoon wore on, with the lake a half-hour hike away from the field where they practiced their magic. A wind kicked up from somewhere, announcing its coming with a distant roar growing closer and closer until it pushed against Chris's left, nudging him closer to Alycia.

His thoughts dwelled upon all of the times they'd held hands during the crisis in May, when Nabu had threatened their lives. More than that, there were at least two instances when they had almost kissed, including in the hospital in Dubai after defeating Nabu.

Back then, he'd thought they would finally be together.

But he'd never asked.

Never made a move.

Since then, they'd drifted apart somewhat. Still friends, and still friendly, but never romantic. What had changed?

The silence between them felt increasingly unbearable, so he searched for something to say, something to break the awkwardness and try to reclaim their once-easy friendship, if only as a start. He glanced at her, and then glanced again, noticing that her fingerless gloves were still on.

"That was pretty cool," he nodded to the gloves.

That earned him a friendly smile. "Thanks!"

His mind raced, and he latched on to the topic. "What other enchantments are you going to try?"

"I've studied most of the book Shara gave me by now," she replied, "and I've learned with these gloves that intent and desire can actually modify the outcome. Initially this defensive enchantment was just supposed to act as another shield, but I thought it might come in handy if it deflected whatever attacked me back at whomever cast the spell.

"So I want to try to combine a couple of enchantments on one piece of clothing next."

He blinked his surprise. "That's…ambitious." She eyed him coolly, and he quickly added, "But if anyone can pull it off, it's you."

One of Alycia's eyebrows peaked in her usual curious look that always reminded him of Mister Spock. "Yeah, well, we'll see. I was thinking tonight of embroidering my trousers with enchantments that will both increase my running speed and leg strength, so that I can run faster. I dunno, though, what do you think? Would that disqualify me tomorrow?"

Chris thought about it for a second, and then shook his head. "Shara said it herself when we started on this crazy gig, our training would be unique because we're the first new Sentinels that can use magic. Showing advanced enchanting skills to help you succeed tomorrow would probably give you positive marks." He thought about what Shara had just told them, about some Sentinel leaders being angry with them for dismantling the Barrier. "Well, from some of the judges, anyway."

She nodded. "Yeah, I suppose you're right." Glancing at him, specifically at his pants, she shook her head. "I suppose if I did it for you and Emmi, they'd disqualify you both."

He nodded agreement. "Since it isn't our own powers, yeah."

Conversation turned casual after that, and they discussed the upcoming test and how much they looked forward to returning to the city. Chris in particular missed his own bed.

Eventually they came to the lake, which was relatively small, one they could circumnavigate in fifteen minutes or so. They saw no evidence that Emmi and Shara were there, but that didn't mean anything, and they walked along the shore silently, waiting for Emmi to get her fill of magic play.

After a few minutes, a beaver suddenly appeared from beneath the water and let out a few short barks at them. Glancing towards where the lake outpoured into a stream, he saw no evidence of a beaver dam. With a warm smile, he said, "Hello, Emmi."

The beaver barked again, and crawled up on shore. It shook itself, spraying water all over Chris and Alycia. "Hey!" he protested.

"Not funny, Emmi," Alycia added.

The familiar press of magic against Chris's inner core signaled Emmi's shapeshifting, and then she was lying on the grass laughing her ass off. Her hair was soaked, as were her clothes, forcing the cloth to cling to her skin.

"Ha-ha," he mimed, narrowing his eyes at her, but then finding himself chuckling along with her. Alycia giggled a little, too, and the mood was suddenly far more at ease.

A very strange creature broke the water's surface a moment later. It looked like a scaly seahorse, but considerably larger, almost mermaid-sized, with a pair of clawed feet on the front and a long, sparkling blue tail on the end. As soon as it clambered out of the water, Shara shapeshifted into her humanoid self.

Chris had to try really hard not to stare at how her wet tank top clung to every curve…

"Well done, Emmi," Shara smiled while wringing out her hair. "You've shapeshifted eight times in half an hour, that's definitely a record for you."

"Thanks," she grinned. "It's getting easier and easier."

"Just remember, though," Shara warned, "magic always comes with a price. Not terribly, like it does in a lot of human fantasy novels, but you *are* drawing magic from nature. Someday nature may demand something in return."

Emmi's eyes widened. "Seriously? Like what?"

Shara shrugged. "It's really hard to say. I think you're still years away from learning what all animal shapeshifters eventually do, and that's how to *communicate* with nature. It'll ask you favors, someday. And you definitely never, *ever* want to ignore those requests, or your shapeshifting might not go so well in the future."

Emmi visibly shuddered. "Duly noted," she repeated Alycia's earlier words.

"Well, then, I think that's all we need to do today," Shara finished wringing her hair out and whipped her hands down to throw excess water off. "There's one last thing, or really two things, I should tell you about tomorrow's test."

Shara nodded back towards the cabin to indicate she wanted to head that way, and the four of them fell into step together. Chris braced himself for more bad news.

"It's not going to be quite the same as all of your training. You'll work together on a single running course, but that course will be designed to test you on your physical fitness, your combat training, and your magic abilities."

That *would* be different. They usually kept their magic training separate, and that's why Benson was so pissy with Chris over using magic instead of his pistol during his runs.

"Additionally, the Sentinel leaders are bringing one or two Sentinels with them to, um…" Shara hesitated and looked sheepishly at them. "Hamper your efforts along the course."

Chris grimaced. "What exactly does that mean?"

"It means you'll have to get by some of…us."

He blinked in surprise. So Shara would be one of the ones standing in their way. This was going to be an interesting test.

At least it's better than sitting nervously in a testing center, he mused with a grin.

CHAPTER 5

The afternoon wound down quickly, and as evening approached, Chris found himself growing more and more anxious. He wanted to talk to Naomi again, to find out what was bothering her during his last vision.

Chris, Emmi and Alycia had a light snack and gulped down copious amounts of water, and then decided to go on one final hike around the training grounds to wind down. *Go figure,* Chris thought ironically. *We're exhausted, so we physically exert ourselves to relax.*

The Sentinel training camp was an area of land southwest of Denver by some distance, near Taylor Park Reservoir. They were surrounded by mountains, and had who knew how many acres to themselves, so the chances of being observed by outsiders was considered minimal, and ample fencing and signs were meant to deter hikers and other explorers from wandering onto Sentinel lands.

Which meant that for several miles, the trio, along with Shara and Benson, were the only people. It was a rare slice of privacy in an over-populated Earth, and as much as Chris missed the city, he realized he would miss moments like this just as much.

Idle chatter fell easily amongst them, with Alycia and Chris's earlier spat seemingly forgotten. After an hour, they returned to the cabin, and prepared a fire outside near the picnic table to cook the evening's meal.

Shara joined them once the fire was roaring, but as usual, Benson was absent. The trio often wondered where he went in the evenings or what he ate, since he never had anything cooked off the fires. The main cabin *did* have a stove and oven, however, so Chris thought that maybe he cooked on his own inside.

Once the fire died down to hot coals, they put a grate over it, and Alycia retrieved boneless chicken breasts from the fridge inside the cabin for them to season and cook.

By the time they ate, it was almost six in the evening, according to Chris's watch, and the sun was still plenty high in the late summer sky. They built up the fire again, and enjoyed the blaze from a healthy distance until the mountains cast long shadows over them.

Gazing into the wavering orange-white embers, Chris's mind wandered to his dreams again, and a question he had asked himself almost daily wound its way into his thoughts — why wasn't he having visions of the future anymore?

Did it have anything to do with Naomi's attitude? Or was there something else going on, something else he was missing? Those visions had proven vital to finding and stopping Nabu. They had let him save Emmi.

His best friend sat to his right, and he glanced at her. She stared with a distant gaze into the flames, her bright blue eyes reflecting the flickering blaze and the dying light in the sky. To anyone who didn't know her, she was expressionless, but Chris knew better. Something weighed heavily on her. Something that had been there ever since Babylon.

She never spoke of what Nabu had done to her, other than to say that the wound he had inflicted in the Sentinel tower was healed through magic immediately, to ensure she didn't die. Beyond that, she refused to say anything.

Then again, he thought, *we never really pressed her about it.*

Drawing in a deep breath, he turned and lost himself in the fire again. The answers still had to be somewhere in his dreams. If Nabu's leftover cultists were gaining ground, he wanted to know what their long-term plans were. He wanted to know who led them, whether it was Alycia's mother Mia or someone else.

Which meant it was time to find answers.

He stood up from the lawn chair and stretched. "I think I'm going to turn in early," he said, half-smiling as he glanced around at the others. Both Alycia and Shara frowned at him, and he shrugged. "It's been a long day. And tomorrow's going to be even longer."

"Right," Emmi commented quietly.

"G'night everyone," he smiled and walked off.

While the main cabin served as their main structure, there were two other cabins on the edge of the clearing that served as dorms, and Chris walked to the one that he and his friends used. Once inside, he flipped on a light to combat the growing darkness, and checked his phone.

No messages, no missed calls. His parents never talked to him these days. The most he'd heard from them all summer was when he told them that he passed his classes and would be graduating. When his mom asked when the ceremony was, he had told them that he had received an internship that started right away, and he wouldn't have time to walk with his class.

His father didn't care, of course. After all, Chris was the least favored of his children, and sometimes Chris wondered if his father blamed him for Naomi's death, even though he'd had nothing to do with it. His mother was a little more despondent about Chris not walking and demanded to know who he would be working for, but his father talked her down, stating it was better and more efficient for Chris to immediately get to work.

Whatever he had wanted to tell them about magic and his adventure, he had decided in that moment not to say a thing about it. They never understood him before, and they certainly never would now. They didn't even mention the crazy things happening all over the world or the freak blizzard that had buried Denver in four feet of snow in a matter of hours, and subsequently flooded the city after all of the snow melted the next day.

It wasn't normal, so why would they acknowledge it?

They would never understand him. But Naomi did.

So after a quick shower in the single bathroom in the cabin, Chris shut off his light, got in the covers of his horribly uncomfortable bed, and started meditating.

Within minutes, he found his golden core and followed it into his inner being. Sometimes he would try to encourage himself by thinking of the swirling gray and white mists as his mind palace, like Sherlock Holmes from the newer British television series, but this was more magical then that, and he knew he wasn't as brilliant as Holmes. Maybe he rated a Watson, at best.

Surrounding him within the gray mists, he saw black shadows moving about. Naomi had to be amongst them, so he called out to her. Once. Twice. Again, and again.

When she didn't show up for what felt like ages, he started to panic. "Anyone?" he asked desperately. "Will someone come and talk to me? Is Naomi okay?" He realized the irony in asking if a dead girl was okay, and if his spiritual self could blush, it did.

Finally, when he felt like he couldn't keep his calm well enough to remain, one of the dark shadows shimmered, and his sister appeared before him.

She didn't look happy.

"Naomi," he rushed towards her and wrapped his arms around her spectral form. "Thank God. Are you okay? Why didn't you come?"

When he pulled away, she looked at him with sad eyes. "You didn't listen last time," she said, her voice low. "And now you've left Emmi all alone."

Frowning, he shook his head. "What do you mean? She's fine. Alycia and Shara are with her."

Naomi's jaw clenched and she clutched her eyes closed, shaking her head. "Chris...I love you very much, but sometimes you're such an idiot."

He stepped back. "I...what?"

Opening her dark eyes, she glared at him, a frightening visage within the strangely-lit spiritual plane. "She's your best friend! She doesn't need Alycia or Shara, she needs you! How can you not see that? Do you not care? I thought you said she was like your sister after I died!"

His stomach twisted and turned uncomfortably at her accusations, and he took another step back. "She is, she was, I mean, but now I have you again. And besides, she's fine!"

"Even from in here, I know that's not true," Naomi waved her hands around in exasperation. "For crying out loud, you should know her better than I do, right? I've only caught glimpses over the years when the Barrier let me, but even *I* know she's hurting!"

It was true that Emmi hadn't acted the same since Babylon, but would anyone after coming that close to death? "She's recovering just fine," he shook his head, and then changed subjects. "Look, I know that you're unhappy with me, but I needed to ask you about the visions I used to have."

She folded her arms defiantly, and he clamped his mouth shut at that. He knew that look. He remembered it well, and his stomach sank to new depths. She was stubborn, more-so than he ever was.

But the stubbornness quickly turned to a saddened look. "Chris…I've loved catching up with you, I really have. It's been wonderful. But I can't let you keep going like this."

Dread filled every fiber of his being, and the desperation of panic started to sneak into the edges of his thoughts. "What…what do you mean?"

She shook her head, and let her hands fall limply to her sides. "I mean you're not living your life anymore. And it's time to force you to. I know you won't like me for it, maybe you'll even hate me for it…"

"I could never hate you," he protested, and tried to step closer, but some invisible barrier stopped him cold. And then suddenly she was further away, like one of those strange dreams where a hallway stretched endlessly before you.

"I'm sorry, Chris," Naomi shook her head. "But this is for your own good. And Emmi's good." Her voice was almost a whisper.

"Naomi?!" His heart rate raced, and he knew he couldn't keep himself in the dream much longer.

"I'm not going to appear before you again," Naomi said. "I love you, brother, make no mistake about that. So go. Live your life."

And suddenly she was gone, and Chris sat up in bed, sweat dripping from his face and soaking his sheets. "Naomi!"

She was gone. He felt it. It wasn't just that he'd woken up, but she was no longer looking over his shoulder, or watching through his eyes, or whatever it was she had done for ten weeks straight.

Her spirit was absent.

For the first time since all of this began, he felt alone.

CHAPTER 6

Chris turned on a lamp on the wooden nightstand and stared into empty space. An anxious energy overcame him, and his heart raced. Not the kind where it thumped hard in your chest, but rather the kind where it beat a million miles per second and left you behind, wondering how you could possibly catch up and take a breath.

Naomi is gone. Again!

Throwing the covers off, Chris was on his feet in an instant, pacing back and forth while trying to find a modicum of control over his pulse.

She was gone, and there was no way he could make her come back. That much was apparent – from all of the times he'd talked to her, it had always been her choice to emerge from the shadows and talk to him. He couldn't control the spirits of the countless millions trapped in his soul.

If she didn't want to come back, he couldn't force her.

He thought about trying anyway, and he stopped pacing to stare at his bed. A second later, he dismissed that notion only because he knew he couldn't sleep now, nor could he meditate. As long as he panicked over the thought of never seeing Naomi again, he'd never find his center.

Worse still, his ability to use magic would be hampered until he calmed himself down. Could he calm down? This wasn't fair!

The instant he thought it, he chastised himself for thinking such a childish thought.

Still, he couldn't stop thinking about it, and the horrible empty feeling in his chest refused to go away.

The only thing he could think to do was go for a walk. He threw on his boots, and then checked the time on his watch. Just after 10 PM. Everyone would be in bed by now, and the last glimmer of sunset would be long-gone, so it would just be him.

Snagging his phone off of the charger, he shut off his lamp and turned on the phone's flashlight feature, and silently slipped out of the cabin so that he wouldn't wake Emmi or Alycia. Then he stood at the doorstep and stared into the pitch black of night. He couldn't remember if it was a new moon tonight or not, but no moon had risen yet, and if he shut off his flashlight, he would be treated with a gorgeous view of the stars.

He almost did, but he needed to walk off some of the nervous energy first. And tea. Herbal tea would do him some good right about now. So he set off for the main cabin, to raid the kitchen cabinets. He knew that Shara kept them well-stocked with countless variations of teas and instant coffees.

However, as he drew closer to the cabin, his pace faltered. Through the windows, he saw light inside. Someone was either awake, or someone had forgotten to turn the lights off. Frowning, he trounced on, thinking that he would be annoyed if someone had been careless enough to leave the light on.

When he entered a minute later, his eyes scanned for any evidence that someone was there. The main cabin was somewhat like a clubhouse in that it was a wide-open structure, with only one area closed off with restrooms. Half of it was a big kitchen, with a large island with stove burners, and multiple bar stools on one side. The other half, which in a normal clubhouse might have included a pool table or something similar, instead had locked gun cabinets and other weapons lockers, along with ammo crates and lockers full of tactical gear. A giant map of the surrounding lands was plastered against the only windowless wall, opposite of where Chris stood.

As far as he could tell, no one else was around. Then he heard the clink of glass. Walking around the kitchen island, a pair of legs in black yoga pants appeared, and he moved further to find Emmi, sitting on the floor with her back against the island.

And a bottle of Jack Daniels in her hand, half-empty.

"Oh hi, Chris," she waved at him with the bottle, sloshing the golden contents around. Her words were clear enough to instantly tell him that she wasn't drunk, but she was definitely tipsy, and well on her way beyond.

"Um...Emmi?"

She grinned, and then took a swig, wincing a second later. "Oye. This stuff isn't great, but damn is it strong!"

"What are you doing?" He shook his head and looked around, hoping she wasn't here drinking alone.

Her pleasant smile faded into an exaggerated frown. "What's it look like I'm doing? I'm drinking my problems away." He stared aghast at her, but she merely shrugged and commented, "Better than wallowing in self-pity in my bed again." She took another swig.

Chris could hardly believe it. Emmi hardly ever drank, let alone to this point, and certainly never to bury her feelings. Even during the worst of her breakups, she never turned to alcohol. Had she been doing this all summer long, or was this her first night? He glanced at a cabinet, half-open still, and saw countless bottles of various liquor in them, full except for one spot in the front where he surmised the Jack Daniels had come from. That allowed him a sigh of relief, thinking that this must be her first.

She offered him the bottle, and he walked over to her. "Here, try it," she smiled.

He took the bottle, placed it on the marble counter top, and slid it away.

That earned him a sour look, Emmi's face scars accentuated by her frown. "Hey!" She started to push herself up, heaving up on the counter ledge but already unsteady. "I wasn't finished."

"Here, let me help you," he reached for her, but she shoved his hand away violently.

"Don't!" Fire burned in her eyes, and her red hair, no longer in a ponytail, fell loosely around her face. "The fuck you doin'? Helping me? Psht. Since when do you help me?"

His heart crashed to the bottom of his stomach. The words slammed into his chest and he staggered back a step, his mouth opening and closing wordlessly.

She almost managed to get back onto her feet, but now the bottle was forgotten, and her enraged eyes glared at him. "You heard me! Go back to your dreams, you...you..." She flipped her hand around, searching for an appropriate word. "Dreamer boy. Whatever."

Turning, she stumbled away from him, towards the half-open cabinet. He closed the distance as fast as he could and slammed the cupboard door shut before she could grab another drink. "You've had enough, Emmi."

She bodily shoved him away, and he tripped and nearly fell down, grasping and clawing at the counter to steady himself. "Fuck off," she spat out. "I'm tired of feeling this way, so I'm gonna do this, just this once, just tonight!" She waved her hands about helplessly. "Just for one night! I can't..." She shook her head rapidly, and stumbled backwards. "I can't keep going like this." And suddenly a sob came out. "I can't keep feeling like this! Don't you see?" And her face soured again. "No, I don't suppose you do."

She stumbled back across to the island and stretched across it to grab the bottle. Chris didn't stop her this time. Not yet. He was too shocked by what she'd said and done. She had never shoved him like that, and despite the arguments they'd gotten into at the apartment, nothing like this had ever happened.

"Emmi," he started, shaking his head, finding himself at a loss for words. "What's...what's wrong?"

She stayed stretched on the counter for a second, but then turned around bodily on it and pushed herself up to sit atop it, her legs dangling. A cackle issued forth, and she held her tummy as if she were laughing too hard. "You really don't know? After everything? No. No you've had your head too far up your ass."

"Stop that!" he grumbled. "Unless you've got something specific to say, stop saying things like that."

"Fine, I'll say it, then," she spat out at him. "You've left me behind! When I needed you!" Her voice rose with each statement, until she shouted at the top of her lungs, "I NEEDED you!" She slammed the bottle down on the marble counter top, but it didn't break. Her voice dropped to a whisper. "After Iraq. After he..." She drew in a sharp breath. "After that bastard...that evil, loathsome..." She drew her arms in and hugged herself.

So this was about her time in captivity. This was about Nabu.

About what he'd done to her in those precious few hours after her capture. Tears flowed freely down her face, and she rocked herself back and forth. He had the urge to hug her, but he knew she wouldn't let him.

This is what Naomi was talking about. Emmi was pissed because she hadn't, in fact, recovered from that experience.

He'd been so blind.

Chris tried to think back to what they had said after rescuing her. How she acted. Nothing had been the same after that. Sure, Emmi still had a sense of humor now and again, she still smiled. But she had been withdrawn, too, and she frequently turned into an animal anytime something went wrong. Especially...

Oh God, he thought, horrorstruck. The way Emmi had acted after Babylon. Her words. Her avoidance of talking about Nabu and what he did after he healed her. The way she recoiled whenever Benson drew near her during his shouting sessions.

A terrible dread filled his stomach, and he felt dizzy and had to use the counter for support.

"Emmi," he spoke quietly. Her eyes darted towards him, but then turned away. "Did Nabu...? Did he? I mean..." She clutched her arms around her body tighter, eyes clenched shut. "Oh God, Emmi, I'm so sorry."

He knew now what had happened. What Nabu had done to her in Babylon. Not just torture, not just pain.

"I can't," she choked out, hiccuping over her grief. "I can't even...look at myself in the mirror anymore," she continued. "I see...him, his h-hands all over m-me. It disgusts me. It makes me sick, and I find myself hating it. Hating myself. I HATE myself!" She pushed off the counter onto her feet. "I was so God damn WEAK!" She flailed her arms. "I wasn't strong enough, don't you see? I couldn't stop him, I couldn't save myself, I couldn't...I couldn't..." She screamed, roared and railed, rage bursting from her heart. The bottle suddenly sailed from her hands across the cabin, smashing into the far wall, the glass shattering and golden liquid splattering everywhere. "I HATE MYSELF!"

Emmi lost her balance and collapsed to her knees, a horrible, wailing sob issuing forth. Chris wanted so badly to go to her, to wrap his arms around her and hold her until she stopped crying, but he feared that was exactly the wrong thing to do. The last thing she would want was another guy touching her without her permission, in any way.

He'd missed the signs. Chris had been so obsessed with having his real sister back in his life, that he'd missed all of the signs of what Emmi had endured.

I'm an asshole, he thought.

Slowly, making sure to not startle Emmi, he sat down on the cold floor and leaned his back against the island, keeping a few feet between them.

He deserved this. All of this. She should have said worse things to him.

An apology right now felt like it might be too little, too late. But he did so anyway. "I am so sorry, Emmi," he spoke between her sobs.

She drew in a sharp breath and glared at him. He braced himself, prepared to take any verbal abuse she might levy towards him. It was the least he could do. He met her enraged gaze, and didn't waver.

"Say it again," she demanded, and drew in a heaving breath. "Say it all…"

"I'm sorry," he said again. "I was so centered on myself, I didn't see how much you needed me. You were there for me through all of my worst times, but I failed you." He wanted to hang his head in shame, but he stared at her instead, looked right into those fearsome blue eyes.

Emmi looked ready to hit him, and maybe that's what she needed. To work out her emotions on him.

Instead, she deflated, casting her eyes downwards and slouching, her back curling up.

"I don't know what to do, Chris," she whispered. "I…I don't know how to stop this. I don't want to feel this way anymore. Every day. Every night. It…it n-never ends. It never f-feels better."

He didn't know what to say. So he just listened, and let her keep talking, as much as she needed.

"Meditation, running, turning into animals," she shook her head and pawed at her face, wiping tears away fiercely, as if they were offensive. She felt her scars, shuddered, and curled her fingers into a fist. "Nothing helps anymore." She glared up at the liquor cabinet. "Not even that. I just feel worse." Her eyes fell upon him again, reddened and puffy. "And it won't get better even if I drink more, will it?" She shook and hiccupped over her grief as she said, "I w-won't ever get over this, w-will I?" She clenched her fist tighter, and punched the wooden island frame, startling Chris.

"I thought killing him would have made it better. We tore him apart, piece by piece." She looked at him again. "Atom by atom. I should feel better, I should feel safe. But I don't," she shook her head. "I'm so afraid now. I'm always afraid. I see him everywhere."

His heart welled up, and he decided to speak again, hoping it was the right thing to say, hoping it would help her feel better. "You're not alone," he said, and quickly added, "not anymore." She looked into his eyes again, but the rage she felt towards him had apparently evaporated. "I promise, I won't leave you again. We'll get through this together. From here on out, I'll be by your side, whenever you need me." Chris resisted the urge to reach out for her hand. "I promise."

Emmi didn't smile, but neither did she scowl. She simply nodded. And then she broke down into another stream of tears and sobs. Much to his surprise, she slid over to him, and buried her head in his shoulder.

He let her stay there as long as she needed, not caring about his t-shirt getting wet or full of other things. But he swore he wouldn't let this happen again.

Turning her head so she could breathe and speak, Emmi said, "I was so scared at first. He didn't use any protection, and I thought...maybe...but no. A few weeks later, I bled and I knew it was okay. I thought I'd feel better then, but I still didn't," she shook her head. "I was relieved, but still hated myself. Hated him. I'll never stop..."

Chris thought he understood what she meant, but he realized he could never relate. That sort of violation was incomprehensible for anyone who had never experienced it.

He thought then of Alycia, too, and realized that even from the grave, Nabu still plagued his two best friends. Alycia's mother was still at large, still brainwashed by Nabu, and still a threat. Surely Alycia thought of that every day.

And Emmi...she thought of him every day.

Had they really defeated Nabu? Or would this legacy plague them both forever?

Emmi sobbed into his shoulder for a long time, but when her tears had almost completely run out, he realized that they still had a big day ahead of them. "If you're up for it," he said, "we should get back to the cabin."

She nodded, and together they stood up. Glancing back at the shattered bottle, she asked, "Should we clean it up?"

"We'll take care of it in the morning," he said. "I think we both could use some sleep. Some real sleep."

Nodding, she let him lead her out. Chris made sure to flip the lights off, and then used his flashlight to guide them back to the cabin. When they silently slipped inside, he led her to her bedroom door, but she shook her head. "No. No I don't want to be alone."

Recalling a similar comment from her back in the Sentinel tower, he nodded, and led her to his room. There, she shapeshifted into a black cat with stunning bright-blue eyes, and she curled up at the foot of his bed.

Ensuring this time to plug his phone back into the charger, he flipped the light off and laid down. When he finally fell asleep, it was to the rhythmic vibrations of purring.

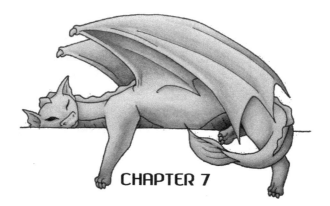

CHAPTER 7

When morning arrived, it was to the sound of knocking on his door. Chris started awake, rousing from his normal dream-state within his own soul, but finding no sign of Naomi.

Cat-Emmi was already awake, sitting on the edge of the bed and staring at the door. Chris stretched and let loose a great big yawn. Emmi took up the challenge, and stretched her cat body the way only a cat can do, winning by a long reach.

While he wasn't entirely sure how Emmi was feeling, he thought it might be fun to start the day off with a laugh, and he threw the sheets over Emmi. She immediately set to playfully batting through them.

Chuckling, Chris stood up and walked over to open the door, finding a refreshed-looking Alycia, wearing the same kind of pants as yesterday, but this time she had switched to a white tank top. "G'day, sleepy-head," she said, grinning at his hair.

Patting down the offending strands, he grinned sheepishly. "Uh, g'morning."

The tumbling sheets must have caught Alycia's attention, as she frowned over his shoulder. A familiar pulse pushed against Chris's soul, and Alycia's eyes softened into a grin as Emmi suddenly grew to her full-size, the sheets pushing off automatically.

Then, Alycia asked a question with her eyes, and Chris nodded and mouthed, "I think she's okay."

Turning to watch, Emmi stood up and stretched again, her shirt riding up enough to show the bottom-most scar on her tummy. She instantly caught herself and covered it with her hand, before tugging the tank top down.

47

"Good morning," she said through embarrassment.

"Well I'll be up at the main cabin making breakfast," Alycia started, "if you two wanna get ready for the day. Omelets?"

"Oh, yes please," Chris smiled. "That sounds fantastic!"

"Don't forget chives for me, please," Emmi added.

The moment Alycia left, Chris turned to Emmi wide-eyed. "The bottle…"

Emmi's eyes drooped, and she shrugged. "I suppose we better hurry."

While Emmi ran to her room to change into fresh clothes, Chris threw on a clean pair of army-green pants and a white t-shirt.

Less than a minute later, he met Emmi in the hallway, and they ran out and up to the cabin. There they found Alycia listening to a steampunk band that Chris recognized on the stereo system while warming a pan on the stovetop. "Oye, that was quick," she smiled, but seemed otherwise unconcerned.

Emmi and Chris exchanged glances, and headed to the far side of the cabin where Emmi's bottle had shattered against the wall. It was completely clean, not a sign of stain or broken glass anywhere.

"The hell," she whispered. "I didn't imagine it, did I?"

Chris shook his head, but there really was only one plausible explanation – either Benson or Shara had already found it and cleaned it up.

No sooner had Chris thought that than did Shara walk in the same door they had come through, refreshed with her cerulean hair pulled back into a ponytail and a smile on her face.

"Good morning, everyone," Shara sang above Alycia's music.

"G'day," Alycia beamed. "Usual omelet?"

Shara nodded and sat at one of the barstools at the other side of the island. Chris and Emmi joined her, and when she met Chris's eyes, he searched hers for any sort of hint that she had found the broken bottle. He wasn't sure what would be worse, Shara or Benson having found the mess.

It had to be Shara, he thought. *Benson would have made us clean it up ourselves.*

Shara looked from Chris to Emmi, and then winked.

Emmi and Chris exchanged worried looks, and then she asked Shara, "Did you…?"

Nodding, Shara motioned to her pointed ears, reminding them of her superior hearing. She must have heard Emmi's shouting last night and come to investigate, cleaning up after them once they had left.

"Thank you," Emmi whispered.

Alycia finished up the first omelet, Emmi's, in quick order, and then set to making another. When she put diced tomatoes in, Chris knew that she was making Shara's next, not his. *She must still be mad about yesterday,* he thought. Thinking about last night, Chris didn't say or do anything. *I deserve it.*

After finishing up Shara's, Alycia made Chris's just the way he liked it, with bacon, cheese, and mushrooms. Then she set to making her own, which, in classic Alycia style, included pouring honey on top once her omelet was cooked. He'd never get used to seeing that, but Alycia's sweet tooth knew no bounds.

Halfway through breakfast, Shara's cellphone rang, and she answered it. "Hey hey, you guys on the road yet?" A pause. "Oh. Well yeah, that would be faster." Another pause. "No, he and I were up with the sun this morning setting things up. He's putting finishing touches on the course now."

It must have been Thomas, Alycia's dad, on the line. They were likely en-route now, along with the representatives from the Sentinel Council.

"Right," Shara nodded. "Did you guys eat yet?" Another pause, and then rather indignantly, "Yeah, I know, I just thought, you know, jetlag and such. Anyway, I'm finishing up another one of your daughter's famous omelets. See you soon!"

She hung up then, and nodded and said with a smile, "We're in for a treat, Tiana's flying them in."

Chris smiled, looking forward to seeing the Denver Sentinels' pilot and sniper. But then he frowned, and asked, "They were able to all fit in the helicopter?" If it was the same one Chris had flown in, it could hold up to six passengers. Seven, if you counted the copilot's seat that Thomas favored.

"Three leaders, and each of their best team member," Shara nodded. "It's a helluva shorter trip than driving."

Chris nodded, recalling their own road trip through the mountains. It was normally just over three hours long, but thanks to insane west-bound traffic, it had actually taken them four hours of crawling along mountain passes and two-lane highways to get to the training camp. By air, it probably was only an hour flight.

Finishing up his breakfast quickly, Chris jumped off of the bench and set to washing dishes, not wanting Alycia to have to do them after cooking, and wanting to do *something* other than stare at the countertop. He then quickly made a pot of coffee for everyone, as well as a cup of tea for Emmi.

To Chris, it felt like forever before they finally heard the distant hum of an approaching helicopter. The four of them, grudgingly leaving their half-finished caffeinated drinks behind, headed out to greet the new arrivals.

Shara and Alycia walked ahead, and Chris beckoned for Emmi to slow down. When they were at least out of earshot of Alycia, he asked, "How are you feeling today?"

Giving a half-hearted shrug, Emmi replied, "I'm okay." Then, she met his eyes and said, "Thank you. I really appreciate what you did last night. Especially stopping me from drinking anymore." Scowling at herself, she added, "I can't believe I did that..."

Resting a comforting hand on her shoulder, he shook his head. "Hey, don't beat yourself up so badly. But I meant what I said. I'm here for you through to the end, okay?"

She smiled, the first genuine, warm smile he'd seen on her face in weeks. "Thanks."

The distant hum grew louder as they walked out to a clear, level field next to the main cabin. A second later, the helicopter appeared over the tops of distant trees. The hum grew to a deafening 'WHUMP-WHUMP-WHUMP-WHUMP' as Tiana slowed down and brought the chopper lower. Wheeled landing gear extended, and as graceful as ever, she touched down. The loud whine and hiss of the engine was deafening, even from fifty yards away, but as soon as they were down, Tiana began cycling the engines down.

Chris felt his fists clench nervously, and he tried to force himself to release the tension in his shoulders. *This is it,* he thought. *Either I pass today, or I'm on my own.*

Something about that made him more nervous than anything else, and it took him a second to realize why. If he was alone, if he didn't have the backing of the Sentinels, that would mean that whenever Marduk attacked Earth, he would have to face the god-like entity without their support.

Going toe to toe with a god was unappealing on the best of days.

It felt like it took ages for the rotors to slow and the engine whine to die, but when it did, the right-front door opened, and Thomas stepped out, pulling off his headset and hanging it up inside. Tiana, wearing a helmet and sunglasses, appeared to be writing in her log book, but took a moment to smile at the trio and wave.

Thomas walked back and opened the side-door for the passenger compartment. The first pair to step out appeared to be the Brazilian Sentinel leader and his second-in-command. The leader looked older than Thomas by at least a decade, but his second looked like he was no more than twenty-five, with surprisingly light skin against his black hair, and he looked very tall and very muscular. Build-wise, it made Chris think of Jason Momoa, and Chris didn't look forward to trying to get by him in the test.

Next came the Australians. Their leader was a severe-looking woman, her chin sharp, her eyes hard-set. Yet when Tom helped her out, she gave him a friendly smile. A man that looked almost as old as Chris's dad followed her out, which placed him close to Tom's age. Chris wondered if Tom knew him from his time in Australia, but that would be a question for later.

Finally, an elder Japanese man stepped out, his once-dark hair now pure silver, and kept in a very neat cut and style. The young woman who followed him out had to be in her late twenties, and for whatever reason, Chris thought she might be the most dangerous of the trio that would stand against Chris and his friends. She carried herself with confidence, and her hair was cut about as short as Chris's, which made him wonder if she favored utility above all else — long hair could easily get in the way, which was what had prompted Emmi to chop off her hair in April.

As Tom led them all towards Chris and the others, Tiana pulled her helmet off, revealing very dark, curly hair on top, with cropped sides, before she exited the helicopter as well and followed behind.

The six guests lined up in front of the trio. Tom nodded to Shara, and then motioned to the trio. "May I introduce our new recruits. My daughter Alycia, Emmi Dubois, and Chris Tatsu."

Chris noticed that the Japanese man in particular stared at him, but his stoic expression was difficult to read. What was he thinking about Chris? Why was he zeroing in on him?

Starting with the Brazilian representatives, Tom introduced them, "This is Lucas Silva, leader of the Brasilia Sentinels, and his second-

51

in-command Joao Oliveira." The Brazilians nodded curtly to them.
There was no sneer or look of discontent on either of their faces.
"This is Amelia Jones, leader of the Sydney Sentinels, and her second,
Jack Lee." Amelia gave Chris and the others a surprisingly friendly
smile. The older man, Jack, not so much. "And Sato Tanaka, leader
of the Osaka Sentinels, and his second, Yua Saito." Sato was
impassive, but something in his eyes reminded Chris of his father's
expressions. He had the feeling Sato disliked him.

"Pleasure to meet you all," Alycia said through a smile. *Good,* he
thought. *One of us needs to be diplomatic.*

"I believe you all know my second," Tom motioned to Shara, who
smiled and nodded to the leaders.

"It's good to see you all again," she lied. Chris remembered Shara
telling them that most Sentinels didn't like or trust Shara, a
xenophobic reaction to her that never waned amongst them.

Sato suddenly spoke in Japanese, his eyes fixed on Chris, who
gulped in response. Chris was a fifth-generation Japanese-American,
and he had never bothered to learn the language. Obviously, Sato
expected him to know it.

When Chris didn't reply, Sato looked at Yua and said something
else in Japanese. Apparently he didn't speak English, but Yua did.
Instead of looking to Chris, Yua looked at Tom and said, "Mister
Tanaka says we are to begin at once, no delay."

Not a request, not a suggestion, a demand. More and more, Sato
reminded Chris of his father.

Tom took the demand in stride. "Of course. Shara, would you be
so kind as to show the seconds to their positions?" He paused and
looked around. "Where's Benson?"

Shara shrugged. "I'm guessing he's still out doing something on
the course. He was grumpier than usual this morning."

Flashing her a warning look, Tom said, "Find him, please. Let
him know we're about to begin."

"Right." Nodding to the other seconds, she gave a fake smile. "If
you'll follow me to the cabin, we'll get you ready and then head out.
Chris, Aly, Emmi, come with me too. I'll explain everything to you
all at once."

Chris and his friends immediately fell in around Shara, while the
newcomers followed closely behind.

"T," Chris overheard Tom talk to Tiana, "Get the drones out of the 'chopper and set them up."

"You got it, boss!"

Chris gave a questioning look to Shara. "Drones?"

"They brought a pair of remote-controlled drones to monitor your progress," she explained. "They'll fly overhead, hopefully high up enough that you won't even hear them."

Nodding, Chris thought, *That depends on how new they are.*

He noticed then that Alycia was walking much faster than the rest, pulling ahead of Shara. "Uh, Aly?" Shara asked. "Got a fire to put out?"

She blushed a little, and hung back to let them catch up. "Sorry," she said sheepishly.

Chris frowned, but then remembered Alycia's plans for last night. He glanced at her pants, but saw no sign of new embroidery. Had she succeeded, and now was still getting used to enhanced speed and strength in her legs?

The seven of them filed into the cabin and headed for the weapons lockers in the back. "Alright," Shara said while she fished keys out of one of her pockets. "Lockers over there have tactical vests and holsters," she explained to the three newcomers. "I'll unlock the weapons cabinets." As she moved to the cases and began unlocking, Chris and his friends stayed back and allowed the visitors their pick of gear.

As they did so, Shara explained, "We'll be using simunition for this exercise."

Chris and Emmi gave her blank stares, but Alycia nodded once. "What's that?" he asked. Yua gave him a horrified look, as if to say, 'you don't even know that?!'

"It's basically training ammo," Shara explained while still moving from cabinet to cabinet. She pointed to one in particular that Chris hadn't been in before, which contained multiple steel ammo canisters. "Best way to explain is think of paintballs, but...not. It fits into standard magazines for each given weapon, and is non-lethal."

Shara opened a canister and pulled out a box of ammo, and then opened it and pulled out a single round to show Chris. It had a standard brass case, but the 'bullet' was brightly-colored red.

Eyeing it, and then Shara, suspiciously, he asked, "Will it still hurt?"

A placating smile crossed her face, and he knew the answer before she said it. "Yes. But that's why you'll be wearing goggles and helmets this time, along with inserting armor into the vests. You'll aim for center-mass only, no headshots, no extremities. And absolutely *no* hitting below the belt."

Chris nodded solemnly, unconsciously covering his crotch with a wince.

Turning to the more experienced trio, he watched as, after they put on their tac vests, they inserted dark ceramic armor pieces into slots on the vests. After those three finished gearing up and moved to the weapons, Chris led his friends over to put on their own vests and holsters. Shara joined them a second later. He'd forgotten that she, along with Benson, would stand in their way.

While they all prepared and started loading up magazines with simunition rounds, Tom brought the leaders in and setup a pair of laptops on the island countertop.

Once finished, Shara led the six outside again, while nodding to Tom. Once outside, Chris saw Tiana setting up two black-colored quadcopter drones, each the size of a laptop. Shara led them over to the bench that had marked the starting point of their last training course, and then brought the group to a halt. She placed a radio piece into her ear, and then tapped it. "Tom, can you hear me? Alright, I've got the kids in place, I'll take the others out into the course. Give us a five minute lead, okay?"

Then she turned to Chris and his friends. "Tom will come out in a second, and he'll give you the signal when to start. This is pretty much what you've come to expect, and it'll be a very straight forward test. Making good time is important, but even more important is taking few, if any, hits, so be cautious. Remember, especially you, Chris, not to use lethal-powered magic, but otherwise you're free to do what is necessary. Most important is that the three of you make it together. Emmi, that means you can't just race the course as a jaguar and leave them behind."

"I know that," she said defensively. "I wouldn't leave them behind…"

"Alright," Shara nodded. Then she stepped closer, and clasped a hand on Chris and Emmi's shoulders, while nodding encouragingly to all three of them. "You can do this. I want you to know that both Benson and I think so." Chris gave her a skeptical look. "It's true.

He's a hard-ass, and damn annoying, but he's also been impressed by all three of you."

"Bugger if he doesn't ever show it," Alycia griped.

"Well that's his job," Shara said. "To always make you think you need to do better, because he believes you *can* do better. If he went easy on you, it would be because he thinks you're a lost cause. Likewise, he wouldn't let you three take this test unless he thought you had a good chance at passing, and I'd say you three have *more* than a good chance." Squeezing their shoulders, she let go, and added, "Good luck, be safe. See you out there." She winked at all three of them, and then led the other three off into the woods.

Chris grimaced at the thought of facing against Shara. Would she just shoot them? Or would she use an animal form against them?

Then he looked to the others, and saw the uncertainty, especially on Emmi's face.

Pushing through his own doubts, he gave an encouraging smile. "Hey. We've got this."

They met his eyes, and they both nodded.

Alycia cracked a smile. "May the Force be with us."

Emmi rolled her eyes.

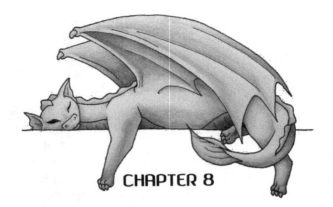

CHAPTER 8

Chris's heart raced. The moment was at hand.

He had to breathe. If he lost self-control, his magic would suffer considerably.

Scanning the tree line ahead, he found a red cone with an arrow attached to the top pointing straight into the forest. That was where they would start, and he pointed it out to the others.

Tiana finished setting up the drones, leaving them parked in the grass, and headed into the cabin. She waved at them moments before disappearing inside. A few seconds later, both drones took to the air. From here, they could barely hear their buzz. One immediately flew over and hovered a good hundred feet above them, while the other took off after Shara, no doubt to track her progress.

The tension was killing him. Chris wanted to go *now*, get it over with and be done, and finally find out his fate.

The look on his face must have been concerning. Emmi's hand lightly touched his forearm. "Hey, you okay?"

Feeling the sudden need to hop up and down to expend energy, he nodded once. "Yeah. I think so."

"It's just like training," Alycia reassured, probably as much for her own sake as theirs.

After what felt like ages, the cabin door opened, and Tom marched out. Chris noticed that the commander still had a slight limp from his gunshot wound back in May, but otherwise he seemed to have weathered those events well.

"Right," the commander started when he came within easy earshot. "Don't screw this up, yeah?"

"Gee, thanks Dad," Alycia smirked.

An uncharacteristic grin crossed Tom's face, and he clasped a hand on her. "You know me, all about those speeches," he looked at Chris. *Nice recall.* "You all ready?"

Everyone nodded, and Chris said, "As we'll ever be."

"Right." He touched a finger to the radio piece in his ear. "Shara, you far enough ahead?" A pause. "Alright, here they come."

Tom had a stopwatch on a bungee cord around his neck, much like one of Chris's old gym teachers, and he held it up. "Okay, get ready," he nodded to them.

Chris's heart rate raced ahead of him, but he held back. He grasped at the automatic rifle strapped to his vest, knowing that he'd have to hold on to keep it from smacking awkwardly as he ran.

A beep from Tom pressing the button. "Go!"

And they ran for their lives.

Alycia bolted ahead of them, lightning-fast and, Chris swore, becoming a blur. She made the tree line in seconds, and shouted out, "Woooooh!" She slid to a stop just as she passed the first direction cone, kicking up dirt into a cloud.

"Damn," Chris laughed, his voice still coming easy despite running full-out to catch up. Alycia waited for them, staring back in wide-eyed disbelief.

"Shit, Aly," Emmi called out as they ran past. "When you do an enchantment, you do it right!"

Alycia fell into a run beside them as they bolted into the forest, but as soon as they were out of sight of Tom and the cabin, Chris cautioned, "Ease up, ease up! We're not just running this time," and they slowed to a jog.

"Right, any one of those buggers could be waiting for us around a tree," Alycia remarked.

Another cone and marker pointed them left, which was not wholly unexpected. They would probably follow along the outer edge of the forest, and then loop back around further inside. And where the marker sent them, there was no discernable trail.

The fir and aspens weren't too tightly packed, but once they turned inward, that would change. For now, the shade from the ever-warming sun was minimal, but blessed.

The trio had spent plenty of time drilling in field tactics, and they set to moving silently, with Chris, defaulting into the lead role, used hand motions to direct them to spread out and follow the signs.

They knew time was of the essence, so they kept pace at a jog, and that did little to conceal them. It was a risk they'd have to take. At the very least, Chris wasn't breathing hard yet, since he was used to running through the trees, not jogging.

Then, much to their surprise, another cone sent them deeper into the forest much earlier than expected. With Emmi and Alycia just a little behind, he was able to halt their advance with a closed fist, and then pointed the sign out.

This was different from any other course they'd run. Which made him suspicious. Off to the right was a 30-foot-tall boulder, with the kind of thin, crusty-looking moss found at high, dry altitudes covering half of it. If there was an ambush waiting for them, it would be near there.

They could have used standard tactics, and Chris almost defaulted to it. One go straight in, the others flank to either side and sweep in.

But they weren't ordinary people. It was time to take advantage of that.

He signaled the others to come close, and they crouched down. "I'm betting we'll run into trouble here," he explained, and the others agreed. "Emmi, take to wing and dart around to come up from behind. Call out if you see someone. Alycia, with your new speed and strength, how fast do you think you can get on top of that boulder?"

"In a heartbeat," she grinned.

"Alright," he nodded. "I'll go 'round left. Go now!"

A familiar pressure burst against his soul, and after a green flash, Emmi was a sparrow. She fluttered up higher into the canopy above, and zoomed away.

Chris and Alycia darted for the boulder, Alycia easily racing ahead of him, before she leapt up high, much higher than anyone should have been able to do. She didn't quite make the top of the thirty-foot-tall boulder, but she scrambled up the rest of the way.

That much noise would, of course, distract anyone hiding around the boulder, but only for a moment, so Chris rushed to the boulder's side, and then hurried around the edge. The boulder was set deep into the ground, an ancient, well-worn stone façade.

Chris kept his rifle up, looking down the sights while keeping both eyes open, and edging away from the boulder just enough to 'pie the corner,' ensuring he would get a bead on anyone first. No tweet or other call came from Emmi, so he assumed it was clear, but it turned out that wasn't entirely true.

A humanoid, vested figure appeared, and he almost fired, but before he could, a green flash in the air heralded Emmi's arrival and shapeshift into a black panther, as she descended from the air to smash into the mannequin and tear it apart.

Bright blue eyes flashed in his direction, while a piece of tac vest hung from panther-Emmi's mouth. A second later, she dropped it and flashed to her normal self, a proud grin on her face.

"Nice move," he grinned.

"Look out," Alycia warned from above.

A loud bang echoed, and Chris felt a punching impact straight to the chest. Alycia fired off into the tree line, with Emmi spinning around to bring her rifle to bear. A curse in what Chris thought must be Portuguese issued forth. It must have been Joao that ambushed them, using the mannequin as a diversion.

The Brazilian emerged from behind a tree, three red splotches on his tac vest and his rifle hanging loosely from it, while his hands were up in defeat. "I surrender," he said with a heavy accent. A grin drew across his face as he looked at Chris's chest, "But at least I got you!"

Chris looked down, and sure enough, there was a splotch dead-center on his vest, blue instead of red, no doubt to differentiate which side fired a shot.

"Goddammit," he slouched.

"Don't sweat it," Joao encouraged. "There's always at least one casualty, but you're supposed to continue anyway." He pointed past the mannequin. "You'd better get moving!"

Chris gave a mock salute as thanks, and after Alycia slid down off of the boulder, they jogged into the forest. He couldn't believe he'd let his guard down like that. It was a stupid move, and if it were real, he'd be dead. He nervously glanced up to see one of the drones following along just below the tops of the trees.

They were headed into denser forest now, with older, thicker trees forcing them to maneuver around more. They spread out again, but continued to jog and kept one another in eyesight.

The gurgling of a stream soon came into earshot, one of the streams that fed into the lake. Seconds later and it came into view, with a cone and arrow pointing them downstream. They were meant to use the stream to continue on.

It was only a good six feet wide, and shallow enough that the deepest parts would only come up to their ankles. It looked like it was deeper in the spring, but for now, it provided unobstructed access to the lake. Maybe that was their final destination.

The risk was that they would be exposed if they walked down the center of it. Chris drew the others back in at the edge of the stream, and they huddled in crouches. "Another trap?" Alycia asked.

"I think so," Chris nodded. "Ideas?"

"Well, keeping with the Star Wars quotes," Alycia grinned, "Spring the trap."

He searched his memories, and then recalled Obi-Wan saying the same thing in one of the prequels. "What do you have in mind?"

"I'm fast, and I can cast a shield," Alycia said. "I go down the middle of the stream, you two cover the flanks."

It was a sound plan. "Alright. As long as you don't use your enchantment until an attack comes, you set the pace, and Emmi and I will keep up."

"I'll go critter again," Emmi said with a grin, "and take up the far side, okay?"

Chris nodded. She shapeshifted into a sparrow again, and flitted across the stream in a flash, before perching on a tree branch. That was a brilliant form to take in this situation, he realized. Those kinds of birds were all over the mountains, and since their brown, black and white coloring were patterned in a way that made them damn difficult to see against a tree trunk, it gave her a considerable advantage.

Alycia started for the stream, but Chris grabbed her hand. He was surprised at himself, but when she didn't recoil, and instead merely looked at him curiously, he felt his cheeks burn. "Be careful, okay?"

A warm smile lit up her face, followed a second later with a mischievous grin. "Hey, it's me!"

"Alright, Solo," he remarked wryly, and then let go.

She splashed down into the stream, and held her rifle up and ready, before she started downstream. Her pace wasn't as fast as he'd hoped, but she was contending with uneven, loose rocks and flowing water. *As long as no one else gets shot*, he thought, grimacing down at his own paint-splattered chest.

Keeping a good twenty feet away from the stream, he followed in the concealment of the trees. Every now and then, rapid movement caught his eye from across the stream, as bird-Emmi flittered from one tree to the next.

If they were lucky, whichever of the remaining opponents was next would be on Emmi's side of the stream, and she'd be able to warn them of it. If they weren't lucky, Chris would come toe-to-toe with someone on this side. He tried to move quietly, but moving silently in a forest was definitely not his forte, and he was afraid that a stationary enemy would get the drop on him.

Get the drop on me, he though, remembering Yua. She looked small, lithe, and being youthful, he wondered how she might get the drop on him. His eyes darted up.

Just in time to see a muzzle coming to bear on him.

He leapt and rolled to the side, a jutting rock painfully poking his back as he did so, just as Yua fired off a round. His roll had positioned the tree trunk between him and Yua, and she hopped down quickly.

Another, more distant shot echoed into the forest, and he heard Alycia yell out in pain and surprise. Chris panicked, and realized he'd made a mistake believing they would only come up against one opponent again.

Yua spun around the tree and aimed at Chris, whose rifle was decidedly not in position to return fire. He thrust out his hand and willed magic to come forth. Yua knew his plan, her eyes going wide before she ducked behind the tree, just in time as a blast of golden magic smashed into it, tearing bark from its surface.

That gave him time to get up onto his feet and bring his rifle to bear at where Yua had just been, but she spun around to the other side and fired off a quick round that barely missed Chris. He dove for the cover of a fallen tree, consumed by moss, while he resisted the urge to fire off his own errant round, fearful of hitting one of his friends.

"Chris!" Alycia yelled, and gunfire echoed from the stream.

He panicked, and peaked up over the log towards the stream. Alycia wasn't there. Nor could he see Emmi. Had they failed? Were his friends captured?

Yua peaked around the tree and fired again, blasting bark off of the dead tree in front of his face and stinging his cheeks, forcing him to duck again. If he hadn't been wearing goggles, he might have been hurt a lot worse.

Chris was pinned. Time was running out. He had to think.

I'm a mage, or wizard, or whatever. I have an advantage she doesn't.

A buzzing caught his attention, and he looked up at the drone above. And the tree branches between them.

Without thinking further about it, he rolled away from the log to get a better vantage on Yua's tree, and then he unleashed two successive blasts of magic at the largest higher-up branches. Not big enough to hurt Yua, but big enough to distract her. The branches snapped and burned at their bases, and promptly fell down. Yua yelled out in surprise, and just as Chris bolted onto his feet, she dove from cover. He fired, his first two shots missing completely, but the third, fourth, and fifth all found their target.

Yua was out of the fight.

The branches crashed harmlessly beside her, and since he had hit her armored vest, he was confident Yua was fine, so he raced past her into the stream. Only to come up short as Alycia and Emmi emerged from the forest.

Heaving a sigh, he asked, "You two okay?"

"Yeah," Alycia nodded.

"We're fine," Emmi added, "but we took down two more in the forest. Benson and the Aussie guy, Jack."

Alycia grimaced, and showed Chris her back, which had a single blue splotch on it. "When I heard shots from your side, I put up a shield in that direction. Benson shot me from behind."

"And when I tried to take him down, Jack showed himself," Emmi added. Then, with a prideful smile, she added, "Bastard didn't get me, though."

Chris blinked. *Three* of them had ambushed them, from both sides. Which left only Shara for them to contend with.

"Yua's down, too," he told them. "But we're running out of time, and who knows where Shara will be. Same plan?" The others nodded. "Let's go."

He passed Yua on his way back into the forest, who sat on the ground looking rather dejected.

They stuck to the stream for nearly a mile, with each passing minute making Chris feel more and more nervous. The other attacks had been early in the course. Where was Shara?

Eventually, just before the stream emerged into a clearing, and with the lake visible through the thinning forest, they came across another cone and arrow, pointing them to the left. It seemed they were heading for the inner edge of the forest again, and he even wondered if, this time, their course would take them into the open. That might leave Shara with a perfect sniping opportunity.

He was just glad Tiana wasn't in on it. She was a perfect shot and they wouldn't stand a chance.

Several more minutes and a half-mile later, and they found themselves nervously squatting at the edge of the forest. Or rather, Chris and Alycia were, while Emmi perched on a branch above them and kept an eye out.

Chris looked out into the open field, with the lake still visible to their right, another half-mile distant from their current location. Though they couldn't see it, the cabin was somewhere to the left, while the grove they had used for meditation was ahead. The arrow they were next to indicated they should head in that direction, and he reasoned that was their goal.

It was also a lot of open ground to cover.

He glanced behind them, his eyes searching the forest for any signs of movement. It was surprisingly, and eerily, still. That didn't mean Shara wasn't back there.

"Why do I get the feeling we passed her?" Alycia echoed his thoughts.

Chris nodded. "She could have shapeshifted into any number of tiny critters to let us pass by, and intends to shoot us from behind as we walk out." Shooting someone in the back wasn't exactly honorable, but all was fair in war, and Chris was damn sure that the Nabu occultists wouldn't play fair, so why should they be trained to expect otherwise?

"Then again," he looked towards the grove. "She could be there, too. Either way, she'll have a perfect bead on us."

"And I'm not sure I can keep a shield up while we walk. Not yet, anyway," Alycia added with a grimace.

Chris smiled encouragingly. "That's fine, you've already done well today."

She scowled, and must have interpreted his comment as patronizing, but he seriously meant it. Emmi had done just as well.

As long as it's good enough for all three of us to pass, he thought, glancing down at the blue splatter on his chest.

"Well, we can't dawdle," he sighed. "Let's get-"

He paused, a distant sound suddenly catching his attention. Tilting his head to one side, so that his right ear was pointed towards the lake, he listened carefully, and identified it as a distant hum-like sound.

"Is that...a helicopter?" he asked.

Alycia mirrored his concerned looked. Emmi suddenly took to the air, tweeting as she flew out into the field, circled around a few times, and then she came back, swooping low and instantly shape-shifting into her normal self.

"I think so," she said while crouching low beside them. "I can see them in the distance, and they're headed this way." She looked over her shoulder towards the lake. "Fast."

"Wait, 'they're'?" Chris asked.

"I think at least three," she nodded.

"That's not Tiana then," Alycia commented, sounding relieved at first that they wouldn't have to fight against an airborne threat.

But that only made Chris worry more. "Why would they be coming directly for the camp? Are they Sentinel 'choppers?"

There was a sudden pressure from behind, and all three spun towards the forest, bringing rifles to bear. Shara stood there, plain as day only a dozen feet behind them, with her hands high in the air. "Don't shoot!" Chris tensed, but somehow managed not to let his trigger finger slip. "It's not ours," she shook her head. "The rotors are heavy, which makes me think they're Black Hawks, and we don't use those."

Lowering his rifle, Chris eyed her suspiciously. Was this part of the test? "So what are you saying?"

Stepping forward, leaving her rifle dangling from the clip on her vest, Shara passed them by to stand on the edge of the clearing, allowing her superior hearing a more direct line to the incoming aircraft.

"There's definitely three...and I think four more, further back? No, two larger craft." Shara shook her head. "I don't..." Her eyes darted towards the lake, and she tensed. Chris heard a distant hiss from the direction of the helicopters, and Shara darted back. "Aly, shield, NOW!"

Alycia acted instantly, raising her hands and summoning power to her body. A second later, a large, shimmering blue-white wall appeared in front of them. Chris caught sight of a trail of white smoke and something fast heading right for them, moments before it slammed into the shield and exploded in a massive fireball, the concussive wave shaking the trees and the explosion ringing his ears.

This wasn't a test. Someone was trying to kill them!

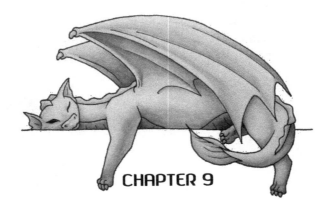

CHAPTER 9

"Keep the shield up," Shara commanded.

Chris looked at Alycia, and surprisingly saw only a minor expression of strain. Her ability to channel magic had improved, and for the moment, they were safe. Two more teeth-shattering explosions followed when a pair of missiles honed in on them, but with a wall in front of them, they were safe until the choppers could swing around or shoot from above.

The attackers appeared to have the same thoughts, and they gave up for the moment. But the trio of helicopters hadn't changed course, and were still headed towards the cabin. They were, as Shara surmised, Black Hawk helicopters, with long, squat bodies and large cabins. All three had their side doors slid open, with the silhouettes of several people within. Each aircraft had a single person sitting on the edge with shoulder-mounted rocket launchers, spent now, but one of their compatriots aboard each took the spent launcher and handed them a freshly-loaded one.

"They're gonna try again," Emmi cautioned.

Surprisingly, they didn't fire upon the four of them, and instead the helicopters rotated clockwise, turning the open doors away from Chris and the others.

Towards the cabin.

Shara's eyes opened wide, and she looked up at a drone still hovering a hundred feet above them. "Tom, take cover!"

Three rockets launched at once from the helicopters, all racing towards Chris's left.

"DAD!" Alycia screamed.

Explosions rocked the air, and beyond the trees to their left, fireballs raced for the clouds.

"Get back, into the forest," Shara ordered, turning and ushering them back. Alycia dropped her shield, and they raced into the concealment of taller trees. The Black Hawks continued on towards the cabin.

Alycia must not have been conscious of her speed, and she disappeared around a tree ahead of the group, but she stopped moments later and allowed them all to catch up. Once the helicopters were out of sight, they felt safe, for the moment.

"The hell's going on?" Chris asked, looking directly at Shara.

"Are they okay?" Alycia demanded intently.

"I don't know," Shara shook her head, "but we have to regroup, head for the cabin and defend any survivors."

With the panic in her eyes intensifying, Alycia bolted away through the forest as fast as her enchantment would let her. "Aly!" Shara called after her, but it was useless. "Shit, she'll get there before us and be alone."

Chris felt the rise of panic threatening to overtake his reasoning, so he forced it back down. He'd be no help to Alycia if he didn't control himself. "Then you two go ahead of me," he said, eliciting surprised looks from them both. "You can shapeshift and get there faster than me. I'll be right behind you."

"To hell with that," Emmi scowled. "We're not leaving you behind!"

"I'm safe here for now," Chris exclaimed, "but Alycia won't be for long, and they need our magic to mount any kind of defense. Now go!"

Emmi whimpered indecisively and looked to Shara, who stared at Chris in both surprise and appreciation. But she didn't move. A second later, her expression changed to a grin. "Yeah, we're shapeshifters," she nodded. "Get on, and then use your powers to cover us."

Bewildered, Chris asked, "What?"

Shara didn't explain, and instead set herself to shapeshifting. A second later, her gryphon form towered before Chris. She cawed at him, and then laid down on her stomach before turning her head back and motioning her beak at a spot just behind her wing joints.

She wanted him to get on and ride!

Blinking and exchanging surprised looks with Emmi, Chris drew in a deep, hesitant breath, but moved forward anyway. He carefully maneuvered around Shara's wings, which she spread out once he was behind them, and then he clambered up. Saying she was the size of a Clydesdale was no exaggeration, and even with her lying down, it was a climb, and he had to be careful not to tug too hard on her feathers for leverage.

Once up, he set his knees behind her wing joints, but was jostled when she stood up, and he leaned forward, smashing his rifle between him and her, while clinging around her neck. Here, the forest wasn't so dense yet, but he was still whacked on the head by a thin branch once she stood at her full height.

"I'm...kinda jealous," Emmi grinned.

At first a smile stretched across Chris's face, but then it faltered when he realized what this would mean. Shara was going to take to the skies, with him on her back.

I hate flying.

"See you over there," Emmi said, and then was engulfed by a green glow. Moments later, a two-foot-tall bird stood in her place, and Chris couldn't help but smile. She had chosen a peregrine falcon! Falcon-Emmi screeched at him, and then took to the air, while a recurring thought crossed his mind.

He bent left to try to catch Shara's eye, and asked, "Where do your weapons and clothes go when you shapeshift?"

Ignoring his question, Shara adjusted beneath him, and he clung on for dear life as she turned back towards the forest's edge. He looked up, and realized they wouldn't easily clear the forest canopy here, so he knew what was next, and braced himself. Shara lurched forward into a near-instant gallop, and raced through the trees. She was so tall that more branches whipped and scratched at Chris's face, and he buried himself in her plumage for protection. His rifle banged against his chest, especially his collarbone, and he knew to expect fresh bruises by evening.

The deep, rumbling rotors of the Black Hawks were noticeably louder now, even with the wind racing by his ears and branches smacking him left and right. That was what she meant by him defending them. She was a large target, and the moment they saw them racing for the cabin, the attackers would open fire.

Chris and Shara burst out into the clearing, and she wasted no time spreading her wings and, nearly throwing Chris off in the process, leapt into the air. He wrapped his arms tighter around her neck, and felt his inner thighs complain with every pump of her wings, jostling him back and forth, up and down uncomfortably.

"Too bad we don't have a saddle," he shouted through the wind, which was now roaring past his ears like a tornado.

Shara half-screamed, half-roared, and she sounded far more alarmed than amused. He looked up, and saw one of the attackers in a Black Hawk aiming a rocket at them.

"Shit," he shouted, thrusting his palm forward and releasing a blast of golden energy. The other guy launched at the same time, and miraculously, Chris's blast hit the rocket just as it left the launcher, detonating the warhead and devastating the helicopter, which immediately started a spin of death towards the Earth below.

Blinking surprise at himself, Chris glanced at his hands, and then at the other helicopters, which they had already passed by – Shara flew insanely fast as a gryphon!

Feeling safe enough for the moment, Chris took the opportunity to look at the cabin, which they approached at a startling velocity. Half of the structure was obliterated, and small fires were everywhere, spreading rapidly. He didn't see any signs of movement within the rubble, but he held some hope, seeing as the kitchen-side of the cabin was relatively intact, debris strewn about the floor and counter tops.

Shara half-tucked her wings to put them into a controlled rapid descent, and he lurched forward to cling to her neck again, moments before they landed roughly just outside of the cabin, Shara's form too big to have easily landed within.

Emmi zoomed by and landed inside, before she shapeshifted back to herself. "Tom!"

Chris dismounted Shara, landing hard on his sore legs, and then he ran towards the cabin's door. Shara, shapeshifted back to her normal self, was right behind him. He ripped the door open, which fell off of its hinges, and then they were inside, staring in horror at smashed remnants of what had basically been their base for eight weeks.

"Holy shit," he heard himself mutter.

"Tom, T, where are you?" Shara shoved past him. They heard groans, and Shara bolted around the island counter, with Chris hot on her heels. They found their companions and the leaders lying awkwardly on the kitchen floor, debris and soot covering them, including a three-foot-long remnant of a support beam.

Shara and Chris worked together to lift the beam up and threw it on the counter, and then helped a stirring Tom stand up.

"Son of a bitch," Tom cursed, wincing from a gash in his shoulder.

Emmi came around the other side of the island, and drew in a hissing gasp. Tiana and Mr. Tanaka stirred, but Lucas and Amelia were motionless, and a large, splintered piece of wood stuck out awkwardly through Lucas's torso.

Once Tom was up and steady, Shara moved towards Amelia, while Chris helped Tanaka up. "Arigatō," he breathed, though he still avoided looking at Chris. Tom helped Tiana up, but it was far too confined in the narrow space between the island and the sink, so Chris backed out of the area to give everyone room.

"Amelia's alive," Shara remarked, and then moved to Lucas and pressed her fingers against his neck. "But Lucas is dead."

The roar of the approaching choppers drew everyone's attention when they changed pitch, and they saw the helicopters pulling their noses up to slow down before they rotated their open doors towards the cabin again.

The choppers were probably only two thousand feet away, and had a clear line of fire into the cabin. At them.

Chris thought of running, but that would mean leaving Amelia behind, not to mention Lucas's body. There were only two choppers left, and he stepped forward, intent on destroying them before they could fire.

"Dad!" Alycia burst in at damn-near light speed.

"Aly!" Tom pointed at the choppers. "Shield, big as you can, now!"

She thrust her hands at the helicopters, and a second later, a massive blue-white wall as tall and wide as the cabin blinked into existence. Rockets, followed closely by rapid gunfire, slammed into it a second later.

If the pilots had been worth their weight, they would have instantly tried to flank Alycia. Instead, the men and women inside ceased fire, and the helicopters merely hovered in place.

Movement way out towards the horizon caught Chris's attention, just as Tom came up next to him. "Chinooks," Tom stated. Just now coming in over the lake, Chris saw two much-larger helicopters, the ones Shara had heard before the first attack. The aircraft were very long, and each had two large rotors overhead, one in front of the other, and were painted olive-green.

"They're likely carrying dozens of troops," Tom commented, "or APC's or other heavy armor." He looked at Chris knowingly, and clasped a hand firmly on Chris's shoulder. "I know you really don't want to kill anyone, Chris, but we're about to be overrun."

A massive, heavy void opened up inside of Chris, and he slumped his shoulders. He'd already taken lives today, and he didn't want to take anymore. But Tom's maddeningly tactical and pragmatic mind was right – if those other helicopters landed, the Sentinels wouldn't stand a chance, even with magic on their side.

Especially if any of the troops on those helicopters could use magic, too.

Chris looked up at the Black Hawks, and surprisingly saw what appeared to be a woman, dressed in all-white compared to the all-black tactical gear of her companions, crouching inside of the one to Chris's right.

A sickening feeling overcame him, a strikingly familiar one, threatening to empty his stomach. Darkness reaching out, clutching at his soul. He'd felt this sensation from another person once before…

"Chris," Tom shook him. "Can you do it? Can you hit them from here?"

He looked at Tom, and then past the Black Hawks at the approaching Chinooks. They were still pretty high up, although they'd already begun their descent. "I don't have to be dead-on," he remarked with a deadpan voice, resigned to his role. "Just gotta aim well enough to make them fall, right?"

Tom nodded, and Chris walked past him. Tiana and Emmi had grabbed fire extinguishers and were spraying them at the bases of numerous smaller fires, especially ones by the weapons lockers, but Chris ignored them and walked to the edge of the destroyed part of the cabin, before leaping down into the charred gravel surrounding the cabin.

He walked along the edge of the shield. The protective wall shimmered and flickered, and he knew that Alycia was straining herself to hold a shield that large, so he picked up the pace. The entire time, he felt like the woman in white bore into him with cold, calculating eyes, but he didn't dare look at her again, not yet.

When he reached the edge, several gunshots thumped out from the Black Hawks, but the rounds impacted the shield harmlessly, or dug into the ground outside of the shield's protective field. The left-most Black Hawk suddenly lurched, maneuvering to get a clear bead on Chris.

They knew what he planned. He had only seconds.

Looking at the Chinooks, still just under a mile out, he drew in a deep breath, focused his energies, and whipped around the shield to release two successive beams of golden magic.

The first blast went wide and missed the fuselage, but he must have hit the rotors, as the helicopter immediately veered off course and rolled to the right, dropping in altitude like a useless stone. His second shot hit the trailing Chinook dead-on, lighting up the cockpit and no doubt killing the pilot instantly.

Chris yanked back behind the shield just as more gunshots thumped into the dirt beside him, but in the distance, he saw both Chinooks nose-dive into the ground, no doubt killing dozens of men and women.

He shuddered.

Pure-white lightning lanced out at him and smashed into Alycia's shield, startling Chris. Thanks to Alycia's enchanted gloves, a single bolt reflected back towards the right-most helicopter. The woman in white took the brunt of the blast and slammed through the closed door on the other side of the helicopter, falling out to her death, while the Black Hawk itself shuddered and shook from the electric discharge. White lightning played across its fuselage, and the engine died, sending the transport spinning and plummeting to its doom.

The left-most chopper was almost in range of Chris, so he thrust his hand around the shield to unleash a plasma ball. The pilot, to his credit, tried to roll the chopper over to dodge it, but all that did was present its belly to Chris's attack, and a massive chunk just beneath the cockpit blew out, sending the entire craft Earthward.

With mixed feelings of triumph and regret, Chris watched the final two enemy craft slam into the ground almost simultaneously. The right-most helicopter, seconds after impacting the Earth, rocked the landscape with a massive explosion, no doubt a result of the electric discharge from magic igniting the fuel.

It was over. They were safe. Five helicopters full of people intent on killing him and his friends, all destroyed. *Magic 1, technology 0,* he thought, trying to find some humor in an otherwise humorless situation.

The blue-white shield dispelled, and that was a reminder to Chris to head back into the cabin. He started walking back towards where he had leapt down, intent on climbing back through, when all of a sudden...

An intense pressure wave of magic slammed against Chris, forcing his golden core to flare brightly. Horrible, blinding darkness seeped into him, threatening to snuff out everything that he was. He thought he must have shouted out in surprise and pain, and he collapsed to his knees, clutching his chest, pushing, *willing* the darkness out of him.

It worked. One second it overwhelmed him, the next, it felt like his own core pushed it out, shoving back against it, before he found its source and assaulted it. It lashed out defensively. Chris, not even realizing how he was doing it, relented, and left it alone, while it left him alone.

He blinked his eyes open. He was on his hands and knees, breathing heavily while his breakfast threatened to return early. Forcing back bile, he looked towards the flaming wreck of the woman in white's helicopter.

No one could have survived that, and surely the woman wouldn't have survived her fall from a hundred feet up?

"Chris!" Tom's voice shouted. He looked up to the cabin and saw the Commander staring down at him. "What's going on? Shara, Aly, Emmi, they..."

"They were paralyzed for a second?" he asked. Tom nodded. "We've felt this once before." *But it can't be!*

Pushing onto his feet, Chris held his rifle ready, pointing it at the flaming wreckage and taking a few steps towards it. Only to stop when a figure appeared from behind it, the woman in white casually strolling, uninjured, around the wreckage and towards the cabin. She was still at least fifteen hundred feet out, which gave him time to assess her.

She was powerful. That pressure wave she had sent out indicated as much, but even now, as he looked at her and fought against the sickening feeling in his gut, he could sense her power thrumming through magic.

"I need the others down here now," Chris called back to Tom.

Suddenly the woman's image blurred and blinked, and she was five hundred feet closer in an instant. He started, and very nearly fired his rifle, as useless as that might have been.

Behind him, Chris heard Tom shouting out orders, but he was interrupted by a booming voice, "Well, well. Leave it to Tatsu to *fuck up* my plans again."

It was the woman, her voice somehow magnified to an overwhelming volume, while it also had an unnatural dual-timbre to it, like a man and a woman speaking at the same time. Chris frowned at her words. She was close enough now that he could better discern her face. Fierce red hair cut at shoulder blade length, fluttering in the breeze. Perfectly tanned face, with a sharp chin and a small, cute nose. And when she suddenly blinked across another five hundred feet, he had a clear view of her eyes, a fierce, bright green.

As far as he knew, he'd never met her before.

But there was also no denying that her soul felt like...

Impossible, he thought. *Nabu is dead! I tore him apart, atom by atom!*

So he shouted the obvious question, "Who are you?"

"You know who I am," she boomed back. She blinked out of view and back in two hundred feet closer. Chris aimed at her chest, and she stopped approaching.

"Answer my question!"

She narrowed her blazing green eyes at him. In a more normal, woman's voice, she replied, "I am Nabu."

He shook his head. "Nabu is *dead!*"

The woman gave him a smirk. "You cannot kill me, Tatsu. I am forever." She leveled a finger upon him, and he tensed, prepared for another attack. Another *white*-colored attack, he realized, thinking back to that pure-white bolt of lightning that had struck Alycia's shield. Just like Nabu's powers.

But then she turned her finger to his right, and he glanced to see that Alycia, Emmi, Shara, and Tom had joined him down in the gravel. The woman's finger pointed at Tom. The only non-magical person of the troupe.

"You," the woman's voice boomed. "You have something I want."

Tom blanched.

Seething, she drew in a breath, and said, "Give me Imhullu, or I will burn everyone you ever loved."

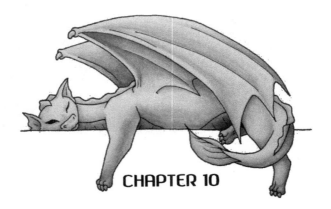

CHAPTER 10

Imhullu. Marduk's divine weapon. The dagger that Nabu had used to murder an innocent man at Centennial Airport ten weeks ago, fracturing the Barrier and setting Chris on a course to dismantle the Barrier.

And Nabu was here, now, at the Sentinel training camp, looking for it.

"What makes you think I know where it is?" Tom called out. He sounded awfully brave for a man without a single weapon on his person.

Nabu had no patience, and suddenly blinked another hundred feet closer. "Do not take me for a fool, old man," her voice boomed across the valley, stinging Chris's ears. "Give me the dagger and I will let you all live today."

Still pointing a finger at them, Nabu opened her hand and faced her palm towards them. Chris tensed, knowing what usually followed, and hoping that Alycia was ready with another shield.

Shaking his head, Tom said, "If you kill us, I won't be able to tell you where it is!"

"I am not a *moron!*" Nabu spat, rage giving her voice an uncontrolled edge. "I know that you have it on you right now!"

Chris blinked, and looked again at Tom. He wore loose khaki pants and a black t-shirt, but there was no sign of a dagger on him. No weapons at all. *What the hell is she on about?*

"It isn't in any of your warehouses," she yelled, "and it isn't in your Denver facility. There's nowhere else it would be." Suddenly Nabu dropped her right hand back to her side, and then lifted her left hand towards the forest. "Give it to me or they die!"

The troupe followed where she pointed her palm, and Chris felt the blood drain from his face. Benson, Joao, Jack, and Yua had emerged a few hundred feet away, simunition-loaded weapons pointed at Nabu. Mind racing, Chris's eyes darted between them and Nabu. Then he looked at Alycia, on the other side of Tom from Chris, but he knew that she would be unable to intervene, even with her enhanced speed.

So he did the only thing he could think of – he kept Nabu talking. "What do you need the dagger for? I already dismantled the Barrier, remember?"

Nabu snickered and, still enhancing her volume, replied, "Yes, I remember. My perfect little pawn."

Chris tensed, his temper flaring. He knew better now, but back then, he had feared that Nabu was manipulating his dreams. Did Nabu know about the souls inhabiting Chris?

She couldn't. If Chris was truly a danger to Nabu, she wouldn't attack like this for just the dagger.

"You didn't answer his question," Alycia called out. "What the bloody hell do you need with that thing now?"

Plaintively, Nabu said, "Do you really think I would take the time to elaborate my whole plot to you?"

Still uncertain how he could save the four by the woods, Chris tried to stall for time, and fell back upon one of his favorite movies. "Isn't that what villains do? Monologue?" Out of the corner of his eye, he saw Alycia grin.

Unfortunately, Nabu saw through his not-so-brilliant plan. "Stop stalling!" She sounded pissed. "Imhullu, now! Or they all die!"

Tom drew in a slow, hesitant breath, and started to speak, but Chris interrupted, an idea finally coming to him. "If you do, you'll leave yourself open to me." He raised his right hand towards their nemesis. "I'll destroy you."

Cocking a curious eyebrow at him, Nabu asked, "What, again?"

"And again," Chris nodded, "and again, and again. Maybe I can't destroy your spirit, but I can destroy your body. That's gotta take a toll on you, and it was easy to do last time."

"Oh, easy was it?" Nabu mocked, and then turned her eyes left, towards Emmi. "Lovely scars, my dear," she smirked. "They really accent your eyes..."

There was a disquieting surge in magic. Chris felt it ripple through him, not from Nabu's direction, but from Emmi's. Something felt very wrong all of a sudden.

"Fuck you," Emmi shouted.

Nabu smirked. "Again?"

Chris very nearly unleashed his full blast upon Nabu for that remark, consequences to others be damned. But he didn't have to.

The ripple in magic grew to a torrent, and Emmi roared. Emmi really *roared*, surging towards Nabu and instantly shapeshifting to the largest bear Chris had ever seen, easily twenty feet tall on all four! But it wasn't a normal, or even healthy bear form. The fur was matted and missing in some places, and the green glow of magic never quite subsided from her, wisping off of her body like a mist off of a mountain stream. The Earth shook from her heavy footfalls, and her roar matched Nabu's enhanced volume.

"Emmi, NO!" Shara screeched, sending Chris's heart leaping into his throat.

Nabu smiled, and turned her palm upon Emmi, unleashing a full-powered white-hot blast upon the charging bear. "Emmi!" Chris shouted.

The blast bounced off of Emmi's hide, lancing harmlessly into the sky. Nabu's confident face turned to abject horror.

Moments before Emmi was atop Nabu, the demigod shapeshifted into her bear form, once having dwarfed Emmi's, but now dwarfed by Emmi's rage-fueled form.

And when they collided, a sickening crunch echoed through the air, as Emmi toppled over Nabu and tore into her fur and flesh. She bashed and clawed, bit and roared madly, Nabu unable to defend against Emmi's frenzied assault.

Somewhere in Emmi's unnatural roar, he heard her cry out. A sign of all her rage boiling over. Nabu's calculated jab had worked better than she had likely anticipated, and now she had bit off more than she could chew, just as Emmi bit off a chunk of Nabu's shoulder.

"We have to stop her," Shara urgently pleaded. "We're losing her!"

Chris's terror and awe turned back to panic, and he bolted out of line towards her. "Emmi, stop!"

His voice somehow got through her raging roars, and she paused mid-swipe to look at Chris, her giant, green-glowing bear eyes blinking in confusion. Nabu acted instantly, shoving with all of her might and sending Emmi tumbling way. Rolling off of her back, Nabu shapeshifted back into her humanoid form.

Emmi recovered quickly, scrambling in a frenzy to her four feet and charging at Nabu with an enraged roar. A white light engulfed Nabu, and just as Emmi fell upon their enemy, Nabu was gone, a portal having whisked her away.

Chris hoped such an escape would have allowed Emmi to find her calm, but it only frustrated her more, and she pounded her wrath into the Earth, gouging out large chunks of mud and stone where Nabu had been moments before. She roared continuously, anguished by her failure to rend Nabu.

Places where her claws had dug in glowed green, and that light wisped up and into Emmi, leaving behind dead grass. As if she had sucked all of the life out of them, and as a circle of green light surrounded her and grew wider, Chris felt a tingle against his soul, a minor tug that left him feeling sick inside.

Shara was at Chris's side, hand on his shoulder. "We have to calm her down now! She's losing control and we'll lose *her* if she doesn't stop!"

"What?!" Chris gaped at Shara.

"I'll explain later, just do something," Shara pleaded. "Help her!"

Chris turned back to the twenty-foot-tall bear tearing up the Earth, the ground rumbling and making his feet unsteady. The strange ripples through magic still resonated into his soul, and the green mist wavering off of Emmi grew thicker as more and more energy from the surrounding grasses coalesced into her.

Magic has a price, he recalled Shara's words. This wasn't likely one Emmi meant to incur.

He walked closer to her, carefully, resisting the pull on his core. Emmi noticed him moments later, stopping her pummeling of the Earth long enough to glare at him. He saw murder in her glowing gaze, unnatural, unbridled fury stripping away everything she was.

"Emmi," he called out, raising his hands defensively. "Stop this, please. You don't want to lose yourself to this."

The roar she leveled back at him was hot and fueled by magic, physically pushing against Chris. He was a hundred feet away from her, but her towering form intimidated him.

Calling back upon their conversation in the cabin last night, he shook his head. "Don't let him win." He thought of Nabu's new body. "Don't let *her* win!"

Another roar, and Emmi pounced at him, closing twenty feet in a single lunge. He backed away a step, suddenly fearful of her unnaturally sharp teeth and claws. "Emmi, please listen! Remember what we said last night? I said I'd be there for you from now on! I know I failed before, I know I screwed up, but I'm here now, and I *need* you!" His voice turned to pleading, desperate as his heart ached. "*Please,* Emmi!" He shook his head. "Fight this, don't give in to it! If you give in, then Nabu wins!" That brought her up short, and Chris keyed on that. "Come back to us. Come back so that we can hunt that son of a bitch down together. *Together!*"

He shook his head and, fighting the urge to cower away from her rage, he stepped closer. "I promised you I wouldn't make you face this alone anymore, and I hold to that promise." Bear-Emmi stepped back from him, as if suddenly afraid. The wave of death surrounding her ceased all at once, and the green glow in her eyes flickered. "Remember what you've always taught me, about finding peace in yourself. Breathe, Emmi. Breathe and center yourself, and stay with me." He looked behind him, at a terrified Shara, at a distraught Alycia. "Stay with *us*," he looked back at the bear form. The eyes blinked out, returning to their normal, if currently giant-sized, blue eyes. "Let's face this together."

Emmi whimpered, and fell back upon her haunches. The green mist bled off faster, and her form began to shrink, inch by inch every second. Once she shrank to an approximately normal size for a black bear, the vapor vanished, and the ripples in magic flattened and disappeared. A green glow engulfed the bear form, and moments later, Emmi returned to her normal self, her legs curled up beneath her. She fell forward onto her hands, crunching deadened grass, and she breathed in and out heavily between sobs.

Rushing to her side, Chris knelt down and wrapped her up in his arms, while forcing himself to ignore the sickening feeling the dead area gave him. "I've got you," he spoke against the lump in his throat. "It's okay. I've got you." She trembled violently in his arms, but he knew then that he couldn't begin to imagine what she must have felt. Adrenaline crashing in her system, rage dying and leaving behind emptiness.

For that moment in time, the world disappeared around them. Emmi grasped at Chris, clutched him in her arms, used him to steady herself.

She didn't speak. He didn't ask her to. He let her have this moment, and said nothing.

Minutes passed by.

Shara came beside them and fell to her knees, gently resting a hand on Emmi's shoulder.

"W-what..." Emmi started, her voice trembling, her eyes looking upon the death she had wrought in horror. "H-h-happened to m-me?"

Shara drew in a deep breath, and then let it out slowly. "You let your rage fuel your shapeshifting. It gave you near unlimited strength, and apparently made you immune to magic, something I didn't know could happen even under those circumstances." Shara looked around, slowly shaking her head. "Magic has a price. If we hadn't brought you back down from that, you could have been trapped that way forever, leaching more and more energy out of every living thing around you. A rage-fueled monster, unstoppable, uncontrollable. Your humanity would have been lost forever."

Emmi's shaking intensified, and she uttered out a terrified moan. Shara shuffled closer then, and wrapped her arms around Chris and Emmi. Emmi leaned into her a little, sharing in the warmth of the hug. A second later, he became aware of Alycia hovering over them. And then she, too, knelt down and joined them in holding Emmi.

"We've got you, mate," Alycia whispered, drawing in a shuddering breath of her own. "It's okay. We're all here for you."

"Please," Emmi cried. "D-don't...let me go like that."

"We won't," Shara reassured. "You're safe, now. You're safe..."

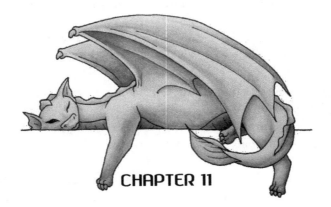

CHAPTER 11

Nabu's attack had left them all with fresh wounds, none so deep as Emmi's.

The cabin itself couldn't be saved, and Chris and Alycia had to step away from their friend to help get the weapons and ammunition out before they lost total control of the fires. They also moved poor Lucas's body out into the open and covered his face with a kitchen towel, the best they could do for the time being. Amelia didn't come to, so Chris helped Tom carry her to the helicopter, which had thankfully been unharmed during the conflict.

Knowing what a severe concussion could do to someone, thanks to Naomi's car accident, Chris turned to Tom as soon as they had her loaded up. "You and T get our guests out of here, and get Amelia to a hospital."

He expected the Denver leader to argue, to make a point that Nabu could return at any moment. For a second, it looked like that was exactly what Tom would do. But then he pressed his lips into a thin line, and nodded. "Right. Load what you can up into the SUV and head for Denver. We'll call local fire and rescue from the chopper and get them on-scene to put out all the fires."

They headed back to the cabin, where the other second-in-commands had joined them in clearing out the cabin of weapons and ammo. Chris walked over to Emmi and Alycia and watched, if only for a moment, as part of their home away from home for eight weeks burned brighter and hotter.

"T, get us ready to fly," Tom ordered Tiana. He turned then to the surviving leaders and their seconds. "Amelia needs a hospital, so we're going to fly to Grand Junction first to drop her off at a hospital. Those of you who wish to leave for your home countries can do so from there."

"I want Lucas's body on the helicopter with us," Joao insisted. His jaw was set tight, but if he had cried, he showed no hint of it. Chris wondered about that, wondered what his culture's views were on men crying. He hoped that, if the man felt grief, he'd be able to express it openly.

Buried grief was not something Chris would wish upon anyone else.

It would no doubt be a tight fit, and a smelly one at that, but Chris understood. He offered to help, but Joao waved him off angrily. "We don't need *your* help," he snarled at Chris, before he and the Aussie second, Jack, hefted Lucas's body up and carried him towards the helicopter.

Chris looked to Tom, uncertainty and even a little worry in his heart, but Tom simply shook his head as if to say, 'we'll talk about it later.'

With Lucas dead, Joao would be the next commander of the Brasilia Sentinels. If he blamed Chris and the others for Lucas's death, which Chris now feared, he might fail them all on principal.

Tom turned to leave, and then, to Chris's surprise, Sato Tanaka stepped in front of Chris, with Yua at the elder leader's side. Tanaka's face was stone, unmoving, unemotional.

He spoke something in Japanese, and Chris looked to Yua for translation. "Sato-sama says that he is grateful for your efforts to defend us from Nabu and his...her forces."

Bowing deeply, Tanaka added in heavily-accented English, "Thank you, Tatsu-san."

Bewildered, Chris didn't know what to do. Thinking back to all of the anime he had watched over the years, and cueing in on Yua's use of '-sama,' Chris bowed back, ensuring he bowed deeper than Tanaka, and said, "You honor me, Sato-sama."

Whether he understood Chris or not, Yua still translated back in Japanese. Tanaka cracked the ever-slightest, almost-invisible smile, and then followed Tom. Yua stepped closer to Chris and bowed to him. "Thank you."

Before Chris could say anything else, she turned and hurried to Tanaka's side.

"Well that was…unexpected," Alycia remarked.

"Yeah," Chris nodded.

While Tom was half-way to the chopper, he turned around and walked backwards while calling, "Shara, get these kids home."

"You got it, boss," she replied. Walking up to them, she nodded, "Go get your things out of your cabin, we'll meet back here in a few minutes."

In all of the excitement, and a nagging fear that Nabu could portal back to the area at any second with reinforcements, Chris had forgotten about his personal belongings.

Emmi was slowly coming back around and registered Shara's words first, and so she was the first to head to their dorm cabin, with Chris and Alycia hurrying after her. When Chris burst into his room, he quickly stuffed errant laundry and his phone charger into the duffel bag he'd brought along, grabbed his phone without checking it for messages, and raced back out. Emmi and Alycia joined him shortly thereafter with their own bags, and they ran back up to the cabin.

By then, the Sentinel's helicopter was just lifting off, and Chris waved at Tiana as she took the leaders of the Sentinels away.

The trio went around the corner to throw their bags into the SUV that Shara had driven them into the mountains with. Shara and Benson came from the other dorm cabin a second later, and while throwing their bags in with Chris's, Shara said, "Keep your weapons on you for now, but let's switch out the simunition for the real thing."

They did as they were told, and then loaded up the rear compartment of the SUV with crates of ammo and weapons. Shara insisted they focus on weapons, mentioning that ammo was easier to purchase.

Once all was ready, Shara and Benson climbed into the front seat, while Chris, Emmi, and Alycia filed onto the bench seat behind them, ensuring Emmi was between the other two. Chris adjusted his rifle on his vest, and tensed. If Nabu was going to attack again, now would be the best opportunity.

Nothing happened. And in silent reverence, they all looked at the burning cabin one last time, before Shara pulled them out and began the three hour journey back to Denver. The further they drove away from the training facility, the more Chris relaxed. For now, they were safe.

As safe as could be with Nabu still alive, anyway. It seemed reasonable, now that he thought about it, that Nabu wouldn't have attacked them after the helicopter left. She seemed intent on finding that dagger, and she was apparently convinced that Tom either had it or knew where it was.

Still, there was no doubt that Nabu would want to hunt Chris and his friends down at some point. They had unhinged Nabu's plans, Chris in particular, more than once.

It occurred to Chris that he now had a target permanently affixed on his back, and that sent a shiver down his spine. He looked towards the rear-view mirror and met Shara's violet gaze briefly. Somehow, the look in her eyes told him that she had the same thought.

At some point early in the drive, Emmi laid her head on Alycia's shoulder and fell asleep. Chris stared at his best friend for a moment and wondered. Were her dreams more peaceful than the real world? Or would Nabu haunt her in nightmares?

He looked up then and caught Alycia staring back at him. She blushed and turned away. If Emmi hadn't been between them, he might have held her hand, assuming she let him.

Chris looked again at the rear-view mirror, and felt his face turn warm as he caught sight of Shara's eyes one more time.

The drive was spent in silence after that. Just like the long drive up to the training camp, Shara didn't play any music, and this time Chris hadn't grabbed his earbuds to use his phone for music. He didn't dare wake Emmi to rustle around in the bags behind their seats, so silence reigned.

Hours later, when they passed over the final pass and descended towards Denver, the familiar cityscape visible ahead, Shara called back to wake up Emmi. "Do you kids need to go anywhere else before we drop you off?"

Chris looked to Emmi, who minutely shook her head, and then he replied, "No, I think we're good."

Alycia nodded. "Home sounds good."

He tensed for a second, and was tempted to ask Alycia to join him and Emmi in their apartment, but he realized then just how exhausted she looked. For that matter, he felt half-dead himself. Maybe they all just needed a good rest.

Over a half hour later, when Shara pulled the SUV up next to Chris and Emmi's apartment building, she put the vehicle in park and looked back at them. "Leave your rifles here, but…" Benson looked at her with a cocked-up eyebrow, and she hesitated. "Look, technically you're not Sentinels yet, but I don't want to leave you three undefended with Nabu on the loose. Keep your side arms and grab a couple of magazines on your way out."

At first, Chris wanted to point out that they had magic to defend themselves. A second later, he remembered how helpful guns actually had been in defeating Nabu the first time, albeit those guns had been enchanted by Alycia.

It couldn't hurt. And now, after so many weeks of using them, Chris was used to firearms, even if he still preferred magic.

They unclipped their rifles from their vests, pulled their magazines and emptied their chambers, and then carefully set them on top of crates behind them, before grabbing their bags and sliding out one side, leaving Alycia alone in the back seat. Chris awkwardly said goodbye to her, and with a weary smile, she returned the farewell. Once he and Emmi had a couple spare magazines, they closed up the SUV and watched Shara drive off.

And then they turned to the apartment building. It was a ten story building, one of the older tall buildings near downtown, and they lived on the eighth floor. Looking up at the stone façade, Chris marveled at being home again, at how ordinary it looked. A mailman carrying an overfull bag stepped out of a nearby mail truck and trudged up towards the front doors, oblivious to the duo and the trials they had endured.

It was all so…ordinary. It felt surreal.

Chris and Emmi trudged in behind the mailman, and automatically headed towards the stairwell, but just as they reached the pair of elevators, Emmi grabbed his sleeve and tugged him to a stop. "Let's just ride up," she said wearily.

That was a surprise. She was the one who had always insisted they take the stairs. Still, as tired as he felt, he didn't complain. After a short ride and even shorter walk, they reached their door, and Chris unlocked it and let them in.

It was weird.

That was really and truly the best description Chris could think of about coming home after so many weeks of Sentinel training. It didn't *feel* the same. The apartment, of course, hadn't changed one bit, except for a fine layer of dust covering the counters, and the lift-up coffee table where, only two and a half months ago, he and Emmi had sat down at 3AM to study for their last final exams.

At first, they stood at the threshold, surveying it. The living room straight ahead, the kitchen to the right, the two rooms divided by an island countertop. Past the kitchen was the hallway that led to their bedrooms and the bathroom. The air was warm and stuffy, the thermostat having been set to eighty before they left. Chris dropped his bag just inside the kitchen and turned the thermostat down to seventy five, an automatic action from previous summers, but he almost laughed at himself. They hadn't had A/C in the cabins, so even being eighty degrees in the apartment was bliss compared to 3PM in the wilderness.

Why did it feel so different now? Why did he feel...out of place?

Emmi stared at the couch for a minute, and then trudged around the island towards her bedroom. Chris heard her pause in the hallway, and then she stepped into the bathroom instead, closing the door and immediately turning on the shower.

He smiled at that, and then opened the fridge door. It was empty, of course. They'd known how long they would be gone and had thrown out anything perishable. Plus, strangely enough, he wasn't hungry.

Closing the fridge, he walked past the microwave hanging over the stove, only to stop short and look into his darkened reflection in the black glass-front door.

That's when he realized why the apartment felt so different. He could see it in his eyes and on his face, and in thinking back, he realized it had been obvious on Emmi's face too.

The apartment hadn't changed.

They had.

For better or for worse.

After a moment of marveling at that fact, he grabbed his bag and headed for his room. Just as he stopped at the doorway, he heard a muffled sob from the bathroom.

It wasn't the first time he had overheard Emmi crying in there, or in her bedroom. In days past, before magic, before Nabu, she had endured many hard breakups, and often locked herself in her room and cried the days away.

It always bothered him that he couldn't help, but now, more than ever, he felt frustrated. His hands automatically clenched into fists as he realized that he couldn't even comfort her right now, it was probably the last thing she wanted. Even if he wasn't afraid of walking in on a naked Emmi, he realized that right now, she wanted to be alone.

Deep down, he wanted to hurt Nabu for what she had done to his friend. For the first time in his life, he felt a need for vengeance.

Throwing his bag on his bed, he gently closed the door, not wanting to startle Emmi, and then sat next to the bag, seething in anger.

In that instant, he decided that his goal from that moment on would be to carry out revenge.

Nabu was his target. If not for the world, then for his friend.

Chris was going to destroy Nabu.

CHAPTER 12

Sleep came in fits at first, with Chris's anger and frustrations making it difficult for him to focus his thoughts and find his core. Finally, when sunrise was only an hour away, he finally found himself standing next to his golden core of magic, surrounded by gray shifting shapes.

Naomi, following through on her promise, was not there. But that was fine. It wasn't Naomi he wanted to talk to now.

"Tattannu!" he shouted into the void. It occurred to him that he hadn't seen or spoken to Tattannu once since the fall of the Barrier, and that further fueled his frustration. "Nabu is alive! I thought I killed him, but he, no *she* is alive."

Nothing. Not so much as a ripple in the mists surrounding him.

"Dammit, you said I'd have the power to destroy Nabu *and* Marduk, but I don't know how!" He swore it felt like a million eyes had turned on him, but the outline of thousands of ancestors still milled about aimlessly, indistinct and useless to him. "This was all your idea, remember? Your doing! I'm here because of you! So tell me what to do, right now!"

The dream world began to flicker, a symptom of losing control of his emotions and his thoughts, which only further fueled his frustrations. He wanted to shout out into the void, to scream.

Until a man's voice startled him from behind. "You are not yet ready."

Whirling around, he found himself face-to-face with his oldest ancestor, Tattannu of Babylon. He looked just as Chris remembered, with worn, cracked dark skin, black hair combed neatly and spotted with streaks of gray, white robes with gold and blue trim, and a turban of like-color atop his head.

"The hell do you mean, 'not ready?'" Chris flung his arms out. "I thought you said you'd help me, I thought you said…"

"You are not ready yet!" Tattannu stepped closer, his voice booming. "To give you the knowledge you seek would destroy you now."

Scowling, Chris scoffed and growled out, "Oh, don't you dare go Master Yoda on me. I've had all that I can stand of self-righteous teachers right about now. I learned to control my existing powers well enough," he stopped short for a second, recalling his failure with the shield, but then he charged on anyway, "I can figure out whatever power you need to teach me to finish Nabu off."

The ancient one grit his teeth, his jaw muscles rippling in frustration. "You do not understand, young one. I do not speak about learning to control a power. It is more. It requires so much more of you."

"Then tell me!" Chris shouted, turning around and pacing back and forth. "For Christ's sake, tell me what I'm supposed to do before that bastard hurts anyone else!"

The dream-world flickered again. He was losing control.

"You must learn patience first," Tattannu lectured, wagging a critical finger at Chris. "Patience, first, and *then* you must learn of acceptance."

The images all around him faded, his golden core the only thing remaining strong. Tattannu's visage turned to smoke, but he held on long enough to add, "Only when you can learn to accept your role will the answers to your questions present themselves."

Chris awoke to golden beams of sunlight reflecting into his bedroom blinds from a neighboring building. With little sleep behind him, but his agonizing frustration rendering him unable to sleep further, he grudgingly threw the covers off and got ready for the day, taking comfort in the warmth of a shower.

Mulling over Tattannu's words, he slumped down and sat on the shower floor, pulling his knees up and wrapping his arms around his legs.

What the hell had he meant? Learn to accept his role? Chris had embraced it whole-heartedly, hadn't he? Wasn't that why he had dismantled the Barrier? Wasn't that why he had trained all summer to become a Sentinel?

With no answers presenting themselves, Chris stepped out of the tub and dried off gruffly.

He paused when he looked in the mirror, wiping away the steam with his towel. Back when the Barrier still remained, he had seen Naomi standing behind him, and he looked for her now. But she never appeared. No spark of magic, no pseudo-motion of a ghost.

Just himself. *No, more than that,* he realized, squinting into the mirror. He saw the same thing he'd seen in the darkened reflection from the microwave.

He was harder, felt less wonder.

Something was missing, something precious.

That simply won't do, he grumbled inwardly. Not after countless years watching sci-fi, reading fantasy, playing games and finding himself lost in the idea of exploring new places, of going on adventures like Bilbo. The trials of this past summer had left him feeling empty, but he would find some way to refill his imagination.

He couldn't let Nabu take away everything that he was.

After a shave and bit of hair styling, his hair having grown at least an inch in the intervening months since he last stood in the apartment, he threw on his old favorite clothes, blue-jean shorts and a black t-shirt, and walked out to find Emmi in the corner of the couch, her knees drawn up so that she could wrap her arms around her legs.

Emmi didn't acknowledge him at first, her eyes were simply unfocused, staring vaguely at the coffee table. "Uh, good morning," he spoke.

There was a pause before she looked at him. Her eyes found focus, and she managed the smallest hint of a smile. "G'morning." Glancing in the kitchen, she said, "We don't have anything to eat."

He'd almost forgotten again. "Right," he stared at the fridge for a second. "Uh, Starbucks?"

Snickering, she nodded and slowly stood up. "Yeah." She looked ready for the day, already having thrown on her once-customary black yoga pants, along with a tight-fitting blue sleeveless shirt. Her growing red hair was tied back in a ponytail, but it looked shinier than it had in weeks, no doubt owing to the ability to take proper showers with whatever products she had left at the apartment.

This time, they took the stairs down, and he beamed at Emmi for her partial return to normalcy. When they spilled out onto the sidewalk and headed for the closest Starbucks, east towards the light rail station, he risked asking the question he was dying to know the answer to. "So, uh, how are you feeling?"

Emmi managed another weak smile, but didn't look him in the eye. "Okay, I suppose. I..." Her voice trailed off, and he saw her force down a lump in her throat. "I thought we were...done with..."

The well of sympathy and longing to help opened up inside of his chest again, and he pressed a hand to her shoulder. "I know. But don't worry. We'll get...them. Her." He almost said 'him,' but caught himself in time. It had always been important to Chris to use proper gender pronouns for everyone, and even if Nabu was their hated nemesis, he couldn't make the mistake of thinking of Nabu as 'something lesser.' That could lead to making mistakes. Possibly catastrophic mistakes, with magic involved.

Another burning question suddenly occurred to him, and for the tenth time that morning, he checked is phone. No missed calls, no messages from anyone.

What was the verdict? Were they Sentinels now? Where was Tom? Had the leaders made it home safely, or on their way?

The burn of frustration rose within him again, and he started to swipe in a text for Tom, but then paused, and changed to sending one to Alycia – 'Any word from your dad?'

He closed down his phone just as they came up to the Starbucks, only to have his phone beep before he could think of putting it back into his pocket. Unlocking the phone, he smiled to see that Alycia was already awake. 'No, not yet. I'll bug him now.'

Blissfully, the line at the counter was short, and they were able to order breakfast quickly. Chris got his usual sandwich and latte, while Emmi got her usual protein box and an açai tea.

When they sat at an outside table, the sun beaming down on them lazily, Chris's phone rang out the tune of the *Final Fantasy 7* victory song. A guy with scraggly hair one table over, someone Chris could only describe as a stereotypical stoner, pointed at Chris's phone and yelled out, "Duuuuuuude!"

Grinning, Chris answered brightly, "G'morning, Alycia." Emmi gave him a curious eyebrow raise.

"G'day. I just got off the tele with Dad. He and Tiana are in the air now, headed for Denver. He said to have all three of us meet him at the tower."

A surge of adrenaline rushed through him, and he felt a broad smile cross his face. "Oh? I take it that means good news?"

A painfully long breath of silence followed.

"I dunno," she finally replied, instantly dashing his hopeful mood. *"He wouldn't tell me, just said to meet him there."*

"…Oh," was all he could muster. Emmi watched him carefully, her expression unreadable.

"Cheer up, mate," Alycia forced optimism into her voice. *"I'm already dressed and all, so I'm about to get in the car. See ya there, yeah?"*

Looking east towards the station, Chris nodded. If they got the next train into downtown, they'd easily beat her there, since she had to drive all the way up from Centennial. "You bet. We'll wait for you in the lobby?"

"Nah, go on in when you get there," she said. *"I'm sure Abby will love to see you both again and will talk your ears off!"*

Some amount of joy wound its way back into his spirit. It had been far too long since they'd last heard Abby's cheerful voice, and he very much looked forward to it.

"Right. Well, we'll see you there!"

"Bye!"

After hanging up, Emmi looked at him expectantly. "We're to head to the tower. Tom will meet us there in a little bit to let us know whether we passed or not."

Emmi neither smiled nor frowned, she simply nodded, and quickly set to finishing up her breakfast. Chris wolfed down his sandwich, and just as he got up to throw his and Emmi's trash away, an idea occurred to him.

"Hey," he said hesitantly. "Um, if today turns out to be our first day, maybe we should make a good impression?"

She eyed him suspiciously, but then realization crossed her face when his eyes darted at the ordering counter inside. Pursing her lips and staring at him with narrowed eyes, she asked, "Make a good impression on 'them?' Or make a good impression on Shara?"

Heat burned in his cheeks. "No," he quickly replied.

Through clenched jaw, she said, "Chris, you…" But then her voice trailed off and she sighed, shaking her head. "She likes caramel Frappuccinos," she drawled.

"Ah," he said hesitantly. At first he didn't move, and simply stared at Emmi. She knew. She knew that he had a crush on two women, now. She'd always known about Alycia, but it shouldn't have surprised him that she knew he had a crush on Shara too.

After all, how many women do you dream about before meeting them?

God, that sounds cheesy even in my own head!

He searched for something to say, but then settled on asking, "Do you know what Abby likes?"

"Peppermint Mocha," she recited. How did she remember these things?

He started for the counter, and then paused. "Wait, I thought that was seasonal?"

Emmi shook her head. "Promoted seasonally, available all year."

"Oh," he said stupidly, and went to the counter, his cheeks still burning.

When it was his turn to order, embarrassment crept into his stomach, and he swore his face burned ever brighter. The barista looked bored, but then did a double-take on his rosy cheeks.

Suddenly wishing not to insult or hurt anyone, he decided to not only order something for Abby and Shara, but for Alycia as well, her favorite drink of a dirty blonde chai tea.

Once the drinks were out in a carrier, he placed his own latte in the last empty slot, and they trekked up to the light rail. A short, awkwardly-silent ride later, and they were in downtown. The Sentinel tower was only a couple of blocks away from the Convention Center stop, so they walked the rest of the distance.

Upon entering the forty seven story building's business lobby, they stopped and stared around. It only just occurred to them that they had never entered this way, and they weren't exactly sure where to go. In the past, they had ridden in a vehicle with Shara or another Sentinel into their special section in the underground parking garage, and then ridden a dedicated freight elevator up. Or they'd come from the roof, which apparently the Sentinels had exclusive use of.

For a second, Chris and Emmi stared at the building directory, until they found "Sentinel Holdings, Inc." listed, and a direction to use 'elevator bank five.'

After wandering around the lobby, with two security guards in particular eyeing them suspiciously, they found the proper elevator.

When they entered, it had buttons for every single floor in the building except forty-seven, so they pressed forty-six, and hoped it would deposit them into the Sentinel false-front lobby. Thankfully, no one else tried to use the elevator.

As the elevator took them up, Chris wondered for a moment what the future of the Sentinels would look like. Would they stay a global shadow organization? Or would they be forced into the light, now that magic was known to the world?

Truth be told, since he had been so intent on seeing Naomi every night of their training, he hadn't bothered to look up much news on his phone. Everything he knew about how everything had changed was relayed through Alycia, not to mention Shara's news about the British Parliament building.

The elevator stopped and thankfully let them out into the familiar lobby, with a grand view of downtown Denver and, beyond that, the mountains visible through wall-to-ceiling windows. The lobby was considerably smaller than the ground-level one, with a shiny marble floor and walls, and a black granite receptionist desk to their right, empty as usual. Above the desk were bold, golden letters stating, 'Sentinel Holdings, Inc.' To the left was the more-familiar, wider doors of the freight elevator.

They approached the granite desk awkwardly, and he saw a single button on it that said, "Press for Assistance." He reached out for it, but before he could touch it, the mantrap door to the left of the desk suddenly slid open, its steel surface painted black.

Out stepped a short, muscular woman with long black hair tied in a tight braid hanging over one shoulder. "Well, well, look who it is," she spoke, her Hispanic accent strong, her face impatient.

Chris stopped short of smiling, and glanced awkwardly at Emmi. "Uh...h-hello, Marisol," he said.

For a second, Marisol looked strained, and then her face broke out into a wide, full smile while she cackled. "Oh God, you are just too easy!" Stepping forward while shaking her head, she held up her hand. Chris thought he knew what she wanted, so he grasped it firmly, and she drew him in for what he normally described as a 'bro-hug,' before she did the same to Emmi. "It's great to see you two again!"

Returning the smile, Emmi said, "Yeah, you too! But I thought you worked nights?"

Marisol shrugged casually. "Yeah, well, with all the daystaffers at the training camp, someone had to fill in, and naturally Jered couldn't be bothered to. Hey, are one of those mine?" she asked, pointing at the tray of coffees in Chris's hand.

Regretfully, he replied, "I'm afraid not. I didn't think we'd be seeing you here."

"Oh, well," Marisol glowered. "I guess I'm just not good enough, eh?"

"N-no, that's not it at all," he stammered, "I seriously thought it would just be Abby and Shara in today, and, and, I mean, I..."

Another mischievous grin crossed Marisol's face. "I'm just kidding, don't get your undies in a twist, Tatsu! Do you mind if I call you Tatsu?"

"Uh, sure, I..."

"Good, 'cause that's what I'm calling you either way. You're the plebes now, right?" And then she faltered. "Uh, you did pass, right?"

Chris and Emmi exchanged worried looks. "We don't know yet," Emmi replied.

"Tom's supposed to tell us when he arrives," Chris added.

"Oh," Marisol shrugged. "Well, if he asked you to come here, chances are you made it." That brightened Chris's morning. "Come on, let's get you inside."

Marisol led them through the mantrap then, and Chris noted that from inside, it looked like the new doors were a lot thicker than the old ones that Nabu had melted through. Once through the second set of doors, they found themselves in what was known as Ops. Directly to the left was a row of windows for a conference room/observation room that looked out over the rest of Ops. To the right were two rows of desks facing away from the conference room, with enough computers to seat eight people and an aisle down the middle. In the far left-front, they heard someone furiously typing away on a keyboard.

The rapid-fire clack-clack-clacking ceased, and a head popped up over the back row of LCD monitors. Abigail Turner's hair was long, blonde, and curly, her makeup bright and expertly applied, and even though Chris couldn't see it from here, he knew that instead of a chair, she sat in a powered wheelchair.

"Chris!" Abby called out excitedly. "Emmi!" Wheeling around

quickly towards the back to meet them, Abby looked like she would have flown at them if she could. "It's so wonderful to see you!"

"Hello, Abby," he smiled broadly, meeting her halfway and stooping down to give her a hug. Emmi followed suit a second later.

Identifying the correct label on the coffees, Chris pulled Abby's drink out and presented it, "This is for you."

"Awwwwww, how sweet!" she smiled and took the drink. She popped the stopper out and drew in a deep breath through her nose, her eyes fluttered blissfully. "Oh my God, Peppermint Mocha? You two are the best!"

Chris grinned and motioned to Emmi, "She remembered it was your favorite."

"Awe, well thank you, sweetie," Abby beamed.

"I've got paperwork to fill out," Marisol interjected and sat at a computer station in the back right. "It's great to see you two again!"

"You too," Chris and Emmi said in concert.

"Well, then," Abby said. "I still don't know whether you guys got in or not, so I can't make accounts for you yet. But I know Shara's in the kitchen, if you want to go bug her about it." Abby's eyes darted to the only iced drink on the tray, and she beamed. "And you have the perfect bribe, too."

"Hey, now," Chris started. "That's not why I..."

"Sure, sure," Abby grinned, and then spun around to head back to her desk.

Emmi nudged Chris, and he felt his cheeks burn again.

Together, they continued ahead, past the desks and the conference room, towards the other half of the forty-sixth floor. Beyond Ops, they quickly found the double doors into the small kitchen. Sitting at one of two round tables was Shara, her brow furrowed as she stared at one of the standard tablets found all over the facility.

When they entered, she looked up, and smiled briefly. "Good morning, you two."

Chris felt his cheeks warm yet again. Shara's smile faltered. "G'morning," Emmi stated, and plopped down in the chair to Shara's right.

Setting the drinks down, with Shara peering at them with eager eyes, Chris pulled out her iced drink and presented it. "We got you a Frappuccino."

Her smile was only half-hearted. "Well thank you," she said to him, and then nodded to Emmi. "Both of you?"

Emmi's eyes darted between Chris and Shara, and then she pulled out her phone and set to browsing whatever social media platform was first in her list.

Feeling awkward, Chris sat down. "So, uh…what's the deal?"

Now Shara's smile disappeared completely. "Honestly I don't exactly know," she replied while pulling the lid off to start sipping it. Chris cursed himself, realizing he had forgotten to grab a straw. "I probably shouldn't even say this, but I know there was a little division." Her eyes darted cautiously towards the door, and then she looked into Chris's eyes carefully, her violet irises captivating him. "All I can say for sure is that both Tom and I lobbied hard to bring you onboard."

His cheeks burned again, but Emmi hardly looked up from her phone. Chris frowned at that, but then looked to Shara. She hadn't turned away from him, and when their eyes met, he felt his innards rush in excitement. Their gaze held far longer than he expected, and despite some voice in his head warning him to look away, he didn't.

He couldn't.

And then Shara blinked. She frowned, and looked down thoughtfully at her coffee before taking another sip.

Chris turned away then, and now wondered just how hot a human face could grow from embarrassment. It was stupid to think she was interested in him, wasn't it? She was easily a century old. He was a child by comparison.

And he liked Alycia.

Dammit, I don't know what to think, what to feel…

Clearing her throat, Shara turned very obviously to Emmi. "Could you give us a moment to talk alone?" A rushing sensation washed through Chris's chest.

Emmi's eyes darted up again, lingering on Shara, before they glanced at Chris. "Sure," she said, pushing back up and walking out of the room.

As soon as the double doors closed behind Emmi, Shara looked again into Chris's eyes. "Alright, kid. We need to have a chat."

CHAPTER 13

A giant lump bulged in Chris's throat, and he tried his best to swallow it down. Her calling him 'kid,' especially when she knew he didn't like being called that, was not a promising way to start the conversation.

"Um, okay," he tried his best to smile and hide his nervousness. "What about?"

With a deadpan stare, Shara replied, "I think you know what."

Warmth coursed into his cheeks, and he wondered just how bright his face looked now. "I…" He stammered. "Well, I mean…"

Shara heaved a sigh of annoyance and leaned back in her chair, rubbing her face. "Look, it's obvious to *everyone* that you have a thing for me. What do you kids call it these days? A crush?"

White-faced, Chris nodded, embarrassment sending jolts of tingles all up and down his arms and legs.

"Well, here's the thing," she continued on, "I don't know how old I am exactly. Not anymore," she rolled her eyes at herself. "Days last longer on Earth, years are shorter, and I've lost track of how old I would be on my world, and I never could figure out how old exactly I was in Earth-terms when I arrived." She leaned forward, placing her hands flat on the table. "But I'm old by your standards, right?"

A sinking feeling started yanking down on his heart, pulling the rest of his chest with it in a painful, heart-wrenching sensation. She still thought of him as a kid, through and through. Not knowing what he could possibly say to her question, he simply gulped and nodded.

"Which also means that, as much as I…" She hesitated, and

probably for the first time since he met her, she blushed. "As much as I think you're cute, I think is the modern vernacular." His stomach did a summersault, and then her violet eyes were looking longingly into his. "As much as I miss someone's company," she said a little slower. The way she spoke, the words she used, and those eyes, God those eyes! Chris was under her spell.

And then she blinked furiously and broke eye contact. "Look, I know I've said it around you before," she rushed on, no longer willing to look him in the eye. "Even after eighty years, I still find myself uncertain about how you humans handle romance and love, and I swear, it changes every decade. Nevertheless..." She paused, a rather dramatic affect given the conversation topic. And then she looked Chris in the eyes, but this time the hunger was gone. Hunger he hadn't even realize had been there earlier, but it was notable now that it was absent. "I'm willing to bet you're a one-person kind of guy." She nodded. "And I'd bet everything that Alycia is the same."

A one-person kind of guy. It hadn't even occurred to him that he should be anything else. But the moment she said it, he knew exactly what she referred to. Maybe even what she hinted at wanting.

He sat back and considered her words for a second, and thankfully, she gave him that moment by studying her iced coffee carefully, before she took a sip from it.

There was no denying his feelings for both Alycia and Shara. In different ways, they both appealed to him, both attracted him. Alycia's was slow-burning, a crush he had nursed for over four years while allowing it to be tempered somewhat by friendship. His crush on Shara was fiercer, born from magical dreams and an intense draw towards her that he couldn't explain except, maybe, through magic.

However, despite how much society's stance had changed over recent years, he had no desire to enter into a polyamorous relationship. As much as he respected the idea, he'd known for some time that it just wasn't for him.

"You're right," he nodded, meeting her gaze again and trying not to let the butterflies send his thoughts elsewhere. "I'm not. I mean, I am, a one-woman kind of guy." He thought further about Alycia, and honestly didn't know one way or another how she felt on the topic. So he erred on the side of caution and chose not to try to supposition her feelings on the matter.

Shara leaned forward, then. "Good. Know yourself, kid." He

flushed at being called 'kid' again, and she faltered for a second. "Which brings us to the truly vital question – what *do* you want?"

He didn't look away, but he certainly didn't have an answer.

"I'd figure it out quickly, too," Shara pressed on. "Because right now, you're breaking Alycia's heart, slowly, painfully, like a small knife twisting inside of a wound. And I'll tell you what, I like her, and if you keep hurting her, I'm going to end up beating your ass senseless."

Chris's eyes grew into wide circles, and he swallowed another lump away. He believed she actually would.

Worse still, if Shara was right, if he was hurting Alycia, it meant that he had hurt *both* of his best friends this summer without realizing it.

"I...I'm an idiot," he looked down at his hands, stared at them while the sinking sensation set in and drew him down into self-loathing. "God, I'm an idiot..."

"No argument from me," Shara encouraged.

Ignoring the playful or not-so-playful jibe, Chris felt a shudder course up and down his spine. For all that he had learned and accomplished over the summer, he felt now more than ever like he had learned nothing. Nothing of true importance, anyway.

"I..." he began, but was interrupted when one of the doors swung open, permitting a small man inside.

Or rather, a small gnome.

Babbar Nurin was a self-indulgent, formerly wealthy gnome that had helped the Sentinels track down and defeat Nabu the first time. His help hadn't been out of any sort of desire to save the world, but rather out of a desire to save himself from the demigod and Marduk.

Which was why Chris was more than a little surprised to see him still skulking around. At just over four feet tall, Babbar sported a short tousle of green moss-colored hair, combed neatly with a part down one side. He also had a rather obtrusive nose, the kind Chris would have expected on a dwarf from *Lord of the Rings* rather than a gnome, and his eyes were the golden color of autumn birch leaves.

And those eyes searched the room intently. "Has anyone seen Nina?" he asked, his voice distant and vague-sounding, though Chris wondered at his London accent.

Shara sat up straight and looked around. "Uh, no, but I've only just gotten back last night," she replied. "Has she gone missing?"

"Sort of," Babbar said. A frown drew down his equally moss-green eyebrows, and he looked at Shara. "Wait, you were gone?"

With sarcasm oozing from her voice, she replied, "Ha, ha. I'm sure you've been up to all sorts of mischief in my absence, you little fungus."

Babbar smirked, and then narrowed his eyes upon the kitchen in the back. "I wonder," he said slowly. "Niiiiiina," he called out soothingly. "Are you in here?"

Chris hadn't seen hide nor scale of her since he'd come in, but Nina, a small emerald-colored dragon, was rather noticeable for her size. A little dragon wasn't something you usually missed, but then again, Nina could also turn herself invisible at-will, and apparently only Babbar could see her when she did so.

And maybe he could smell her, based on how his already-large nostrils flared. Two obvious, whistling sniffs later, and Babbar's searching face stretched into a grin. "I know you're in here, little one," he called and continued towards the back. Chris watched the gnome's progress with interest.

A shuffling and clanging sound came from within a cabinet on the floor next to the fridge. Curiosity drew Chris to stand up and follow behind Babbar. They inched, closer and closer, to the cabinet, Babbar slowing and walking on his tip-toes. A child-like grin was plastered upon his face.

Finally, when only a couple of feet were left between Babbar and the cabinet, he leapt forward and threw the doors open. "Ha!"

There was no sign of a dragon within, but Chris immediately knew they had just found Nina's hoard. In an empty space at the bottom of the cabinet, a bunch of used bottle caps lay in a pile six inches tall.

Something shifted atop the caps, flattening the pile somewhat, and a tiny little chirp escaped. "Oh, moving right in, are we?" Babbar asked. There was a minor pressure against Chris's soul, and the emerald form of a foot-long dragon curled inside wavered into existence. Nina looked much like a European-style dragon, with ridges and spines and foot-and-a-half wide wings when they were spread out, but unlike the European depictions, her tail ended by spreading out into a tiny little fan that could generate quite a little breeze when she was excited, just like she was now.

She tilted her head upside-down and blinked her lizard-like eyes, and then turned to focus on Chris. Another adorable chirp escaped her, and Babbar looked at Chris. "Oh," he said, genuinely surprised. "You're back as well."

Chris grumbled about not having been noticed before, but replied with a jab of his own. "Wow, nothing gets past you, does it, Sherlock?"

Babbar arched a curious eyebrow at him, and then shrugged and looked back to Nina. He sighed and planted his fists on his hips. "What am I going to do about you, young lady?" Nina looked at him curiously and chirped again. "And where did you get most of these caps this time?" Chris swore she looked at Babbar indignantly as she chortled, a tiny squeaky sound that vibrated her gullet. "Oh really? And I'm sure *no* one else in the floors below will open fridges to suddenly find sodas without caps?" She curled up tightly around her hoard and gave out a satisfied growl. "That's what I thought."

Chris chuckled lightly, and then turned back towards Shara just as the double doors opened again, permitting Alycia and Emmi into the kitchen. Alycia's eyes met Chris's for a brief moment, and then they flicked down towards the dragon, and she went into insta-cute mode. "Nina!" she squealed and rushed past Chris to say hello. Emmi grinned and followed along, and Chris got out of the way so they could pay Nina all the adoration that the little dragon engendered.

Nina, of course, loved every moment of it, while Babbar grimaced.

Shara's head perked upwards suddenly, and Chris followed her gaze towards the ceiling with a frown. "What is it?"

After a moment of listening, Shara nodded. "Sounds like a helicopter. They must be here." She cleared her throat and stood up, looking knowingly at Chris and then at Alycia, before she gathered her tablet and coffee up. "Alright, folks, let's head for the conference room."

Alycia looked at Shara with disappointment while still stooped by Nina. "Aww. Okay, well I'll come pet you later, okay Nina?" Nina chirped happily. "Maybe I'll bring you a present," she added with a whisper while motioning at the mound of caps.

She and Emmi stood up then, but Babbar frowned. "Why would I need to go to the conference room?"

"Not you, fungus," Shara scowled at him. "Them," she motioned to Chris and the others, and then, with an exasperated sigh, headed out.

The trio began to follow, but then Chris remembered the coffees. "I almost forgot," he exclaimed, and pulled Alycia's drink from the tray and presented it to her. "We got you a coffee."

A great big smile blossomed across Alycia's face, her amber eyes beaming at him. Emmi cleared her throat, and said rather poignantly, "Actually, *he* got you a coffee." And then she winked at him.

Chris blushed, and then he noticed Alycia do the same. "Thank you," she said softly.

Lost in her smile, he walked next to her as they left the room. A second later, he remembered his own coffee and ducked back in to snag it from the table before he hurried back to Alycia's side.

Once the four of them were settled into the conference room, with Shara sitting to the left of the head chair, they waited, somewhat impatiently, for Tom to come down and join them.

Shara took out her phone to swipe in a message to someone, and then set it down on the table next to her tablet and looked out upon the ops floor with a frown, before looking back to the table. "I wonder why Tom's keeping Babbar around," she muttered absently. The silence in the conference room ensured that the trio heard her.

"Why wouldn't he?" Alycia asked.

Shara blinked in surprise and looked at Alycia. "I said that out loud? Sorry."

"It's a good question, though," Chris nodded. "Is he still technically under arrest?"

With a brief shake of her head, she said, "No. Despite my protestations," she emphasized those words, "Tom agreed to give Babbar clemency for helping us find and defeat Nabu."

A grimace drew down Chris's face. They *had* defeated Nabu, but not as completely as they had thought.

Still, Shara's question was more than legitimate. Babbar was known for making illegal or underhanded deals. It truly didn't make sense to keep him around once he was released.

From the corner of his eye, Chris noticed movement out in the ops floor, and he craned his neck up to see Tom and Tiana chatting with Marisol and Abby. Marisol pointed up at the windows, and Tom turned to look directly into Chris's eyes.

Anxiety overwhelmed him, and Chris sat down sheepishly. It was now. Now they would find out if their efforts had been for naught. If they would be Sentinels from here on out, or if they'd have to find another path in life.

What would Chris do? What *could* he do? The idea of going back to job applications and trying to find 9 to 5 work just didn't sound appealing to him anymore. *Then again, it never really did,* he thought. All last spring, he'd dreaded the interviews, dreaded finding a job. Worse, he had dreaded failing to find a job and being forced to move in with his parents.

The glass and steel-framed door from Ops opened, and Tom stepped up, leaving Tiana down with the others. He made a show of closing the door behind him, and then took his customary chair at the head of the conference table, his back to the window.

Despite what Chris thought to be an agonizing pace and a grim look upon the Commander's face, Chris frowned. If he had bad news that might not go over well with them, wouldn't he have closed the blinds? Chris had seen him do that at least once before.

"Well, then," Tom nodded to them. Chris glanced at his friends, saw the same nervous energy written in their eyes. Alycia met Chris's eyes for a second, and he lingered there, drawing strength and hope from her and trying to project the same feelings to her.

And then they all stared at Tom, who took a really, really inordinate amount of time to look into the eyes of everyone present. His face was stoic, unreadable, maddeningly so. Chris felt his leg begin to twitch.

Finally, he couldn't take it anymore. "Well?!"

Tom quirked an eyebrow at him. And then a grin cocked the edge of his face. "You're in."

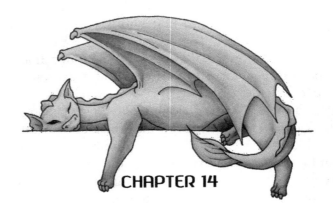

CHAPTER 14

Waves of relief washed through Chris's core, easing bunched-up muscles that he hadn't even realized he'd tensed until they melted. Alycia cheered, loud enough to startle everyone – she must have been more nervous than anyone thought.

Tom allowed the trio a moment to enjoy their success, and Chris beamed about, glad that, for the first time in a long time, something had truly gone right for him. He had set his mind to something, worked hard at it, and instead of backfiring in his face, it finally, *finally* paid off.

If only moments like these could happen more often, he thought, but then shook his head, forcing the self-defeating thoughts out of his mind. It was a day to celebrate, not self-flagellate.

"We should totally go out tonight to celebrate," Alycia declared. "Though I know *you* won't have a beer," she poked into Chris's side.

"Hey, that stuff's nasty," he defended. "It tastes like-"

"Piss?" Alycia smirked. It had become an inside joke for them, since Aussies nick-named beer as piss, and Chris thought it an appropriate analogy.

"Alright, alright," Tom finally interjected, bringing them back to reality. "Congratulations are certainly in order, and I hate to kill the mood, but..."

"You're gonna anyway, eh Dad?" Alycia eyed him.

Tom made a sour face at her. "Well as of this morning, you're officially on the payroll, so yeah, time to go to work."

Chris blinked. "I thought we already were when we started training?"

"That was probate pay," Tom replied. "Now you get the full ticket."

He'd thought the deposits already made into his bank account were a good pay, a living wage for Denver, which in and of itself was a rare thing to find these days. They were going to get paid more?!

"Being a Sentinel comes with a lot of hazards," Shara explained. "Naturally that means hazard pay."

"After all, if you consider us a company, we're the oldest on Earth," Tom added. "The Sentinels are very, very well-funded after millennia of management." He paused, and added, "Despite the losses betrayers incurred during World War II."

Chris's eyes darted to Shara. He knew only a little bit about that piece of Sentinel history, and it involved Shara's arrival on Earth. Sentinels sympathetic to Hitler and the Nazis had told the Axis powers all about magic and the Sentinels. When a rip through reality brought Shara to Earth, the Nazis captured and tortured her.

It was also part of how Imhullu, and the Dragonstone, had left England – the Nazis had sunk the cargo ship leaving England for the U.S., with both artifacts aboard, and later, someone had stolen them.

"So," Tom interrupted his thoughts, "If you three haven't already figured it out by now, I am a rather curt and to-the-point leader amongst the Sentinels."

"That pretty well describes the others we've met," Emmi remarked.

Tom narrowed his eyes at her, but then exchanged a quick glance with Shara before he conceded, "True. But on that note, I do wish to be forthright with all of you by saying that you *barely* were accepted."

That sobered everyone up quickly. Chris even felt a tinge of indignation, since they had used magic to save the lives of everyone at the camp.

"I had to argue vehemently to have you three accepted," Tom stated poignantly. He looked specifically at Emmi. "To be clear, it isn't your talent they doubt. During both the test and initially against Nabu's attack, you all performed admirably. But your emotional response to Nabu is what made some of the others hesitant to accept you."

Emmi visibly blushed and looked away. Chris actually expected her to shapeshift after that, but she managed to stay in the present. Maybe that long talk in the cabin the night before the battle had done her some good.

Chris turned his eyes to Tom, and was about to point out that *all* of them, Tom included, had a personal stake in Nabu's demise. Before he could, he realized that Tom hadn't actually let his personal feelings about his wife or Nabu interfere with his work. He had control of his feelings, or at least could direct them into something productive.

For Chris, that could be difficult. Nabu had taken his sister before Chris even knew about magic. Nabu had hurt his best friend in unimaginable ways. And had taken and twisted Alycia's mother. Last night, Chris had promised himself he would destroy Nabu, for vengeance's sake. Could he control that rage, control himself and not give in to that need?

Did he even want to?

"Having said all of this," Tom continued, "I fully support all three of you. Yes, even you, Emmi," he added when she gave him a surprised look. "I know what it's like to feel absolute rage towards Nabu." The Commander's fists slowly clenched, tight enough to pop a few knuckles. "And believe me, no matter what anyone says, *we're* gonna be the ones who bring that bastard down."

A twisted sense of glee welled up in Chris.

"Which brings up an obvious question," Alycia said. "How the *hell* is Nabu alive? And what's with his...or her body?"

"Is it possible to shapeshift into another human form?" Emmi asked Shara.

"Normally if you can shapeshift into an animal, you're not one of those rare beings who can change their personal appearance," Shara replied, shaking her head. "But if anyone could, it's Nabu. That doesn't explain how she's alive now. Nor does it explain this." She tapped something on her tablet, and the video screen on the wall opposite of Tom flickered on, showing a profile of Nabu in her new body.

"Her name was Kenzie Robertson," Shara declared. "Born October of 2004 in Edinburgh, Scotland."

Chris gawked at the visage. "It looks just like Nabu's new body," he remarked.

"It may actually *be* her body," Shara said with a grimace. All eyes fell upon her again. "Nabu isn't exactly human, after all. A part of him...her...*them* is ethereal like we suspect Marduk is."

"A part of Nabu *is* Marduk, isn't it?" Chris asked, recalling when Tom had first told them about Nabu and the Barrier. "Didn't Marduk use some sort of divine pregnancy or something to create Nabu, half-human, half-god?"

"The details aren't very well recorded, but essentially yes," Tom replied.

"Which could easily mean that Nabu truly cannot die," Alycia said quietly, a tinge of fear in her voice. Chris reached out and patted her hand resting on the tabletop, and then felt his cheeks warm a second later from the act. She smiled weakly in response.

Shara cleared her throat, and the screen changed to show what looked like a still image from security footage. "This was taken on the night of the attack against parliament in England." A woman was on the screen, facing towards the left of the camera. They barely could see her face, and her hair was gray-toned thanks to the night vision of the security camera, but it looked like *her*.

Like Nabu.

"Damn, Nabu gets around," Alycia remarked.

"Yeah," Tom nodded. "The ability to create portals certainly helps. The next question would be 'where will Nabu strike next?'"

Chris turned to him. "She'll be coming back here next."

The sound of creaking chairs echoed in the suddenly silent room. Everyone looked at him, and he felt suddenly awash with nervousness. "Care to explain?" Tom asked.

"I think it's safe to say we pissed off Nabu something fierce," he replied. "Twice now, we've messed up her plans. And she seems to think that *you*," he nodded at Tom, "have Imhullu."

More creaking chairs. Everyone looked at Tom again. He took it in stride. "I don't have it," he stated. Chris was about to ask why Nabu would claim he did, but Tom held up a hand to forestall Chris, and continued, "But it's not in any of our storage facilities, like Nabu said. I had a...a feeling about it. That Nabu's cult would want it again. So I worked with someone they assumed I would never trust to hide it."

Chris frowned. That was probably a long list of people. He couldn't explain it, but somehow Chris had the feeling that Tom was a bit on the paranoid side.

"Either way, Nabu's coming after us," Chris declared. "I'd be surprised if she wasn't."

His friends nodded in agreement, and even Shara didn't debate the matter. Tom stared at the tabletop for a moment, interlacing his fingers in front of him in a slow, thoughtful movement. Finally, he nodded. "I think you're right. Which means we really need to be ready to defend."

"I've got some thoughts on that," Alycia volunteered. Now all eyes turned to her, and her tanned face darkened with a blush. "I, uh, have been doing a lot of reading and cross-referencing, and some experimentation." She nodded at Shara and added, "With some guidance, of course. Anyway, I think I could enchant parts of the building to create defensive wards. Make it, for instance, so that if someone triggered a ward, it would erect a magic wall and contain whomever breached it."

Tom looked upon her with prideful eyes, his face quirking up into a grin. "That sounds intriguing. Any specifics that you can give us?"

"Um," she stopped short and glanced at Chris and Emmi before she shook her head. "Not yet, just some vague ideas."

"Then make them specific," Tom ordered. "And put them into a report. Abby can show you what kind of format we use for such reports."

A wry sort of grin stretched across Alycia's face. "Yes, sir," she said mockingly.

Movement in the corner of Chris's eyes caught is attention, and he looked out behind Tom at the far video wall in ops. For a second, he thought that Abby had, for whatever reason, put up a strange monster movie on the wall. What looked like two giant, serpentine monsters, as wide around as a smart car and about as long as two city busses, were thrashing around in a neighborhood.

A second later, he remembered that magic was real. And the fact that a news headline at the bottom said 'Terror in Greenwood Village' made him second-guess his assumption.

His face blanched.

Greenwood Village. His parents lived there!

The chime on Shara's tablet chirped, and she pressed a button. Abby's worried voice called out, *"You guys better get down here!"*

Tom frowned and turned, catching Chris's horrified look as he did so, and then everyone gawked at the terrifying video. One of the snakes coiled up, and then struck at a car that had just come around a corner and screeched to a halt, its fangs tearing the car, and the occupants within, to shreds. It must have been a live transmission, and suddenly it cut to an anchor on a news set, who looked as pale as Chris felt.

"Oh shit," Tom's startled outcry echoed Chris's thoughts.

The troupe scrambled up and filed quickly onto the ops floor, lining up along the back of the room to stare.

"This just happened," Marisol stated, looking up from her computer screen, which showed a cellphone video of the snakes thrashing about, demolishing cars and smashing up the fronts of houses. "Witnesses report two brilliant flashes of light, and suddenly these monsters were there."

Chris stepped closer to her, his eyes darting between the news feed on the wall and the cellphone video on Marisol's computer. "W-where exactly in Greenwood Village are they?"

Marisol frowned at his near-panicked voice and set to work looking up the information. "Two witnesses place it on Cherryville Road."

His stomach sank and a giant well of emptiness opened up in his chest. Darkness even edged into his vision as blood drained from his face, his head, his extremities. Even after everything he had seen and experienced, never before had he felt such a horrible emotion.

Terror. Unbridled, fear. And a kind of worry for others that he had never known before.

"My parents live on that road," he whispered through the shock.

An oppressive silence filled the room.

Chris had been right. More than he realized. Nabu was coming after them. After *him*.

After his family.

"Gear up," Tom ordered everyone. "Now. We move out in ten minutes."

As the others scrambled and Chris stared dumbfounded and paralyzed at the video, a heavy, firm hand clasped onto his shoulder. He looked up at Tom, whose blue eyes blazed determination at him. "We're gonna save them, Chris. *You're* gonna save them."

Clenching his jaw, Chris nodded. This was why he had joined. To save people. To make a difference.

He just hadn't expected his first official mission as a Sentinel would be to save his parents.

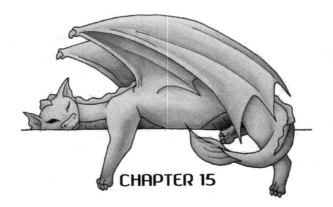

CHAPTER 15

Phasing between dazed and determined, Chris was led up to the locker rooms on the forty seventh floor, his mind still focused on the horrors attacking his parents' street. Once they reached the locker room and began gearing up, the dazed sense finally vanished, and a steel resolve set in – this is what he had trained for. All he had to do, as Tom kept reminding him, was remember his training. Focus on the task at hand, and conquer each new task with steadfast resolve.

The pair changed into familiar BDU pants, though Chris kept his black t-shirt on, and then they pulled on their tactical vests, which Chris realized was the same one he had worn to Babylon, and still was fitted to his size.

Once he and Tom were finished, they met the women down in the armory, where they set to filling their vest pockets with as many ammo magazines as they could carry.

Chris glanced at Alycia, who gave him a worried grimace, and then he looked at Shara, noticing that her eyes were a blazing blue, no doubt covered by color-changing contacts again. She also wore a black bandana over her cerulean hair to cover up her pointed ears.

At Emmi's suggestion, the troupe elected to use the same enchanted pistols from Babylon, Alycia's first real enchantments. The enchantments ensured that every round fired from the guns would freeze their impact points instantly, which had been crucial in finishing Nabu off. Rounding off their gear were P90 rifles clipped to their vests, their small sizes perfect for urban combat, and finally radios with earpieces.

Chris, Tom, Shara, Alycia, Emmi, Tiana and Marisol. *Helluva task force, even if we are going face to face with giant snakes.*

Despite the mission ahead and the risk posed to his parents, Chris couldn't help but feel rather bad-ass. Fully-geared, armed, and brimming with magic. And this time, he and his friends had the training necessary to make a bigger difference.

They were ready for this.

As the troupe marched out and headed towards the garage, Chris glanced at Emmi. Her face betrayed no misgivings, only the same determination he felt. Was she worried about his parents? She knew them almost as well as Chris, but not actually being related to them, she had the good fortune of not enduring a lifetime of berating and disinterest from his father.

"Good luck, guys," Abby called out and waved as they passed through ops.

"Keep the home fires burning, sweetie," Shara waved back.

"Of course. I'll be monitoring your frequencies!"

Chris grinned at the Star Trek quote, thankful that he and Alycia wouldn't be the only pop-culture referencing geeks in the building.

Once they were through the mantrap, they took the freight elevator down to the garage, and loaded up into the same white windowless van that had taken them to safety after the gargoyle on Sixteenth Street. Shara took the driver's seat this time, while Tom sat in front, and Chris and the others piled into the back, taking up the benches on both sides of the van, their knees touching one another.

Come on, hurry, hurry, he mentally urged Shara. Seconds later, they were through the garage door and out onto busy downtown streets.

But there was a monster terrorizing suburban Denver, and Shara wasn't going to let traffic stand in her way. Horn blaring, cursing in three languages, she weaved them through traffic as best she could.

"Dammit," Tom cursed, looking at his phone. "Stay off the interstate, it's backed up."

Chris grasped the grip on his weapon anxiously. Maybe they should have flown. How fast could Tiana have gotten the chopper up and running? He hated how densely packed Denver traffic had grown over the years. It had never been this bad when he was a kid...

"Hey," Marisol, who sat across and to his left, reached out a calming hand, pressing it against his white-knuckled grip on his rifle. "Easy there, okay? We're gonna get there in time."

He nodded his head, but it did little to sooth his nerves. Worse still, it made his core being fluctuate, and before he knew what was happening, a golden static shock leapt from his hand to Marisol's and she yanked it back. "Ouch!"

"Sorry," he grimaced. "I'm sorry, I didn't…" Shaking his head, he drew in slow, deep breaths and began the rigors of calming his mind. Uncontrolled magic wouldn't help *any*one.

"On the bright side, you're ready to blast the snakes," Alycia remarked.

Marisol shivered. "I hope that works." Under her breath, she added, "I hate snakes."

"It's too bad I didn't have time to enchant some rifles," Alycia remarked. "I'm betting that could do some damage."

Emmi shrugged. "I think between your pistols and Chris's powers, we'll be fine."

There was a brief pause amongst the group, but then all of a sudden, Alycia burst out laughing and snorting. Chris's eyes opened wide, and he stared at her, along with everyone else. Finally, when she managed to control her laughter enough, her face turned pink upon noticing the attention she had garnered.

"Wanna let us in on the joke?" Emmi asked.

Snickering, Alycia remarked, "It's too bad we didn't have Naked Snake on the team." Chris gave her a puzzled look. "You know, from *Metal Gear Solid 3*? He could just eat them for us, yeah?"

It took two seconds of awkward silence before someone in the group got the joke, and surprisingly it was Tiana who first burst out laughing. Chris grinned, while Emmi gave her trademarked eye-roll.

Still, the break in tension was welcome, and Chris found it just a little bit easier to center himself after Alycia's bad joke, the weight on his chest just a little bit lighter.

The rest of the trip slothed by painfully slow, and what was normally a half hour drive took them closer to an hour. At one point, Abby piped in through their linked radios, *"Alright, I've spoken to the DPD chief and he's passed on our info to the Greenwood Village PD. They know you're coming, and they know you're the experts."*

"Fantastic," Tom complimented. "Thank you, Abby."

"That's what I'm here for! Also, you should know that local S.W.A.T. already went in." There was a dreadful pause. *"It didn't go so well for them."*

Chris heard both Tom and Marisol curse, and he felt his face draw down remorsefully. How many cops were already dead from this single attack? How many of his old neighbors?

How bad would it have been if the snakes had been summoned in downtown?

When they finally arrived on-scene, a police barricade halted them on the six-lane-wide University Boulevard that blocked all traffic onto the much smaller two-lane Cherryville Road. Shara nearly ran over a cop frantically waving for them to stop, and then she and Tom hopped out, while Tiana hefted her sniper rifle up and opened the back door, letting Chris and the rest of the team spill out onto the hot asphalt. To the east was a red-brick fence that ran the length of the neighborhood on that side, but west, along Cherryville, were open green lawns and numerous trees, with a brick-encased sign next to the road that said 'Greenwood Acres.'

There was a heated exchange at first between Tom and the officer, who had drawn his pistol upon seeing armed civilians pour out of a white, windowless van, but as soon as Tom said who they were and the officer radioed it in, he holstered his pistol and motioned to the brick-encased neighborhood sign. "My captain's that way," he stated curtly.

Weaving between cop cars, and being extra careful to keep their weapons pointed down, the Sentinels followed Tom across University and up onto the grassy entryway. *This is what we trained for,* he reminded himself anxiously. *I can do this. I can do this...*

Those words died in his thoughts, however, the instant he heard a hiss-roar and a deafening crash down the road. Cherryville Road curved first towards the north and then west, hiding his parents' house and the snakes, but in that instant, he saw one of the monsters arch its head high over the trees, and then it came crashing down on something else.

No, they *hadn't* in fact trained to face off against giant snakes.

"Well, um," Alycia said, pale-faced. "Jafar, eat your heart out?"

The police captain was a stout white man with graying hair who grumbled at them, "You guys the specialists?"

Tom took it in stride and nodded, shaking the officer's hand, while the rest of the Sentinels made a half-circle around the captain and two of his officers. "That's us," Tom affirmed. "What's the situation?"

"Bastards take everything we throw at them and keep on smiling," the captain waved vaguely down the road. "We've closed off the area, but evacuations are damn near impossible, and they've trashed three houses."

Chris felt the color drain from his face. "Which ones?"

The captain eyed him with a grumpy expression, and then rattled off three addresses, saying that's according to the latest info from the choppers buzzing overhead, of which two were police helicopters, and the third was a news chopper.

Chris felt simultaneously tense and relieved. None of them were his parents' house. But each address belonged to a next-door neighbor or to one across the street.

"Goddammit," he shuddered and looked up the street. "That's...they're surrounding my house..."

The captain again eyed him, this time with suspicion. "You live here?"

"It doesn't matter," Tom cut them off. "What have you thrown at them?"

Looking rather miffed at being side-railed, the captain folded his arms. "And just who *exactly* are you people, anyway? Other than 'experts?'"

Tom grumbled and exchanged a heated glare with the captain. "We're the ones who'll beat these things back for you, but I have to know if you've found a weakness in them yet."

"If I had, do you think I'd let your asses in there?" the cop waved his arms around in exasperation. "We've shot them with everything, including armor-piercing rounds from S.W.A.T., who by the way took significant casualties assaulting those things. Sons of bitches even took a rocket to the mouth and just ate the man who launched it like he was a midnight snack."

Chris rolled his eyes. *Christ, this guy's a thesaurus of clichés. Not very good ones, either.*

Heaving a sigh, Tom looked at Chris for a second, his mind no doubt working through tactics. "Alright, here's the plan. T, you're with us until we get close, then find a roof you can climb onto and provide overwatch. Your gun won't do us any good, so just keep an eye out for any of Nabu's goons."

"Whose goons?" the captain asked.

Tom ignored him. "The rest of us haul ass up the road. Our

116

priority is to get our big hitters," he nodded at Chris and Alycia, "In range. We'll use our pistols-"

The captain planted a heavy hand on Tom's shoulder and tried to reel him around to face the cops, but Tom didn't budge, and instead he glared at the captain's offending hand. To the captain's credit, he didn't remove his hand. "Hey, I asked you a question."

"Captain, there are two magical monsters tearing up the neighborhood and we have the only people who can stop them. Now do you want to keep interrupting us, or are you going to let us do our jobs?"

The captain's face flared red, and he gnashed his teeth down in anger. "Who the *hell* do you think you are?"

"If you haven't been told by your chief, then you don't need to know!" Tom barked, and then shoved the captain's hand off. He turned back to the team, and ordered, "Three meter spread, T in back. Move out!"

If the captain took issue at being brushed off, they gave him no more time to complain, and with weapons raised and pointing up the road, the troupe spread out to take up the two-lane road, and moved at a steady, fast-walk pace.

Whatever complaints Chris had about Benson's methods, the man had drilled unit tactics into them quite well, and Chris found himself complying with Tom's orders without having to think about it. Tom and Shara took up the center, while Chris and Alycia took to the right, Emmi and Marisol to the left, and Tiana walked behind.

The ground literally shook when another snake rose above the trees and crashed down on something. A car alarm went off, and he heard both snakes hiss-roar at it, before there was a horrific screech of rending metal, and the alarm was silenced.

They went around the first bend and continued up the road, at which point the lane markings disappeared. This was a richer neighborhood in Denver, though the houses were still just barely valued under a million dollars these days. His parents had bought early, before prices all around Colorado had skyrocketed.

There were great big houses of brick and finer materials, large yards, ample tree cover, and fancy cars in the driveways of most houses, and they were most definitely not packed in tight like other neighborhoods. Eventually the Sentinels came upon the neighborhood's roundabout, made to look 'nice' with a small, sad-looking tree in the middle, and they continued past it.

Abby startled them with faux-cheer, *"Smile guys, you're on camera!"*

Chris glanced up at one of the choppers flying closer to them. Great. The whole world would get to see them. What would populations around the globe think of well-trained magic wielders?

Before they reached the leftward bend ahead, the snakes came into view, blocked partially by trees but still clearly visible. Their scales were black, as pitch as the night, and their bulbous eyes were like a pair of onyx stones, reminding him of some of the snakes he'd seen pictures of from the deserts of the Middle East.

In fact, he wondered for a second if these were giant versions of snakes from around Babylon. If these were summoned by Nabu, it would make sense. Somewhere, he thought he remembered some lore revolving around Marduk and snakes.

And then Chris's heart skipped a beat when they came around the bend enough that he could see the front of his parents' house. It was a single-story ranch-style house with a pull-through drive that connected to the road at two points, and had a very large, ancient ash tree in the front yard that had somehow survived the boring insects that invaded Denver almost a decade ago, and another tall fir tree just beyond the driveway.

Two houses across the street were completely flattened by the snakes, with nothing but a hint of their foundations visible beneath great piles of rubble. He wasn't sure where the third reportedly destroyed house was, maybe further down the road, but the house next to his parents' on the right was the snakes' new target, and was already half-destroyed, brick crumbling under a powerful bashing from the monstrous reptiles. A flash of movement to their right caught their attention, and Chris saw Mr. and Mrs. Davis running with their children, the owners of the house currently being demolished. *Good,* Chris thought with some relief. *They got out.*

Mr. Davis saw Chris and the others advancing up the road, and then did a double-take on Chris, wide-eyed.

Turning back to the snakes, Chris drew in a shuddering breath when one of them slithered up high, towering at least twenty feet off the ground. *Oh God, this is crazy...* It crashed down on the house a second later, demolishing more of it. Mr. Davis's BMW lay upside down in the street, its underside ripped out, with pieces of sheered metal and fiberglass jutting skyward.

And then one of the snakes saw the Sentinels advancing, and it snarled and hissed menacingly at them, at the same time alerting its companion to their presence.

The entire line stopped their advance as two pairs of onyx eyes fixed upon them, and Chris heard Marisol utter with a shaking voice, "Dios…"

For a second, it was a faceoff. The snakes both drew up so that they towered twenty feet and glared down upon the comparatively tiny humans, while the Sentinels all gaped upwards, uselessly pointing P90's.

"Pistols," Tom reminded everyone, lowering his weapon ever-so-slowly and unclasping his tactical holster.

Most everyone followed suit, but other than lowering his rifle, Chris didn't move to draw his pistol. He wanted to keep his hands free. *In fact,* he thought, *my rifle will only get in my way.*

Terrified of startling the beasts into action before he was ready, Chris very slowly unclipped the weapon from his vest, and gently eased it down onto the asphalt. Tom's eyes darted at him, but he didn't object. The snakes watched them carefully, swaying back and forth hypnotically.

The other five Sentinels raised their pistols, although when Chris looked behind him, he noticed that Tiana was gone. *Damn, she's sneaky.*

And then he turned his full attention back to the snakes.

Giant. Fucking. Snakes.

This hadn't been in the job description.

The snakes coiled back in unison.

Tom took that as their cue. "Fire!"

The roar of enchanted pistols filled the once-peaceful neighborhood, and the icy rounds slammed into the snakes, flash-freezing individual scales at every impact point. They recoiled like bent-springs, writhing in agony and hiss-roaring at their attackers. Chris drew power from within, touching his golden core and letting its power fill him.

The barrage of enchanted bullets ceased seconds later, and the snakes took advantage of the lull and lunged at the Sentinels, only to smash face-first into a giant blue-white wall of light.

They recoiled, no doubt surprised by the sudden appearance of an immovable object, and then Chris was ready. "Aly!" he shouted.

The shield fell. He thrust both palms forward, and golden bolts of lightning lanced out with a clap of deafening thunder. Chris *felt* the expulsion of energy, an instant discharge that made him feel noticeably fatigued.

The bolts caught one snake square in the face, sizzling its scales and physically throwing it up off of the ground and back towards his parents' house, slamming into the ground hard enough to shake the foundations of every neighborhood house.

The other snake changed tactics. Slithering at dizzying speed, it darted around to their left and tried to strike them from the side, uprooting a fifty-year-old tree in the process, but it met with another of Alycia's shields.

The Sentinels tracked it with their pistols, fresh magazines loaded, but with Alycia's shield up, they couldn't fire. It struck again, the shield flaring and Alycia grunting with effort. The struggle against such raw strength was probably overwhelming, and Chris knew they had to finish the second snake off fast if they wanted any hope of surviving.

But the snake was smarter than it looked. While their attention was rightly on its dangerous mouth, when it had swung around to their left, its tail had remained on the road. Chris felt the wind forced from his lungs from an impact that sent him and the others flying down the street, where they rolled and slid across asphalt. They skid to a stop in gravel on the side of the road, which tore through Chris's BDUs and skinned his legs painfully.

The snake didn't wait for them to recover, it raced towards them and towered above a second later. Acting solely on instinct, Chris unleashed a beam of golden energy at it, aiming and scoring a direct hit on its left eye, which exploded in a sickly pop of gore. It hiss-roared in agony and recoiled backwards, arching its head skyward.

Where it saw a news chopper hovering closer than it should have been. Now half-blinded, it must have thought the helicopter had taken its eye, and it drew down into a coil.

"No, stop it!" Tom shouted, firing his P90 despite how useless it was.

Too late.

With an incredible burst of speed, the snake sprang up into the air, its entire body clearing the ground, while its head reached up, up, and up. The pilot panicked and tried to roll the helicopter out of the way, but when a civilian helicopter hovers, maneuvering fast isn't their forte, and fangs as thick as Chris's legs pierced the fuselage.

The jet engine powering the helicopter had numerous moving parts, and the spinning rotors didn't help, so even as the snake crashed down to the Earth with the chopper in-mouth, the mechanisms tore its face apart. When it slammed the length of its body down from one grassy yard, across the road, and into another yard, the remains of its head and the chopper crashed into what was left of the brick house, engulfing it in a teeth-shattering explosion when the jet fuel finally spilled out and ignited. A secondary explosion followed, no doubt from an exposed gas line in the house.

Horrified, Chris gaped at the headless monster and the burning wreckage.

But Chris's lightning hadn't quite killed the first snake. It was moving again, this time keeping low as it slithered towards them stealthily, surprisingly effective despite its immense size, but the Sentinels saw it coming with moments to spare.

"The eyes," Tom called out, "aim for the eyes!"

Most of the Sentinels had lost their grip on their pistols when the other snake hit them, but not Emmi. She unleashed a rapid-fire torrent of rounds at the advancing snake. First its right eye instantly froze and then popped, followed by its left.

But Chris remembered that second Harry Potter movie. The thing could still hear, and it honed in on Emmi.

"Emmi, look out!" he shouted, and drew in power for another attack.

She could have shapeshifted to get away. She *should* have. But she didn't, and instead she dove out of the way as the snake lunged for her, fangs flashing and dripping venom and barley missing her leg. It tried again, and she rolled along the ground to dodge it.

Too fatigued to try another blast of lightning, Chris instead unleashed another golden beam, strong enough to bash the snake's head away and hopefully disorienting it.

A screeching roar filled the air, then. A great shadow cast by giant wings soared overhead as gryphon-Shara gained altitude, and then dove down to drive her beak and talons into the snake's head.

It recoiled violently, but Shara somehow held on, whipped around by the snake's flailing. She slashed some more, yanked scale and flesh and then bone from the snake, exposing its brains while fluid sluiced out and sprayed across asphalt and grass.

Finally, the snake gave up the fight, its life ended, and it collapsed to the ground just as Shara let go and spread her wings, giving her a jarring, but at least survivable landing next to the snake.

She stepped up to it, and nudged it with her beak. It didn't move again, and she roared in triumph.

It was over.

Except that Chris had the feeling that his parents still weren't safe.

CHAPTER 16

With his heart racing, Chris ran to where he'd set down his P90 and picked it up from a fine layer of dirt that the battle had kicked up. As he did so, he heard Tom over the radio, *"T, any other movement?"*

Chris didn't bother to clip the rifle back to his vest, and instead turned towards his parents' house. It was completely untouched by the snakes, but that only made him more nervous.

"Negative," Tiana called back. Chris searched around for her, and saw her somehow perched up on top of the second story roof two houses behind them. She was knelt awkwardly on the top of the pitch and had her rifle pointed towards his parents' house. *"I'm guessing that the intact house is the Tatsu house, and nothing's gone in or out..."* She paused without warning, and Chris tensed. His eyes darted back and forth, his neck popping from the effort. *"Hold on,"* she said, and started clambering to her left to get a different vantage. *"The front door looks like it's been broken down."*

Fresh adrenaline surged into Chris's blood, and without thinking, he broke into a run for the house. "Tatsu, wait!" Tom shouted, but Chris ignored him and ran as fast as he could. Horrific images played through his mind. Would he find his parents' broken bodies on the ground? Or would Nabu have strung them up? Or were they still alive, at the mercy of Nabu who was prepared to execute them in front of Chris?

Scrambling over the corpse of the first snake they had killed, Chris heard Tom's voice came through the radio, *"Abby, tell the local PD to stay back, we might have a hostage situation."*

That did nothing to soothe Chris's panic, but before he could reach the front porch, gryphon-Shara landed in front of him and screeched. He skidded to a halt just as she shape-shifted back to her normal shape.

"Hold on, Chris," she held up her left hand, her right gripping her rifle tightly. "We go in as a team, alright?"

Impatient, Chris reeled around to point out that everyone was still spread out and there wasn't time to wait for them, but was surprised to instead find that everyone had already recovered their pistols and were hot on his heels.

Tom didn't look happy with him, and as he limped to Chris's side, the commander clamped down on Chris's shoulder painfully. "Alright," he said impatiently. "We go in, two-by-two. Shara, take Alycia around back. Chris with me, Emmi and Marisol together." Chris nearly bounced out from under Tom's grip, he was so anxious and afraid for his family. They didn't have time for this!

"Come on," he started to walk towards the house, but Tom's grip cinched down painfully and rooted him in place.

"We don't know what to expect," Tom spoke, emphasizing each word. "Nabu could have any number of tricks up her sleeve, so be extra cautious."

"You got it, boss," Shara nodded, and waved for Alycia to follow her. Alycia's gaze lingered on Chris for a moment, before she followed Shara around to the right side.

Tom forced Chris to look him in the eye, but his impatience grew stronger by the second. "Focus, Tatsu," he stated firmly. "If you want to save your parents, we need to get it right, okay?"

"Breathe, kiddo," Marisol added. "Just breathe."

Emmi came up beside him and took his hand, squeezing it tightly in reassurance. "We're all with you."

Chris drew in a deep breath, and slowly let it out. The adrenaline surging through his veins wasn't helping, but he knew they were right. If Nabu was in there, he needed absolute control over his magic to ensure no collateral damage. His parents needed him to be calm.

"Alright," he breathed. "Alright. I'm okay."

"You know the layout," Tom stated, "So you and I go in first. What can we expect?"

He glanced at the double doors, which looked splintered and smashed inward, as if some giant had broken them down or simply just walked through them. "Sitting room by the front door with a fireplace. Kitchen straight ahead and right. Dining room to the left once in the kitchen, and a living room further left, past the dining room. Um, hallway immediately on the left when we first enter, leading to bedrooms, along with stairs to the basement."

It was the most succinct description he could give of the house's layout, and he had to keep himself from giving any more details. It didn't do the house justice, the history, the sadness that came after Naomi's death. The unnerving arguments he and his father used to have. The feeling of being trapped until adulthood.

Yet now, more than ever, he wanted back in there.

Please, please be okay, he thought.

Releasing his vice grip on Chris's shoulder, Tom hefted his rifle up and said, "Alright, lead the way."

He nearly bolted in, leaving everyone behind, but Chris somehow controlled that impulse. Drawing in another deep breath, he readied his rifle, pointed at the door, and slowly advanced. It took every ounce of will he had to keep his pace measured and steady.

Chris examined the splintered and smashed remains of the door, looking for but failing to find any hint of what to expect inside. His boots crunched on broken glass from the small oval window inset into each of the doors.

He sidled up on the right side and looked at Tom, who darted past the entryway while pointing his weapon inside, and then he too sidled up beside the door. Looking in, he nodded, and Chris spun around the corner and pointed his rifle into the sitting room. Tom rushed past him into the room as well, and they examined the ornate, cherry redwood and patterned cloth couches for a second. No one there, no sign of blood, just a little bit of splintered wood on the closest couch. The fireplace sat unused in the far left corner, the summers too hot for his parents to bother with it.

They heard crunching glass as Marisol and Emmi followed them in. Tom used hand signals to direct them down the hall to the bedrooms, and then motioned for Chris to lead them into the kitchen.

The hall to the kitchen was short, but the instant he started moving down it, he heard movement from within, and what sounded like a whimper.

With such a narrow hallway and the kitchen opening to the right and the dining room to the left, clearing the area safely would not be easy. Chris kept to the right, almost sliding against the wall, so that he could see more easily around the left corner. That was when he saw his father, Ken Tatsu, seated opposite of Chris at the dining room table, but facing the kitchen instead of the table. His eyes darted at Chris, and widened in shock. Ken looked much like Chris expected himself to appear thirty years from now, but with neatly-trimmed hair and a slight balding spot on top. His chin was sharp, his eyes deep and dark, and he wore a gray business suit with a midnight-blue tie.

Chris advanced until he came to the kitchen's threshold, and that's when he saw his mother, Hana Tatsu, seated just beside his father. She was shorter than anyone else in the family at exactly five feet, and had long, black, silky hair. She wore far more makeup, especially blue eyeshadow, than Naomi ever thought appropriate, but it was smeared now, with tears streaking down her stained face. She drew in a deep gasp upon seeing Chris.

"No," Hana whimpered and shook her head. His father shushed her instantly, and remained silent.

They were okay. They were alive. But they were terrified.

Ken looked into the kitchen with a deliberate motion, and Chris felt the terror return. Glancing back at Tom, who waited just behind him against the left wall, Chris used hand motions to indicate he suspected a target around the right corner.

Tom nodded, lifted his rifle, and used the standard 'pie-the-corner' tactic to round it while keeping his weapon trained on any possible threat. Then he came up short, his eyes growing wide and his head tilting upwards.

Chris frowned impatiently, and started to nudge Tom, willing him to move further in so that Chris could see what was going on. When he finally was able to peak around the corner, he felt his insides seize in horror.

The kitchen, dining room, and living room were all one open space, an open floor plan, with vaulted ceilings. It was a good thing, too, because the...*creature* in the kitchen was very, *very* tall. It stood on the other side of a marble-topped island with a gas stovetop. The creature was sort of a man, or man-shaped, with hulking shoulders and blocky, bulky muscles, almost like a super-deformed game character from the old Playstation 1 days, and it stood easily ten feet tall. It had no neck, its head smoothly forming into those hulking shoulders, and its eyes, glowing pure-white, were shaped like upside down triangles. Its lips were big and protruded unusually far out.

And it looked like it was made entirely of clay.

Dried clay, cracked and flaking. The creature stood absolutely still, inhumanly so, without drawing in any sort of breath.

It wasn't alive.

It was animated matter.

Chris felt his heart beat faster as the possibilities of what it was raced through his mind. The only thing that made sense was a golem, but that was Jewish folklore, wasn't it?

"Whatever you do," Ken's deep, aged voice stated, "Do not leave this house."

Chris turned back to his father, but Tom kept his rifle on the unmoving goliath. "What do you mean?" Chris asked.

Ken's eyes bore into his. What was his father thinking now? What did he think Chris was doing here, armed and wearing tactical gear?

"A woman," he said quietly, cautiously. "She came with that thing. Told us to sit here and not to move. She told *it* to stand guard, to not let us move, and to let none who enter leave. If anyone tries, it'll kill us." Chris's mother whimpered again.

Chris involuntarily gulped, and glanced back at the smashed front door. It really looked like something had simply walked through it, and now he knew that it was probably an accurate assumption.

"Where's the woman?" Tom asked without taking his eyes off of the creature.

"She left," Ken said. "Said she had to get…our *son's* attention." He frowned at his son.

Chris felt his jaw drop.

"Nabu wanted us here," he said. "Wanted *me* here."

"The snakes were meant to draw us in," Tom nodded. He tapped his earpiece. "T, be careful, Nabu may be around still."

"Got it," she replied. *"No other movement so far, though."*

"We're at the back patio door," Shara added. Chris looked left, past the dining room table, and saw Shara at the back door, with Alycia behind her. *"Want us to come in?"*

"Negative," Tom replied. "Mr. Tatsu says if anyone leaves the house, this…*creature* in the kitchen will attack."

"*Creature?*" Shara asked. She tried to peak in through the patio, and then disappeared. A second later, her face appeared in the window over the kitchen sink, and her eyes opened wide. "*Holy Toledo! Is that what I think it is?*"

Chris tapped his earpiece and said, "Could it be a golem?"

"*That's exactly what I was thinking,*" she nodded. Chris heard movement behind him and saw Marisol and Emmi in the hallway, listening intently. "*But it isn't a well-formed one, it barely looks humanoid.*" Shara turned her head, possibly because Alycia asked her something without turning her radio mic on, and Shara replied, "*I researched Judaism after I was rescued from the Nazis. Including their myths and legends, though,*" she paused and regarded the stone-still creature in the kitchen, "*maybe not entirely myths after all. Maybe the kabbalist golem was really created thanks to a crack in the Barrier.*"

"Threat assessment," Tom remarked tersely. "I need a threat assessment, Shara. How dangerous is this thing?"

"*Hard to say,*" she replied morosely. "*A lot of the texts I've read about them contradicted one another. But if Nabu thought it could contend with us, I doubt it'll be easy to defeat.*"

The muzzle on Tom's rifle lowered. "What if we stuck a grenade in its mouth?"

"Good luck getting its mouth open," Chris replied. "If it follows what I know of golems, the script containing its name is in its mouth, and destroying or taking that would destroy the golem. I doubt it's just going to open up and let you put anything in *or* take anything out."

Chris glanced back at his parents, and noted somewhat comically that they stared at him with deeply-furrowed brows. His mother's tears had stopped, her terror momentarily giving way to surprise and confusion regarding her son's presence.

"Hang on," Chris frowned. "Did you say you can't move from that spot?"

Ken nodded. "That woman said it would attack us if we moved."

Chris looked at Tom and grimaced. "So we couldn't move them to cover before using a grenade anyway." He didn't like the idea of destroying the golem before it hurt anyone, only to have a grenade fragment hurt or kill one of his parents, or both.

For that matter, anything they tried would risk his parents, and they had no idea what the golem's capabilities were.

"Uh, guys," Abby's voice came over the radio. *"Looks like the local PD aren't waiting anymore. I've got cops moving in from all sides of the neighborhood."*

"Shit," Tom glared at the golem. "If they muck around in here, they could set it off and not know it. Or worse."

"Then whatever we're gonna do, we have to do it now," Chris stated.

Tom nodded. "We'll keep the island between it and us, which puts us between it and your parents." He looked back at Ken, the first time since they had entered the kitchen that he took his eyes off of the golem. "You two get ready to run for the patio door, my people out back will help you get to safety. Got that, Shara?"

"Yes, sir!"

"Wait, just who are you people?" Ken asked indignantly.

Tom's jaw tensed and he looked at Chris with annoyance. "Why do people keep asking me that today?" He turned back to Ken. "If you want to live, do as I say!"

"Now you listen here," Ken started.

"Enough!" Tom hollered, pointing his finger at Ken and eliciting a sharp gasp from Chris's mother. "I don't have time to argue! When I tell you to run, you get your asses in gear, understand?"

In another time and place, Chris would have laughed his butt off from the look of shock on Ken's face. *No* one talked to his father like that!

Looking at Marisol, Tom ordered, "See to it they move when I say," and then he turned to Emmi, "And be ready to turn into something big and bulky."

Emmi blanched, but nodded. "Um, okay..."

There wasn't time to ask about her hesitance. Marisol edged past Tom and Chris and stood by Ken, her rifle lowered but vaguely pointing towards the golem. "Is that door unlocked, Mr. Tatsu?"

"What? I, uh, no."

Marisol shuffled past them and flipped the lock latch on it, and then slid it open.

That was a mistake. The golem must have taken that as her attempt to leave the house, and it suddenly lurched to life, sounding like stone grinding across stone.

"Shit, go, go, go!" Tom roared at the Tatsus. "Open fire!"

Chris rushed around Tom to his left, putting the island between him and the golem, and together they pulled their triggers, the P90's spitting a flurry of fire that deafened them.

Cupboards splintered, glasses and windows shattered, everything around the golem took ricochet fire, but the golem itself only looked pissed. It grumbled and roared a low, gullet-vibrating howl, and walked *through* the island, crumbling the marble countertop and rending the metal of the stove as easily as if it walked through a finish-line ribbon.

Tom grabbed Chris's vest and yanked him aside just as the golem made a lumbering swipe at him, crashing through the final remains of the island and gouging into the floor, revealing the basement beneath.

Chris's mother screamed as she headed out the patio door, with his father ushering her quickly from behind. The golem took note of this, and after pausing for just one second, headed directly for his parents.

Tom let his rifle drop, suspended by the clasp on his vest, and he drew his pistol, firing off two successive rounds that slammed into the golem and froze sections of its clay flesh two inches in diameter. Chris channeled power into his hands, dropping his weapon with a clatter onto the tile floor. Before he could unleash his powers, the golem, incensed by Tom's enchanted weapons fire, grabbed the heavy oak dining table and threw it at them. On reflex alone, Chris blasted the table apart with magic. Splinters and chunks of wood pelted them, forcing them to shield their faces.

A great crash drew their attention back to the golem, just as it *walked* through the wall into the backyard.

Tom hissed, "Son of a *bitch*!"

Pistol fire banged from outside, and Chris, Tom and Emmi rushed out through the hole the golem had made. The backyard was almost as large as the front yard, covered in grass except for the back half of the yard, which had an in-ground pool.

Shara and Alycia were popping off round after round at the monstrosity, with Shara in particular aiming for its head, but it had raised its right arm to protect its mouth, ensuring that nothing could harm the named paper inside.

Horrified, he watched as the first two frozen spots from Tom's pistol thawed rapidly, leaving no visible marks behind. Even Shara's precision shooting proved useless, since unlike with Nabu or the snakes, hitting the same spot twice didn't cause it to shatter.

Was it that resilient to magic?

Only one way to find out.

Channeling more power from within, Chris opened his left palm and, before the golem could try to hurt anyone else, he unleashed a barely-refined blast upon it.

The beam ricocheted off of its hide like it was a mirror and lanced to the left, gouging a burn line into the grass and barely missing his fleeing parents. His mother tripped over the fresh mark, falling with a screech.

The golem roared a challenge, and then reached into the Earth and scooped the turf out like it was soft ice cream, before it hurled a sizeable chunk at Alycia and Shara, only to have it smash into Alycia's shield.

That was when Chris noticed that the creature's right arm, where all of those freezing shots had hit, was immobile. As long as it was frozen, it couldn't move it.

And then it turned back towards his parents, intent on killing them.

"Shoot its legs," he shouted, drawing his pistol and aiming, but it was surprisingly fast! Belying its size and weight, the golem seemed to *flow* across the ground, covering the hundred feet of distance between it and his parents in a heartbeat. Before Chris could think to fire off a round, it wrapped its bulky fingers around his mother and ripped her from his father's grip. Her scream was blood-curdling, but as the monster began to squeeze, he swore he heard something pop, and her terrified scream changed pitch to one of pain.

"Mom, NO!"

Chris froze, terrified, helpless. His magic was useless, even dangerous against it, and if he shot it, he could miss and hit his mother. Ken's usual stoicism was lost, his face contorted into fear and rage as he leapt at the golem's arm and tried to pry her from its grasp.

All his powers, all his training, and when he needed it most, it was useless.

Another sickening pop, and his mother's legs stopped kicking.

He looked at Emmi, saw the horror in her eyes as her pistol was gripped limply in her hands, pointed at the ground. Why hadn't she changed yet? Why hadn't she grown to a bear and ripped the golem's grip from his mother?

It was Shara who finally made the change. Shara who shapeshifted into a great gryphon again, and fell upon the golem, digging claws into its left arm and cinching the clay, razor-like claws cutting through, inch by painfully-slow inch.

No doubt fearing the loss of limb, the golem released his mother, who collapsed like a ragdoll to the ground, his father trying and failing to catch her. And then the golem used its right arm, freshly-thawed, to bat Shara off of it, sending her splashing into the pool.

"Emmi, help!" Chris shouted at his friend. "You've got to shapeshift!"

She looked terrified at the request.

With the golem no longer holding his mother, Tom had stopped only a dozen feet from the monster and started firing at its head. One shot hit right on its mouth, stunning it momentarily. Another shot hit just below.

It used its wounded arm to shield its face, but this time, with deep, unhealed gouges in the arm, the ice had more affect. The arm visibly and audibly cracked. It was about to break!

But then Tom's magazine ran dry.

It raised its other arm up, prepared to smash down upon Tom.

"Dad, no!" Alycia screamed. Using her enchanted pants, she blurred forward and projected a shield in front of Tom just in time to intercept the fist, but her distance must have made the shield weaker. It tore through the shield and slapped Tom on the shoulder, sending him spinning and hurtling to the ground.

It seemed unstoppable, and Emmi still hadn't shapeshifted! The golem whirled around again and reached for his father. With its bulk between Chris and his parents, he felt a little safer, and he emptied his pistol magazine into the monster's back. It reared back, dozen two-inch ice spots on its back, but it did nothing more than delay it and piss it off.

Thankfully, the distraction lasted long enough. Shara extracted herself from the pool and pounced upon the golem again, yanking back and bringing it down hard onto its back. She then raked her claws across its face.

As suddenly as it had started moving in the kitchen, it froze. A deafening silence fell upon the backyard while everyone stared at the monster with bated breath. Chris glanced at gryphon-Shara, and noticed that a tiny piece of parchment-type paper was caught on one claw, having been ripped from the golem's mouth.

Its life force.

Its name.

At first, nothing happened. The monster was as still as the stuff it was made from. But then Chris noticed that the dry, cracked sections he had seen in the kitchen were growing, slowly at first, but accelerating at a smooth, exponential rate.

Within seconds, the entire monster was nothing but powder, and it disintegrated into the breeze, just as a flurry of tactical-geared police officers rushed around both sides of the house. They had seen it, but only at the end of its life.

They also saw a gryphon towering above the scene, and they stopped cold and gaped.

It was over.

But were they too late?

"Mom!" Chris called, dropping his pistol and rushing to her side. Her eyes were closed, and her chest wasn't moving. "MOM!"

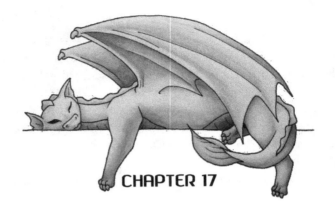

CHAPTER 17

The world around Chris became a blurry haze. His mother lay motionless on the ground. There was a dull pulse of magic against his soul, which he later reasoned was Shara returning to humanoid form.

Had he knelt next to his mother for a second? A minute? An hour?

There was a flurry of conversation around him, shouts, orders, demands. He ignored them all.

Paramedics arrived at some point, kneeling down and asking him and his father to step aside so they could work. His father, his stoic attitude having momentarily returned, complied. Chris had to be pulled away by Emmi and Tom. The paramedics quickly examined her, and immediately placed a brace around her neck before splitting their stretcher apart down the middle and carefully maneuvering it underneath to reconnect.

Then they lifted her away. Chris started to follow, but a firm hand stopped him.

The fiery glare he shot at Tom might have been terrifying, but instead of the impassive, unemotional face he expected, the commander's face was downtrodden. "Let them do their work," he said with surprising softness. "We'll meet them at the hospital."

Hospital. There weren't any nearby. The closest was Littleton Adventist, almost five miles away, but he wondered if they could handle the damage to her body.

A terrified shudder rushed through his body, leaving a sour feeling in the bottom of his belly. *Damage to her body,* he thought. It was an engineer's thought, he realized. Think of a body as a physical machine, damaged but repairable, and it made it easier to deal with it, right?

Except the human body was more than that. His mother's life was in the balance.

He couldn't lose another family member, especially not his mother's.

More than ever, he wanted to go into his dreams, to hide in there and see his sister and find comfort. He needed her.

But then warm arms wrapped around him. Emmi held Chris, tightly, shaking a little with her own despair. The woman who had been like his sister for over a decade.

Emmi was as scared as he was, he realized. She was his family now.

Ignoring his father, Chris nodded at Tom. "Let's go."

"Hold on," a voice demanded. It was the police captain they had spoken to earlier. "I need statements from all of you. I need to know just who the hell you people are!"

"Fine," Tom barked at the captain. "Shara, take these two to the hospital. Grab T on your way out. The rest of us will stay to collect weapons and give statements."

The police captain shook his head. "I need their statements too. Especially his," the man pointed an accusatory finger at Chris, and he noticed a scowl upon the cop's face. "What did you do? How did you do it?"

When the captain moved towards Chris, Tom stepped in his way. "That woman is his mother." There was something in Tom's voice, not just determination or resolution, but the slightest waver of emotion. A second later, Chris remembered that Tom had thought his wife, Mia, murdered by Nabu twenty years ago.

This no doubt brought back memories. As that realization sunk in, he looked at Alycia, who watched her father sullenly before meeting Chris's gaze.

"Send officers to meet them at the hospital," Tom demanded. "They'll give their statements there."

Whether the captain abated or not, Chris didn't know. Shara gently pressed on his shoulder and led him and Emmi away from the scene. And then another presence joined them.

His father. Ken Tatsu.

Still emotionless.

After all, it wouldn't be proper to shed tears in front of so many people, would it?

Chris glared at Ken and almost demanded his father leave them alone.

Ignoring the heated look from Chris, Ken asked Shara, "May I accompany you? I do not believe the police will allow me to drive my vehicle out of the garage."

There was something in his voice. An edge that Chris had never heard before. Was he mad? Was he sad? *What the hell are you feeling? Shout! Cry! Do something, you unfeeling bastard!*

The anger boiling within startled Chris enough that he kept his thoughts to himself.

Shara nodded, "Of course." Then she tapped her radio earpiece. "T, meet us at the van."

"On my way," her voice replied.

They had to walk some distance around the bodies of the snakes before finally heading back down Cherryville to University Boulevard. There were uniformed police everywhere, trying to hold back countless news reporters. Chris remembered the helicopters, and looked above to see at least four choppers still orbiting the intersection.

His hatred redirected towards them. More than ever, he wanted to be left alone, left to his grief and worry without having to worry about what the entire human species would see.

But his secret was out. He was a magic user, and now the whole world had seen him take on giant snakes.

Tiana waited for them by the van, having already placed her rifle under the benches in the back. Shara looked between Chris and his father, and then asked Tiana, "Would you mind riding in the back with Chris and Emmi?"

Quirking a curious eyebrow, Tiana shrugged and nodded. "Sure."

"Mr. Tatsu," Shara turned to his father, "Would you care to ride up front with me?"

Still refusing to look at Chris, he nodded curtly and walked around to climb into the passenger door.

Chris nodded at Shara and muttered, "Thanks."

After everyone else climbed in and Tiana closed the doors, Shara started the van and slowly eased them away from the scene. Two cops tried to stop them, but whatever Shara said to them convinced them to let the van through southbound.

After a ten-minute silent and awkward ride, they arrived. Tiana had to remind Chris and Emmi to leave their weapons behind, and that included their tac vests and holsters, to ensure they didn't accidentally alarm hospital staff.

They checked with the front desk of the E.R., and were told that Mrs. Tatsu was in surgery now. A part of Chris was relieved, thinking that they would have only taken her into surgery if she was still alive and had a chance. Had they managed to restore her breathing in the ambulance ride?

Then his father was asked to fill out paperwork. Chris, Emmi, Shara and Tiana found a corner of the waiting room to sit in silence, while his father sat as far away from them as he possibly could, and the dreadful task of waiting began.

He and Emmi sat on a small couch together, her arms wrapped around him comfortingly. It wasn't until ten minutes passed by that he suddenly realized that even as recent as three months ago, he would have never let her hug him, let alone hold him like this.

Such acts always reminded him of Naomi, and how much he missed her. Now more than ever, his heart ached for his sister's presence.

Tiana and Shara sat across from them, with Tiana reading a magazine and Shara staring into nothing. He watched Shara for a second, wondering why she wasn't busying herself with her phone or a magazine, but then he realized she was meditating while keeping a watchful awareness of their surroundings.

She must have sensed him staring and met his eyes.

"Sorry," he muttered, stirring Emmi out of her own reverie.

"It's okay," Shara spoke softly. "Are you okay?"

His first reaction was to lash out - it was a dumb question. But it was one he would have asked if the situations were reversed. He drew in a deep, shuddering breath. That was when he realized the tears hadn't come yet, and he wondered why. Glancing behind him, towards his father, Chris wanted to blame him. Blame his father for trying to make his son never feel emotion, or at least never show it.

"I don't know," he admitted, looking back to Shara. "I just..."

Tiana had set her magazine down and looked at him with cool eyes. That was when he realized she probably didn't know everything that had happened, no one had explained to her why they were at the hospital. She simply had come along, silently and patiently, not questioning anything.

"The golem crushed..." His voice faltered, and finally, the tears came, blurring his vision. "My...um, mother," he managed to croak out, and felt everything come crashing down on him all at once.

It played out in his head again, and again, and again, no matter how hard he tried to suppress the images. The golem picking his mother up, crushing her, the crunch of breaking bones, her legs hanging limply, like a ragdoll. Her screams suddenly silenced. Her body crumpling to the grass. Her motionless chest.

And her face. He knew he had looked, but before now he hadn't *seen* the look on her face. The horror. The terror. The pain. A twisted and contorted expression, stained and mired by running makeup.

If she died, her final hours on Earth would be looking absolutely dreadful, and for some reason, that made him feel worse. Angrier.

No, anger wasn't the right word. It was too soft. Even rage fell short of how he felt, the boiling sensation within making him want to find Nabu and disintegrate her again. And again. And again. If she could come back in another body, over and over, he could just destroy her over and over again. Make her feel his pain. Make her suffer...

Shara blinked and broke her gaze on Chris, looking towards the hospital entrance. "That took them a minute," she muttered. Chris blinked his tears away and saw a man and a woman enter, both wearing plain clothes suits, but both visibly showing detective badges on their belts.

Cops. No doubt there to get Chris's statement.

A shudder shook his frame. He had never actually given an official statement to police before, so he wasn't sure what to expect.

"What do we tell them?" Emmi asked. "How truthful can we be?"

"I'll talk to them first," Shara stated, standing up. "I'll see if I can convince them not to talk to you two, at least not for now. Besides, I recognize one. He knows who we are." She paused, and amended, "Sort of." Looking towards the other side of the waiting room, she nodded to Chris. "Looks like the doctors are talking to your father."

While Shara moved to meet the cops, Chris bolted to his feet and looked towards the reception desk to see his father standing with two white-coated doctors. One was much younger, an attractive woman with long brown hair and light blue eyes, and the other was an older graying man with neatly-trimmed hair and no hint of facial hair.

He and Emmi rushed towards them, leaving Tiana behind.

But when they approached, the doctor placed a sympathetic hand on his father's shoulder, and then looked at Chris with hollow eyes. Feeling his stomach drop down from underneath him, Chris stopped short, his boots squealing on the tiled floor. "What's happening?"

The doctor started to speak, but Ken reeled on Chris, uncontrolled wrath contorting his face. "You!"

It stunned Chris. Never before had he seen his father show such powerful, overt hatred. Never had he heard such venom in his voice. "Wha-"

"Stay away!" Ken roared. "It's your fault! It's all your fault!"

Chris stepped closer, looking to the doctor. With a shuddering voice, he asked, "Where's my mom?"

With Ken visibly shaking, and tears welling in his eyes, Chris dreaded the next words. The doctor spoke with a soft voice, trained in patience and sympathy. "We did what we could," he stated. "but her spinal cord was severed in eight different places, her vertebrae crushed..." With each word, Chris felt his heart thunder against his chest, slow and painful. His legs felt weak, and he sank down to his knees, Emmi trying to catch him while whimpering, barely containing her tears. The doctor continued listing everything that was broken on his mother.

Broken. But unfixable. Unrepairable. The pieces added to one whole truth.

A terrible truth.

The doctor stopped his long explanation and lowered his head remorsefully. "She's still alive, but only because we have her on minimal life support. I'm afraid she will never breathe on her own again. And given her internal injuries, even life support might not fully sustain her for long."

Chris slouched forward, wanting to collapse completely but unable to with Emmi holding him. Tears splashed down onto the tile with every blink of his eyes. It clutched at his heart, crushed his chest. He *hurt*. That's all he knew. Terrible, aching, wrenching pain overwhelming his senses, his reason.

His mother was alive, but for all intents and purposes, she was gone.

"I am so sorry," the doctor stated. "It is entirely your father's decision what to do next, but my recommendation is to..." He trailed off. He didn't have to finish. There was nothing left to say.

"You can see her again beforehand if you wish," the other doctor spoke, her voice sweet and soft and caring.

Chris nodded, and stood up. But the moment he stepped forward, his father interceded, the rage on his face creating a terrifying vision. He shoved Chris back. "Don't you dare," he growled. "You have no right, no right at all! This is your fault."

Stunned, Chris shook his head, mouth hanging open. "I...didn't..." But he did. His father was right, it *was* his fault. Nabu had targeted them to get back at Chris.

And Chris had failed to protect them.

Pointing towards the exit, Ken growled, his voice hoarse, "Leave! Go now, before you hurt someone else!" When Chris gaped at Ken, he roared, "GO!"

Chris didn't move. He was too stunned. Too shocked, too empty, too hurt. How could he leave without seeing his mother one last time?

"Dad," he pleaded, using the name for the first time since childhood. "I..."

"Do not call me that," Ken retorted, tears splashing down onto his gray suit jacket. His voice shook as he slowly, deliberately said, "You. Are no son. Of mine. You're no son of hers."

His first words didn't bite. But those last words, they struck at Chris like a sledgehammer. He staggered backwards.

But whatever he felt, Emmi stepped forward, enraged. "That's not fair!"

Ken reeled on her, "Stay out of this!"

"Screw you, asshole," she snapped. "He tried to save her! Chris has become someone special, and if not for him, *you'd* be dead too! You owe your life to your son!"

"HE'S NOT MY SON!"

"Sir, please," the doctor rested a gentle hand on Ken's shoulder. "Please keep your voices down. This is no place for this argument."

Ken gruffly rolled his shoulder, forcing the doctor's hand off. Then he glared at the doctor and said, "No one else is allowed in to see her. As Hana's husband, it is my decision, *my* will."

The doctor's mouth hung open, but then he drooped his shoulders and sighed. "It is indeed your choice." He looked at Chris sympathetically. "I am so sorry."

Chris couldn't believe it. He *wouldn't* believe it. "That's…my mother in there!" He started forward, but suddenly there were two burly security guards emerging from somewhere, standing in his way.

"Please," the doctor said. "I know this is hard, and I don't agree with it, but I have to abide by Mr. Tatsu's wishes."

His father walked away, towards the door leading into the rest of the hospital, following the younger doctor. "Dad, please," Chris called. "Let me say goodbye!"

Ken didn't pause, didn't look back. He walked through the doors, and left Chris behind to his tears and emptiness.

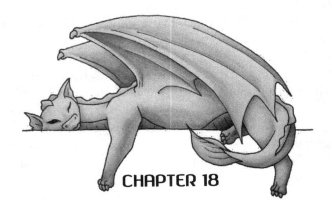

CHAPTER 18

Even in the coldest winter, Chris's body never shook as much as it did now. A tumult of rage, despair, and guilt broiled around inside of him. The older doctor gave Chris one last apologetic look, and then followed Ken further into the hospital.

Leaving Chris with a kind of emptiness that he was all too familiar with.

He hadn't had a chance to say goodbye to his sister, either.

Both his mother and his sister had been taken from him, *ripped* from him by the same person.

He should have felt unbridled fury towards Nabu, but the angrier he felt, the more he directed it towards himself. The more Chris blamed himself.

His father…*Ken* was right. More than he knew.

A gentle hand on his back startled Chris, a sympathetic touch from Emmi. Seconds ago she looked ready to tear Ken apart, piece by piece, but now her expression had softened into compassion. Emmi, his one friend, his *sister,* who could go from serious to joking to sympathetic in a matter of seconds, and be absolutely genuine about each emotion.

Chris marveled at her. He almost envied her, but then he remembered the horrors she had recently endured. His self-loathing grew stronger when he thought, *I failed her, too. I should have saved her before Nabu ever had a chance to…*

Knuckles popping from clenched fists, Chris turned away from the doctors, from the front desk, away from his mother and father. Away from the pain, away from the agony of feeling, of caring. He couldn't bear it any longer. He wanted to stop feeling, he wanted to stop crying.

Countless eyes in the waiting room watched him, and he scowled at them all. "What are you looking at?!"

Some glared, some looked away sheepishly. Shara looked on remorsefully while the detectives watched dispassionately.

He wanted to go. He *needed* to go, now.

Tiana had joined Shara's side at some point during the exchange, so he marched over to them, studiously ignoring the cops. "I need to get out of here," he pleaded, his voice shaking.

Shara opened her mouth, clamped it shut, and then looked at the detectives. "Is that good enough?"

The lead detective considered her for a moment, and then nodded. "Yes, ma'am. We'll come find you if we need more." He looked at Chris and added, "I'm very sorry for your loss, sir."

Chris wanted to scream at the cop, but somehow he contained himself. It helped when he saw Emmi next to him in his peripheral vision.

Nodding to his partner, the detective headed back towards the desk, no doubt to wait for Ken.

It was the strangest sensation after that. Before, Chris had felt in a fog, but now everything was in hyper-focus. The smell of disinfectant in the hospital was overwhelming, and he saw every detail of every face that gawked at him. He remembered walking out of the front door with the others, freshly-laid asphalt on a nearby road stinging his nostrils. Two pigeons cooed noisily in a nearby tree. The summer heat felt oppressive, closing in all around him, suffocating.

They loaded up into the van, and the discarded guns still smelled strongly of discharged gunpowder. Tiana drove while Shara sat in the passenger seat, but no sooner had Tiana put the van in drive than did Shara's cellphone ring. The tone, which Chris remembered sharply from when he had first met her in an alley behind the arcade bar, he recognized now as a Beethoven piece.

"What's up, Tom?" she asked upon answering.

Somehow Tom's voice carried – Chris couldn't make out exactly what the commander was saying, just that his voice was loud.

"We've already left, headed for the tower," Shara said. Another pause, and she glanced back at Chris. "Yeah. That's probably a good idea, it's just that…Chris is in no shape." Another short pause. "I'm afraid so."

Part of him was curious what they were talking about, but part of him didn't care, or rather didn't *want* to care. He just wanted everything to be over. His bedroom called to him, and for the first time in his adult life, he understood why Emmi used to lock herself in her room after a bad breakup. He just wanted the world to leave him alone.

But the world never stopped, and the war against Nabu had just begun.

"Right. I'll talk to her about it." Shara hung up, and then twisted around to be able to look at Emmi, who sat to his right and held his hand tightly. "Emmi, when was the last time you heard from your parents?"

Chris felt his face grow pale. He hadn't thought of that. If Nabu had targeted his family, surely she would target Emmi's parents as well.

"Oh, um," Emmi faltered as color drained from her face. "Shit, it's been a while. I called them two months ago to let them know about graduating but not walking, and that I had an internship with you guys. That was it."

"We should bring them into protective custody," Shara said grimly. "I'll GPS your house, but you should call them to let them know we're coming, and to pack lightly."

"Sure, but they probably aren't even in the States," Emmi said with a casual shrug.

"Don't they usually go to Europe over the summer?" Chris asked.

"Yeah," Emmi nodded, searching her pants pockets. "Umm, I don't have my phone, it's at the tower."

Shara tossed her phone back. "Do you remember their numbers?"

"I think so," Emmi nodded and brought up the app to dial a number. The phone immediately started ringing, and a second later, Chris heard a voice answer. "Mom! Are you guys okay?" Emmi paused and smiled. "I didn't know. How's the wine?" Another pause, and he heard Mrs. Dubois's voice cheerily responding. "Okay. Well, I know this is going to sound strange, but be extra careful out there, okay?"

"Where are they?" Shara asked.

"Marseille," Emmi replied.

"Good, there's a Sentinel detachment in Paris, they can get to them quickly."

Emmi nodded. "Mom? Something's happened and your lives are in danger." A beat, and Emmi rolled her eyes. "No, I'm not exaggerating, you're just going to have to trust me. Some people will come find you and take you into protective custody." Another pause. "No, Mom, this has to do with my internship." Another pause, and her voice grew frustrated. "Dammit, no, Mom, I'm not in trouble with the law. This has to do with all the strange things happening all over the world now." She nodded. "Yes, magic. No, the news isn't lying, it's real. I promise." Her mom spoke some more, and Emmi interrupted sharply, "Will you just listen to me? Trust me on this, okay? I'll text you the names of who to expect as soon as I know, they'll be coming from Paris."

Chris had met Emmi's parents on multiple occasions, and after getting past the awkward stage where her mom had wanted to set Chris and Emmi up as a couple, they settled into accepting him as her best friend. Her parents, especially her mom, sometimes didn't seem to live in the real world. Excess wealth could do that to some people, he supposed.

"Alright, good," Emmi nodded. "Pack your bags, but *only* what you need, okay? Are you in our summer house?" An affirmation came across the line. "Okay, I'll let them know the address. Be safe. I love you, Mom. Tell Daddy I said hi."

And the conversation was over. She tossed Shara's phone back, and Shara immediately started looking up another number.

Denver traffic was even worse than before, and while Shara called Tom back, and then reached out to the Parisian Sentinels, Chris and Emmi leaned against one another and stared into nothingness.

What had their lives come to? Their families were in danger, and a psychopathic, body-switching half-god was hunting them down. Chris could just imagine what conversations he might have with some of his old college buddies. 'What'd you do this summer? Went camping? Traveled? Interviewed with prospective employers? Cool! I learned how to fight demigods with magic, and then watched a golem crush my mom!'

Pain cinched at his chest, contorting his heart into the feelings of rage, despair, and regret again.

This was his life, now. These feelings would be with him for years to come.

But what if he could direct them? Channel those emotions? It was something Emmi had tried to teach him with meditation, to focus his thoughts and feelings, to use the energy from them to achieve what he needed.

What did he need?

To destroy Nabu, once and for all.

That would protect *everyone,* so that's what he would do.

Whispering just loud enough for Emmi to hear, he said, "Her days are numbered."

"What?" Emmi asked with a frown.

"Nabu," he clarified. "I'm going to find her, and I'm going to destroy her, once and for all."

"I agree, that's an appropriate goal," Shara suddenly called back. *Damn those ears of hers.* "But if there's one thing I've learned over the past eighty years, it's that Nabu doesn't do something unless it's part of a larger move." Shara looked back at him, her phone conversations apparently finished.

"What are you saying?" Chris asked, just as they pulled into the underground garage beneath Sentinel tower.

"I'm saying that I don't think Nabu did all of this just to go after your parents," Shara spoke with a grim expression. "I think this was part of a larger scheme. She's planning something bigger, and much more dangerous."

Chris drew in a deep breath and nodded. "Then I guess we better figure out what it is."

CHAPTER 19

When they arrived at the tower, the others had already returned. Chris, Emmi, Shara and Tiana rode the elevator up and met Tom, Alycia, and Marisol in the armory, just as the latter group had finished putting away their weapons and other gear.

Alycia must have heard from Tom about Chris's mother, and the moment she saw him, she rushed at him and flung her arms around him. At first he simply stood there, arms hanging limply at his sides, but the longer she held the hug, the more he felt like collapsing into her.

"I'm so sorry, Chris," she whispered, fresh pain in her voice. "I know there's nothing I can say. I wish there was..."

He finally wrapped his arms around her and squeezed back. Choking back tears, he tried to speak, but nothing came out.

When they finally pulled apart, Tom stopped next to him and rested a hand on his shoulder. "I think we could all do with something to eat, yeah?" Chris didn't feel much like eating, but he nodded. "Good. I'll have Abby order something to be delivered."

Chris and the others from the van put away their weapons and gear after that, and then Chris went to the locker room to get rid of his sweat and blood-soaked clothes. Tom hadn't followed, so Chris took the opportunity to soak in the shower alone.

After a few minutes of letting the hot water relax his muscles, Chris sat on the shower floor, his legs drawn up to his chest and his arms wrapped around them. He didn't cry, not again. Instead, he focused on his anger. He drew it in, let it fuel him, let it give him clarity.

Nabu wanted revenge, true, but she wanted something else. Chris and Emmi's families were convenient avenues to get what she wanted. And it couldn't have just been the dagger.

Determined to poke at the others over it, Chris shut the water off and dressed quickly, thankful for the familiar feeling of blue-jeans on his legs after spending so much time in BDU's over the past two months.

When he reached the kitchen, everyone was already present, including Abby and Babbar. A soft chortle from under the cabinet by the fridge let Chris know that Nina was still enjoying her hoard. Abby had apparently ordered a catering package from a Mexican restaurant nearby, and on the kitchen counter, a taco bar had been set up, with everyone already making their own meals.

They all looked at him when he entered, and scarlet warmth rushed into his face. He hated the extra attention. So he deflected, and instead asked one of many burning questions on his mind.

"Babbar," Chris began, intentionally sitting next to the gnome just as he had settled down to eat. Chris faltered then, while Babbar only half-paid attention to him, intent more on fixing his soft-shelled tacos up. There was something bizarre about seeing a green-haired gnome eating tacos.

Snapping himself out of his amusement, Chris asked, "Why was Nabu afraid of Nina?"

Babbar's eyes opened wide and he looked at Chris. "And why, precisely, are you suddenly interested in that?"

"Because if she can help us destroy Nabu once and for all…"

"I thought you were the chosen one in that regard," Babbar narrowed his eyes. A flash of anger passed through Chris, and he suddenly found himself wanting to reach across and grab the gnome by the collar.

"Yes, but I can't do it alone, and now…" Chris paused, forcing clenched fists to unravel. "Now she's hurting the people we love."

His tacos forgotten, Babbar interlaced his fingers and drew them up to his chin, studying Chris with what looked suspiciously like judgmental eyes. This was an unexpected turn.

"What did you think was going to happen?" Babbar asked just as Alycia sat down to Chris's left.

Blinking, Chris asked, "Excuse me?"

"You gave Nabu his, or rather *her* powers back," Babbar stated.

"You gave a demigod the ability to use their full powers, and then helped thwart their plans. Did you think Nabu would simply shrug her shoulders, say 'oh darn,' and adjust her plans without plotting revenge against you?"

"Hey," Alycia growled. "Chris did what he was *supposed* to do, the only thing he *could* do."

"Wrong," Babbar pointed a finger at her. "He didn't have to dismantle the Barrier."

Emmi had come to the table to sit next to Alycia, but stopped as soon as Babbar pointed that out. She stared at him, her face emotionless for the moment. Alycia defended, "If Chris had refused, Nabu would have killed Emmi."

"But the Barrier would have remained intact, especially without the dagger," Babbar countered. "Emmi's sacrifice would not have been in vain."

Chris's eyes darted to Emmi, searching her face for some reaction to Babbar's statement. Her expression remained blank, but she still didn't sit or even set her plate of tacos down.

"Hey, fungus," Shara called from the other table, where she and Tom had just sat down after clearing a chair away for Abby. "Shut the hell up, will ya?"

"No I will not," Babbar retorted hotly, his autumn-gold eyes flashing at Shara. "This is a war that the boy has brought upon us all." He looked at Chris, "And in war, there are casualties. Did you think to yourself, 'it doesn't matter, as long as it isn't people I know and love?' Did you truly not realize that people would *die* while you fought Nabu and Marduk, oh great chosen one?"

"I'm not the chosen one!" Chris shouted, slamming his palm on the table. "I never said I was chosen!"

"But it still falls to you," Babbar shouted back. "Your choice to destroy the Barrier. Your job to somehow destroy beings that are impossible to destroy!"

A familiar fear cinched at Chris's chest. He had wondered about that, and it was one of the many terrors that had plagued him last night.

"Nothing is truly invincible or immortal," Tom stated just as Abby rolled up next to him and studiously set her plate down. She seemed not to want to get involved in the argument, and Chris couldn't blame her.

"Oh really?" Babbar asked, folding his arms. "Tell me, mister know-it-all, do you know what a celestial is? Or an infernal?"

Tom frowned, and just about everyone around the tables grew silent. Marisol uneasily pulled up a chair to Babbar's right, and Emmi finally snapped out of her reverie and sat down. Tiana was the last to join the group, sitting at the other table next to Abby.

There was only one other person who apparently had any idea what Babbar was talking about. Shara asked, "Wait, you think Marduk is an infernal?"

Babbar nodded. "I do. It's obvious, isn't it?"

Chris narrowed his eyes, trying desperately to control the growing frustration he felt inside of himself. "You...you knew this, and didn't tell me?"

"Or any of us," Tom added, the edge in his voice unnerving.

"He didn't because it's not true," Shara stated. "Marduk can't be an infernal because infernals were defeated before the dawn of civilizations."

"Not true," Babbar replied hotly. "They were defeated *because* of civilizations."

"Hold it, hold it," Chris held up his hands to stop the two from arguing further. "Who are the infernals? Who are the celestials?"

Babbar and Shara exchanged glances. She nodded to him, and set to eating her first taco, ensuring Babbar watched her take her first slow bite.

Narrowing his eyes, and then looking at his own abandoned tacos, Babbar sighed. He took a moment to consider his words, and then looked at Chris. "On Earth, most human cultures have some sort of origin mythology, correct?"

Chris felt his right eyebrow arch curiously. "You mean creation myths?"

"Yes, that's what I meant," Babbar nodded. "Stories about how humans were first created, usually by one or more gods." Chris nodded. "Well on my world, we have creation myths about the celestials. How they came to be, the first ethereal beings, long before the existence of corporeals like you and I. Like human myths, there are many different versions, but that fact isn't as important as the fact that celestials are *real*. And the infernals are real," he looked pointedly at Shara. "No one is quite certain if the infernals are fallen celestials, or if they simply came into existence to balance against the celestials."

The gnome grew silent, and Chris pressed him, "But what *are* they?"

"I'm getting to that," Babbar replied grumpily. He sighed again, and started, "They're gods, essentially, but not in the fashion you humans think of gods. They are the source of magic. Specific celestials embody and create specific magics. There is a celestial who enables your ability to cast arcane magic," he nodded at Chris. "There is one for shapeshifting, for conjuration, for enchanting, for displacement, better known as portals. Each type of power has a sort of patron god, the one who...I don't want to say creates it, because that's not accurate. They make it...possible, I suppose is the correct word. From them, the essence of magic permeates the universe."

Thinking back to when Chris first met Babbar, he asked, "If there are more than one, why do you always say 'goddess,' like a specific one, while Shara says 'gods?'"

"I worship a specific celestial," Babbar replied. "The goddess who embodies luck and fortune."

A frown drew down Chris's face. "Luck and fortune? That's not a magic power."

Alycia cleared her throat, and Chris glanced at her. She lifted her eyebrows up knowingly, but when Chris didn't get it, she said, "Domino?"

Chris's frown deepened. "What?"

"From Marvel? Deadpool 2?"

"Oh," he replied, snippets of the movie flashing through his memory. Not having read the comics, he'd never known if Domino had the same powers in the comic books or not.

"Right," Babbar nodded. "See, some humans get it."

At first, Chris felt a little surprised that Babbar knew Deadpool 2, but then he remembered that the gnome's underground house was built to mimic the Resident Evil mansion.

"In any case," Babbar continued, "other gnomes worship other gods or goddesses."

"While my people worship all of the gods," Shara volunteered. "Or celestials, as some legends call them."

Babbar opened his mouth to say something in response, but clamped it shut a second later. Chris looked back and forth between the two, but then asked, "So what about the infernals?"

"According to most of our lore," Babbar replied, "the infernals are the opposite. They feed on energy, they feed on *magic*, to gain power. When the first corporeal civilizations arose, the celestials blessed them with magic. Some say they did so to ensure the corporeals worshipped them, and they gained power from such worship, but that assertion is very much contested. What *isn't* contested is the fact that infernals could consume the souls of specific corporeals, and which species they could consume appeared to be tied to whichever celestial was tied to the species. When the infernals absorbed the souls, they absorbed their magical essence along with it. So the infernals began to consume every mortal they could, in hopes of gaining enough power to contend with the celestials and tip the balance in their favor."

"Let me guess," Alycia said. "The celestials didn't like that."

"Exactly," Babbar affirmed. "But just like celestials, infernals cannot be destroyed. So the celestials did the next best thing – they imprisoned them. Trapped and bound their ethereal essences where they could no longer harm anyone."

"Maybe that's all true," Shara interjected impatiently, "but that doesn't mean that Marduk is an infernal."

A shiver ran the length of Chris's spine. "But Marduk feeds on human souls," he said quietly.

"Precisely," Babbar sat back in his chair and nodded triumphantly. "And Marduk was unable to directly affect anything on Earth, which is why he created Nabu."

"I'm telling you, it can't be an infernal!" Shara stood up, her chair screeching across the tiled floor while her arms waved around. "They were defeated, they're *gone*, Babbar."

"Why can't he be one?" Babbar asked simply. "Other than your mistaken belief that they simply don't exist anymore?"

"Isn't that reason enough?" she replied. "For crying out loud, you're talking about an entity that, if he is an infernal, is immortal! Unkillable!"

"Oh, so that's it, is it?" Babbar mocked. "Marduk isn't an infernal because you simply don't want him to be?" He scoffed. "You elves and your arrogant-"

"I'M NOT AN ELF!" Shara screeched, glowering over Babbar as she took a threatening step towards him.

"Easy, Shara," Tom cautioned. "Easy."

"I'll stop calling you an elf when you stop calling me a fungus," Babbar spoke with narrowed eyes.

"Babbar, back off," Tom turned on him. "Arguing and insulting each other isn't gonna solve a damn thing. Now sit down." When Shara didn't comply, he added more forcefully, "Sit!"

Shara scowled at Babbar for another few seconds before she finally slumped back down into her chair.

"Now let's say you're right," Tom pointed at Babbar. "Just for argument's sake," he cut off Shara's objection. "What can we do about it? How do we stop Marduk?"

Half-laughing, Babbar replied, "You don't!" He shook his head adamantly. "You cannot kill a god, evil or good."

The twist of fear in Chris's gut turned just a little harder, tightening everything inside. "That... I don't believe that," he shook his head. "Tattannu said-"

"Your ancestors made a mistake!" Babbar reeled on him. "They made a mistake, and now thanks to *their* arrogance, we're all going to die at the hands of Marduk."

"I disagree," he replied, his voice shaking along with his hands. "I'm sure no one thought they could pull off the Barrier, either, and they did. *And* they tied all of Tattannu's descendants to it, believing whole-heartedly that it would be enough to destroy Marduk."

"Yet they don't know how," Babbar countered.

Chris paused, thinking back to last night's brief dream. "I don't know. Tattannu implies he knows how."

"Then why hasn't he told you yet?" Babbar folded his arms again. "If there's a way, why doesn't he tell you now, so that you can do it *now* before Nabu or Marduk murder anyone else?"

"I..." Chris faltered, his mouth hanging open. "I don't know," he conceded, unwilling to go so far as admit that Tattannu had told Chris that he simply wasn't ready.

An uneasy silence fell upon the room, broken only by the occasional crunch of someone biting into a hard-shell taco. Babbar took the opportunity to start eating his meal, though he scowled after one bite, his food no doubt cold by now.

After a second bite, he set it down grumpily and sat back again, before he fixed his eyes on Chris. "Right now, the most important thing we can do is keep Marduk from devouring more souls."

A frown drew down Chris's face. "What do you mean?"

Babbar didn't answer, but instead glanced at Tom, who answered, "If Babbar is right, then Marduk is still in whatever prison the celestials set for him. He cannot directly influence Earth, which means he'll rely upon Nabu. We don't know what sort of influence he'll have on others, but our best guess is that Marduk can't just eat the soul of anyone who dies."

"The dagger," Emmi suddenly blurted out. Chris stared at her, and she looked at him. "Imhullu. That's why Nabu is looking for it. She needs to use it to feed souls to Marduk."

"That's our thought," Tom nodded at Babbar.

"And that's why you've kept him around," Shara stated bluntly. "Because he already told you all of this, and you believe him."

Tom hesitated, and then uneasily said, "Not everything. But let's just say it's safer to act as if he's right. If he's wrong but we take precautions, no big deal. If he's right and we don't keep the dagger from Nabu, well, then..."

"Bad for us all," Chris finished.

"Yeah," Tom nodded, and then took the last bite of his second taco.

If Chris hadn't lost his appetite before, he certainly had now.

"So where is it?" Emmi asked.

Tom shook his head. "I'm sorry, it's better if no one else knows."

It instantly clicked in his head, then. He glanced at Babbar, and then back towards the cabinet by the fridge. They must have used Nina's portals to hide the dagger, and they might even need Nina to retrieve it, if they should ever want to.

Alycia visibly shuddered. "Oof. If Marduk realizes Nabu lost the dagger..."

A small grin cracked Chris's face. "There'll be hell to pay."

"Yeah," she smiled. "I almost feel sorry for the bugger."

"You didn't answer Chris's first question," Emmi went off on a separate tangent. Chris had to search his memory to remember what he had even asked in the first place, and thought of it moments before Emmi said it. "Why was Nabu afraid of Nina?"

Shrugging helplessly, Babbar replied, "I honestly don't know. Other than the fact that she could still use magic even with the Barrier up."

"And you've no idea how she did that?" Chris asked.

"None whatsoever," Babbar replied helplessly. "I was just happy she could. It gave me a competitive advantage."

Chris smirked. "Right. Never mind that you might have been cracking the Barrier every time she used her powers, possibly helping Nabu and Marduk out..."

Babbar started to object, while all eyes fell upon him, most everyone grinning and waiting for his retort. He stopped himself, looked around, and slouched down, hiding in the well of his chair. "Touché, Tatsu."

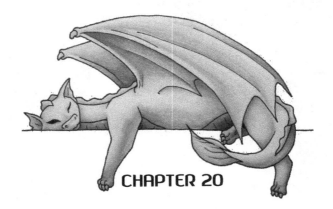

CHAPTER 20

Chris tried to eat, he really did, but every time he looked at the taco bar, a giant well of grief grew within his stomach, and all thoughts of hunger were banished.

With the impromptu meeting over, it came time for the three new Sentinels to get setup as legitimate employees. Including, most importantly, their own computer accounts, which Abby cheerfully helped them with.

In particular, she asked Chris if he would be willing to put his technical knowledge to good use and help her out as a sys admin.

"Of course," he replied, managing a weak smile for her. He, along with Alycia and Emmi, were out on the ops floor, hovering behind Abby's wheelchair as she worked on their accounts. "Although, won't I be in the field most of the time?"

"Not likely," Marisol said from her station behind them. "Most of our time was spent here, searching for hints of magic going on out there." She hesitated, and added, "But these days, there's magic everywhere and we've been called in to consult with Denver P.D. a lot, so, who knows."

"Alright," Chris nodded. "I'm always game for more I.T. experience."

"Excellent," Abby beamed, enunciating every syllable. "Then you can help me make their accounts, too!"

So the afternoon was spent, with Chris being given the 'keys to the kingdom' and then overseen by Abby as he made his own standard-level account along with Emmi's and Alycia's.

Once he was finished, Abby pointed out to them all, "Your

accounts will replicate to every server the Sentinels own throughout the world, so you'll have base-level access even if you're…I dunno, in Osaka or Adelaide or something like that. Except for your admin account," she pointed out to Chris. "That's only valid here and…in…" She trailed off. "Well, in a secret place you're not supposed to know about just yet."

That piqued everyone's interest. "Secret place?" Alycia's eyes lit up. "Ooooh, where's that?"

Barely containing her grin, Abby arched an eyebrow up. "It's a secret, as in you can't know."

"Then why mention it?" Emmi asked.

"Because Chris will get access to the computers there, *if* it becomes necessary," she replied. And then she looked at him with a serious face, "But don't you dare go nosing around the system trying to figure out where it is!"

A part of him was tempted to defy her orders, but for the moment, he didn't feel like getting into any more trouble. They had enough to deal with as it was. "Alright, Abby, I promise."

"Aww, Chris!" Alycia faux-pouted. "I was hoping you'd let us in on the secret once you found out…"

"Riiight, ladies," he smirked playfully.

"So," Abby changed subjects, spinning her wheelchair around to look out over the other workstations in ops. "Marisol and Jered usually use those two stations in the back, and Shara usually sits next to me. The other four stations are yours to choose from."

That basically left two in the front right and two in the back left. He nervously glanced at Alycia, hoping she'd choose to sit next to him. "Well you'd better sit up front with Abby so she can make sure you don't go snoopin' around," Alycia joked. "Emmi, shall we take the back?"

"So we can also keep an eye on him?" Emmi grinned.

And so, despite Chris's wishes, he was up front with his best friend and his crush sitting in the back. For a minute or two, the banter and having tasks to perform helped him forget about what had happened that day.

It didn't take long for it to all come crashing down again. While setting up his workspace and arranging his pair of monitors to the right height and angle, the weight of losing his mother sank down into his gut again, especially when he had one terrible thought —

which side of his family descended from the Tattannu line? Would he see his mother in his dreams tonight? Was she even gone yet, or was his father still holding on to her, making her live as an empty shell?

The grief he had seen in his father's face was fresh on his mind, the one and only time Ken Tatsu had outwardly shown Chris anything other than disappointment.

When day stretched into evening, he felt ready to retreat to the apartment. That's when Tom and Shara came out to ops.

"Hey there, cutie," Shara said to Abby, caressing her neck as she walked by.

"Hey sweetie," Abby beamed a bright, beautiful smile right back at her, eliciting a grin from Chris.

Tom walked to the front of ops just as Shara sat down, and he nodded to Abby. "Abby, bring up the Denver Post website, please." He motioned to the center 75-inch TV behind him.

"You got it, boss," she said brightly.

After a second of furious typing and clicking, suddenly all noise ceased from her, and she looked up at Tom with wide, shocked eyes. Tom nodded, and Chris craned his neck to try to see what she saw, but a second later, the website and its headline appeared behind Tom.

It was an aerial photo of their battle against the snakes earlier in the day, no doubt taken by one of the news choppers. The one helicopter that had been downed by the snakes lay amidst smoking ruins in the photograph, while Chris saw himself blasting a snake in the face with his powers.

The headline said, 'PEACEFUL NEIGHBORHOOD DESTROYED BY MAGIC-WIELDING CITIZENS; FIFTEEN DEAD, INCLUDING CHILDREN.'

"What?!" Alycia shrieked.

"That's not fair," Emmi added. "We didn't cause all that!"

"I know," Tom nodded calmly. "But things are getting worse out there."

Chris frowned and asked, "Worse how?"

His eyes fell upon Chris, and there was something in his expression that gave Chris a chill. This was about him again. This was about his decision in Babylon.

"You three really haven't kept up with the news, have you?" Shara asked.

Chris blinked at her and shook his head. "Just what little you told us. Panic around the globe. Five percent of the population can wield magic."

"Seems that early estimate was wrong," Tom volunteered. "We're looking at more like ten percent, if some news outlets are to be believed, and even *that* may be underestimating." He drew in a hesitant breath, and then rubbed at the bridge of his nose. "Magic users everywhere are finding themselves under persecution, so most have tried to keep their powers hidden. Now people are accusing others of using magic, whether there's evidence or not." Tom hesitated again, and looked first at Emmi, and then at Chris. "And some whacka decided to dox you two."

It took Chris a moment to realize what a whacka was, recalling it was an Aussie slang that Alycia had used more than once, and then he realized what 'dox' meant. "Wait, what do you mean? Doxed us?"

"Doxing means publishing private info about you for all to see," Abby volunteered, "usually so people can retaliate against you for some perceived offense."

"I know," Chris nodded, and then realized the implication. "I mean, you say someone doxed us..."

"Scroll down, Abby," Tom said.

The article on the screen scrolled down, and another photo came into view. It was of Chris and Emmi's ten-story apartment building, with a massive crowd outside bearing hand-painted or markered signs. A line of police stood in front of the entrance, barring the protestors from entering the building.

"That photo was taken an hour ago," Tom stated.

In the foreground, one sign in particular caught Chris's attention. Above a crude drawing of a Christian cross, the words, 'Magic Users Are Servants of the Devil.'

"Son of a bitch," he heard himself say, realization dawning on him.

All eyes fell upon him again. He looked around, and then nodded at the scene. "I'm sorry, but ever since I found out magic was real, I've stopped believing in coincidences. That sign...and the fact that there were two giant snakes."

A grim look soured Tom's face, and he nodded. "Yeah, I caught that too. As if someone meant to reference the Garden of Eden and the serpent. It's too perfect, and too fast."

"Which means someone's orchestrating this," Chris spoke through a tightened jaw. "Someone's manipulating all of us, everyone," he motioned to the crowd in the photo. "Someone's pulling our strings."

"And it's a good bet we know just who that someone is," Shara stated.

"It would stand to reason Nabu would do exactly this sort of thing," Tom said. "It's just that, she's never had the power to do something on this scale."

There was a quaver in Tom's voice that Chris had never heard before, a hint of fear that was completely unlike the Sentinel commander. "There's more than just this, isn't there?"

Tom gave him a stone-faced stare, reminding Chris of his father for just a split second, before the commander nodded. "Abby. Please bring up the headline for international news on the New York Times website."

The solemn tone in his voice sent a shiver of anxiety down Chris's spine, and he looked past Shara to watch Abby's reaction carefully. Just as before, her eyes grew wide, her face going pale, and she looked up at Tom with her mouth hanging open. "Oh my god…"

A second later, she pushed the headline up onto the wall.

The headline read, 'CITIZEN VS. CITIZEN – MAGIC VS. NON-MAGIC. RIOTING IN LONDON STREETS.'

An image to the right of the article's body showed buildings blazing and people throwing bricks, bottles, and other objects at one another. Absolute rage contorted their faces, even in the pixelated image.

The first paragraphs of the article read, 'After the attack on parliament, ordinary citizens have taken to the streets demanding justice. At first the protests were peaceful, with citizens holding signs and silent vigils for those whose lives were lost in the attack. However, when a woman was seen shooting fireballs into a crowd, violence erupted across the city in a matter of hours.

'Matters grew worse when anonymous tips started flowing across social media of names and addresses of magic-wielding citizens, a tactic known as doxing, and the riots were drawn to those person's homes and places of business.

'Now the magic wielders have begun to unite against their would-be attackers, and they have used their abilities to slaughter citizens wholesale. Police have been overwhelmed and suffered casualties, and so the British Prime Minister has called in the army to help regain control of London.'

A stunned silence had fallen over the ops center. Tom let everyone finish reading as much of the article as they could, before he sighed and nodded to Abby, who closed the window.

"As you say," Tom looked at Chris, "I have a hard time believing in coincidences. We know now that Nabu was the one who attacked parliament. We know that Nabu set up the attack on Chris's neighborhood. And I'd bet a coldie that Nabu and her cult have been dropping the social media tips."

Chris clenched his jaw. "So we were right. This has all been part of a larger strategy."

"Right," Tom replied.

"Unfortunately it still leaves us with the question of what her long-term goals are," Shara pointed out. "We know she wants the dagger, but this feels like it's part of something even larger."

"In any case," Tom folded his arms, "it's probably best if you kids stay here tonight."

Chris's spirits slumped to a new low. Of course, Tom was right, he knew it. There wasn't a chance that Chris and Emmi could get into their apartment safely now, but he had so looked forward to locking himself in his room and sleeping in his own bed again. For one thing, the mattresses in the Sentinel guest rooms were horribly uncomfortable.

Heaving out a dejected sigh, Chris looked back at Emmi and Alycia, who looked right back at him, and then at each other. "Well then," Alycia faked an encouraging smile. "Just like old times, yeah?"

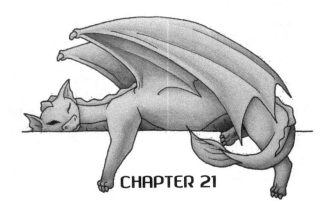

CHAPTER 21

Despite Alycia's remark about old times, it really didn't feel like it to Chris, not anymore. When dinner time rolled around, Chris found that he still had no appetite, so he didn't join everyone else in the kitchen. Marisol decided to stay the night as well, but Chris was more than a little surprised when Jered never arrived to relieve her. He worried at first, but Tom assured him that Jered was okay, and that he simply was working from a different location for now.

With nothing else to do, Shara decided to give the trio a full, legitimate tour of the facility, pointing out all of the different rooms and their roles on the forty sixth and forty seventh floors. They had already seen most of it in their previous visits, but this time they were told what a lot of the different labs on the forty sixth floor were really for.

Most surprising was that at some point, the Sentinels had tried to explain magic with science, and there were chemistry and physics labs setup to help test their theories. So far, nothing had panned out. *Maybe in the future, I can find the scientific link to magic,* Chris thought. Frowning, he wondered, *can magic be engineered?*

Alycia grew more than a little excited, however, when Shara showed her a small storage closet of sewing supplies. "I've been wanting to work on a few more things," she jabbered excitedly. "I might as well work on them while we're stuck here, yeah?"

Shara nodded, "By all means!"

With the tour pretty much concluded, Alycia grabbed what she thought she'd need, and took them up to her room. Shara wandered away, leaving Emmi and Chris alone.

Smiling and shaking her head, Emmi looked at Chris and said, "Well for once, I'd rather not be alone. Mind hanging out with me?"

He really didn't want to. Not because of Emmi, but because of the anguish and grief that kept bubbling up inside. A big part of him wanted to hole up in his room and never see or speak to anyone again, even though he knew that was childish and impossible.

But he also couldn't say no to her. Not when he had made a promise to be with her. "Of course," he said, smiling despite himself.

Tension in her shoulders that he hadn't noticed before instantly eased. "Good," she said, relief washing over her face. "Want to see if we can catch a sunset from the lobby?"

He started to nod, but then a grin drew across his face. "Better yet, let's watch from the roof."

Excitement lit up her face. "Yeah!"

Together, they headed for the stairwell and tromped up to the rooftop landing pad. The helicopter was still there, its rotor blades moored to hooks at the edge of the pad by thick lines to keep them still against the wind.

It was a lot warmer than the last time they were up here, but then again, last time, there had been a freak, magic-induced blizzard that had dumped several feet of snow on Denver in a matter of hours. Now, there was hardly a breeze, even this high up.

They wandered over to the western corner of the building, since like all of downtown Denver, the building didn't align straight east-to-west. Before them lay an incredibly gorgeous view of the setting sun over the distant mountain peaks. The orange and yellow light was already fading to deep purples and blues.

Because the rooftop was a heliport, there was no chain link fence to block their view, only a horizontal fence attached to the sides, meant to catch anyone who might accidentally fall off.

They sat down together on the corner of the concrete pad. The sun was still bright enough to force Chris to squint, but it rapidly grew dimmer.

The vibrant colors brought him peace, and he looked inward to touch his own golden sphere of energy. It had become like old leather, the kind of comfort that calmed his nerves and helped him find his focus. The dread and grief were still there, but that current of magic somehow soothed it, took the edge off.

Until Chris heard a shuddering sigh from Emmi. When he looked at her, she avoided his gaze, but her eyes kept darting towards him. Before he could ask what was wrong, she finally drew in another deep breath, and met his eyes.

"Chris, I am so sorry," she began, her voice shaking. The instant she started talking, wetness collected along the bottom of her eyes. "I...I should have shapeshifted, I should have done *something* to stop that monster." She spoke faster and faster, her voice rising. "It's all my fault, I should have saved her! I should have done *something!*"

Confusion contended with his growing grief, but he dove into his memories, flitting in and out of them to figure out why Emmi suddenly blamed herself.

"Hey, hey," he cooed, reaching out to gently touch her back, but she recoiled away from him.

"No, I don't deserve your sympathy," she crawled away, getting perilously close to the edge of the concrete. "I was too afraid, and I let that monster crush her!"

"You couldn't have done anything else," he defended, his hand outstretched in caution. "Emmi, why in the blazes would I blame you?"

"Because I'm afraid!" she yelled at him, tears now flowing freely. "I'm so goddamn afraid!"

Feeling his own temper rising, Chris barked out, "Of what?"

"Of turning again!" She stopped her backpedaling just as her right hand reached the edge of the concrete.

He blinked his surprise, and in an instant, it all made sense. Emmi's raging bear form, her loss of control, and the harm she had brought to the surrounding life.

"Your rage form," he said, not knowing what else to call it.

She nodded fitfully. "Y-yeah, that. I...I didn't..." Emmi shook her head furiously. "I can't shapeshift again, Chris, I *can't*. At least, not in battle. Not against Nabu or his minions or whatever the *hell* that thing was." She looked at him through reddened, tear-filled eyes, and all of his earlier emotions, all of his remaining grief, sorrow, and hatred died. All he wanted now was to help her.

"It's okay," he said, as quietly as he could. The breeze kicked up for a second, and he was afraid her slender form would be blown over the building, but the wind subsided after only a few seconds. "You'll control it next time, right? You know what it's like, you know how it feels."

"Y-yeah, I do," she nodded, sniffling. "I do, and that's the p-problem." She looked down for a moment, but when she looked up, it was only with her eyes, her head downturned, her expression ominous. "That's the problem. I...I want it again."

Chris stopped short of replying, his mind trying to process what she had just said. "What?"

"I know that if I shapeshift, and I feel that rage again, I'll gladly go into it." She shook her head. "Y-you don't know what it's like, Chris. It felt so pure. Everything else washed away. It...it was just me and my rage. No other feelings, no other memory. I didn't even remember *why* I wanted to rip Nabu apart, I just knew that I had to. Such clarity of thought and feeling, it was so wonderful compared to the hell I've lived in since that...since Nabu..."

Then he realized what she meant. It was like giving up on life. Hiding in a hole, or in a bedroom, like Chris wanted to do. Let the emotions consume him, fill every fiber of his being, *feel* it and nothing else. No guilt over crying, no shame. Just the grief. The pain. The fury towards Nabu for inflicting it all upon him, and the promise of release after succeeding.

It was so tempting.

That was how Emmi must have felt now. Even if he could never understand what she had been through, never fully understand what it felt like to have been so violated and used, he understood the temptation to escape from it all.

How had he brought her back from the brink last time? *That's right, I remember.*

"Just remember one thing, keep this fact *burned* into your mind," he said quietly, allowing a little of his hatred for Nabu to give his voice an edge. "If you give in to that desire, you let Nabu win. It's exactly what she wants from you." He faltered then, realizing that, as his anger boiled up and his desire to completely *destroy* Nabu grew ever stronger, he was likewise playing into her hands.

Because if he acted out of anger, if he let his emotions control his actions, he wouldn't be *thinking*. That would be all the opportunity Nabu needed to win.

Emmi's eyes met his, and somehow, he knew then that she understood it, just the same as he did. She knew him as well as he knew her.

Stretching out his hand, he repeated what he'd said at the training camp. "Let's work together to get that bastard. But we'll do it the right way."

She sniffled again, and pawed away the tears from her eyes and face. "Alright," she took hold of his hand, shuffling closer. "Alright, together."

They held that position for a second, and then were startled by the sound of the rooftop door slamming closed from another breeze. They both jumped and looked to find Alycia standing there, her face lit up orange against the almost-set sun.

The trio stared back and forth stupidly. "Er, did I miss something?" Alycia asked.

Wiping the last remnants of tears away, Emmi smiled, and stood up, urging Chris to stand as well through their joined hands. She then reached out her other hand towards Alycia. "Just a promise," she said to Alycia. "One I'd like us all to make."

With a confused frown on her face, Alycia stepped closer, trepidation slowing each step. "Okay...?"

Emmi urged her closer with a wave of her hand, and once he realized what she was doing, Chris likewise held out his other hand. Alycia hesitantly took up both, and then Emmi squeezed.

"I'm scared," Emmi began. "No, scratch that, I'm *terrified*. Of so much, but especially of myself. I don't trust myself anymore. But I trust you two. You both have my back, and I probably wouldn't be here if it weren't for both of you. So. Chris, Alycia, I'm promising you now, that I won't let you down. I won't fail you. You can count on me to be there for you."

Whatever confusion Alycia felt, it melted into understanding and appreciation. She squeezed their hands as well. "And I promise the same to you two."

It felt wonderful to have Alycia's hand in his again. And it felt right that the three of them now stood together, atop a roof, with a red sun easing behind the mountains. Looking around, and then looking each of them in the eye, he nodded. "I promise. We'll get through all of this *together*."

The moment lasted forever, and simultaneously not long enough. It was a moment of calm amidst a storm of action, and Chris reveled in it. He had his friends. His grief was still there, but as long as they were there, he felt like he could withstand it.

It wasn't over. Not by a long shot. But maybe, just maybe, they had a fighting chance against Nabu, even if she *was* one of those infernals.

The trio turned then to watch the final glimmer of sunlight fade behind the mountains, and they gently squeezed one another's hands to remind each other that they weren't alone.

"Now," Alycia squeezed their hands again. "If you two will permit me, I've an idea to help you both in the future. Mind coming down to the armory with me to pick out gloves?"

Chris looked suspiciously at her. "Gloves?"

"Yeah," she beamed. "I think it's time you two had your own shields."

She must have been speaking about enchantments, and Chris felt the bubble of excitement building up. With his failure to create his own shield, any help in that department would be most welcome.

So they followed Alycia down, and picked fingerless tactical gloves that fit each of them. She promised to work on them through the night, but the embroidery would take time, and she needed to concentrate on the enchantment. Bidding them good night, she retreated into her room again, gloves in-hand, and left Chris and Emmi standing in the hallway.

At first Emmi glanced at her bedroom door, but then she looked at Chris pleadingly.

Laughing, he nodded. "If you feel up to it, yeah."

Grinning, she closed her eyes and focused for a second. A green glow engulfed her body, and a second later, she was a pitch-black cat with bright blue eyes.

That night, she slept at Chris's feet.

Just like old times.

The warmth of his core of energy washed over Chris like a blissful hot shower, washing away everything and leaving behind only pure feelings and rejuvenating him better than any normal sleep could.

The surprise came when he felt her presence. Turning away from the core, just like he used to do before he knew magic was real, he felt elation fill his chest when he saw his sister, forever locked in her teenage form.

"Naomi," he said through a broad smile. "You're here!"

But she didn't smile, and he realized instantly that she somehow knew.

Without another word, they rushed forward and clung to one another in a tight hug. It was always a strange sensation – Chris knew this was just a dream, and there shouldn't have been any physical sensations, but he could feel the warmth in her skin as if she were still there, still alive and really hugging him.

"I'm so sorry," she whispered.

Squeezing her tight, he looked around into the gray mists surrounding them, at the hazy shadows of his ancestors shuffling about on the peripheral of his perception. "Is...she...?"

He felt Naomi shake her head. "She's not here."

Slouching in her embrace, Chris nodded. He figured he wouldn't be so lucky. Or perhaps unlucky, as it would be doubly hard to live in the real world if he could have come back to talk to his mother every night.

"I don't..." He started and stopped. "I don't understand why this is so hard. I wasn't ever close to either of them."

He felt her body jerk as she chuckled in his ear, and she pulled out of their embrace. "That's precisely why," she explained. "You were never close to her, but there was always time to make up for that later. Now, there is no more time. Now, there are no more chances."

Nodding, he frowned and asked, "How much do you know?"

"I only get flashes of your life, significant moments. I saw something big crushing her. I saw...your argument with Father."

With involuntarily clenched fists, Chris glowered and looked away from her. "I hate him."

"Chris," she chastised.

Shaking his head furiously, he said, "No, there's no excuses this time. No reasoning. He's an asshole for what he said and did, and I swear I will *never* forgive him."

Stepping close to him again, she pressed a hand against his chest. "Forever is a long time. Be careful with that anger." Then she glanced over his shoulder, at the golden core of magic that was his center. "You've seen what it can do to Emmi, what if it does something similar to you?"

Something inside of him wanted to argue against that, to say that he could control such rage-fueled magic.

That was a lie, and he knew it.

Sighing, he craned his neck around to look at the core again. It pulsed rhythmically, a constant vigil in his soul. More than that, he knew it was tied to thousands, maybe millions of souls. Would he taint them with his growing anger, too?

Those souls. His power. All of this came down to his ancestors, the legacy left behind for him. He looked Naomi in the eyes and asked, "Where is Tattannu?"

Her expression turned to one of sympathy. "I don't know. I mean, he's always with you, but I don't know where he is when he's not...here with me, if that makes any sense."

Gritting his teeth in frustration, Chris looked around at the shadows again, frustration bubbling up within. "Tattannu!" No reply, not even so much as a ripple in the shadows. "Get your ass out here! No more games, no more delays."

Still nothing. "Chris," Naomi started, but he pulled away from her and walked closer to the shadows.

"I'm only doing this because of you!" Still nothing. "Get out here and tell me what the hell I'm supposed to do!"

The shadows finally rippled. Maybe it was Tattannu, coming to tell Chris how he was supposed to end Nabu. A faint voice called to him. *"Learn to let go."*

Before he could contemplate what that meant, a deafening bang startled him, echoing in the shadows.

Jerking out of his sleep, Chris's eyes shot open against the dark. Someone banged urgently on his door, and then, without waiting any longer, it flew open. Harsh light beamed in from the hallway, casting Alycia's shadow upon Chris and cat-Emmi.

"Chris!" Alycia shouted, fear in her words.

"Oye, hey, what?" he asked unintelligently, the fog of sleep still pressing against his consciousness.

"We need your help," she said urgently, flipping on the light. He and Emmi both hissed against the bright white LED illumination.

"Whassgoinon?" He wiped his eyes, but alertness was coming faster now that adrenaline surged into his system. "Alycia? What's wrong?"

She unlocked her phone and showed him the screen. It showed a single text message from 'Eric,' whom Chris knew to be Alycia's brother.

Blinking sleep out of his eyes just as Emmi shapeshifted back to human form, he looked closer at the message. It read – 'Why didn't you tell me Mum was alive?!'

At first the significance was lost upon him. But then it all rushed back to him. Mia Taylor was in league with Nabu, and she hadn't been seen since Babylon.

Now Eric Taylor knew his mother was alive.

Which meant that their enemy had caught up with Alycia's only other family.

CHAPTER 22

"We have to wake your dad up," Chris stated, blinking the last of his sleep from his eyes.

Emmi let out a great big yawn, stretching her arms out wide, but as soon as she heard that, her sleepiness was gone. Alycia showed her the message as well, and just like with Chris, it took moments to register upon her what was wrong. Her eyes opened to wide ovals and she cursed.

"Dad's already awake," Alycia explained. "He was the first person I woke up, and he wanted you two up as well."

With a nod, Chris grabbed his cellphone off of the charger on the desk and shoved it in his back pocket before he ushered the others out into the hallway. Tom had apparently been sleeping in one of the guest rooms as well, but now he was banging on Marisol's door while simultaneously talking on the phone.

"We're gearing up," he said into the phone. "Meet us down in the armory."

Hanging up, he looked at Chris, and then at Alycia. "I'll use one of Abby's programs to try to geolocate his phone," Tom stated. "And then we'll-"

The theme song from the anime *Fullmetal Alchemist: Brotherhood* suddenly rang out from Alycia's phone, and everyone stopped. She gaped wide-eyed at the screen, and then showed it to everyone else, revealing that it was Eric calling.

After a solid two seconds passed, Tom nodded. "Put it on speaker."

Alycia complied, and then, with worry edged into her voice, she spoke, "Eric?"

"He's here," a woman's voice replied. Chris felt the icy grip of fear return to his stomach as he and everyone else, including Marisol who just came out of the door Tom had been knocking on, gathered around in the cramped hallway.

"Mum!" Alycia cried out. "Mum, where are you? What have you done with Eric?"

A soft, low laugh rang out. *"My sweet, he's just fine. He's standing next to me. Do you have an answer for him?"*

Hesitating, Alycia frowned at her father, and then asked, "An answer for what?"

"His question? Why didn't you or Tom tell him I was alive? I'm rather disappointed in you for not telling him."

"Mia," Tom interrupted. "What are you going to do with him?"

"Oh good, you're there too," her voice purred. *"That makes this so much easier. Tell me, dear heart, do you have it?"*

There was no questioning what 'it' was. She intended to ransom Alycia's brother for Imhullu.

"Never mind that now," Tom shook his head. "It isn't too late. Nabu's hold over you isn't unbreakable. Come home!"

"But I already have," she replied, heat rising in her voice. *"I went home, dear heart, and someone else lived there. You sold our house. You left our home, and you left our baby here."*

Chris felt a frown crease his brow. That was a rather strange thing for her to point out. Why would she have gone looking at Tom and Alycia's former house in Australia?

"I'll tell you when I see you," Tom insisted. "Tell me where you are and I'll come get you."

"Yes, you will," she replied, the rising anger in her voice leveling off. *"And you'll bring it with you, and we'll have a* lovely *family reunion. I know you have the means to get here fast. Tell me, is Babbar listening?"*

Tom blinked, and looked beside him just as Babbar, whom Tom had apparently already awoken earlier, sidled up into the group. He didn't speak, but he looked white as a sheet.

When Tom didn't reply, Mia continued, *"Come to Melbourne Airport in fifteen minutes, terminal two. Eric and I will meet you there, dear heart, but if you come without it, I'm afraid our reunion won't be so happy."*

Opening his mouth to reply, Tom was cut off when the call ended. "Shit," he rubbed the bridge of his nose. "God dammit," he folded his arms.

"Wait, why the airport?" Emmi asked.

"To make sure we don't come fully armed," Tom sighed, shaking his head.

Chris thought about that for a moment, and then shrugged. "So we don't go in with typical weapons. Notice she didn't say anything about coming alone?"

Tom quirked an eyebrow at him. "Good point. That seemed like a bit of an oversight for her."

"So take us all in," Chris nodded.

"But you heard her," Alycia interjected worrisomely. "You have to bring the dagger, or..."

"I know, I heard," Tom unfolded his arms and stepped up to Alycia, placing his hands squarely on her shoulders. "Look, we're gonna get 'im. Both of them. But you and I both know, they can't have the dagger, not without risking everything."

Chris saw Alycia's jaw clench, but she nodded. "Right. I know. I just...we know what Nabu is capable of." Her eyes darted at Chris, and then at Emmi. "I know neither of us are on the best of terms with Eric, but-"

"But nothing," Tom shook his head. "He's coming out of this alive, alright?" An idea appeared to spark in Tom's eyes, and he grinned. "We're going to bring them home, Aly. *Both* of them, yeah?"

Nodding slowly, she gave him a half-hearted smile. "Yeah. You've got a plan?"

"The start of one," he nodded. "Let's get to the armory. Except you," he pointed at Marisol. "I need someone here on the computers, and since we're all awake, I'd rather not have to call Abby back in."

"Sure, boss," she nodded. "Want me to get T or Jered on standby?"

Tom shook his head, "Not Jered, no, he's still on special assignment. But text him, let him know what's going on. And let T get some sleep."

Marisol nodded. "You got it, boss." With that, she edged past the group and down the hall.

"Let's go," Tom waved them all on.

Together, the group headed for the armory, where they met Shara, who had thrown on BDU pants and a black tank top, but hadn't fixed her bedhead hair yet, nor put in her color-changing contacts. Tom filled her in as quick as he could, and then said, "Since we can't go in fully armed, here's the plan. We'll stick with civilian clothes. It's winter down there, so we'll put on concealed carry harnesses covered with jackets."

"Ooh," Babbar suddenly quipped in. "Do I get a gun, too?"

"Like hell," Shara shot at him hotly.

"Hey," he scowled at her. "Considering you can't do this without Nina or I, I think you should show me some more respect."

Gritting her teeth, Shara turned to rebuke Babbar, but Tom placed a cautioning hand on her forearm just as she pointed a finger at Babbar. "Let it go, Shara. We don't have time."

She stopped short and stared into Tom's eyes. After a second, the hardness in them vanished, and she nodded. "Do I need to go get my contacts on?"

"No time," Tom replied. Then he turned to Babbar, "And yes. I want you armed, but with a tranq gun."

As Chris moved to the lockers with the tactical gear and found the one locker with multiple shoulder harnesses, he heard Babbar start to retort, "A tranq gun?!"

"Yes, a tranq gun," Tom grit out, just as Chris started handing shoulder harnesses to everyone. "I want Mia alive. That goes for all of you, especially you and your powers, Chris," Tom looked directly at Chris just as he passed one of the harnesses to Tom.

Nodding once, he replied, "I'll set my phasers to stun." Alycia managed a wry grin at his remark, and he felt glad to have helped ease her tension.

After handing the last harness out, to Babbar no less, Chris threw on his own and began the awkward process of adjusting the straps to fit him.

"I'll also have a tranq gun as well, and I want you three to do so as well," Tom continued. "But just in case Nabu shows her face, I want you," he nodded to Shara, "to carry one of Alycia's enchanted pistols."

"Crap," Alycia's eyes widened. "Speaking of, I need to grab some things from my room."

"That's fine," Tom nodded. "Hurry up, and meet us out in the lobby. We'll grab a tranq gun for you."

"Right," she nodded. She grabbed a black BDU jacket from another locker, and then ducked out of the room.

"Melbourne Airport isn't super massive, and if I know Mia, she'll put us right in the center," Tom added.

Shara finished pulling her harness on and walked over to a locked case. Keying in a code, the case opened, revealing several pistol-sized tranquilizer guns. Chris still didn't know a whole lot about the history of firearms, but he had trained with tranquilizer guns for a few days at camp, and knew that these were heavily modified from their original rifle designs. The tranq pistols suffered a few drawbacks with their concealable size, not the least of which was a shorter effective range, and just like their rifle counterparts, a lack of a magazine. Darts would be reloaded one at a time.

As Shara handed him a gun and a packet of darts, Chris frowned and looked at Tom. "Where exactly are we going to portal in that won't draw attention?"

Tom hesitated, and then glanced at Babbar before he accepted a tranq gun from Shara. "It's a risk either way, but I think our best chance will be on the roof of the parking lot across from the terminal. Someone might see us, especially..." He glanced at his wristwatch. "Shit, it's gonna be busy. It's 5 PM in Melbourne."

Chris blinked, and checked his wristwatch. It was 1 AM Denver time. That was a hell of a time difference. He loaded a dart into the chamber of the gun, and then secured it in his holster, having to adjust a few more straps to make it fit right, while he pocketed the dart pack. It would be awkward, trying to get off more than one shot, but that's what his powers were for.

"Well, there's nothin' for it," Tom spoke at the end of a long sigh. "We're just gonna have to give it a go and hope we don't make a blue."

Make a blue, Chris thought. *Make a mistake. That's what Alycia told me once.*

When everyone else had a tranq gun and packet of darts, Shara closed the case and opened another, pulling out one of the enchanted Glock 9mm pistols and shoving it into her harness holster, while grabbing two spare magazines to place in magazine holsters under her other arm.

Emmi had accepted a second tranq gun and packet for Alycia, and once everyone found a BDU jacket that fit from the lockers, they all

175

headed out. The Sentinel tower was eerie at night, with most of the lights shut off. It reminded Chris of the night Nabu had attacked it.

They stopped by the kitchen on their way past so that Babbar could retrieve a sleepy Nina, who chortled grumpily until Babbar extracted one of his antique copper coins from a pouch he apparently always kept on him. That got her excited, and she nipped up at his hand.

"Ah, ah, not yet!" Babbar replied. He patted his right shoulder, and by pumping her leathery wings once, Nina zoomed up onto it and sat perched like a pirate's bird, eyeing her treasure greedily.

The troupe passed through ops after that, saying their goodbyes to Marisol. Once they hit the mantrap doors, Tom pulled out his phone and brought up a map app, centering in on Melbourne, Australia.

Alycia was waiting for them in the lobby, wearing gloves and holding two more pairs. "Here," she smiled, handing a pair each to Chris and Emmi. "They're both enchanted to create shields on command. To activate them, you..." She paused, and frowned at Emmi. "Have you ever watched any Spider-man movies?"

Emmi blinked. "What? Uh, yeah, Chris made me watch the Andrew Garfield ones once."

"Ah," Alycia frowned. "Um, do you know what Spider-man does to activate his web shooters?"

"Oh," Chris nodded, images from the Toby Maguire films passing through his head, especially in the first movie when he first learns how to magically shoot webs from his arms, rather than inventing web shooters like he was supposed to. Chris held out his right hand, wrist-up, and drew in his middle and ring finger while leaving his pinky, index finger, and thumb sticking out, and pressed those middle fingers into his palm. "That action?"

"Yup," Alycia beamed. "I knew you'd know it."

Emmi frowned, and emulated the action. "Nerds. Like that?"

"Exactly. Wearing the gloves, if you press in the center like that, it should activate and deactivate the shields. I've tested it myself, but maybe you two should as well."

Chris nodded and carefully pulled the fingerless gloves on, black like his BDU jacket. There was a Norse rune embroidered in gold thread into the palms of each glove, and he examined them. They were identical on each glove, but he didn't recognize what it was exactly, just that it was the most complex rune design he had seen yet, with multiple 'spokes' extending from the center like a wheel.

Backing away from the others, he did the 'Spider-man thing' and felt a pulse of magic press against his insides, just as a blue-white shield appeared in front of him.

"Nice!" he exclaimed.

Emmi tried as well, and grinned wildly upon having both arms covered in shields.

Chris turned his off, and then tried activating it by clenching his hand into a full fist, but nothing happened. Somehow, Alycia had managed to make it so that the shield only activated with the proper hand action.

"These are freaking awesome," he said, eliciting a bright smile from Alycia. "How strong are they?"

"Well, um…I don't know, actually," Alycia replied. "I guess this could be their first field test, though." She shrugged at everyone else and added, "I'm sorry, I didn't have time to make any more for anyone else."

"It's okay," Shara smiled, and then tapped her nose. "They'll come in very handy." Chris grinned sardonically at her.

Clasping a hand on Alycia's shoulder, Tom added, "Well done, Aly. Proper good job."

She smiled sheepishly, and even in the relatively dim light of the two always-on lights left in the lobby, he could see her cheeks flush.

"Right," Tom turned back to his phone, and then showed it to Babbar. "That mark there is where the parking lot is. Can Nina put us on the roof?"

Nina and Babbar squinted at the phone, a rather comical image, all things considered. Then Babbar looked at Nina and asked, "What do you think?" She twisted her head ninety degrees to the side and chirped. "That's my girl," Babbar grinned, and then nodded at Tom. "We can do it."

"Alright," Tom looked into the eyes of everyone present, but then he hesitated. "This is asking a lot, I know. It would be easier to ignore Mia, it would be easier not to go to them. But…"

Something swelled in Chris's heart, and without really knowing why he did it, he clasped a hand on Tom's shoulder, stopping him mid-sentence. "After what you all did to help me? And Emmi's family? It's our turn to help you."

Emmi stepped up next to Chris and smiled at Tom. "He's right.

We'll make this right."

Tom looked at them, and then at Alycia and Shara. "Thank you." Drawing in a deep breath, he looked down at Nina and Babbar, and motioned to everyone. "Gather 'round." Once Babbar was surrounded, he said, "Take us in, Babbar."

Without another word, Babbar flipped the copper coin up, allowing Nina to expertly snatch it out of the air. A burst of red light engulfed Chris's vision, just as an intense pressure pushed against his soul. White noise engulfed his senses after that, while a strong copper smell assaulted his nose and the tip of his tongue. Something tugged on his stomach, like a car jolting to a stop.

And then he was wet. Rain drenched down upon them when they appeared on the top level of a multi-tiered parking garage, just as a giant airliner roared overhead. They were smack in the middle of the lot, and a car slammed on the brakes, skidding to a stop mere inches from where Alycia stood.

"Oye, watch it!" a voice roared out.

Welcome to Australia, Chris, he grinned.

CHAPTER 23

The startled driver blew his horn a couple more times, apparently unaware that the crowd in front of him hadn't been there seconds ago. At first Chris thought the tiny dragon on Babbar's shoulder would have stopped him short, but as they shuffled out of the way and the driver pulled up next to them, he smirked at the Sentinels and commented, "Oz Con was last month," before he rolled up his window and screeched down the exit ramp.

Chris blinked in confusion, wondering if the driver had been angry or bemused, and then he blinked again to keep rain from getting in his eyes. The downpour was frigid-cold, as he'd expect for winter, but at least there wasn't snow. Shivering and wrapping his arms around his torso, he looked about and spotted a few more people in the parking lot, but they didn't bother to pay attention to the mysterious newcomers.

"Charming," Chris remarked above the rain. "I thought this was supposed to be a friendly country."

"His accent wasn't Aussie," Alycia defended. "Must not be a local."

Ignoring their banter, Tom asked Babbar, "Can she go invisible in this rain?"

Babbar didn't even have to ask, Nina simply chirped, and then disappeared. There was a strange optical illusion in her place, like looking through crystal-clear glass that bent the light ever so slightly, or like an improved Predator cloaking device, but for the most part, she was impossible to see.

"Alright, follow me," Tom waved them towards a pedestrian

stairwell near the northwest. At least, Chris guessed it was the northwest, it was difficult to tell where the sun was through the overcast. They were already soaked to the bones, but as they splashed through the parking lot, Chris drew in a deep breath and, for a moment anyway, he relaxed into the smell of fresh rain. The downpour must have only just started, and that smell of new rain on dry ground always smelled wonderful to him.

When they reached the entrance into the top floor landing, the troupe squeezed past a couple walking out and shook the rain off. The inside boasted broad windows that showed the busy arrival and departure streets below, and their boots squeaked noisily on the tiled floor, their hurried footsteps resoundingly loud in the confined corridor.

They found the stairs down to the next floor and passed through a set of aluminum and glass doors into an enclosed pedestrian bridge that passed over the road and into the terminal. Chris stopped short for a second and blinked at a sign, and then looked ahead at where the bridge connected with the airport-proper.

"Come on," Alycia tugged on his arm urgently. "What's wrong?"

Falling back into step, he said, "Nothing, it's just that…the sign back there said this leads to the first floor of the airport, but that's clearly the second floor."

"That's more of an American thing," Emmi pointed out. "What we think of as the 'first floor' is considered the ground floor in a lot of other countries, and the 'first floor' is considered the first floor above the ground floor."

That sounded more than a little weird to Chris, but he shrugged it off and trusted Emmi. She had travelled internationally with her family multiple times, while Chris hadn't ever left the United States until this year, and both times he had done so illegally.

He almost came to a stop mid-stride again. "Shit, we don't have passports."

One pedestrian blinked in surprise at him, but the others in Chris's party kept rushing along. "Move it, Tatsu!" Tom barked.

Chris really hoped they wouldn't be detained by local PD, or they might be in bigger trouble than anyone thought. Particularly Shara, who was a literal alien.

The sound of rain pelting the aluminum roof of the bridge let up just as they reached the airport, and then they passed through glass and aluminum doors into the airport-proper. There were physical and electronic signs everywhere directing wayward visitors, including signs to go to the 'ground floor' for arrivals and baggage services. Directly ahead of them was one of many check-in counters.

Tom's eyes surveyed the bustling, busy early evening crowd, his near-six-feet giving him a height advantage over most visitors. Chris mentally readied himself, and gently touched his golden core, prepared to summon magic at a moment's notice. He glanced at his new gloves as well, and smiled at Alycia, but her eyes were darting from face to face in the crowd.

From Babbar's shoulder, Nina chirped and chortled, and Babbar nodded. "You said it, Nina. Just too many people. I think I'll find a quiet corner…"

Tom stopped him with a quick, halting hand. "No. We stick together, and you need to have a coin ready. The moment we have Mia and Eric, we all gather and you get us back to the tower."

Babbar opened his mouth to argue, but the urgent and intense look upon Tom's face made him clamp it shut, and he nodded. "Alright." He dug out another coin, and Chris suppressed a snicker when Babbar's shoulder shifted and he protested against Nina's sudden interest. "Hey, hey, no, *nooooo*, you need to wait. And stay invisible!"

"Keep your eyes open for anyone who looks suspicious," Tom added. An impatient traveler shoved past Chris, and he realized they were blocking the bridge exit. "Let's go."

Cautiously, the group ventured further into the airport's international departure area. It was an open design, with support pillars interspersed but otherwise very few walls, and mostly either half-height cubicle-type walls or lots and lots of glass partitions. Shops of various types lined the edge like a mall, many bearing names he didn't recognize, and some strikingly familiar. The smell of fresh coffee wafted over to him, and he instantly craved some. Following his nose, he saw a place called 'Hudson's Coffee,' and he wished dearly that they could stop for some. Near it was another kiosk for a place called 'Sushi Sushi.' Beyond and behind them against the wall was a more familiar sign, a McDonald's, and he blinked in surprise.

At only five foot eight, Chris found that looking through the crowd was difficult for him on a good day. Faces, clothes, everything flashed by in a jumble, and he did his best to watch for a familiar face. He knew to expect Mia, and her features were burned into his memory from that first fateful night in the Centennial Airport hangar. He had no idea what Eric looked like, since Alycia had never shown Chris pictures of her brother.

Tom had said to watch out for anyone suspicious, but in the international terminal of the airport, that was like asking someone to watch out for a cosplayer at a comic convention. Everyone looked so different and had such different cultural customs that he couldn't begin to figure out what was normal and what wasn't. He felt an adrenaline surge when he saw one man in particular using a cellphone camera, pointing it apparently straight at Chris. But after taking a picture, the man turned it towards another area and took another picture. Just a tourist.

They came across some interesting, brightly-colored murals in the floor, but most of the visitors ignored the artwork and stomped over them, rushing to whatever destination awaited them. The Sentinels turned right at the murals and started walking past zig-zagging lines of passengers waiting to check their luggage.

That was the key, he suddenly realized. Granted not everyone here would be travelers, some maybe came to see other travelers off, but anyone without luggage might be worth a second look. Of course, as soon as he thought of that, everywhere he looked, there were countless people sans luggage, so that was a bust. Either that or they were hopelessly surrounded and outnumbered.

The moment he thought of that, he felt a creeping sense of fear, and his arm hairs stood up on end.

This was a trap. It had to be.

And they had walked right into it.

Tom came to such an abrupt stop in the exact middle of the terminal that the others almost plowed into him. Looking ahead, Chris saw her then. Standing a dozen feet in front of a luggage store stood their target, the woman who had evaded the Sentinels for ten weeks.

"Mia," Tom whispered. His voice was no doubt lost in the hustle of the crowds, but Mia Evans Taylor must have seen him speak, as a broad smile crept across her face.

Standing next to her was a man closing in on his thirties, with long sandy-blonde hair and blazing blue eyes, just like his father. He wore a white hoodie underneath a tan parka and donned faded blue-jeans.

Mia looked much the same as Chris remembered - tall and somewhat slender, despite the well-defined muscles he knew she had. She wore a white t-shirt under a black faux-leather jacket, and likewise wore blue jean pants, along with rugged leather boots.

Eric saw Tom then, his eyes flashing with anger, and then he turned his scowl upon Alycia. He started towards the group, but Mia raised her arm to block him. "Not yet," he thought he heard her say through the crowd.

Tom's fingers curled into fists, and he very slowly, very cautiously approached, with Alycia at his side. Shara glanced at Chris, Emmi and Babbar, and said quietly, "Spread out."

Chris and Emmi walked to the right of Tom and Alycia, while Shara and Babbar spread out to the left. Mia saw them, her eyes very deliberately tracking Chris's movement in particular. Behind her sly smile, he saw something he recognized from when he had last looked in a mirror – rage. She hated Chris, with such passion that he was afraid his presence was going to make matters worse, not better.

"Here I thought you'd come alone," she called out. A couple that was just about to walk between the two groups suddenly stopped, glanced back and forth, and then went around behind Mia and Eric. "But I suppose bravery hasn't been your thing for a long time."

"Hello, Mia," Tom said, his voice even.

"Hello, *darling*," she replied, her smirk growing. Mia looked at Alycia, and for a split second, the smirk faltered. "Alycia…"

"How long have you known?" Eric interjected, his voice much louder than everyone else's. Similar to his father's, there was a deep quality to it that helped it carry over the white noise of the crowd. His Australian accent was a lot thicker than Tom or Alycia's, but that wasn't a surprise since the latter two had spent years living in the United States.

"Eric," Tom centered his eyes upon his son. "It isn't what you think."

"How LONG?!"

Tom's jaw clenched. Alycia answered for him, "Just over two months."

That apparently wasn't the answer Eric expected. Like his father, his hands had been clenched into fists, but they relaxed after Alycia spoke. He appeared to fumble with his thoughts, but finally he asked, "You couldn't have called me to tell me? Texted me? Email or even bloody post a letter?!'"

"I didn't want to tell you until we got her back," Tom replied.

With an incredulous look, he motioned at Mia. "She's right here. Got her back from where? She said you tried to kill her!"

Chris felt his eyes widen at that. No one had tried to kill Mia in Babylon. When the Dragonstone blew apart in a surge of magic, she had slammed into the wall and slumped down. That was the last Chris had seen of her.

"That's a lie," Tom defended. "I tried to save her from Nabu."

Nabu, Chris thought with a start. His eyes darted around the terminal, searching for bright red hair and trying to *feel* the overwhelming presence of the demigod. Surely Nabu would be here, too, wouldn't she? But other than a carrot-topped man rushing through the terminal, he didn't see a hint of red hair nearby. He did, however, notice a ring of people dressed similarly to Mia closing in around them, men and women who no longer tried to hide their intent looks upon Chris and his companions.

"And that was another lie," Eric flung his arms out in frustration. "You told me a man named Nabu killed her, but she says Nabu saved her!"

The surrounding goons weren't visibly armed, but then again, they might not need weapons. He tensed, and reached out a hand to lightly brush Emmi's. She looked, and followed Chris's sight to one guy in particular, a bulky-looking man with cropped hair and deep, black eyes. He grinned at them, and stopped about twenty feet out, with his companions to his left and right likewise doing so. They effectively created a screen that the airport patrons weren't willing to penetrate.

Chris's eyes darted left, past Tom and Alycia, but Shara had seen their enemies approaching from her side as well.

They were surrounded.

"Nabu tricked you," Tom said to Mia. "And continues to do so."

Mia's composure faltered for a second, and her eyes darted down at the ground. She rubbed her right hand with her left in a worrisome manner. "He never tricked me," she defended.

"He isn't even a he anymore," Tom pointed out. "Did you have something to do with that? Did you arrange for that girl to sacrifice her life for Nabu?"

Eric's face turned into a bewildered frown, while Mia averted her gaze again. When Eric searched her for a response and she didn't give one, he shook his head. "What girl?"

"Even before the Barrier fell," Tom pressed on Mia, ignoring Eric for the moment, "Nabu had unrivaled powers of persuasion. You're a good person, Mia. There was a time when you wouldn't hurt a fly, magical or not." Her eyes met his then, but she didn't stop nervously working her hands together. "So tell me, did you force that girl to sacrifice herself? For that matter, did you arrange for the attack in Adelaide? How many people have died by your hand since Nabu *infected* your mind?"

Movement caught Chris's attention, and he looked right to see a security guard approaching the ring of Nabu's goons. He tensed again, and worried that things were about to go south. If security involved themselves, this would turn into an all-out brawl, and there were far too many innocents in the airport.

"It...that's not the point," Mia shook her head.

"And what about us?" Alycia asked, her voice shaking. "You almost helped Nabu kill me in the hangar."

Mia tensed, and Eric gawked at Alycia. "She did *what?!*"

Nodding, Alycia continued, "And she helped Nabu hold one of my best friends hostage." Emmi looked down at the floor, her gaze growing distant.

"That's not," Mia started and stopped.

The guard approaching the group stopped a foot shy of the crop-topped goon Chris had seen earlier, his eyes growing wide when he heard the word 'hostage.' The guard reached for his baton, and said, "Ladies and gentlemen, you're impeding traffic. Kindly move out of the way, and-"

Crop-top jerked out his hand and slammed it into the guard's throat. He let out a choked cry and instantly fell to his knees, before the goon twisted and kneed the guard in the face. The hapless guard spun around and fell to the ground, blood splattering everywhere, and somewhere someone screamed.

Their peaceful, friendly chat was over.

"None of that matters," Mia snapped out of her uncertainty and suddenly grabbed Eric by the scruff of his jacket, no mean feat since she was four or five inches shorter than him. Then a gun was in her hand, though she kept it pointed at the floor instead of at her son. "Give me Imhullu."

"I can't do that, Mia," Tom shook his head, his hand slowly rising up into his jacket.

"Don't!" Mia shouted, pointing the gun at Tom. *She won't point it at her son, but she'll point it at her husband,* Chris thought. *Interesting.*

"Oye!" someone shouted from behind. Chris craned his neck around and saw two more airport security guards rushing towards the encircled group, batons already in-hand.

One of Nabu's cultists, a woman with long black hair and dark eyes, turned and lifted her hands. Then, utter horror filled Chris when the felt the familiar press of magic against his soul. A second later, a golden plasma ball shot out from the cultist's hands and slammed into one of the guard's chest. He was taken completely by surprise, and as he flew backwards, one of his flailing arms smacked his partner in the face with the baton.

Without thinking about it, Chris shouted, "Shields!" and turned on both of his gloves. Blue-white quarter-spheres appeared against both hands, and he raised them just as the arcane-wielding goon turned back on them.

Chaos erupted in the airport. More travelers screamed or yelled, more guards came running, and the goons all turned around to face the outside distractions. That thankfully included the one Chris was prepared to fight, and left them all with just Mia holding Eric hostage.

Emmi had turned her shields on as well, and darted left to help cover Shara and Babbar. But to everyone's surprise, Babbar had drawn his dart gun and fired it at Mia as quick as lightning. The dart struck her mid-stomach, and she lurched forward in surprise, eyes opening wide.

The tranquilizer solution was fast-acting, and she wavered in her stance, her grip on Eric loosening enough that he extracted himself, horror-stricken. "Mum? Mum!"

"Go, now!" Tom shouted.

But as all of the other Sentinels rushed towards Mia and Eric, Chris felt multiple pressure points against his soul. Two of Nabu's cultists shapeshifted, one into a large wolf-like animal, the other into a silver-backed ape. The arcane-wielding cultist launched two more spheres of energy into the panicked throng of people. The large, muscle-bound one Chris had noticed earlier lifted his hands and thrust them out at a crowd, and before Chris's eyes, two people turned into solid ice and fell over, shattering into a thousand chunks of frozen flesh.

None of the goons paid the Sentinels any attention. They focused on the crowds. As if that had been their real mission from the start.

This wasn't about the dagger, he thought.

"Tatsu, get over here!" Tom roared.

Chris looked back and saw that everyone had gathered around Mia and Babbar in front of the luggage shop. They were ready to leave. But if they left now, what would happen to the innocent civilians? Nabu's goons were here to hurt others, not the Sentinels.

It was another setup, a part of Nabu's larger game. Chris was sure of that.

Their original mission in the airport was accomplished, so Chris shouted back, "Go!"

"What?!" Alycia screeched.

"I've got to stop these people, but you need to get Mia and Eric out of here!"

"What the bloody hell do you mean?" Tom gaped. "They're not our concern!"

A man screaming in agony before he fell silent turned Chris's stomach, and he looked back at the arcane-wielding woman. She must have heard Chris, because while all of the others ravaged the crowd, she looked right at him, and unleashed another plasma ball. Chris threw his arm out instinctively, and Alycia's enchanted shield gloves saved him from the brunt of it, though it still nearly shoved him off balance.

Clicking his left glove off, Chris drew upon his ample source of magic and focused it into a retaliatory strike, unleashing a controlled beam of golden energy right into the woman's stomach. With a loud "Wuff!" she flew back and slammed into one of the automated check-in kiosks, sending it crashing onto its side and her tumbling, hopefully unconscious, out of the fight.

"God dammit, Tatsu, get your ass over here!" Tom ordered.

"I'm not leaving innocent people to die!" Chris shouted back. "This is what I signed up for, to save people from Nabu! Get your asses back to Denver, I'll handle these goons!"

But he was outnumbered, and his attack upon the arcane woman caught someone else's attention. The giant wolf glowered at him, strange green eyes flashing with feral rage. A roar to his left drew his eyes away from the wolf long enough to see the mammoth-sized silver-backed ape charging at him. The wolf barked menacingly and rushed him at the same time.

CHAPTER 24

Chris thrust his arm up, shield held high, but he knew that it would do little to dissuade two monstrous shapeshifters barreling down upon him.

A giant body smashed into the ape, sending it careening into the wolf so that they both slid across the polished airport floor. A giant bear roared and placed itself between Chris and the attackers.

The thump of compressed air rang through the airport, and Chris gaped as Alycia and Tom, dart guns drawn, rushed to reload. Two of Nabu's cultists, who had just turned their attention to the deafening spectacle surrounding Chris, fell onto their sides, unconscious. Chris couldn't find Shara, but he guessed that she had shapeshifted into something smaller than her Clydesdale-sized gryphon and was terrorizing cultists elsewhere.

The silver-backed gorilla recovered quickly, scrambling to all four limbs and roaring a challenge at bear-Emmi. She roared back, but Chris, inspired by his companions, drew his dart gun from inside his jacket and fired a dart at the ape. His aim was near-perfect, and it embedded itself into the ape's neck. It roared a challenge at Chris and rushed him, but Emmi swiped a massive paw against its face and sent it spinning across the slick floor. It tried to stand again, but the dart's affect became apparent, and its movements grew slow and uncertain.

The wolf, on the other hand, took advantage of their distraction and leapt up onto Emmi's back, where it tried to sink its teeth into her hide. Using her bulk and weight to her advantage, instead of trying to throw it off, Emmi merely rolled over the wolf. A hapless yelp escaped, and when she finished her roll and was up on her paws again, the wolf lay momentarily stunned upon the floor, with one leg bent at an unnatural angle.

Chris fumbled to pull out another dart and reload his weapon, but the blue-white shield still active from his glove blocked him. He thought about deactivating it, but a blast of magic from the arcane wielder slammed into it, and this time he lost his balance and careened onto his side. His right glove grew super-heated, setting his hand burning while the shield sputtered and died.

Cursing, Chris dropped the tranq gun and peeled the polyester and cotton glove off seconds before it burst into flames, leaving his hand raw and red.

The arcane wielder smirked at him and prepared to unleash another strike at him, but months of training and cultivated instinct allowed him to instantly unleash another golden beam of energy upon her, sending her sprawling.

That answered the question of how much punishment the gloves could take. A strong enough plasma ball would destroy them, and possibly burn the wearer in the process.

Yelling in rage, the woman tried to scramble to her feet again, but a blur of movement and a sudden impact on her neck surprised her, and a second later, she slumped back down onto the ground.

Looking back at his friends, Chris saw Alycia's tranq gun pointed at the woman, and she smiled and winked at Chris, before pulling another dart out to reload. Tom had fired his tranq gun at another one of Nabu's goons, but the attack was moving further into the airport. At least until a great, beautiful gryphon suddenly grew into existence halfway towards terminal one and interjected itself between a fleeing traveler and a pursuing cultist.

Bear-Emmi roared, drawing Chris's attention back to that battle just in time to see her standing at her full height just so she could use her powerful front paws to throw the wolf against a glass partition, which shattered upon impact. The wolf spun and flailed across the floor and came to a stop a good fifty feet away. This time it didn't move again.

There were four or five cultists left, so Chris picked up his gun, finished fumbling a dart into the chamber, and readied his weapon.

Another thunk of compressed air, and Chris gaped as Babbar fired another tranq round at one of the goons. His aim was dead-on, and the gnome's target fell unconscious.

Leaving just four of them left, and as the cultists surveyed their numerous fallen companions, they must have realized they were outclassed and now outnumbered. It helped when gryphon-Shara swiped at one and bear-Emmi roared a challenge. Glancing at one another, the cultists stopped using whatever magic they had and simply ran for the exit.

Not content to simply let them all get away, Chris carefully aimed and fired. The dart struck true in the butt of a particularly large, muscle-bound minion, and he yelped before stumbling and then crashing to the ground, sliding unceremoniously into a support pillar.

Allowing himself a satisfied grin, Chris pushed up onto his feet, and looked at Emmi. The rage in her unnaturally blue eyes died and she looked at him, and the strangest, disjointed grunting noise escaped her. It took him moments to realize she was laughing, and in any other circumstance, he might have laughed right back.

But Tom wasn't interested. "Satisfied, Tatsu? Get your asses over here so we can go!"

Stowing his tranq gun back in its holster, Chris rushed towards the group, bear-Emmi right beside him, while Shara shapeshifted back to herself and darted across the airport to join them. Eric, who was worrying over his mother's unconscious form, looked horrified at the giant, furry bear barreling down on them, but a familiar pressure pushed up against Chris as Emmi shapeshifted back to her human form.

Not once had she lost control.

A shimmering image appeared on Babbar's shoulder as he produced his copper coin again, but then the gnome's eyes grew wide. "Look out!"

Chris turned back just in time to see a pair of local police, who probably had no idea who the good guys were, taking aim with pistols and shouting, "Stop!"

But a second later, a shimmering blue-white shield stood between the group and the cops, and no doubt on instinct, the cops fired. Their rounds slammed helplessly against Alycia's summoned half-sphere shield.

Chris lost his balance when he tripped over something, and he crashed to the ground, sliding to a stop inches away from Babbar's feet, while Emmi came to a stop next to him. Babbar grinned down at Chris, and then looked at Nina, who had fully reappeared on his shoulder.

"Take us back, Nina," he requested, just as he flipped the coin into the air. She snatched it in her mouth easily, and quickly munched down on it.

Blinding red light. White noise. Pressure and the peculiar taste of copper on the tongue.

In an instant, they were back in the darkened lobby of the Sentinel tower, the chaos of the airport gone.

They were home. They were safe.

Eric dry-heaved, falling forward onto his hands and trying desperately not to retch all over his mother. Chris was already accustomed to the rigors of portal travel, but he sympathized with the older man, recalling his own first experience through one of Nina's portals.

It was over. Not only had they rescued Eric from the clutches of Nabu's trusted lieutenant, they had said-lieutenant in their hands now, and they had stopped a massacre at the airport. A sense of pride he never recalled feeling before filled him with joy, and despite lying face-first on the ground, he smiled.

Emmi's face still held a bemused grin, and she offered him a hand. He gladly accepted it, and she heaved him back up onto his feet. When she chuckled, he asked, "What?"

"Did you really have to shoot him in the ass?"

He wanted to roll his eyes, but instead he burst into laughter along with her. "Well, ya know, it was kind of a big-*ass* target."

"Oh God," she playfully shoved him. "That was terrible!"

Suddenly another hand cinched down on his shoulder and spun him around. He faced Tom, who glowered at him. "What the hell did I tell you about following orders, Tatsu?"

Something snapped in him, he wasn't sure what, but before he knew what he was doing, he shoved Tom's hand away and backed up. "Get off me!"

"You endangered the mission and all of us!" Tom yelled, a vein in his forehead bulging prominently. "You're bloody lucky none of us got hurt!"

"And I'm glad none of us did," he replied. Then he jabbed a finger into the larger man's chest, "But a lot of innocent people can't say the same, can they? I saw at least two people killed, and I know I heard more than that die!"

Tom opened his mouth to retort, but stopped short. What was he going to say? Was he going to say that wasn't any of their business? Was he going to say they had larger fish to fry, or some other excuse to let a massacre happen?

When the commander didn't say anything, Chris scowled and turned around to face the windows. Clenching and unclenching his jaw, he looked at Tom's reflection in the window and said, "I didn't sign up to watch others die for our actions. I didn't sign up to let Nabu have her way with the world." Turning back to Tom, he continued hotly, "I signed up to stop Nabu, to *save* people! Isn't that what the Sentinels are about? Or are we still about 'secrecy at all costs?' For Christ's sake, the secret is *out*," he flailed his arms around. "People know about magic, and now they know about *us*, thanks to our news debut yesterday! So I made a choice." He looked at the others, at Alycia kneeling next to Eric and their mother, at Shara who had the slightest grin on her face as she watched Chris, and at Emmi, who stood shyly behind Tom, one hand reaching across her torso to grasp at her other arm.

Looking again at Tom, Chris continued, "I chose to save who I could. I chose the lives of others over my own. I didn't ask you to stay and help. Though," he looked again at the others, particularly Emmi, "I'm grateful you did or I'd probably be dead right now. Thanks."

Emmi smiled. "What are friends for?"

Tom started to talk, but Chris interrupted, "But I have a purpose now, and a power. A power that can be used to help others. What is the *point* of it all if I don't actually *use* it to that effect?"

His piece said, he folded his arms and waited for Tom to reply. Chris searched the commander's face, looking for some hint of what Tom was thinking. In a way, Chris knew he wasn't entirely in the right. He had signed up with the Sentinels knowing that he would have to follow orders, and less than twenty-four hours in, he had disobeyed them.

But seeing all of those people, especially after seeing that couple shatter into a thousand pieces... The sight itself and the memory turned his stomach, but the idea of letting such an affront go unanswered sickened him even more.

No, he had done the right thing, consequences be damned.

After a moment of mulling it over, Tom nodded. "You're right."

Shocked, Chris took a step back and felt his eyes open wide. A triumphant sensation buzzed through him. "I am?"

"Yeah," Tom nodded, though he wasn't looking Chris in the eyes. "You have a power. And you have a purpose." Finally, he looked into Chris's eyes, determination and certainty in them. "Your purpose is to save the world from Nabu and Marduk. You can't bloody well do that if you're dead, can you?"

Chris's cheeks burned, and he gulped. So Tom *wasn't* actually agreeing with him.

"What would we have done if you'd been killed, eh?" Tom shook his head. "You've said it yourself, the power you possess is all that can stand against them. So I'm only going to say this once – don't *ever* risk yourself like that again. If we are to win in the long run, you are our *only* hope."

The commander turned away from Chris and walked back towards Mia. He bent down and almost effortlessly picked up her unconscious form.

Staring the whole time, Chris felt an emptiness open up inside of him. A part of him wanted to deny Tom's logic, the part of him that was proud of his actions. But was Tom right? Was he foolish and selfish for putting himself in danger like that?

No, he thought, shaking his head. "You're wrong."

Eric and Alycia stood up, and they along with Tom gaped at Chris. "Excuse me?" the commander asked, a warning tone in his voice. Tom might not have magic, but the way the room suddenly chilled had him wondering about that.

"I said you're wrong," Chris stated resolutely. He unfolded his arms and planted his hands on his hips. "If I start to think like that, if *we* start to think like that, we've already lost."

Through narrowed eyes, Tom stared icicles at him. "And how do you figure that?"

"If I start to think only about myself, about my survival, about my *mission,* and nothing else," he shook his head, "then Nabu has already won." He looked specifically at Emmi, allowing his gaze to linger upon her. "I can't just think about myself, about preserving myself. If I just duck my head in like a damned turtle, or bury it in the ground, the world is still going to burn around me."

He drew in a deep breath and continued on, eyes boring into

Tom's. "I don't know how to destroy Nabu. I don't know how to destroy Marduk. But I *do* know that Nabu has a plan, and that airport massacre was part of it. If we just let her get away with everything she wants to do, then it won't matter if I'm alive, she'll have won anyway. The only chance *any* of us have is to fight Nabu every single God damned step of the way."

The adrenaline from the fight had worn off, but now a fresh surge coursed through him as he thought of the final words to say on the matter. Screwing up his courage, he lifted his chin and said, "If that's not your goal, if you don't want me out there fighting her and her cultists, then I made a mistake and I don't belong here." His voice shook when he spoke those last words, but he held his chin high and prepared for the consequences.

Someone drew in a sharp, surprised breath, but his eyes were fixed on Tom, who stared back at him with a stone-faced expression. Chris waited impatiently for Tom to say something, to tell him to leave or to say that no, Chris was right to fight. Those were the only answers, weren't they? The only ones Chris would accept, at any rate.

To his surprise, it was Shara who interjected. "He's right."

Surprise crossed the commander's face. "Not you too, Shara."

Planting her fists on her hips, she eyed him intently. "You once said that the purpose of the Sentinels was to protect the Barrier, but that's gone now. So what do we have left?" She pushed on, not letting him reply, "We have the *spirit* of that mandate, that's what. We were meant to protect the Barrier to protect *humanity*, and all of the Earth. To save people. Shutting ourselves into a vault to hide won't save people. It won't help anyone, and it'll let Nabu and Marduk move unhindered. We have to stand against them."

Something caught her attention, her expression turning to a frown when her eyes darted to the windows. Chris glanced behind him, but it was still dark outside, and all he could see were the city lights below.

Tom let out an exasperated sigh. "Dammit, Shara, why do you always take their side?"

Her frown deepened and she looked back at him. "I thought we were all on the same side?"

Now Chris heard something from outside, which considering the triple-paned windows, was a feat in itself. It was a reverberating sound that he couldn't place at first, but after a few seconds, he realized it was a helicopter. It might have been strange to hear a helicopter flying around at this hour, near two in the morning, but then he remembered that there was a hospital nearby with a roof-top helipad, and he figured that it was their chopper either bringing in a patient or going out to an emergency.

"We are," Tom tepidly agreed. "But we're up against a god, for Christ's sake." Somehow Chris managed to stop himself from grinning at Tom's choice of words. "We need to be cautious."

The helicopter grew closer, but Chris ignored it. "I'm not saying I'm going to go head-first into a battle against Nabu," he said, "not until I know for sure I can beat her. I'm just saying-"

Nina suddenly chirruped and shifted uneasily on Babbar's shoulder, her eyes fixed on the windows. Something spooked her, and she apparently dug centimeter-thick claws into the gnome's shoulder. "Ouch, Nina!"

The helicopter was close enough that Chris could almost feel it. He, along with everyone else, looked outside at the same time, but if the helicopter was nearby, they either couldn't see it, or…

Or it's running without its navigation lights.

There was a flash of bright light from a spotlight outside, blinding them all. Nina roared and leapt from Babbar's shoulder, but at that exact instant, there was a pop of breaking glass, and a bullet tore through Nina's hind-section, sending her tumbling onto the tiled floor.

"NINA!" Babbar yelled.

"Aly, shields!" Tom yelled.

And a hailstorm of rapid gunfire filled the lobby.

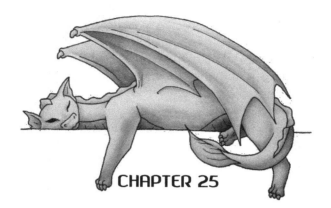

CHAPTER 25

Chris dove for the floor just as a shimmering blue-white half-sphere placed itself between the group and the windows. Glass shattered, and chunks of marble or granite spattered harmlessly against the shield. The roar of the weapon firing upon them was constant, and he instantly pictured the mini-gun from Terminator 2 in his head.

Pushing through terrorizing fear, he looked up and saw Alycia standing over everyone else, her hands outstretched and a glowing bright blue light surrounded her. Unlike him, unlike *everyone* else, she stood fearless against the onslaught.

Except the gun fire never once touched her shield. The only impacts came from glass and stone and marble.

They aren't aiming for us, he realized. With his fear abating, replaced by another fresh surge of adrenaline, Chris sat up and turned. Outside, he saw blazing flame spitting from a revolving barrel, which at that instant ceased fire. The spotlight died, and the glowing tips of six barrels became the only outward illumination, barely visible thanks to the afterimage of the spotlight burned into Chris's vision.

The entire outside face of the lobby was shattered and open to the whipping wind coming in from forty six floors up, and from the surprisingly soft thumping of helicopter blades. Whatever was out there, it was quieter than any helicopter he'd ever seen or heard, which was how they hadn't even noticed it until it was right next to them.

Pushing himself back onto his feet, Chris touched his core of magic and readied his powers to defend, but somehow, he knew that wouldn't be necessary. Not yet, anyway.

Whomever they were, and he had a good idea of who was out there, they wanted the Sentinels alive. Especially Tom.

Behind him, the others stood back up, although Tom left Mia's unconscious form lying on the floor, with Eric cowering next to her. Shara drew her pistol, while Emmi stepped up beside Alycia. Babbar knelt next to Nina's unmoving form, and Chris felt a surge of rage and fear intermixing to produce a strong desire to hurt whomever had shot the beloved dragon.

A bright white light flashed into existence, but through Alycia's shield, he couldn't feel the press of magic from it. Someone within the fuselage had just made their presence known.

Nabu.

Her wild red hair billowed out around her against the wind, and she stepped out of the helicopter, her entire body aglow. She hovered inches from the chopper now, illuminating it and revealing that it was a black-skinned Black Hawk helicopter, somehow modified to run a lot quieter than standard Black Hawks.

As easily as walking, and heedless of the whirling blades of death overhead, Nabu floated gently across the forty- or fifty-foot gap, and landed a few inches inside of the broken windowpanes. If he hadn't known just how evil Nabu was, he would have thought the imagery angelic.

Instead, his fury grew ever-stronger, and he stepped up to the edge of the shimmering force field, his fists clenched tight enough that fingernails dug into skin on his ungloved hand, inducing stabbing pain on the burns. Nabu stepped closer, leaving only a few inches between them.

"You," Chris glowered.

Nabu's glow dimmed somewhat, but she didn't let it die completely. Quirking an eyebrow at him, she asked, "Is that really the best you can do?"

His mother's broken body flashed through his memory. Emmi's tears at the camp. Alycia's mother. Chris's entire body shook, and he wanted to wipe the smug smirk off of Nabu's face in the bloodiest way.

"I told you," she growled, and then turned her attention to the rest of the Sentinels. "I told you, Taylor," she shouted at Tom. "Hand over Imhullu or watch your world *burn!*" Stepping aside so that Chris no longer stood between her and the others, she waved

CHRONICLES OF THE SENTINELS - RETRIBUTION

casually at him, "And now you see I am as good as my word. His family. Your family. Next will be Emmi's family."

"I'll kill you before I let you touch them," Emmi surged forward, but Shara held her back with a restraining hand. "Don't you go near them!"

"I own them!" Nabu screeched. "I own all of you, you just don't know it yet! And now that your parents are in Sentinel custody, when I destroy them, I'll have to go through the French Sentinels as well. And that's only if you *don't give me what I want!*"

Her last words were directed at Tom, who held his tranq gun in both hands, the muzzle pointed directly at Nabu. He said nothing, and only watched as Nabu continued her tirade.

"Oh, going for the stoic, silent trope, eh Tom?" She shook her head. "It suits you, but in this case, it'll hurt you. I'm done playing games. I need that dagger *now.* So either hand it over, or I destroy everyone you ever loved right here, right now. A flick of my finger, and this entire building falls, with you all in it."

"You'll never find it then," Tom finally spoke. "Kill me, and the dagger is lost forever. No one else knows where it is."

"*Someone* does," Nabu slammed her fist against the shield. "You wouldn't have left it unattended for someone to accidentally find. And I'm sure I know who, since he hasn't shown his face in the tower in months. So where is dear Jered, eh? Where have you hidden him?"

The pieces clicked together, and it made sense. Tom had hidden the dagger using Nina's portals, that much Chris had deduced earlier, but the commander must have sent Jered along with to watch over it. That was why Jered was never around, even at night.

But how did Nabu know that?

"You've kept a close eye on us," Tom remarked.

"I *own* everything, I told you!" Nabu shook her head, and began pacing in front of the shield, back and forth past Chris, like a caged animal. "Dear Ada gave me all of the access I needed, don't you see? I'm in your system, in all of the Sentinel's systems, I know *every* move you make, where you go, when, how much it costs, how many packets of Kleenex you use! I know everything!"

"Except what you need most," Tom smirked. "Because I kept that strictly off the books."

A sudden sob escaped from Babbar, drawing everyone's attention.

The sob was a happy one, Chris realized, as Nina moved ever-so-slightly. She was alive. For now, anyway.

Chris remembered the first time Nabu assaulted the tower, how scared Nabu was when Nina appeared. That was why she shot Nina, to neutralize whatever threat the little dragon posed.

"You're gonna pay for that," Chris growled just as Nabu passed him by.

She stopped short and looked at him in a bemused fashion.

"And you," she narrowed her eyes at him. "You were immune to my powers back in the mountains. You are something special."

Shrugging casually, Chris said, "If you truly have access to the system, then you've read my report."

"Indeed," she nodded solemnly. "Which is why I need you out of the picture, too."

Suddenly she struck the shield with both of her hands, a bright white glow intersecting with the shimmering blue. Alycia cried out, and just as Chris looked back at her, she fell to her knees, her face screwed up in concentration.

So Nabu wanted a fight? Chris was more than happy to oblige.

He prepared a plasma ball between his hands, and looked into her bright green eyes, lighter than normal due to her entire body glowing white. She stared right back, and something dark and vicious grew behind her gaze. A hatred for Chris born not of personal vendetta, but of his ability to interfere, blazed within.

That was fine. His hatred towards Nabu *was* personal.

The shield fell, allowing Nabu to fall inward. He unleashed his plasma ball, but it splashed harmlessly against a white shield. Several tranq guns thumped, and Shara unleashed three rounds from her enchanted gun, but nothing penetrated Nabu's shield.

She moved fast, at least as fast as Shara when she used her special speed ability, and Nabu grasped one of Chris's outstretched hands, and then she twisted it around behind his back until they both faced the gaping windows and the helicopter. Her lips were right next to his ears when she whispered, "Goodbye, Child of Tattannu."

Pain seized through his arm as she twisted and shoved, and before he could stop her, Nabu shoved him out of the open window, the darkness below swallowing him whole.

Voices shouted his name, but they were mostly lost in the downblast from the helicopter rotors. His stomach took forever to catch up with him, but panic solidly gripped his chest.

Streetlights below grew closer and closer at dizzying speeds, and he raced for an answer. Could Alycia's shield protect him? He still had one glove on, but he knew it wouldn't do a damn thing, recalling how hard he had been jostled when magic had plowed into his other shield arm.

He couldn't fly. He couldn't shapeshift. There was only arcane powers.

Powers that he hadn't yet tamed. In the fields in the mountains, he had tried to create a shield around himself, failing miserably and exhausting himself in the process, but now his life depended upon it. It would scorch the ground, maybe even gouge into the road below, but he didn't have a choice.

Drawing as much magic as he dared from his core, he concentrated on encasing himself in a focused plasma field, surrounding his body. Somewhere above he thought he heard a bird screech, but he couldn't lose his focus, not now.

Golden energy flared to life all around him, his vision swam with it, and later he realized his eyes must have glowed with his power. It flowed out of him more rapidly than he thought possible, fueling the arcane shield with more energy at once than he thought possible.

And he slammed into the street, *hard*. His shield held just long enough to cushion his impact, gouging a half-sphere crater into the concrete, but when the shield failed, he still smashed hard onto his right side, and he heard and *felt* something break, sending fresh surges of agonizing pain into his body.

But pain was good. Pain meant he was alive. Pain meant that Nabu had failed to kill him.

It also meant she was alone with his friends forty-six stories above. He tried to push up, but fresh pain surged from his broken arm, and he involuntarily cried out.

His hasty shield had cushioned the impact enough that it wasn't a clean break, but *damn* did it hurt! Trying not to use his right arm muscles at all, he pushed up using his left hand, and looked upwards. There was a fluttering of wings, and from the shadows above, a giant barn owl emerged into the glow of the streetlights and landed effortlessly next to his small crater in the road. A familiar press of magic later, and Emmi appeared.

"Chris!" she cried out, half-relieved, half-panicked, while she stooped over the edge. "Oh God, are you okay?"

"More or less," he groaned, and craned his neck to look up. The helicopter was practically invisible above them, but a very distinct glow shone, cast from within the broken windows of the forty-sixth floor. Even from all the way down here, that glow was familiar. It was just like the power he had used in the Collector's place, and just like what Nabu had tried to use in the field two days ago.

She was enthralling the others. Using her powers to do who-knew-what to them.

Being careful not to cut himself on any sharp-edged chunks of concrete, he tried to stand, and accepted Emmi's outstretched arm to help him up onto the street. Thankfully, there wasn't a car in sight, not one being driven at any rate. There were a few parked on the side of the road, but at this time of night, they were sparse.

"We've got to get up there," he said. Looking at Emmi, he asked, "I don't suppose any of your flight forms are strong enough to lift me up?"

"Not a chance," she laughed. "No gryphons or anything like that on Earth."

He looked at the building lobby ahead, just as a night security guard opened the front door to gape at Chris and the fresh crater in the road. "I guess we're taking the long w-"

Something crashed and shattered glass down the road, followed quickly by the screech of rending steel. A roar followed, and as Chris, Emmi, and the guard looked to Chris's left, panic surged into his veins when a small smart car flew out of the shadows into the glow of the nearest streetlight, headed right for Chris and Emmi.

"Look out," he shoved Emmi down with him, his arm screaming upon jarring impact, just as the car missed their heads and tumbled further down the road with a horrifying crash.

Scrambling back to their feet, they gaped at a giant monster lumbering towards them. It was easily twelve feet tall, roughly humanoid, gray with a heavy brow, jutting chin, and sharp, pig-like tusks. Its eyes looked mean, yellow, and were fixed on Chris and Emmi. The security guard yelped and ducked inside, uselessly locking the glass door before pulling his cellphone out.

Staring up at the monstrosity as it lumbered towards them, thankfully unarmed, Chris shook his head. "I...don't believe it."

"What?" Emmi asked.

"They have a cave troll!"

She frowned at him. "Did you just quote a movie? At a time like this, Chris?"

Smirking, he charged up his powers, only to hear another crash from directly behind them. Chris and Emmi looked at each other, and then behind, and his spirits sank. Another, nearly-identical troll was barreling towards them at full speed. "Shit..."

"I don't think Boromir said that," she remarked. After a second, he gaped at her. "What?" she shrugged. "You've watched that movie how many times at home? Of course I know it!"

The first troll roared at them, and she turned her attention back to it. "Tell you what. I'll take on Tweedle-dee, you take on Tweedle-dumb?"

He nodded, hoping the monsters weren't somehow immune to magic. Then he remembered his tranq gun, and gingerly pulled it from his holster, wishing it hadn't been his dominant arm that had broken. "Let's see if this slows them down," and he took aim at the second one, dubbed 'Tweedle-dumb' by Emmi, and pulled the trigger.

Nothing happened. Almost too late, he remembered he hadn't reloaded his gun. "Dammit!"

Emmi, seeing his idea, drew her own and, seeing Tweedle-dumb as the greater threat since it was closing the distance rapidly, she twisted around and fired at it. The dart implanted dead-on in its neck, right where a left artery should have been, and hopefully was.

But for the moment, all that did was piss it off.

"Move!" he shoved her away, and then dove in the opposite direction, crying out in pain when he slammed down again on an already-broken arm. The troll's fists, coupled together, came down right where they'd stood and created a fresh crater in the concrete.

Twisting onto his back, Chris thrust out his good hand and unleashed a golden beam of energy, but was horrified when it bounced off of the trolls head and smashed into the second story of the Sentinel tower, shattering glass and setting off a deafening explosion.

"Oh, not good." Chris scrambled back onto his feet, prepared to meet Tweedle-dumb's retaliatory strike, but Chris's attack had momentarily blinded it, and it pawed uselessly at its eyes.

Emmi shape-shifted into her giant bear form again, and with a great roar, charged at Tweedle-dee, just in time to stop it from barreling over Chris. Its momentum didn't quite stop, and together, bear-Emmi and Tweedle-dee careened into the lobby of the shorter tower across the street, shattering glass, rending aluminum door frames, and setting off a noisy building alarm.

By now, Tweedle-dumb had recovered some semblance of vision, and looked menacingly at Chris. Wide-eyed, he backed up as the monster drew back its lumbering arms and swung from the side. Chris tapped his left shield to life and tried to jump up and hide behind it, Captain America style, and to his credit, it somewhat worked. The shield absorbed most of the troll's hit, and it sent Chris flying like a baseball down the road and onto the sidewalk. He tumbled and rolled, the pain of his broken arm joined by fresh bruises and scrapes.

When he finally stopped rolling, he was next to the destroyed smart car, and his vision blurred from tears of pain. Somewhere in the back of his head, he knew he could go into shock if he wasn't careful. But the trolls were immune to magic!

Or were they?

Sitting up and tapping the shield off, he realized it was immune to his beam, maybe his plasma, but what about other magic forms?

Tweedle-dumb looked confused for a second that Chris was still alive, but it recovered and roared a renewed challenge before barreling down on Chris. Except it stumbled and very nearly fell flat on its face, barely catching itself on its fists and coming to a stop. It shook its head, trying to clear whatever was bothering it, and Chris grinned when he realized the tranq was finally slowing it down.

Standing up, he watched as it stumbled to the left, and tripped when its left leg fell into Chris's crater. Frustrated, it roared again, and scrambled back up onto the street. Turning back on Chris, it lumbered towards him clumsily.

It may not be at 100%, but it was still dangerous! Not knowing what else to do, Chris tried his only other form of magic, raising his left arm and focusing more golden energy into it. With seconds to spare before he was pummeled again, he unleashed golden arcs of electricity upon the beast. They weren't reflected, and instead lit up the troll, which arched its back as its muscles seized.

He tried *really* hard not to quote Emperor Palpatine, but he was very glad when the beast finally succumbed to a combination of his magic and the tranquilizer dart, and it fell over and gave out a moaning, pained breath. Chris ceased his onslaught, and slumped onto his knees, grateful for the momentary break.

Until a cacophony of roars and splintering wood reminded him that Emmi still had her own troll to fight. Suddenly they rolled out of the smaller building's lobby, Emmi's bear form smaller than the troll, but managing to put up a hell of a fight. She roared and bit into its neck, and it cried out a roar back at her before bashing her head. Somehow she kept herself latched on, and pulled hard. The troll's flesh must have been a lot harder than normal flesh, since it didn't rip apart, but even still, black-green blood oozed from the puncture wounds.

The troll rolled them around some more, knocking them into a streetlamp and sending it crashing into the middle of the street, the bulb and its cover shattering with a loud pop.

From the looks of it, Emmi and the troll were evenly matched, at best, so he had to help even the odds. He searched for his gun, and found it several feet away. Rushing over to it, he yanked his dart container out and fumbled with his broken arm, gritting teeth against the intense but thankfully numbing pain, and finally managed to get a dart out. He dropped the packet and picked up his gun, and fumbled some more while loading a fresh dart into it.

It simply didn't want to cooperate! "Come on, dammit!" he shouted, looking up just in time to see the troll bash Emmi's ribcage. "Piece of shit, come on!" She howled in pain, letting go of its neck, and it threw her off then.

Finally, the damn dart went in the chamber, and he cocked it and took aim. The troll, grasping its wounded neck, ambled up onto its feet and let loose another deafening howl of a roar.

Chris fired. The dart struck the back of its neck, and it winced and slapped at the dart like a bug, smashing it and swiping it out of its neck. It stared dumbly at the remnants of the dart in its hand, and then looked back at Chris.

"Oh," he said, and involuntarily took a step back.

It fully turned towards him, growling.

Knowing it would at least slow the thing down until the tranquilizer took hold, Chris dropped the tranq gun and raised his hand, and unleashed another blast of electricity at it. Golden bolts of lightning leapt out at his command and seized the troll. It roared in agony and fell over, its body rigid.

Feeling mentally exhausted from focusing his will, Chris's lightning faltered, and he let his arm drop. He was outright drained, and hoped that his assault had been enough. The troll whimpered and stirred, still awake, but not particularly willing to move again.

Bear-Emmi had made it back onto her feet during Chris's attack, but she kept her distance from the troll, and slowly circled it to come towards Chris.

He must have taken the fight out of it, and it groaned, raising a hand to reach towards Chris, but otherwise it didn't move or attempt to stand up again. Finally, with a huff of breath that blew considerable concrete dust out, Tweedle-dee slumped and let himself rest.

A green glow engulfed Emmi, and she returned to her human form. Her face, and particularly her mouth was smeared with the sickly green blood of the troll, and she spat and wiped her tongue with her hand. "Ew, yuck!" she scowled. "That tastes *nasty!*" Chris opened his mouth to comment, but she pointed a finger at him. "Don't! Not one God damn word, Tatsu. I swear, if you say 'that's what she said,' I'm gonna…"

"I didn't say anything," he retorted defensively. "You said it, not me!"

She glared at him, but then slumped and sighed, before her body shook with a silent laugh. Looking upon the unconscious troll, she planted her blood-stained hands on her hips and said, "Well, then. Even Gandalf would be proud, young padawan." He blinked and frowned at her mixing of pop culture references. "Crap," she sulked. "I got it wrong?"

He grinned, and used his good arm to touch her shoulder. "You get a golden star for trying."

She narrowed her eyes at him. "Don't patronize me," and then she stuck her green-stained tongue out at him.

A laugh escaped him, but he winced when doing so jostled his arm.

Remembering Nabu, he looked up. The warm glow from her enamor spell was gone, but there was still a white glow from Nabu's entire body, which floated lazily between the building and the helicopter.

Which probably meant only one thing.

Nabu must have already found out where Imhullu was.
And she was escaping.

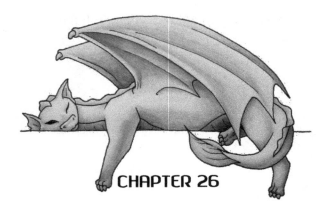

CHAPTER 26

The nice thing about Nabu's glowing body was that it illuminated the black helicopter rather nicely, and gave Chris a perfect target.

"Oh no you don't," he said, raising his good arm up while Emmi followed his gaze.

The instant Nabu was inside of the helicopter, he unleashed a golden beam of energy. He missed at first, the beam lancing harmlessly into the night sky, but he kept at it and ever-so-slightly adjusted his arm, scything his power across the fuselage diagonally.

He must have hit something vital. There was a bright flash, followed by a resounding bang, and the stealth helicopter's engine suddenly groaned louder than it ever had. The tail rotor instantly lost its ability to counteract the rotational forces of the rotor, and the chopper careened out of control while simultaneously falling from the sky like a tumbling fall leaf, swaying back and forth as the pilot struggled to regain control.

It nearly crashed into the top of the lower building across the street, but somehow the pilot pulled the careening aircraft away, despite the dizzying spin, and brought it back over into the street. That was where their luck ended. The pilot overcorrected, and the rotors smashed into an upper floor of the Sentinel tower, shattering glass and tearing through concrete. When the rotor blades caught a steel beam, it jerked the helicopter around and slammed the tail into the building. Rending steel screeched into the night, and now, with the engine seized and no more lift or control from the rotors, the Black Hawk helicopter plummeted towards the street like a lead weight.

Towards Chris and Emmi.

"Shit, move!" she shouted, wrenching on his broken arm to yank him away.

"Owe, hey!" he protested, but managed to keep up and leap away just as the fuselage smashed to the street, flattening with a horrific crash and sending debris scattering all around, with one gear skipping by and almost cracking into Chris's ankle.

Surprisingly, there wasn't a single explosion. A small flame ignited somewhere from within, but the jet fuel in the tanks didn't catch, not yet.

Still, anyone mortal within the chopper wouldn't have survived such a violent crash. The cockpit faced towards their left, and Chris could see the pilot and copilot slumped in their seats, their necks bent at awkward and unnatural angles.

He forced back guilt-induced bile, but reminded himself that they were Nabu's cultists, and would have killed him and his companions in a heartbeat, if given the chance.

Still doesn't make me feel any better about it, he thought, the bile continuing to work its way up and around his throat.

Unfortunately, there had been one occupant that was more or less immortal. After a protracted stillness, broken only by the flicker of some flame within, someone stirred inside the ruins of the cabin. A second later, the dirty, battered, pale form of Nabu climbed out, her white clothes covered in engine oil, grime, and blood.

And she directed a loathsome glare at Chris.

The moment her eyes locked on him, he *felt* the fury flowing off of her through the magic spectrum. The white glow from moments earlier returned, but unlike ever before, it pulsed rhythmically. Some distant pop-culture-obsessed part of him, hidden behind the dual sensations of terror and determination, likened her glowing rhythm to a Star Trek warp core thrumming. But then, as Nabu clambered off of the fuselage and onto the broken street, he noticed the thrumming steadily grew more rapid.

Warp core breach imminent?

Chris looked around at the surrounding skyscrapers, and felt the icy stab of terror. A massive energy discharge here in the core of Denver would be devastating. Desperately, he hoped he was wrong.

"You just can't leave it be, can you?" Nabu spat out. "Either of you?"

Emmi came up next to Chris, unwilling to hide behind him. "You can't stop us," she defiantly replied. "We'll come after you again, and again, and again, until there's nothing left of you."

In the distance, the wail of sirens grew audible. Police and other emergency services were on their way, and that actually made Chris more worried – they would become targets for Nabu. Whatever was going to happen, it needed to happen now.

"Emmi, go check on the others, please," he murmured.

"What? No!"

He flashed intent eyes on her, and said, "I'm going to unleash all of my strength against her. There *will* be collateral damage."

A sudden cackle escaped Nabu, drawing their eyes back to her. "You must know by now that you cannot kill me, no matter *what* your ancestors told you."

Impatient against Emmi's unwillingness to leave, he stepped forward, intentionally placing himself between her and Nabu. "Maybe, maybe not, but I can slow you down."

Drawing in his will and touching the golden core, he created a conduit from the spirit world to the living, and drew up his good arm, knowing full-well that the pain in his right would be too great to be useful.

"Emmi," he spoke curtly without taking his eyes off of Nabu. "Run. Now."

He sensed more than saw Nabu ready her strike, and with only moments to spare and only two dozen feet between him and his nemesis, Chris unleashed the most powerful blast of magic that he could.

It leapt from his palm violently, and he struggled to keep it pointed at Nabu, just as she used both of her hands to release a pure-white blast of magic at him. The two beams collided in the middle, just like what had happened in Babylon.

But Chris had been stronger in Babylon. He hadn't been worn down by grief and anger, not to mention a pair of trolls and a fall from a near-fifty story building.

The point of conflation didn't remain in the exact center, but rather it very steadily moved towards Chris, pushing his stream back further and further. His entire arm shook from the effort, and his thoughts grew foggy, turning into that feeling of disorientation after being abruptly awoken from a deep sleep long before your body was ready for it.

This time, he was going to lose the battle of wills. And unlike

Nabu, he wasn't sure he could survive a full-powered blast of arcane magic. This was the end for him.

Unless.

Alycia.

With seconds to spare, Chris ceased his stream of power and tapped his palm, yanking his arm back just as the blue-white shield appeared. Nabu's foot-wide blast slammed into it, flinging Chris through the air while deflecting and diffusing the blast to his right. He skidded along concrete on his back, ripping his jacket and shirt to shreds and digging into his flesh until he finally came to a stop just beyond the sleeping form of one of the trolls.

His back and broken arm spasmed in pain, and his left hand burned! Crying out in agony, he used his wounded arm to peel the nearly-incinerated glove from his hand and tossed it aside. It had worked! Alycia's shield had saved his life.

But now he was fresh out of shields, and was left to Nabu's mercy.

When he managed to look back at his nemesis, however, she was not in human form anymore, nor was Emmi. Both had changed into their bear forms, Nabu's being twice the size of Emmi's, and were locked in a battle to the death.

Shattering glass and the twang of snapping metal drew his gaze to the Sentinel tower, and he gaped in horror at the damage Nabu's deflected blast had wrought. A large chunk of the building, starting on the second floor and reaching up to the sixth, had been carved out of its southern corner, leaving floors and pipes and conduits exposed. The streetlights and ambient city lighting cast odd shadows into the craggy, half-destroyed interior.

And as the entire building appeared to lean closer to him, he realized its structural integrity was compromised. He didn't have to be an engineer to know that if you lose a chunk of a building that big, it wasn't going to remain standing for long.

The enormity of that fact took seconds to set in, but as it did, an overwhelming dread welled up inside, growing into a monster of horror and shock. *The tower is going to fall…oh God, a fifty story building is about to fall over!*

A roar that sounded half-pained and half-surprised snapped him out of his shock, and he saw Emmi fall to the road with a great whump. He couldn't see the telltale matting of fur that would indicate blood, but Nabu must have hit her so hard that it knocked her senseless for a second.

Beyond the wreck of the helicopter, several police vehicles, including a S.W.A.T. van, raced closer. The giant bear craned its neck over the wreckage at them, and then looked at Chris. A familiar white glow engulfed the bear's body, and it shrank down to normal human size and shape, hiding her form from the incoming police behind the Black Hawk.

"That's my cue, Tatsu," she smirked at him. "As much as I'd love to stay and play, I can't really be seen here right now. You know how it is," the white glow grew intense around her body just as he scrambled onto his feet, his body aching and complaining every step of the way. "Daggers to steal, innocents to sacrifice. What's a girl to do?"

Before he could bring his powers to bear, she was engulfed by a white semi-sphere of light, and then was gone. She had used her portal ability to flee.

The terrifying sound of stressed metal on the brink of snapping reinvigorated him, and he rushed towards Emmi as she stirred, shaking her giant bear-head and looking around. Somehow, she had kept herself from going feral, and he was grateful for that, even if it meant that Nabu had gotten away.

"Emmi," he shouted, drawing her gaze to him just as he withdrew his cellphone from his pocket. It was smashed, no doubt from one of his many impacts, and was completely dead. "Shit, is your phone in one piece?"

After a second of staring dumbly at him, she tried to reach a clawed paw towards her backside, and gave out a weird sort of startled noise. Then a green glow engulfed her body until she emerged as her human self. For probably the hundredth time that year, Chris thought, *What the hell happens to their clothes and electronics when they shapeshift?*

Once human, she reached into her back pocket and withdrew an intact smartphone. "Call one of the others," he pressed.

The tower groaned and a chunk of stone fell from six stories up, drawing her gaze. A horrified expression drew across her face, no doubt mirroring Chris's own look from moments ago. "Emmi, hurry!"

"Uh, right," she shook her head, and set to dialing out. It looked like Alycia was on her speed dial, and a second later she switched it to speaker phone. It rang, and then again, and each time it made Chris's pulse redouble.

When it went to voicemail, he cursed and looked inside the lobby. Somehow, the glass doors were still intact, though they all had spiderweb-cracks across every facet. The lobby itself was likewise intact, and he knew there was a security guard inside. "Come on," he called, rushing for the lobby, "And keep trying!"

Screeching tires signaled the arrival of emergency services on the other side of the chopper wreckage, but the cops wisely stayed clear of the teetering skyscraper. Chris wasn't so wise, and when he made it to doors, he used a small pulse of magic to finish off the door, blowing the glass into the lobby which itself was covered in concrete chunks, stone dust and other debris. Most of the lights were off, indicating that the building was without power now, but emergency lights still worked, casting deep, dark shadows into any place not directly beneath one.

He heard Emmi's phone start ringing out again just as they rushed up to the security desk. "Anyone still in here?" Chris called, rushing around the desk without waiting for an answer. There he found a terrified night security guard, the bags under his eyes indicative of how hard night shift was on him. "Hey, sir, I need your help!"

"W-w-what?" The guard was bewildered, clutching at his baton with both hands like it was the only thing keeping him alive.

Moments before Alycia's phone would have sent them to voicemail, he suddenly heard a voice answer her phone, *"Hello?"*

Chris blinked in surprise. "Babbar?"

"Chris!" Babbar shouted. *"I thought you fell to your death!"*

"Yeah, I'm still alive," he nodded, briefly wondering if Babbar knew who GLaDOS was. Then his stomach cinched for a second. Why was Babbar answering Alycia's phone? "What about everyone else?"

"Nina's hanging on," he said grimly. "Everyone else appears to be alive, but Nabu rendered them unconscious with her spooky mind control power. I woke up before anyone else."

Relief mixed with terror filled Chris. If everyone was unconscious, no one could escape. "Try to wake them up, especially Shara," he said. "She can shapeshift and ferry you all out!"

"And if I can't wake her?"

"Then hold on, because we're coming up."

Emmi gaped at him wide-eyed. "Forty-six stories? With the power out, which means we're taking the stairs?"

He nodded. "I'm not leaving them all to die." As if to accentuate his determination, the building shook, concrete dust filtering through the emergency lights.

Babbar sighed. *"Alright, Chris, I'm on it."* And then he hung up.

Looking at the guard, he asked, "Is there anyone else in the building tonight?"

The guard blinked furiously at him, as if surprised that Chris addressed him again. "W-what? Oh. I m-m-mean, yes, no, no!" He shook his head furiously. "Night cleaning…they're already gone."

"Good, now get yourself out now! There's cops and ambulances outside, go check in with them, and tell them to stay clear!"

"W-what about those m-m-monsters?!" the guard countered, clutching ever tighter to his baton.

"We took care of them," he assured the guard. "It's safe, but it won't be for long, so MOVE IT!"

Startled by his shout, the guard scrambled around the other side of the desk and, with his shoes slipping and sliding on the dust-covered granite floor, he fled as fast as he could.

Chris started towards the back, where he knew an emergency stairwell was next to the main bank of elevators near the west corner, which should have been undamaged.

This was crazy, but he couldn't let anyone else die tonight.

Not if he could help it.

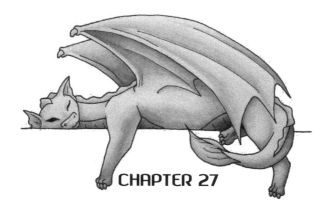

CHAPTER 27

An emergency light shone brightly over the emergency stair entrance, and Chris didn't hesitate, he blasted the door open with a plasma ball, sending it careening inward off of its hinges.

An instant later, he was in the stairwell, barreling up the steps two at a time, with Emmi right behind him.

"You know," she shouted, her voice echoing loudly in the concrete-bricked column and off of painted concrete steps, "it was an emergency exit. It would have been unlocked."

"No time to worry one way or another," he shouted back, racing past the second story landing. "Better to just blast the damn thing and be done with it."

They huffed their way up, both of their breaths starting to come harder. They raced past the third floor at full speed, and quickly came up to four. Just as he was about to head up the stairs past four, something unexpected happened – the concrete stairs, and the far wall past them, cracked and separated, as the entire building groaned.

"Oh shit, move, move, move!" he shouted, leaping over the growing crack. Emmi leapt the growing separation of the stairwell, while Chris rounded the back-and-forth stairs just as chunks of concrete bricks fell off the wall.

Adrenaline was starting to wear thin on him, but on the plus side, the pain in his broken arm was gone, if only temporarily. On the downside, his extremities felt a little numb and his hands shook uncontrollably. But he rushed ahead, heedless of his body's warning signs that he was close to running on empty.

His friends were in danger. *Alycia* was in danger. He wasn't going to give up yet.

All of the stairs between four and six were crumbling and cracking, no doubt from those floors bending over. Their time was rapidly running out, and if the building literally fell over with them still in it, he put their odds at survival as close to none.

Finally, when they made it past the sixth floor, the stairs were a little more solid, and the walls intact. It seemed like between four and six was the weak point from Nabu's deflected blast.

By the time they hit the tenth floor, Chris's chest burned, along with his oxygen-starved leg muscles, his quads more than anything else. He was in damn good shape, thanks to their weeks of training, but it didn't make climbing endless flights of stairs any less difficult.

"Oh, fuck this," Emmi breathed, and a second later, she shapeshifted into a dog and raced ahead of him up the stairs. The flash of black, white and gray fur told him she'd chosen a husky or similar dog.

After a few more flights, he lost sight of her dog form as she easily bounded ahead of him. When he rounded the next flight, he saw her sitting at the top, waiting for him. As soon as she saw him, she darted up to the next landing. She repeated this over and over, always ahead of him, and he found himself insanely jealous of her abilities.

Somewhere between twenty-two and twenty-three, the building shook violently and lurched to one side. Panic clarified itself in his stomach, just as he lost his balance and fell back three steps to the previous landing, and then smashed his already-broken arm into the wall, sending fresh jolts of pain into his weary body.

Somehow, miraculously, the building stabilized again, but he noticed a distinct slant to the stairs. The building was leaning, and unfortunately, it leaned in such a way that would make climbing the stairs even harder.

Emmi was braced on all four legs on the next landing, but once the building stabilized, she yipped at him, as if to say, "Hurry your ass up!" and then launched herself up the next flight.

Grumbling, Chris cradled his wounded arm for a second, and then pushed against burning legs to fly up the next flight.

When his legs starting giving out at about thirty, he heaved a terrible sigh and just about collapsed. He had to stop, adrenaline no longer sufficing. It didn't matter how much he tried, his body simply wouldn't move anymore. Emmi came back around after having already disappeared and gave him an 'awoo,' as if that would encourage him.

Heaving in breaths, trying to suck in oxygen to replenish his muscles, he shook his head, halfway between stairs. "Just...give me a...a second," he huffed, wondering how the hell firemen managed to climb even higher carrying full gear back when 9/11 happened. "I'm gonna...try something."

It was the only chance he had left now, the only chance his friends had. Closing his eyes for a second, and trying desperately to ignore the weird false-lights playing around in his vision, he looked for his golden core, his center. Could arcane magic be used to fuel him? Could the energy from hundreds of thousands of souls push his exhausted body beyond its limits?

Finding the core of energy had become routine, easy. But using it in a way he had never done before was another matter. How could he direct it? Was it even possible?

I just need a boost, he thought. *Consequences be damned, I need to get to Alycia, I need to save them all!* He thought of Naomi, and of Tattannu, and he shouted into the nether realm, *Help me!*

Someone answered back. Some*thing* answered back. Whether it was one of his known spirits or something else, he didn't know, but all of a sudden, his aching, cramping leg muscles relaxed just enough to reduce the pain he felt, and a surge of renewed energy coursed into every inch of his body.

Standing upright, he looked at Emmi, whose wolf-like head tilted curiously at him. Could she feel that surge of magic?

No... It was something else. Because in the gloom of the emergency lights, he noticed something else A golden glow.

He looked at his hands, but it didn't come from his body. Instead, as the light shifted, he realized it was his eyes.

They had become bright gold pinpoints of energy.

With more determination in his voice than he actually felt, he said, "Let's go," and he charged up the stairs, Emmi lunging ahead a second later.

Whatever fueled him now felt like an unlimited source, surging fresh strength into his body, somehow keeping his muscles functioning. His breathing was still labored, but he could control it better.

When they finally made it to forty-six, the building had shook and lurched two more times, and there was a distinct canter to the stairwell, to the entire building.

Emmi waited for him next to the door, still in her husky form. He huffed past her and tried the door handle, but the door wouldn't budge. Looking at her with a smirk, he said, "See? Told you."

She growled in reply. He backed away and blasted the door into the Sentinel Holdings lobby. Emmi preceded him in a bounding rush, but he was right behind her, and he came upon a scene of everyone still lying on the floor, except for Babbar, who shook Shara violently.

"There you are," the gnome sighed in relief. "What in the blazes kept...you?" He gaped at Chris, no doubt at his glowing eyes, which faded as Chris's need for extra energy finally abated.

"Forty-six flights of stairs, that's what," Chris growled, rushing over and stopping first by Alycia to check on her. Emmi shapeshifted back to her human form next to him and started checking on the others.

Lifting Alycia's head up carefully, Chris asked, "Alycia? Aly! Wake up!"

Her eyes seemed to dart back and forth behind her eyelids, and he wondered if this was more than just a case of being unconscious. "Babbar, what exactly happened?"

Abandoning his frantic attempts to wake Shara, he shook his head, "Nabu used a light to enchant everyone, like what you did at the Collector's. It worked on everyone, including me. Next thing I know, she's face to face with Tom," he motioned to Tom's unconscious form, "Made him give up the dagger's location. Then I wake up to Nina licking my face." Babbar stepped over Shara's body to Nina, who lay on her side anxiously licking her bullet wound.

"Is she okay?" he asked while easing Alycia's head back down onto the ground. "Can she portal us out of here?"

"I don't think so," Babbar shook his head, kneeling next to his beloved Nina. She turned to look at him mournfully, a high-pitched whimper escaping her throat, before she resumed licking her wound. It didn't appear to be bleeding anymore, and in fact there wasn't even a hole. "She's healing rapidly, but I doubt she'll be ready in time to save us."

"Dammit," Chris sighed, and then moved over to Shara. "Why

are you awake and no one else?"

Just as Chris knelt next to Shara, Babbar shrugged. "Gnomes are better than you?"

Giving him a tired look, Chris looked closely at Shara's eyes. They were also moving rapidly beneath her eyelids. Everyone was dreaming.

No, not just dreaming. Their breathing was shallow and rapid, and their skin was clammy. They were stuck inside of nightmares.

Somehow, Nabu must have induced a persistent nightmare state. The building lurched, and a mostly-round piece of debris nearby started rolling towards the gaping windows behind Chris. He watched it for a second, his heartbeat racing along with it.

There wasn't time for this. He needed to wake Shara, if no one else.

The only thing he could think to do was dangerous, but it was better than waiting for the entire building to collapse. He bent down closer and placed one hand on her forehead, and another on her chest, not quite sure how he knew what to do.

The instant both hands connected with her, he felt his golden core connect with her off-green center. In his mind's eye, he saw the colored spheres side-by-side, with a tendril of translucent energy connecting between them. Her core looked much like his, if less energetic and smaller, which didn't surprise him, since his was fueled by millions of souls. What *did* surprise him was a black, oily substance coalescing around her sphere, squeezing it, crushing it, tightening like a snake coiled around its prey.

Nabu had left something behind within Shara, a stain tarnishing her essence, blackening her soul. He shuddered to think of what might happen if she and the others remained in this state. Would it destroy them? Would it darken them to such a degree that they would never be normal again?

Was that what had happened to Mia?

As if to answer him, several of the vague shadows around him suddenly came into sharp focus. People, souls of his ancestors, all of a sudden taking an interest in what he was doing. As if this was something important. Something vital.

"Chris," the familiar sing-song voice of his sister spoke. He craned his neck around, unwilling to drop his focus from Shara. Naomi reached her hand out, offering it to him. Was she offering to help?

Not quite realizing what he was doing or why, he touched her hand. His connection to Shara strengthened, but something else happened then. Naomi reached her hand away from them, to the left of the dual spheres, and a golden arc of energy lanced out and connected with another sphere that hadn't been there before, but now came to life in an instant.

It was a soothing, calm orange color, like that of a setting sun. It radiated warmth at first, but the same dark stain morphing over Shara's had befallen it. Only this stain was darker, far more concentrated, eclipsing the orange glow almost entirely, and it had penetrated all the way down to the center.

One of Chris's ancestors, a tall man with a receding gray hairline dressed in a Victorian-style gentleman's suit, stepped up to Naomi and touched her shoulder with one hand, while reaching out with his other.

A spark of light, and another sphere appeared next to the orange one, this one the familiar blue of Alycia's powers, and Chris instantly felt her familiar presence. Like the others, hers was stained black.

Yet another man stepped forward, this one donning ancient samurai armor, beautifully crafted with red plate armor pieces connected to one another by leather chords. His helmet, which Chris thought was called a kabuto, held large horns pointed upwards, and he wore a terrifying painted mask portraying some kind of red and black monster.

The samurai touched the Victorian-era man's shoulder, and projected yet another sphere, this one a softer shade of orange, and likewise stained. That sphere in particular was smaller than everyone else's, and somehow, Chris intuitively knew it was Tom's, and like the others, it was tainted with oily darkness.

Another person, an elderly woman that reminded Chris of one of his grandmothers, appeared and likewise touched the Samurai's shoulder, projecting out yet another, weaker sphere, likewise tainted. *Alycia's brother,* Chris thought.

Startled, he realized he had just made a Sherlock-esque deduction. Mia had power. Hers was the brighter, larger orange sphere, but tainted worse than anyone else's.

"This is how Nabu enthralls people," Naomi explained. "And through us, you can break the chains before they ever form. You can free them."

"How?"

"By letting go," she said, her face sympathetic but her voice pained. "By giving in. Accept who you are. Accept *what* you are."

She smiled weakly, and suddenly more figures in the hazy crowd came forward, more of his ancestors. Tattannu was nowhere to be found, but at least a hundred others came forth and linked arms, ensuring that everyone present was somehow linked to Chris and the spheres of light.

"I...I don't understand," Chris shook his head.

"It's like a good man once said," Naomi volunteered. "It's easy if you try." She closed her eyes, bracing herself for something, though he didn't know what.

Emotion. That was part of the key, the hint in the song she had quoted. Emotion was as interwoven with the soul as any other part of the psyche, but she had quoted John Lenin, and he knew what that meant.

So he focused on Alycia's soul, on her tainted blue sphere. He focused on how he felt about her. The feelings welled up within him, and passed through his soul into that of his ancestors, becoming amplified by each person it passed through, reverberating back like an echo chamber, coming into sharp focus.

It wasn't as simple as that, he knew, and he recognized what was happening. His ancestors were infusing their energy into that emotion, he could see it, he could *feel* it, giving their strength over to his feelings. The mechanical engineer in him marveled at it. It was like a transducer, converting one form of energy into another, and back again.

And he directed that energy outward, at all of the external spheres. His golden core surged, the tantalizing bolts of inner electricity flashing brighter and more frequently. The connective conduits flared bright, and the other spheres shuddered violently.

And then, like ash peeling and flying away from a burning log, the dark taint floated away from each sphere.

Shara drew in a sharp breath and clutched at Chris's hand on her chest. He withdrew from the spirit world and opened his eyes, staring into her deep violet ones and pulling his hands away.

Alycia, Tom, Eric and Mia likewise jerked awake, but Mia, no doubt still feeling the effects of the tranquilizer, immediately fell back unconscious.

"What the hell?!" Tom murmured, bleary as if waking from a deep sleep.

Chris, on the other hand, felt like falling asleep. The effort of breaking Nabu's hold over them had drained him, drained *more* than him. The souls of a hundred ancestors were likewise drained. The weight of it all grew heavy, his shoulders sinking down low and a dizzy spell overcoming him.

"Oh, shit," he wobbled on his knees. Emmi, who had come up behind him, steadied him.

"What did you do?" Emmi asked. "I...I *felt* that! Your magic went into them, or something!"

Chris blinked away tears, the kind that come when your nose itches fiercely inside from allergies, and looked at Shara, hoping she had an answer.

She shook her head slowly, as confounded as he was.

He thought he knew what had happened, but he didn't know how to explain it to them. Not yet, anyway.

What he *did* know was that the answers he had sought from Tattannu were there, barely on the peripheral of his consciousness. Something about what he had done was the path to defeating Nabu and Marduk.

Turning, he locked eyes with Alycia, his heart suddenly aching to be with her. He stumbled onto his feet and nearly fell over. And then he *did* fall over, when the building suddenly lurched beneath them.

"We need to go," Chris stated. "The building's about to collapse."

"Wait, what?!" Alycia gaped in horror.

Stumbling back onto his feet with Emmi and Alycia's help, he nodded. "There's a chunk missing on the lower levels, aaand-"

His explanation was cut short as a sense of free-falling suddenly took hold of him. His feet slid out from under him, and he realized that it was too late. The building was falling almost directly south. The plus side to that was he and the others weren't sliding directly for the window, but rather the corner, towards the reception desk.

That was where the good news ended. Emergency lightbulbs popped from twisting and warping frames, and one of the neighboring buildings, shorter than the Sentinel tower, loomed ahead and below, what few lights illuminated within it blazing as a warning that they were rapidly descending towards it.

The troupe, with Babbar holding tight onto Nina, grabbed onto the desk and tried to hold on precariously to the overhanging granite lip, but it was smooth, and the building tilted faster and faster.

Until some section several floors below them slammed into the neighboring building, jarring them all loose.

"Chris!" Alycia screamed, her grip slipping first. He tried desperately to reach out for her, but it was with his broken arm, and it simply refused to work anymore.

Emmi caught her, but she lost her grip on the desk, and they flew out of the shattered windows.

"ALY!" he yelled, and was sorely tempted to let go. He almost didn't have a choice.

But then, barely visible in what little light there was, he was astonished to see them land on top of the neighboring building's roof. It was short enough that from their floor, they hovered over it, almost too far, since Alycia and Emmi had nearly fallen over the *far* side of the neighboring building.

Unfortunately, it wasn't a good resting spot for the Sentinel tower, and with a terrifying groan and the shriek of wrenching metal, the tower suddenly jarred downwards, 'shrinking' as the lower floors collapsed.

"Now's our chance, go now!" Tom shouted, and he pushed off from the desk. It was still a long drop down, and when he hit the rooftop, his feet gave out and he collapsed into a haphazard roll. Babbar followed, but just as he did, the tower began to slide left, tearing the safety of the other roof to their right. Moments later, a gaping chasm of darkness and the glow of streetlights *far* below filled their view.

Chris looked at Shara, and then blinked and looked around. "Where's Marisol?"

Shara's eyes met his, and they looked up at the sealed mantrap doors.

"She must be trapped inside," Shara shouted.

Cursing, Chris held on as tight as he could with his good arm and grit through the pain as he pointed his broken arm at the mantrap doors. He unleashed as strong of a blast as he dared, blowing open the door, but wrenching his arm back and sending fresh surges of pain. He lost his grip, caught his foot on the desk and suddenly tumbled and summersaulted through the air.

A giant, clawed, three-toed bird's foot caught him. Shara had just shapeshifted into her gryphon form and caught him with one front claw, while her other dug talons into the marble floor, halting their fall.

Until the entire building jostled and jerked, and her talons started to give way, gouging deep lines into the floor.

She needed both claws, he realized, while forcing his eyes up and away from the deadly drop beneath them. He had to climb up onto her back.

The tower must have been wedged in between two other towers, but the structure was definitely *not* going to hold. Screeching steel and crumbling concrete told him as much, and every few seconds, the entire building lurched, threatening to tear Shara's claw free.

So he grasped at Shara's muscle-bound arms, feeling absolute strength and power beneath them beyond anything he'd ever felt before, and he tried to scramble safely from within her grasp.

"Hey!" a familiar voice called down to him. He grabbed onto the front of the base of Shara's left wing, and then looked up at the freshly-opened mantrap door. There Marisol peaked out, looking down at them. "Thanks for opening the door for me, it wouldn't budge when the power went out. Any chance for a lift?"

Shara roared back in response, and through gritting teeth, he replied, "I'm working on it!"

It was next to impossible to climb up Shara's back with how fatigued he was, and his broken arm didn't help, but it was better than falling what he guessed was thirty stories down to the road below. He might not survive such a fall again, not with how depleted he felt.

Once he had a good grip, Shara released her grasp, just as they slid down to the edge of the floor and her back legs dangled out the window. She dug her left claw's talons in, and halted their slide.

Somehow, Chris managed to clamber up and wedge his armpits over her wing bases, ensuring he wouldn't fall. Freed of his burden, Shara jerked up and dug claws into fresh floor. Then she did so again with her other, and again, and again.

They made quick progress, halted only once by the tower shuddering and jerking several times. Chris's right arm demanded more attention, and he was sure it was moments away from finally breaking clean through.

When they were level with Marisol, Shara climbed onto the reception desk, the side of which gave her a modicum of 'level' ground to stand atop without digging claws in.

Chris looked down at the street below, and instantly felt his stomach flip. Even in the dark of night, streetlamps illuminated the spread of debris regularly falling from the tower, and highlighted what would happen to him if he let go.

Looking back at Marisol, whose face looked pale even in near-total darkness, he nodded. "I don't think we can safely get closer, you'll have to jump!"

"I was afraid you'd say that," she sighed. But then, surprising him, she didn't even hesitate, and she leapt across the distance, wrapping her arms around Shara's neck while letting her feet land on the wooden side of the desk.

Except, the desk wasn't meant to hold that kind of weight, and it finally creaked, snapped, and gave way, the wood base splintering and the granite top falling away in pieces. Marisol cursed, Chris yelled in surprise, and Shara screeched.

Chris reached up and grasped Marisol's hands, helping her hold on to Shara's broad neck as she dangled beneath Shara's beak, while Shara used her last bit of footing to turn around and point her beak towards the street below. The tower shuddered and jerked downward with them, but Shara dug her claws into the floor and propelled them out of the windows, and then spread her massive wings wide to catch the air.

Marisol's grip faltered, but again, she didn't cry out or scream, she just cursed up a storm. "Shara, I'm slipping!"

They were still under the tower, and it was falling faster and faster, wedging down into the cross street, until the structural integrity simply gave out, and the building collapsed inwards and downwards. Debris and glass shards fell upon them as they raced away, the ground rushing up at them as Shara used their downward momentum to help them pickup speed.

And then they were clear, just as the last spire of a radio tower from atop the Sentinel tower whistled past them, barely missing Shara's left wing. The tower crashed below and behind them with a horrendous boom, expelling a massive cloud of debris and dust that billowed out and occluded the streetlamps, which all died a second later.

Shara dipped them lower and pumped her wings against their momentum, slowing them down just in time, as Marisol's hands slipped out of Chris's, and she fell the remaining distance to the road below, invisible to Chris in the darkness.

With a terrified screech, Shara landed fast and rough, jostling Chris enough that he lost his own grip and slid off to the side, landing hard on his good arm and eliciting a loud "Oof!"

But they were down.

And everyone was alive.

A green glow illuminated the street when Shara shapeshifted back to herself, and then she raced over to Marisol's side. "Are you okay?"

Barely visible in the moonlight, Chris saw Marisol stir. Just as Shara knelt down, Marisol managed to lift her head and, with a thumbs up from both hands, she said, "That was a wild-ass ride, chica!"

Shara let out a breathy laugh and lowered her forehead to Marisol's. "I'm glad you enjoyed it," she managed to say between chuckles.

"Yeah," Marisol nodded, and dropped her head and hands back down. "Let's do it again, only next time, leave the falling building out of it."

Chris looked at where he knew the remains of the tower was, as did Shara, but the moonlight couldn't penetrate the cloud of dust, which very quickly blew over Chris and the others, stinging Chris's eyes.

"No promises," Shara remarked dryly.

CHAPTER 28

Shara's phone broke the oppressive silence on the street, Beethoven's ancient music blasting out into the night. When she pulled her phone out, it illuminated both her and Marisol in a haze of dust.

Chris limped over to them just as Shara answered and put it on speaker.

"Emmi?"

"Hey, you're alive! Thank God." Waves of relief likewise flooded Chris.

"Yeah, we're fine, but-"

"You need to get up here right now." The steely tone to her voice washed away the flood of relief, and Chris tensed, his shoulders bunching up and pulling at worn and weary muscles in his wounded arm. Marisol's head shot back up, and she scrambled to sit up.

"What's wrong?" Shara asked, her tone falling back into her commanding presence.

"Just...get up here," Emmi said, her voice shaking. *"Now."*

Shara hung up, stood, and then offered a hand to Marisol to help her stand. "Do you two feel strong enough to ride on my back again?"

Marisol and Chris exchanged worried looks. "I think so," Marisol replied.

Chris experimentally shifted his arms, and winced. "I'll make do. Can you see enough to get us there safely?"

Just as a pale green glow engulfed her body, Shara nodded. "Once I'm above the dust, yeah. I have *excellent* night vision as a gryphon." And then she grew into her beautiful white-gold gryphon

227

form. She let loose a combined roar and shriek, and then lowered herself down.

Marisol clambered up to sit in the more comfortable area behind Shara's wing joints, while Chris had to sit a little further back and wrapped his arms around Marisol's midsection, which was pure hardened muscle.

He nearly lost his grip the moment Shara began to move, and his broken arm screamed in pain, but he held on for dear life. A second later, Shara galloped along the street, away from the ruins of Sentinel Tower, and spread her wings along the wide avenue, pumping them hard until they were airborne.

Chris and Marisol had to clench their eyes against the sudden blowing dust, and he felt some get into his mouth, gritting between his teeth. Finally, they soared up above it, revealing a starry night sky oblivious to the terror that had just befallen downtown Denver.

When Chris opened his eyes, he gaped down below at the city, or rather at where the city should have been. The moonlight illuminated the dust somewhat, making it look like they soared above a dull cloud, but more shocking was just how much of the city had lost power. Multiple blocks, a black tarnish on the city not unlike the stain upon the souls of Chris's companions earlier.

It was more than a little disorienting to fly so blindly, and an age-old terror of flight suddenly took hold. *This isn't a tin can. This isn't a tin can.* Over and over he repeated that to himself, clutching to his assertion ten weeks ago that it wasn't flying that scared him, but the thought of being in a tin can that could fall from the sky at any moment. Considering how many aircraft he had personally downed over the past few days, maybe that fear was well-founded.

But whenever Shara adjusted her course, and especially when she changed whether she was ascending or descending, his stomach didn't know where to go or how to follow, and bile rose up again, threatening to force him to retch.

He must have groaned aloud without realizing it. Marisol turned her head to try to look at him, and shouted back at him, "You okay, Wey?"

"Uhhhh," was all he managed to reply, fearful that if he opened his mouth anymore, something would come out.

"Hey, don't hurl on this jacket, okay? It's my favorite!"

Shara screeched her agreement.

Forcing open eyes that he hadn't realized he'd clutched shut, Chris desperately searched for some sort of light source nearby that he could orient himself upon. He found beams of light moving around on a surface, and as they dove closer to those lights, he realized they were from flashlight apps on cellphones.

Shara expertly landed them atop the roof several feet away from the lights, all of which darted up towards them upon hearing the crunch of gravel and glass under Shara's massive hooves and taloned feet.

Without the wind in his face, the need to let loose the contents of his stomach grew frighteningly stronger, and Chris quickly dismounted and fell to the side, not caring about the rubble that pierced his pants and scraped his knees and hands as he fell down, dry-heaving. His throat burned with the effort, but nothing ever actually came out.

"I'm okay," he managed after a moment, feeling Marisol's hands on his back. "That was…"

"Disorienting," Marisol agreed. "Yeah."

He glanced at her and frowned accusingly. "You seem okay."

With a shrug, she replied, "Space Mountain in Disney, man. It's my favorite ride."

A snort of a chuckle escaped his throat, and he managed to stand up just as Shara shapeshifted back to her normal self and rushed towards the others. "Tom!"

Something inside of him clutched tightly at his chest, as the image of Tom falling out of the building onto the roof, and his legs giving out beneath him, flashed through Chris's memory. He and Marisol looked to one another in the ambient glow from the flashlights, and then hurried after Shara.

When they saw him, with Alycia hovering over his body on her knees, he felt his face grow ever-more pale and clammy. The landing must have hurt, yes, but when the tower slid down, a small piece of rebar must have been flung down from above, and pierced the commander's abdomen on the lower right side. Blood stained his ripped shirt, which Chris guessed the others had done to more clearly see the wound, and a pool had formed beneath him, soaking into otherwise dry concrete dust and debris.

Emmi stood above them, holding her flashlight to look down on their wounded commander, while Babbar was nearby, likewise holding a flashlight but also clutching the wounded Nina in his free arm like one might hold a baby. Nina watched, her lizard-like eyes narrowed to slits as she looked ready to fall asleep in Babbar's arms. And behind them all was Mia's unconscious form, with Eric hovering over her, his face blank, his hand idly holding yet another cellphone with a flashlight app upon the group.

Tom stirred a little and winced, and then he opened his eyes and looked around. Waves of relief washed over Chris. "Shara. Chris!" He winced upon his exclamation, and grit his teeth while his right hand gripped the rebar. "Good, you're alive."

Feeling his mouth grow dry, Chris nodded solemnly. *Oh God, don't let him die, not now!*

Shara knelt on the other side of Tom, but looked up at Emmi and said, "Go! Get down to the street and get a paramedic team up here." Emmi gaped for one heartbeat too long, and Shara shouted, "Now!"

She jumped, but nodded. Handing her phone over to Chris so he could continue to shine the light down upon Tom, she scooted away, and then shapeshifted into an owl and fluttered away, incredibly silent.

"Shara," Tom let go of the bar and gripped her arm, surprisingly tightly from the looks of it. "Nabu. She…she forced me to tell her where the dagger was."

"Shut up," Shara shook her head, wetness welling up in her eyes. "Tell me all about it later."

"You don't understand," he looked at her intently. "Jered." And then he nodded back at Babbar. "Babbar's old home. The underground mansion. Jered has watched the dagger there. Both arrived by portal. Babbar has been taking him groceries all summer with Nina's help."

He must have moved a little too much, and suddenly his face screwed up in a pained look.

"Dad, stop talking," Alycia begged, her voice shaking. Without thinking about it, Chris walked around to her side and rested a comforting hand on her shoulder. She reached up and grasped at it tightly.

"Shara, you need to fly," Tom spoke through clenched teeth. "Go see if Jered's alive."

Alycia managed to say in a half-sob, "W-we tried to call him. Hhe's not answering."

"Nabu used a portal to escape," Chris informed them. "She probably went straight there, and…"

"We have to be sure!" Tom gripped Shara's arm tighter. "Go now. With Nina hurt, you can get there the fastest."

Though tears fell from her eyes, mixing with Tom's blood, Shara nodded and stood up.

"Hold up," Chris shook his head. "You can't go alone. What if Nabu is still there when you arrive?"

"I don't have a choice," she glared at him, her purple eyes literally flashing in the dark, startling Chris. She was mad. No, she was beyond mad, she was *pissed* to have to leave Tom in this condition.

Hesitation filled Chris. He wanted to offer to go with, but he wanted to stay by Alycia's side. She had already suffered enough. Glancing at Eric, he thought for a brief second, *at least her brother is here,* but he sat uselessly by his mother, seemingly unconcerned for his father or his sister.

"Don't," Shara held up a hand. "I know you've somehow built up this hero complex over the past few days, but right now you're far too exhausted and wounded to help. You wouldn't last the hour long flight it'll probably take me to get there, and even if you did, you'd be useless in a fight."

"But," he started, and then stopped. He hated to admit it, but she was right. His broken arm needed tending to, there was no way he could hold on or stay awake for an hour, let alone hold in whatever the contents of his stomach were at the moment. A flight into the dark mountains before sunrise, with no way to truly orient himself aside from a setting moon and starlight?

Heaving out a sigh, he nodded. "Alright. I'll stay with them."

She nodded, and then smiled. "Besides, when I get there, I'll just go in as a mouse or something. Nabu won't see me coming. If it's not already too late, that is."

Chris shuddered, and he thought they were all fools to think Nabu wouldn't already be long gone by the time she arrived. More than likely, Jered was already dead at that very moment, and Imhullu was in Nabu's hands.

"Alright," he nodded curtly, and then looked up at her.

She moved to wipe tears clear from her eyes, but then scowled at her dirt-encrusted hands and arms. "I'll call as soon as I know something," she said, looking down at Tom. "You, sir, had damn well better stay alive."

Wincing, Tom managed a weak smile and nod.

Turning on the spot, Shara stowed her phone, and then shapeshifted back into her gryphon form, before taking off in a flurry of wind. As she faded into the dark of night, she let out one last shriek-roar.

The minutes dragged by after her departure. Chris knelt down beside Alycia, wincing as he did, and tried to wrap his right arm around her, but ended up just awkwardly letting it rest on her back. She leaned into him.

Tom stared at them both for a minute, before he closed his eyes and let out a sigh. "Eric," he called to his son.

Chris and Alycia looked up at her brother, and he looked over at his father, but didn't say anything or move beyond that little motion of the head.

Sighing again, Tom spoke with his eyes closed. "You don't have to say or do anything except listen." His words were slow and measured, his voice weak. "Your sister can explain more about who and what we are, but I wanted you to know that I have always been proud of you." A startled look opened up Eric's face, but then his expression screwed down into one of doubt. "I know you blamed me for your mother's...well," he laughed, and instantly winced, his face growing paler even in the pure-white cellphone light. "She's not dead. But we all thought she was, and I know that you...you blamed me for it." He shook his head. "That's fine. Blame me. Blame it all on me. The lies, the secrets. Don't blame your sister. She knew nothing about my world until this year, and she didn't tell you because I *asked* her not to."

Eric's eyes darted to Alycia, and she looked right back at him. After a second, she hung her head low, and then nodded. Fury etched into Eric's face, fury directed at his father. "You're an ass," he muttered.

Tom's jaw clenched, but he nodded. "I am. I know. And I always will be. But you...don't have to be. Don't be like me. Be something better, yeah? For your sister."

Silence fell upon them again after that. Sirens wailed in the distance, the dust cloud grew up around them, not as dense as down at street level, but still obvious in the hazy beams of flashlights.

Somewhere nearby, there was a loud screech. Then another one. "Hey, a little help here?" Emmi's voice called out.

Chris spun around, and saw that the steel door towards the western corner of the rooftop was partially opened, pushing up against a steel beam that must have fallen from Sentinel Tower. Chris stood up and rushed over, with Alycia following closely behind.

There was no way they could move the beam with just muscle, but thankfully there were other options. Despite still being exhausted, enough time had passed that Chris's power felt strong enough to use again. Drawing on engineering classes, he picked what he thought was a good place to cut the steel beam to the left of where the door was hitting it. He glanced into the door at her and a pair of medics behind her and said, "Stand back, just in case this goes wrong."

The medics looked confused, but followed Emmi's prodding as they backed down the access stairs.

Chris nodded to Alycia to encourage her to likewise backup, and then he drew upon his golden core, focusing his power into a tightly-controlled beam of energy. It lanced out from a glowing spot on his palm, and he instantly felt fatigue wash over him again.

Gritting his teeth, he held it and watched as molten beads of steel started to dribble down. He knew there was a risk of starting a fire on the roof, but right now, all he cared about was getting Tom the medical attention he needed. As Chris cut, he adjusted how much energy he pushed into his beam, concentrating hard enough that his jaw started to ache from clenching, and sweat poured down his face.

Finally, the I-beam snapped, and he stopped his magic a moment later, a tiny gouge appearing in the rooftop, but otherwise no other collateral damage. He grasped the door, but knew it would still be too hard for him to move, so he looked at Alycia. "Help me?"

She rushed over, and together, they pushed. With a grin, and between grunts of effort, she said, "Way to go, Iron Man."

He laughed, and it hurt everything in his body, but somehow it still felt good to laugh.

Once the door was opened, the medics rushed up carrying equipment and a stretcher, with Emmi following close behind. "Over here," Alycia guided them, while Emmi stopped next to Chris.

She looked him up and down and managed to blow a shocked whistle through her teeth. Frowning at her, he asked, "What?"

"You look like hell," she remarked.

Another painful laugh escaped him, and he winced. "Oof. Don't make me laugh, please."

She chuckled and nodded. "Yeah, alright, I'll let you off easy this time."

Exasperated, he shook his head, and together, they watched the medics work. The rebar was a relatively short piece, and hadn't impaled more than a centimeter into the roof, so they managed to get Tom onto the stretcher fairly easily.

"We need to get him to a hospital and into surgery," one of them told the others, a harried-looking woman who no doubt was *very* busy tonight. She looked around, stopping ever so briefly on Babbar and the dragon cradled in his arms, before her eyes honed in on Mia. "Does anyone else need medical attention?"

Eric opened his mouth to say something, stopped for a second, and then shook his head. "She's just...she'll be fine."

Chris hissed when Emmi slapped his arm, and she called, "He could use some attention."

The medic looked Chris up and down, and nodded. "We'll get someone to look at you downstairs, this man needs more attention."

"Ready," the other medic said, after affixing several bandages around the rebar sticking out of Tom's stomach.

Nodding, the two worked together to lift Tom up. Emmi took her phone back from Chris and led them down the stairwell, using her flashlight even with the emergency lights within working, while Marisol followed behind.

Looking at Babbar, Mia, and Eric, Chris asked, "What about you two?"

Hefting up and stowing his phone, Eric started to lift his mother, "I'm getting her out of here."

"You're sticking with us," Alycia said, rushing over to help him lift Mia up.

"Like hell," he spat at her. "I'm getting as far away from you people as I can." He tried to jerk Mia away from Alycia, but nearly toppled over in the process. Mia's head lolled to one side, and her eyes fluttered open as a startled cry escaped her throat.

Panicking, she jerked out of her children's embraces and looked around wildly, before her eyes settled upon Chris. He wasn't sure what to expect, what she would think or feel, but he mostly expected her to still hate him for killing her 'beloved.'

Instead, she gaped at him in awe. "You," she whispered. Clearing her throat, she blinked and shook her head. "You, it was you, you in my head." She shook her head again, and banged her temple with her palm, as if trying to clear away whatever muddled her thoughts. Considering that tranquilizer formula should have left her unconscious for hours, he was surprised she was doing as well as she was.

"What do you mean, Mum?" Alycia asked.

Mia's eyes lost focus for a second, and she glanced at Alycia. Her eyes narrowed, and she cautiously approached, lifting her hand towards Alycia's cheek. "D-daughter?"

A breathy noise escaped Alycia, and then she choked in air. "It's me, Mum," she said, nodding furiously.

Looking to Eric, her smile blossomed. "Eric! My son," and she opened her arms wide to both of them.

Alycia easily fell into them, but Eric, no doubt due to having been threatened by his mother not an hour ago, stayed back. She motioned with her arms for him to come join them in their embrace, but Eric refused.

Remorse drew down her face. "My God, I am so, so sorry, Eric. I...I didn't mean to. I wasn't in control. Same with you, Aly," she let Alycia out of her embrace just enough to look her daughter in the eye. "I...Nabu..." She shook her head, and looked again upon Chris. "It was you. You in my head. You in my heart. You released me."

Alycia looked over at Chris, and blinked in surprise. "Wait, that was real?"

Even Eric looked over at him in surprise.

"That stain, that *need*," Mia shook her head. "It's been with me for so long. I feel...empty without it. I don't know what to do. I've...I've done so many horrible things."

Drawing in a breath, Chris hesitated, and then said, "I'm not exactly sure what I did, but I think I understand what Nabu did to you." The only problem was, she'd been under the spell for so long, Chris worried that there were still consequences to come for poor Mia.

A long road to recover lay ahead for Alycia's mother. For her family.

Babbar huffed. "Well, it's a touching family reunion and all."

Chris and Alycia glared at him. "But I rather think we should be joining the others downstairs." He blinked, glanced down at Nina, and then back up at Chris. "Do you think they allow dragons in the hospital?"

CHAPTER 29

Emmi waited for them at the bottom of the stairs, and then led them outside through a side door that she and the medics had found, which was just as well since tons of concrete, steel, and other materials blocked the main entrance. Plus it had been smashed up by Emmi's battle with a troll. For a second he started, remembering the trolls, only to then relax when he realized they'd likely been smashed by the collapsing building.

They came outside just as the medics finished loading Tom up into one of the ambulances. Medics, firefighters, and police were all over the scene, and down at street level, the dust was oppressively thick, with the strobing lights from atop emergency vehicles creating an eerie light show. Everyone was covered in a layer of dust, their faces gray and haunting.

"I'm going with Dad, okay?" Alycia said to them.

Mia's eyes opened wide, and she stared after Tom mournfully. She looked like she wanted to go as well, but only one person could ride along in the ambulance, and Mia had been gone a long time. She nodded solemnly.

Looking at Chris, Alycia smiled and leaned towards him, kissing him on his cheek. He felt his face flush, but then she started spitting and wiping at her lips. "Damn, that dust is on *everything*," she grimaced.

He didn't care. She'd kissed him, and even through the dust, he could feel on his cheek where she had planted it. A broad smile widened across his face, and she smiled back sheepishly, before loading up into the ambulance.

The medic that had looked Chris over caught another passing medic's arm, pointed at Chris and said, "I think he needs help," before she let go and jumped up into the back, closing the doors.

After the new medic looked Chris over, he was led down the alley to another ambulance at the next street, and was attended to while the others watched on. The medic confirmed that Chris probably had a broken arm, but they'd have to x-ray it back at the hospital.

Emmi wanted to ride along, but she looked at Mia and Babbar, before she asked Marisol, "Will you be okay watching them?"

"Of course," she replied casually, and glanced at Mia. "Assuming this pendejo here doesn't try to get away."

A frown drew down Mia's face. "Pendejo?"

Standing up as tall as she could, Marisol gave her a sour look, "Yeah, it means-"

"It means," Emmi interrupted, "That I should probably stay too, to make sure you two don't kill each other." She looked apologetically at Chris. "We'll see you at the hospital?"

He grinned back and forth between Mia and Marisol, and then nodded at Emmi. "I think that's a good idea."

A ten-minute ride later, and Chris was being wheeled into the nearest hospital on a gurney, much to his chagrin. After filling out some paperwork as best as he could (does it count as a workplace injury when your workplace falls down on you?) he was taken to x-ray, before a doctor and nurse declared the bone didn't need to be set, and they began working on a cast for him.

All the while, his thoughts kept darting back and forth between worry for Shara and his revelations up in the tower. And on the fact that the tower hadn't flat-out collapsed after falling over. Maybe that wasn't the strangest thing to have happened tonight, but it was as if...something, somehow, had held it together just long enough for them all to get out.

But what? What or who could have that kind of power?

Thinking of his friends, he though that at least on the one hand, Shara most likely would be safe, even though Jered was probably already long-dead, slaughtered by Nabu, another casualty in the war Chris had started.

On the other hand, he felt as if he'd reached a significant milestone. The answers he'd sought for over two months felt like they might just be within his grasp now. Whatever that oily black substance was on the souls of his companions, he, along with the souls of a hundred other ancestors, had cleared them.

But it had left him, and those participating souls, exhausted. When he thought of that, his thoughts wandered back to what Tattannu had told him. *I'm not ready to know the truth,* he thought, a grim emptiness settling into his stomach. Thinking further on it, he recalled what else Tattannu had said – he would have to learn acceptance.

Once the doctors had finished setting the cast on his arm, virtually immobilizing it, they treated his burned hands with ointment and bandages, and finally they painfully cleaned his cuts and bandaged them.

After what felt like an eternity, they left him alone on the gurney in a large open area filled with other gurneys, but they had been kind enough to close the curtains to give him a modicum of privacy. He wasn't sure how long before they would come back, hopefully to discharge him, but between the painkillers and the treatment, he felt at last calm and collected enough to settle into meditation.

After a brief spell of controlled breathing, Chris found himself back inside his inner world, staring at his golden core of energy. It hung silently, the golden bolts of electricity lancing inwardly, brighter and stronger than any of the other souls he had seen today.

The usual background of milling shadows looked closer now, even oppressive, and they were sharper than before. Was that a result of what he had done? If he needed to cleanse another soul again, would they overwhelm him?

Gulping, he looked for Naomi, but then he realized that she had spent herself helping Chris cleanse his companions' souls. So he called out to the one who had been conspicuously absent. "Tattannu!" As before, no answers, but this time, he wouldn't take no for an answer. "I think I'm beginning to understand." Again no answer.

So he drew in a breath, and echoed Shara's words of wisdom from the training camp, "All magic has a price. The more powerful the magic, the greater the price."

The shadows around him stirred for a second, and then drew to a halt. An eerie sensation crept up along his spine, and he shivered when he realized they were staring at him. Never in his life could he have imagined just how creepy it would feel to have a million eyes, especially the eyes of spirits, staring at him.

Drawing in a shuddering breath, he asked, "What do I have to sacrifice? What price will I have to pay to defeat Nabu and Marduk?"

Those apparently were the magic words. One shadow directly ahead of him shimmered, and then stepped into focus, the elder Tattannu. His wizened face looked soft, his expression no longer one of judgement or disappointment, but one of relief, and contentment.

The first ancestor's dark eyes reflected the golden core with a renewed intensity. They flicked once towards the core, and then settle back upon Chris. His look turned to a solemn gaze, and he nodded once.

"Everything."

Chris startled awake just as the curtains were drawn back, and a nurse smiled at him. He didn't smile back. He couldn't.

Everything, he repeated in his thoughts. *Did that mean...himself?*

Was that it? Was he expected to sacrifice his life? Would this war kill him in the end?

Given everything that had happened, and the stakes involved, it didn't sound so far-fetched, but the thought sent a terrifying shiver along his back, and goosebumps rose upon his arms.

That had to be it. He *could* defeat Nabu, and Marduk.

But it would cost him everything.

The nurse asked Chris to fill out discharge papers, which he did in a deadpan manner, unwilling to let the nurse know what was wrong. He tried to fill out the paperwork himself, but since he was right-handed, it was a near-impossible task with his arm immobilized, and his left-handed scratches on the paper were illegible. The nurse offered to help him, smiling all the while, and he dictated his answers to her.

She was friendly, overly so, and despite the rigors of a long night shift after a disaster, she kept smiling lightly at him and never once begrudged having to help him with such a mundane task. Somehow, that friendliness warmed his core, and reminded him that it was people, every day people doing small acts of kindness, that made life worth living.

That made life worth fighting for.

A defiant streak crept into his heart. Surely that's not what Tattannu meant! It couldn't be. And even if he meant it, even if that's what 'acceptance' meant, then Chris would find another way.

Once the paperwork was finished, the nurse led him out to a waiting room, where she said his friends awaited.

Alycia and Emmi gave him a warm hug when he emerged, and they, along with Marisol, Mia, Eric, and Babbar, had taken over half of the waiting room. At some point, each of them had been allowed to cleanup, the dust, ash, and other grime mostly cleaned from their faces and hands. None of the staff had questioned the strange-looking Babbar and the fantasy-like creature curled up in his arms, a sign of the times they now lived in. Nina didn't lick her wound anymore, but the spot where the bullet had penetrated was a much paler green than the rest of her body.

No one had heard from Shara yet, but they were afraid to call her, in case her phone rang at an inopportune moment.

Then again, Chris doubted her phone would work if she was shapeshifted.

The group settled in again to wait for news of Tom, and as a pleasant surprise, there was a single three-person couch that everyone else let him and his two best friends have. Alycia in particular snuggled up under his left arm, and he felt his heartbeat race in excitement for a second, before he settled it down with some controlled breathing.

Chris looked back and forth between Alycia and Emmi, the latter of which had pulled out her phone and was browsing social media idly. It seemed strange to think that after everything that happened, the world still spun on, and social media was alive and well, despite the early hour. Would he ever get used to that?

His friends had lost so much, risked everything. The scars across Emmi's face and body was a reminder of the physical toll this war had wrought upon her, but it was nothing compared to the wounds she had suffered within. Nabu had changed her forever.

And then his gaze turned to Alycia, upon the woman he had begun to fall in love with. After Shara had lectured him on breaking her heart, he thought he would have had the courage to tell Alycia how he felt. Before he could, giant snakes had attacked his parents, and then Alycia's mother had made contact, and then the battle of the tower had happened. Something *always* got in the way.

Now that they had a moment, it would be the perfect opportunity, wouldn't it?

A giant weight settled into his stomach, along with an obtrusive lump in his throat, and he cleared it noisily. *No*, he thought. *I can't. Not if…if I'm meant to sacrifice myself, I can't do that to her.*

When he cleared his throat, she looked up at him, into his eyes, her beautiful golden-brown gaze penetrating into his soul. His heart warmed, but more than that, a steely determination asserted itself inside.

She was worth fighting for. So was Emmi.

They all were.

There was still a lot to do, still a lot to learn. He didn't know yet what exactly he would be required to do to defeat his nemesis. But in that moment, he resolved to find the answers as quickly as possible, no matter what the answer ended up being.

For the sake of everyone he loved.

It was well past an hour since Shara had taken flight when she called Marisol's phone. The group was alone in the waiting room, so Marisol answered on speaker.

"I'm okay," Shara assured them. *"But Nabu was definitely here. She ransacked the place, and Jered is missing. Given her powers, I wouldn't be surprised if he's become another thrall."*

Chris cursed. Her ability to infect their souls was a big, big problem, and had plagued them ever since his first encounter with her. But at least now he knew what she was doing, how she was doing it. All Chris would need was a moment alone with Jered to save him.

He looked at Mia, whose eyes were distant as she stared vaguely at the cellphone. If she could recover after two decades as Nabu's thrall…

"How's Tom?"

"We don't know yet," Alycia replied. "He's still in surgery."

"Okay. I'll head back right away. We need to regroup and figure out our next move."

They hung up, and continued the agonizing task of waiting. By the time the doctor, a tall and slender woman who looked to be in her fifties, came out to talk to them, the sun had just started to rise. Most of the group eagerly gathered around her as she spoke.

"He's going to pull through," the doctor explained, and a collective sigh heaved around the group. For the first time since he had been woken up by Alycia at 1 AM, Chris felt his shoulders relax.

"He was very lucky, the puncture was relatively clean and the rebar kept most of the stomach acid out, but for now, fighting the infection will be the most important factor."

"Can I go see him?" Alycia asked.

"I'm afraid not," the doctor shook her head. "Not yet. Give it a few more hours, and even then, we'll need you to wear a mask and gloves. We can't risk introducing additional infections at this time."

As Alycia's face drew down, Chris pulled her close and held tightly.

Then the doctor produced a phone, "This has been ringing off and on a lot over the past ten minutes."

She handed it over to Alycia, and then walked away. No sooner had she left than did Tom's phone ring again, and Chris rolled his eyes upon hearing *Flight of the Valkyrie.*

It was Abby calling, her persistent smile from a photo Tom had snapped of her gleaming back at them.

Alycia answered it and put it on speaker. "Abby!"

"Alycia?! Thank god!" The worry in her voice made Chris's heart hurt. *"I've been trying to get a hold of you all for the past ten minutes! Even calling Tom's phone, only one out of every ten tries rings through."*

Chris looked up at the others, and then suggested, "The nearest cell tower might be damaged or something."

"Maybe," Abby replied. *"You know, I had this wonderful joke lined up for Tom when I saw the news about our building. Like, 'sounds like I won't be reporting to work today,' but he never answ…"* She trailed off for a second, and then asked, *"Hang on, where's your dad?"*

Alycia quickly replied, "He's okay. Well, he's alive. He just got out of surgery from a wound, but the doctor says he should pull through."

"Oh," Abby sounded relieved. *"Good. Well anyway, you all should pull up the news on your phone and watch. The President is about to give an emergency speech, and the pre-brief for the press indicates it'll directly address the, and I'm quoting here, the 'magic problem.'"*

Without another thought, Emmi drew her phone back out and brought up a browser. Her connection was spotty on the cell network, so she connected to the hospital's guest Wi-Fi, and then started searching news sites, until she found a live video.

It showed the ever-familiar podium in the press room at the White House, with the seal of the President of the United States on the front of it. A banner at the bottom of the screen indicated that the President was about to address the nation.

They waited for about two minutes, and while they did, Chris, Alycia, and Emmi filled Abby in on everything that had happened.

Finally, the President's press secretary stepped onto the screen and asked everyone to be seated. A moment later, the President stepped up to the podium. He'd only been in office for less than seven months, and the weight of the office hadn't start to wear him down. He was vibrant, he was steadfast, and he looked determined. Exactly what the U.S. population might need in a crisis like this.

"My fellow Americans," he began. *"As you all know, we live in unprecedented times. The existence of what has been dubbed 'magic' by the general community has shaken global society to its very core. Estimates of the percentage of the population that is capable of utilizing these powers continues to rise, and we now suspect approximately twenty percent of the global population to be capable of wielding various supernatural abilities, to varying degrees of power.*

"I know you're all frightened by these facts. A faction in London calling themselves 'Arcane Dawn' have seized control of key areas of the city and taken multiple parliament members hostage." Chris blinked in surprise. That was new news. *"Terrorists using magic attacked an airport in Melbourne. And now, on our own soil, less than a day after a devastating spectacle of magic in a quiet suburban neighborhood of Denver, magic-wielding terrorists have destroyed the Sentinel Holdings tower in downtown Denver, inflicting massive damage to nearby buildings and killing at least three people."*

Chris glanced nervously at his companions. This wasn't going anywhere good.

"As your President, it is my responsibility to protect you all, and I intend to do just that. We cannot *allow what has happened in London to happen here. As such, this morning I have signed multiple Executive Orders. Registration of all magic-wielders in the United States is now compulsory. For the safety of everyone, this requirement will be quickly enacted, and individuals with magic powers will be required to register at their nearest voting center within forty-eight hours. Anyone who fails to do so will be arrested and treated as armed and dangerous.*

"To assist in this matter, we're mobilizing the National Guard in all states, and reservists will be called to active duty to help."

Drawing himself up, the President continued, *"Additionally, it has been brought to my attention that there is a clandestine organization hidden amongst every nation in the world, including our own, that has used magic to subvert control and influence world leaders."* Chris felt the blood drain from his face. *"These people believe themselves to be above the law and have flaunted society for decades, if not centuries. They call themselves the Sentinels."*

"Oh no," Marisol groaned.

"And as of this moment, they are America's Most Wanted."

Chris's eyes darted amongst his companions fretfully.

"I know you all wish to know more, but for now all I will say is that we ask any citizen who has knowledge of the Sentinels in America to come forward and tell us. I encourage all of our international partners to treat the Sentinels in the same manner within their respective territories.

"Now, if you'll excuse me, I'm afraid I don't have time to take questions this morning."

As the President left the podium, the press room exploded into a flurry of shouted questions, with everyone standing up at once. It was the polar opposite of what Chris and his companions were doing, as everyone in the waiting room simply stared at one another, dumbfounded.

Everyone except Emmi, who stared hard at her phone and peered closer at it. She tapped the pause button on the live stream, and then her eyes grew wide. "Uh, guys?"

The confused looks all turned to her, and she pointed at the phone. "Is that who I think it is?"

They looked down at her phone, and Chris in particular had to squint through the tiredness burning his eyes.

It was Nabu. In the press room of the President. And she wasn't a member of the press, either. She was standing behind the podium, next to the press secretary.

"What the hell?!" Chris gawked.

Lowering her phone, Emmi stared at Chris. "She's on the inside. This has all been a manipulation by her from the fucking start!"

Chris nodded. "London. The airport in Australia. She wanted this to happen."

"But why?" Marisol asked. "What does manipulating the President into this decision do?"

"It renders us useless," Chris grit his teeth. And then his face paled. "And it makes us...oh no."

"Guys," Abby suddenly spoke from Tom's phone. Chris looked down, dread filling every part of his body. *"You should run."*

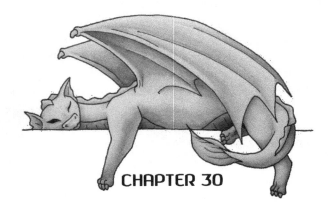

CHAPTER 30

The press conference ended, and Nabu watched with mild amusement as the reporters all roared their questions, even after their President had said he would take none. *Impudence,* she thought. *They allow far too much of it from their subjects.*

And yet, their impudence continued to serve her.

After the torrent of unanswered questions ended, the reporters all gathered up their materials while chattering with each other. Part of Nabu wanted to push them to wild conclusions. All it would take was a little willpower. But no, they would serve their purpose without it. She needed to save her energy for other endeavors.

Pushing off of the wall and scratching at her neckline where the collar of her business blazer itched, she stalked off after the President of the United States.

Some would have considered her bold for enthralling him. Some would have marveled at the genius of it. The idea made her laugh. It was paltry. It was *necessary,* but it was a small matter, as if he was actually anyone of importance.

However, he *did* hold the keys to the kingdom, so to speak. Her kingdom. Her future.

She followed him and his gaggle of lackeys until they reached the Oval Office, and quietly, silently, she followed them in. When the President saw her standing next to the door, he took his cue and ordered everyone out.

"Don't forget, Mr. President," his aide admonished, "You have a nine o'clock with General Kissinger."

"Thank you," he nodded, and shooed her out. The aide eyed

Nabu curiously, but as Nabu was a personal guest of the President, she paid little more attention to the interloper.

He approached her then, a lecherous leer upon his face. Having grown accustomed to her new body, Nabu easily slid into the role, and slipped into position against him. "Oh very well done," she whispered in his ear, infusing more of her will upon him. "You've performed *flawlessly.*"

With the eagerness she had come to expect from her thralls, he grasped her back and held her closer. "I did it all for you," he crooned.

"Yes, I know," she smirked, and pushed him away. Confusion crossed his features, but a little bit of will thrown into her gaze was enough to assuage his uncertainty. She just had to string him along until the day of fire. His soul would never be so wholly bought as Mia's. It wasn't necessary, and the idea of a continued liaison with him sickened Nabu.

Mia, Nabu thought with ire. Nabu would miss her companionship and devotion, but the ploy had been necessary, and well worth it.

Returning her attention to the President, Nabu nodded slowly. "I shall return," she spoke, inflecting as much sensuality into her voice as she dared.

The President's hand shot out and grasped her. "Wait!"

A flare of annoyance exploded within Nabu, and without thinking about it, she unleashed a charge of electricity along her skin, singing the President's hand. He yelped and jerked backwards.

With venom in her voice, she roared, "You dare touch your god?"

Like a small child caught red-handed, he cowered backwards. "I'm sorry! I'm so sorry. Please, forgive me, my master, I just...I need you. I need you *with* me."

Cooling her temper, Nabu sighed wearily. "Yes, you do. But for now, I must attend to other matters." Reaching into her blazer, she touched the cool, ancient hilt of Imhullu, hidden in a shoulder harness's sheath. "My father comes soon, and I must be prepared."

"Yes," the President bowed, mewling like a kitten. "Yes, of course, but...when...when will you come back?"

"Soon," she promised. "Be patient, carry out my will, and you and your nation will be favored by the new order."

"Thank you," he bowed again, and backed up into his ancient, wooden desk. "Thank you, my master."

Scowling at his pitiful apologies, she turned her back upon him, and summoned forth the will necessary to create a portal. White light followed by white noise engulfed her human senses, and her willpower, her divine essence ripped and pulled that human form along, until she stood within a research lab in the middle of a quietly-forgotten laboratory in the middle of New Mexico.

The scientists and engineers there expected her, thanks to the President's orders, and when she appeared, they marveled at her power, but otherwise appeared unimpressed by her sudden appearance.

Unbuttoning her blazer, she drew Imhullu from its sheath, and presented it to the man standing before her, Professor Zamir Ali. He bowed deeply before her, and gently accepted the dagger from her.

"Make it work," she growled at him.

"Yes, of course," he spoke, and turned to walk to the center of the lab, where he addressed his companions, a motley assortment of scientists and engineers from all over the world. Most of them had come with fevered anticipation, a desire to closely examine a magic artifact and try to figure out the scientific reasoning behind magic.

Zamir was different. He worshipped Nabu, a reverence not born from the careful application of Nabu's will upon his soul, but of his own free will. He would lead the team to the ultimate goal.

Nabu's future, her *freedom*, depended upon them.

Satisfied that Imhullu was in good hands, she prepared to leave again for another location.

But at that very moment, searing pain wrenched across her human body, prompting an unwilling cry of pain. The engineers gaped at her open-mouthed, and she knew she could not stay, not for what was to come.

Summoning her will power again, Nabu drew her human body across the sea of space and magic to her temple in Borsippa. The moment the white noise subsided and her vision cleared, she saw before her the tablet that had ensured she would survive Tatsu's attack nearly three months ago.

It glowed, far more brightly than when Nabu had resided within it, and it confirmed her suspicions.

He is here.

Father.

"MY CHILD," a wretchedly powerful and resounding voice echoed within Nabu's head. Her human half nearly exploded from the overwhelming power of the Voice of Marduk. *"YOU HAVE FINALLY DISMANTLED THE BARRIER!"*

Nodding her head out of human habit, Nabu replied through her thoughts, *Yes, Father.*

"YET YOU DID NOT CALL TO ME AT ONCE. YOU HAVE NOT YET FED ME A SINGLE SOUL." Each consonant blazed fire through Nabu's mortal brain, threatening to tear it to pieces within her skull. *"WHERE IS MY SUSTENANCE?"*

Much has changed, Father, she defended, falling to her knees not out of reverence, but out of pain. His voice tore at her human senses, ripping her thoughts to pieces, shredding her nervous system, and it took all of her will power and skill with magic to repair her body as fast as the damage occurred. *The human population has grown in number, but likewise have they grown in boldness and insolence. I confess I had lost the dagger for a time,* red-hot rage seared into her thoughts, echoes of her connection to her father, *but now it is within my possession again!*

The anger subsided just a little. And then she felt the curiosity. *"GROWN IN NUMBERS? HOW MANY NUMBER THE HUMANS?"*

Now to cast the bait. *Billions, Father. Eight billion souls.*

His excitement was palpable and surged through her divine half like a drug, driving immense pleasure. Endorphins and other pleasure-giving chemicals raged within her body. *"BILLIONS. MORE THAN ENOUGH TO FREE ME FROM MY PRISON."*

"Precisely," she spoke out loud, more out of habit, and out of need from her body's reactions to conversing with Marduk. "And to continually feed you as you begin your conquests. All who stood against you before will no longer. With humanity as your fuel, you can destroy your enemies once and for all!"

"YES…MORE THAN ENOUGH TO BEGIN."

Looking up, as if Marduk were a god from above and not from another realm entirely, Nabu smiled. "It pleases you, then, Father?"

"YES. YOU HAVE ACQUITTED YOURSELF FOR YOUR PAST FAILURES AMICABLY, NABU. WHAT PLAN HAVE YOU?"

Now was the time to twist the truth a little, and sink the hook. "The humans have science, they have technology. Implements which could enhance our powers. I can spread Imhullu's effects to multiple implements, and slaughter humans by the hundreds, funneling their souls into you in waves. Their cleverness shall be their undoing."

The pleasure rolling through her body redoubled. *"HOW CLEVER OF YOU, MY CHILD. BE WARNED, HOWEVER. IF YOU FAIL ME AGAIN, I WILL RECLAIM THAT WHICH IS MINE, AND MAKE ANOTHER IN YOUR STEAD."* A pang of fear and pain overcame the pleasure within Nabu, and she seized upon the floor, her body out of her control. *"WORK QUICKLY, NABU."*

"Y-yes, F-father," she gasped. "I will."

With no more to be said, the tablet's glow subsided, leaving Nabu curled up on the sandstone floor in a fetal position. The power it took Marduk to project his voice, even through a medium like the tablet, was immense, and he would be so weak after four thousand years without a single morsel of a soul. Chances were, he would not return for days, if not weeks.

Which meant that Nabu's thoughts were safe, for the moment. "I will, Father," she glared at the tablet, the implement that delivered her from death's clutches, and that which delivered her father's wrath. "As fast as I can. And when I'm done," she set her head down, allowing the cold from the stone to seep into her worn out body, "you will be no more."

DID YOU LIKE THIS BOOK?

Reader reviews play an important role in a book's success by helping other readers discover stories they might enjoy. Please consider taking a moment to leave a review for *Chronicles of the Sentinels - Retribution* on Amazon and/or Goodreads! You'll be making this author's day :D

ABOUT THE AUTHOR

Jon Wasik has been telling stories since he was a little boy, usually with a cookie and milk at his Great Grandma's kitchen table. It wasn't until 5th grade that he finally put pen to paper, and from that moment on, writing has been his greatest passion.

When he isn't writing, Jon likes to read, play video games, and watch insanely geeky movies with his wife. His Gollum voice impressions are eerie, he quotes Doctor Who like others quote the bible, and he can leap terabytes of data in a single bound!

Want to find out more about Jon, or keep up on the latest news about his books? Check out his website, and while you're there, subscribe to his mailing list! Just go to the following website and click "Join Mailing List" at the top!
http://jonwasik.com/

CPSIA information can be obtained
at www.ICGtesting.com
Printed in the USA
BVHW071015100222
628587BV00006B/121